No one knew that better than young Shirley Hollister whose hardworking family had lived with close tenderness regardless of their poverty. And now that they had an opportunity to live in the country, what did it matter if they could only afford to live in a barn?

But Shirley's joy was clouded when their new young landlord seemed to take a charitable interest in their project. She knew that Sidney was too wealthy to understand their humble life.

Could he ever know what it was like to be rich in love as well as money, or would he become bored and return to a world of carefree ease?

Bantam Books by Grace Livingston Hill
Ask your bookseller for the books you have missed

Grace Livingston Hill
The Enchanted Barn

BANTAM BOOKS
TORONTO • NEW YORK • LONDON • SYDNEY • AUCKLAND

*This low-priced Bantam Book
has been completely reset in a type face
designed for easy reading, and was printed
from new plates. It contains the complete
text of the original hard-cover edition.*
NOT ONE WORD HAS BEEN OMITTED.

THE ENCHANTED BARN

*A Bantam Book / published by arrangement with
Harper & Row, Publishers, Inc.*

PRINTING HISTORY

Originally published by J. B. Lippincott 1918

Bantam edition / August 1977
2nd printing .. December 1977   4th printing ... February 1979
3rd printing ...... April 1978   5th printing .. December 1979
6th printing ... July 1984

ISBN 0-553-24199-0

Published simultaneously in the United States and Canada

CHAPTER I

Shirley Hollister pushed back the hair from her hot forehead, pressed her hands wearily over tired eyes, then dropped her fingers again to the typewriter keys, and flew on with the letter she was writing.

There was no one else in the inner office where she sat. Mr. Barnard, the senior member of the firm, whose stenographer she was, had stepped into the outer office for a moment with a telegram which he had just received. His absence gave Shirley a moment's respite from that feeling that she must keep strained up to meet his gaze and not let trouble show in her eyes, though a great lump was choking in her throat and the tears stung her hot eyelids and insisted on blurring her vision now and then. But it was only for an instant that she gave way. Her fingers flew on with their work, for this was an important letter, and Mr. Barnard wanted it to go in the next mail.

As she wrote, a vision of her mother's white face appeared to her between the lines, the mother weak and white, with tears on her cheeks and that despairing look in her eyes. Mother hadn't been able to get up for a week. It seemed as if the cares of life were getting almost too much for her, and the warm spring days made the little brick house in the narrow street a stifling place to stay. There was only one small window in mother's room, opening against a brick wall, for they had had to rent the front room with its two windows.

But, poor as it was, the little brick house had been home; and now they were not to have that long. Notice had been served that they must vacate in four weeks; for the house, in fact, the whole row of houses in

1

which it was situated, had been sold, and was to be pulled down to make way for a big apartment-house that was to be put up.

Where they were going and what they were going to do now was the great problem that throbbed on Shirley's weary brain night and day, that kept her from sleeping and eating, that choked in her throat when she tried to speak to Mr. Barnard, that stared from her feverish eyes as she looked at the sunshine on the street or tried to work in the busy monotony of the office.

They had been in the little house nearly a year, ever since the father died. It had taken all they could scrape together to pay the funeral expenses, and now with her salary, and the roomer's rent, and what George got as cash-boy in a department store they were just barely able to get along. There was not a cent over for sickness or trouble, and nothing to move with, even if they had anywhere to move, or any time to hunt for a place. Shirley knew from her experience in hunting for the present house that it was going to be next to impossible for them to find any habitable place for as little rent as they were now paying, and how *could* they pay more? She was only a beginner, and her salary was small. There were three others in the family, not yet wage-earners. The problem was tremendous. Could it be that Carol, only fourteen years old, must stop school and go to work somewhere to earn a pittance also? Carol was slender and pale, and needed fresh air and nourishing food. Carol was too young to bear burdens yet; besides, who would be housekeeper and take care of mother if Carol had to go to work? It was different with George; he was a boy, strong and sturdy; he had his school in the department store, and was getting on well with his studies. George would be all right. He belonged to a baseball team, too, and got plenty of chances for exercise; but Carol was frail, there was no denying it. Harley was a boisterous nine-year-old, always on the street these days when he wasn't in school; and who could blame him? For the narrow, dark brick house was no place for a lively boy.

2

But the burden and anxiety for him were heavy on his sister's heart, who had taken over bodily all the worries of her mother. Then there was the baby Doris, with her big, pathetic eyes, and her round cheeks and loving ways. Doris, too, had to be shut in the dark little house with the summer heat coming on, and no one with time enough or strength enough to take her to the Park. Doris was only four. Oh, it was terrible, *terrible!* and Shirley could do nothing but sit there, and click those keys, and earn her poor little inadequate salary! Some day, of course, she would get more —but some day might be too late!

She shuddered as the terrible thought flashed through her mind, then went on with her work again. She must shake off this state of mind and give attention to her duty, or she would lose even this opportunity to help her dear ones.

The door of the outer office opened, and Mr. Barnard entered.

"Miss Hollister," he said hurriedly, "if you have those letters ready, I will sign them at once. We have just had word that Mr. Baker of the firm died last night in Chicago, and I must go on at once. The office will be closed for the rest of the day. You can let those other matters that I spoke of go until to-morrow, and you may have the day off. I shall not be at the office at the usual hour to-morrow morning, but you can come in and look after the mail. I will leave further directions with Mr. Clegg. You can mail these letters as you go down."

Ten minutes later Shirley stood on the street below in the warm spring sunshine, and gazed about her half dazed. It seemed a travesty on her poor little life just now to have a holiday and no way to make it count for the dear ones at home. How should she use it, anyway? Should she go home and help Carol? Or should she go out and see whether she could find a house somewhere that they could possibly afford to move to? That, of course, was the sensible thing to do; yet she had no idea where to go. But they did not expect her home at this time of day. Perhaps it was as well that she should use this time and find out something without worrying her mother. At least, she would have time to think undisturbed.

She grasped her little package of lunch that she had brought from home with her and looked about her helplessly. In her little thin purse was the dime she always carried with her to pay her car-fare in case something happened that she had to ride either way —though she seldom rode, even in a storm. But her mother insisted on the dime. She said it was not safe to go without any money at all. This dime was her capital wherewith to hunt a house. Perhaps the day had been given her by a kind heavenly Father to go on her search. She would try to use it to the best of her ability. She lifted her bewildered heart in a feeble petition for light and help in her difficult problem, and then she went and stood on the corner of the street where many trolley-cars were passing and repassing. Which one should she take, and where should she go? The ten cents must cover all her riding, and she must save half of it for her return.

She studied the names on the cars. "Glenside Road" one read. What had she heard about that? Ah! that it was the longest ride one could take for five cents within the limits of the city's roads! Her heart leaped up at the word. It sounded restful anyway, and would give her time to think. It wasn't likely, if it went near any glens, that there would be any houses within *her* means on its way; but possibly it passed some as it went through the city, and she could take notice of the streets and numbers and get out on her return trip to investigate if there proved to be anything promising; or, if it were too far away from home for her to walk back from it, she could come another time in the evening with George, some night when he did not have school. Anyhow, the ride would rest her and give her a chance to think what she ought to do, and one car was as good as another for that. Her resolve was taken, and she stepped out and signalled it.

There were not many people in the car. It was not an hour when people rode out to the suburbs. Two

4

workmen with rolls of wall-paper slung in burlap bags, a woman and a little girl, that was all.

Shirley settled back in her seat, and leaned her head against the window-sash wearily. She felt so tired, body and soul, that she would have been glad to sleep and forget for a little while, only that there was need for her to be up and doing. Her room had been oppressively warm the night before; and Doris, who slept with her, had rolled from one side of the bed to the other, making sleep well-nigh impossible for the elder sister. She felt bruised and bleeding in her very soul, and longed for rest.

The car was passing through the thickest of the city's business thoroughfare, and the noise and confusion whirled about her ears like some fiendish monotonous music that set the time for the mad dance of the world. One danced to it whether one would or not, and danced on to one's death.

Around the city hall the car passed, and on up Market Street. They passed a great fruit-store, and the waft of air that entered the open windows came laden with the scent of over-ripe bananas, late oranges and lemons; a moment later with sickening fumes it blended into a deadly smell of gas from a yawning hole in the pavement, and mingled with the sweat of the swarthy foreigners grouped about it, picks in hand. It seemed as though all the smells in creation were met and congregated in that street within four or five blocks; and one by one they tortured her, leather and paint and metal and soap, rank cheese in a fellow traveller's market-basket, thick stifling smoke from a street engine that was champing up the gravel they fed it to make a new patch of paving, the stench from the cattle-sheds as they passed the railroad and stock-yards, the dank odor of the river as they crossed the bridge, and then an oilcloth-factory just beyond! The faint sweet breath of early daffodils and violets from an occasional street vendor stood no chance at all with these, and all the air seemed sickening and dreadful to the girl as she rested wearily against the window with closed eyes, and tried to think.

5

They slipped at last into the subway with a whir and a swish, where the cool, clean smell of the cement seemed gradually to rise and drown the memory of the upper world, and came refreshingly in at the windows. Shirley had a passing thought, wondering whether it would be like that in the grave, all restful and sweet and quiet and clean, with the noisy, heartless world roaring overhead. Then they came up suddenly out of the subway, with a kind of triumphant leap and shout of brakes and wheels, into the light and sunshine above, and a new world. For here were broad streets, clean pavements, ample houses, well-trimmed lawns, quiet people walking in comfort, bits of flower-boxes on the window-sills filled with pansies and hyacinths; and the air was sweet and clean. The difference made Shirley sit up and look about her, and the contrast reminded her of the heaven that would be beyond the grave. It was just because she was so tired and disheartened that her thoughts took this solemn form.

But now her heart sank again, for she was in the world of plenty far beyond her means, and there was no place for such as she. Not in either direction could she see any little side streets with tiny houses that would rent for fifteen dollars a month. There were such in the city, she knew; but they were scarce, and were gobbled up as soon as vacant.

But here all was spaciousness, and even the side streets had three stories and smug porches with tidy rockers and bay windows.

She looked at the great plate-glass windows with their cobwebby lace draperies, and thought what it would be if she were able to take her mother and the children to such a home as one of those. Why, if she could afford that, George could go to college, and Doris wear a little velvet coat with rosebuds in her bonnet, like the child on the sidewalk with her nurse and her doll-carriage.

But a thing like that could never come to her. There were no rich old uncles to leave them a fortune; she was not bright and gifted to invent some wonderful toy or write a book or paint a picture that would bring the fortune; and no one would ever come her way with a fortune to marry her. Those things happened only in story-books, and she was not a story-book girl; she was just a practical, every-day, hard-working girl with a fairly good complexion, good blue eyes and a firm chin. She could work hard and was willing; but she could not bear anxiety. It was eating into her soul, and she could feel a kind of mental paralysis stealing over her from it, benumbing her faculties hour by hour.

The car glided on, and the houses grew less stately and farther apart. They were not so pretentious now, but they were still substantial and comfortable, with more ground and an air of having been there always, with no room for newcomers. Now and then would come a nucleus of shops and an old tavern with a group of new groceries and crying competition of green stamps and blue stamps and yellow stamps posted alluringly in their windows. Here busy, hurried people would swarm, and children ran and shouted; but every house they passed seemed full to overflowing, and there was nowhere any place that seemed to say, "Here you may come and find room!"

And now the car left the paved and built-up streets, and wandered out between the open fields, where trees arched lavishly overhead, and little new green things lifted up unfrightened heads, and dared to grow in the sunshine. A new smell, the smell of rich earth and young green growing things, of skunk-cabbage in bloom in the swamps, of budding willows and sassafras, roused her senses; the hum of a bee on its way to find the first honey-drops came to her ears. Sweet, droning, restful, with the call of a wild bird in the distance, and all the air balmy with the joy of spring. Ah! This was a new world! This indeed was heaven! What a contrast to the office, and the little narrow stifling brick house where mother lay, and Doris cut strings of paper dolls from an old newspaper and sighed to go out in the Park! What a contrast! Truly, this was heaven! If she could but stay, and all the dear ones come!

She had spent summers in the country, of course; and she knew and loved nature, but it had been five years since she had been free to get outside the city limits for more than a day, and then not far. It seemed to her now that she had never sensed the beauty of the country as to-day; perhaps because she had never needed it as now.

The road went on smoothly straight ahead, with now a rounding curve, and then another long stretch of perfect road. Men were ploughing in the fields on one side, and on the other lay the emerald velvet of a field of spring wheat. More people had got into the car as it left the city. Plain, substantial men, nice, pleasant women; but Shirley did not notice them; she was watching the changing landscape and thinking her dismal, pitiful thoughts. Thinking, too, that she had spent her money—or would have when she returned, with nothing to show for it, and her conscience condemned her.

They were coming now to a wide, old-fashioned barn of stone, with ample grassy stone-coped entrance rising like a stately carpeted stairway from the barnyard. It was resting on the top of a green knoll, and a great elm-tree arched over it protectingly. A tiny stream purled below at one side, and the ground sloped gradually off at the other. Shirley was not noticing the place much except as it was a part of the landscape until she heard the conductor talking to the man across the aisle about it.

"Good barn!" he was saying reflectively. "Pity to have it standing idle so long; but they'll never rent it without a house, and they won't build. It belongs to the old man's estate, and can't be divided until the youngest boy's of age, four 'r five years yet. The house burned down two years ago. Some tramps set it afire. No, nobody was living in it at the time. The last renter didn't make the farm pay,—too fur from the railroad, I guess,—and there ain't anybody near enough round to use the barn since Halyer built his new barn," and he indicated a great red structure down the road on the other side. "Halyer useta use this,—rented it fer less'n nothing, but he got too lazy to come this fur, and so he sold off half his farm fer a dairy and built that

8

there barn. So now I s'pose that barn'll stand idle and run to waste till that kid comes of age and there's a boom up this way and it's sold. Pity about it, though; it's a good barn. Wisht I had it up to my place; I could fill it."

"Make a good location for a house," said the other man, looking intently at the big stone pile. "Been a fine barn in its time. Old man must uv had a pile of chink when he built it. Who'd ya say owned it?"

"Graham, Walter Graham, big firm down near the city hall—guess you know 'em. Got all kinds of money. This ain't one, two, three with the other places they own. Got a regular palace out Arden way fer summer and a town house in the swellest neighborhood, and own land all over. Old man inherited it from his father and three uncles. They don't even scarcely know they got this barn, I reckon. It ain't very stylish out this way just yet."

"Be a big boom here some day; nice location," said the passenger.

"Not yetta while," said the conductor sagely; "railroad station's too far. Wait till they get a station out Allister Avenue; then you can talk. Till then it'll stay as it is, I reckon. There's a spring down behind the barn, the best water in the county. I useta get a drink every day when the switch was up here. I missed it a lot when they moved the switch to the top of the hill. Water's cold as ice and clear as crystal—can't be beat this side the soda-fountain. I sometimes stop the car on a hot summer day now, and run and get a drink —it's great."

The men talked on, but Shirley heard no more. Her eyes were intent on the barn as they passed it— the great, beautiful, wide, comfortable-looking barn. What a wonderful house it would make! She almost longed to be a cow to enter this peaceful shelter and feel at home for a little while.

The car went on, and left the big barn in the distance; but Shirley kept thinking, going over almost unconsciously all the men had said about it. Walter Graham! Where had she seen that name? Oh, of course

9

in the Ward Trust Building, the whole fourth floor. Leather goods of some sort, perhaps, she couldn't just remember; yet she was sure of the name.

The man had said the barn rented for almost nothing. What could that mean translated in terms of dollars? Would the fifteen dollars a month that they were now paying for the little brick house cover it? But there would be the carfare for herself and George. Walking that distance twice a day, or even once, would be impossible. Ten cents a day, sixty cents a week—twice sixty cents! If they lived out of the city, they couldn't afford to pay but twelve dollars a month. They never would rent that barn for that, of course, it was so big and grand-looking; and yet—it was a *barn!* What did barns rent for, anyway?

And, if it could be had, could they live in a barn? What were barns like, anyway, inside? Did they have floors, or only stalls and mud? There had been but two tiny windows visible in the front; how did they get light inside? But then it couldn't be much darker than the brick house, no matter what it was. Perhaps there was a skylight, and hay, pleasant hay, to lie down on and rest. Anyhow, if they could only manage to get out there for the summer somehow, they could bear some discomforts just to sit under that great tree and look up at the sky. To think of Doris playing under that tree! And mother sitting under it sewing! Mother could get well out there in that fresh air, and Doris would get rosy cheeks again. There would not likely be a school about for Carol; but that would not hurt her for the summer, anyway, and maybe by fall they could find a little house. Perhaps she would get a raise in the fall. If they could only get somewhere to go now!

But yet—a barn! Live in a barn! What would mother say? Would she feel that it was a disgrace? Would she call it one of Shirley's wild schemes? Well, but what were they going to do? They must live *somewhere,* unless they were destined to die homeless.

The car droned on through the open country coming now and then to settlements of prosperous houses, some of them small; but no empty ones seemed to beckon her. Indeed, they looked too high-priced to make her even look twice at them; besides, her heart was left behind with that barn, that great, beautiful barn with the tinkling brook beside it, and the arching tree and gentle green slope.

At last the car stopped in a commonplace little town in front of a red brick church, and everybody got up and went out. The conductor disappeared, too, and the motorman leaned back on his brake and looked at her significantly.

"End of the line, lady," he said with a grin, as if she were dreaming and had not taken notice of her surroundings.

"Oh," said Shirley, rousing up, and looking bewilderedly about her. "Well, you go back, don't you?"

"Yes. Go back in fifteen minutes," said the motorman indulgently. There was something appealing in the sadness of this girl's eyes that made him think of his little girl at home.

"Do you go back just the same way?" she asked with sudden alarm. She did want to see that barn again, and to get its exact location so that she could come back to it some day if possible.

"Yes, we go back just the same way," nodded the motorman.

Shirley sat back in her seat again contented, and resumed her thoughts. The motorman took up his dinner-pail, sat down on a high stool with his back to her, and began to eat. It was a good time now for her to eat her little lunch, but she was not hungry. However, she would be if she did not eat it, of course; and there would be no other time when people would not be around. She put her hand in her shabby coat-pocket for her handkerchief, and her fingers came into contact with something small and hard and round. For a moment she thought it was a button that had been off her cuff for several days. But no, she remembered sewing that on that very morning. Then she drew the little object out, and behold it was a five-cent piece! Yes, of course, she remembered now. It was the nickel she put in her pocket last night when she went for the extra loaf of bread and found the store

11

closed. She had made johnny-cake instead, and supper had been late; but the nickel had stayed in her coat-pocket forgotten. And now suddenly a big temptation descended upon her, to spend that nickel in car-fare, riding to the barn and getting out for another closer look at it, and then taking the next car on into the city. Was it wild and foolish, was it not perhaps actually wrong, to spend that nickel that way when they needed so much at home, and had so little? A crazy idea,—for how could a barn ever be their shelter?

She thought so hard about it that she forgot to eat her lunch until the motorman slammed the cover down on his tin pail and put the high stool away. The conductor, too, was coming out of a tiny frame house, wiping his mouth with the back of his hand and calling to his wife, who stood in the doorway and told him about an errand she wanted him to do for her in the city.

Shirley's cheeks grew red with excitement, for the nickel was burning in her hand, and she knew in her heart that she was going to spend it getting off that car near that barn. She would eat her lunch under the tree by the brook! How exciting that would be! At least it would be something to tell the children about at night! Or no! they would think her crazy and selfish, perhaps, to waste a whole day and fifteen cents on herself. Still, it was not on herself; it was really for them. If they could only see that beautiful spot!

When she handed her nickel to the conductor, she felt almost guilty, and it seemed as if he could see her intention in her eyes; but she told herself that she was not sure she was going to get off at all. She could decide as she came near the place. She would have to get off either before she got there or after she had passed and walk back. The conductor would think it strange if a young girl got off the car in the country in front of an empty barn. How would she manage it? There had been houses on the way, not far from the barn. What was the name the conductor had mentioned of the man who had built another barn? She might get off at his house, but still—stay—what was that avenue where they had said the railroad would

12

come some day with a station? They had called it out as they stopped to let off the woman and the little girl. Allister Avenue! That was it. She would ask the conductor to let her off at Allister Avenue.

She watched the way intently; and, as they neared the place where Allister Avenue ought to be, her heart pounded so that she felt quite conscious, as if she were going to steal a barn and carry it home in her coat-pocket.

She managed to signal the car to stop quite quietly, however, and stepped down to the pavement as if it were her regular stopping-place. She was aware of the curious gaze of both motorman and conductor, but she held her head up, and walked a few steps up Allister Avenue until the car had whirred on out of sight. Then she turned anxiously, looking down the road, and there to her joy saw the stone gable of the great barn high on its knoll in the distance.

CHAPTER II

SHIRLEY walked down the dusty road by the side of the car-track, elation and excitement in her breast. What an adventure! To be walking alone in this strange, beautiful spring country, and nobody to interfere! It was her Father's beautiful out-of-doors, and she had paid her extra nickel to have a right to it for a little while. Perhaps her mother would have been worried at her being alone in the country, but Shirley had no fears. Young people seldom have fears. She walked down the road with a free step and a bright light in her eyes. She had to see that barn somehow; she *just had to!*

She was almost breathless when she reached the bottom of the hill at last, and stood in front of the great barn. The up car passed her just as she got there, and the people looked out at her apathetically as they would at any country girl. She stood still a minute, and watched the car up the hill and out of sight, then picked her way across the track, and entered the field where the fence was broken down, walking up the long grassy slope to the front of the barn and standing still at the top in front of the big double doors, so grim and forbidding.

The barn was bigger than it looked in the distance. She felt very small; yet her soul rejoiced in its bigness. Oh, to have plenty of room for once!

She put her nose close to the big doors, and tried to find a crack to look through; but the doors were tight and fitted well. There was no use trying to see in from there. She turned and ran down the long grassy slope, trying to pretend it was a palatial stairway, then around the side to the back of the barn, and there at last she found a door part way ajar, opening into what must have been the cow-stables, and she slipped joyously in. Some good angel must have been protecting her in her ignorance and innocence, for that dark basement of the barn would have been an excellent hiding-place for a whole regiment of tramps; but she trod safely on her way, and found nothing but a field-mouse to dispute her entrance; and it scurried hastily under the foundation, and disappeared.

The cow-stables evidently had not been occupied for a number of years, for the place was clean and littered with dry straw, as if it had fallen and sifted from the floor above. The stalls were all empty now, and old farm implements, several ploughs, and a rickety wagon occupied the dusty, cobwebby spaces beyond the stalls. There were several openings, rude doorways and crude windows; and the place was not unpleasant, for the back of it opened directly upon a sloping hill which dropped away to the running brook below, and a little stone spring-house, its mossy roof half hidden by a tangle of willows. Shirley stood in a doorway and gazed with delight, then turned back to her investigation. This lower place would not do for human habitation, of course; it was too low and damp, and the floor was only mud. She must penetrate if possible to the floor above.

Presently she found a rough ladder, cleats nailed to uprights against the wall; and up this she crept cautiously to the opening above, and presently emerged into the wide floor of the real barn.

There were several small windows, left open, and the sweet spring air swept gently in; and there were little patches of pale sunshine in the misty recesses of the great dim room. Gentle motes floated in the sharp lances of sunshine that stole through the cracks; another ladder rose in the midst of the great floor to the loft above; and festoons of ancient hay and cobwebs hung dustily down from the opening above. After Shirley had skipped about the big floor and investigated every corner of it, imagining how grand it would be to set the table in one end of the room and put mother's bed behind a screen in the other end, with the old piano somewhere in the centre and the big parlor chair, mended, near by, the old couch covered with a portière standing on the other side, she turned her attention to the loft, and, gathering courage, climbed up there.

There were two great openings that let in the light; but they seemed like tiny mouse-holes in the great place, and the hay lay sweet and dim, thinly scattered over the whole big floor. In one corner there was quite a luxurious lot of it, and Shirley cast herself down upon it for a blessed minute, and looked up to the dark rafters, lit with beams of sunlight creeping through fantastic cracks here and there, and wondered how the boys would enjoy sleeping up here, though there was plenty of room down-stairs for a dozen sleeping-rooms for the matter of that.

Foolish, of course, and utterly impossible, as all day-dreams always had been; but somehow it seemed so real and beautiful that she could scarcely bring herself to abandon it. Nevertheless, her investigation had made her hungry, and she decided at last to go down and eat her lunch under the big tree out in the sunshine; for it was dark and stuffy inside, although one could realize how beautiful it would be with those two great doors flung wide, and light and air let in.

The day was perfect, and Shirley found a beautiful place to sit, high and sheltered, where she would not be noticed when the trolley-cars sped by; and, as she ate her sandwiches, she let her imagination build a beautiful piazza where the grassy rise came up to the front of the barn, and saw in thought her mother sitting with the children at the door. How grand it would be to live in a home like this, even if it were a barn! If they could just get out here for the summer, it would do wonders for them all, and put new heart into her mother for the hard work of the winter. Perhaps by fall mother would be well enough to keep boarders as she longed to do, and so help out with the finances more.

Well, of course, this was just one of her wild schemes, and she must not think any more about it, much less even speak of it at home, for they would never get done laughing and teasing her for it.

She finished the last crumb of the piece of one-egg cake that Carol had made the day before for her lunch, and ran down to the spring to see whether she could get a drink, for she was very thirsty.

There proved to be an old tin can on the stones in the spring-house, doubtless used by the last tramp or conductor who came that way; but Shirley scrubbed it carefully in the sand, drank a delicious draught, and washed her hands and face in the clear cold water. Then she went back to the barn again, for a new thought had entered her mind. Supposing it were possible to rent that place for the summer at any reasonable price, how could they cook and how keep warm? Of course there were such things as candles and oil-lamps for lighting, but cooking! Would they have to build a fire out-of-doors and play at camping? Or would they have to resort to oil-stoves? Oil-stoves with their sticky, oily outsides, and their mysterious moods of smoke and sulkiness, out of which only an expert could coax them!

But, though she stood on all sides of that barn, and gazed up at the roof, and though she searched each floor diligently, she could find no sign of a chimney anywhere. Her former acquaintance with barns had not put her into a position to judge whether this was a customary lack of barns or not. There were two wooden, chimney-like structures decorating the roof, but it was all too evident that they were solely for purposes of ornament. Her heart sank. What a grand fireplace there might have been right in the middle of the great wall opposite the door! Could anything be more ideal? She could fancy mother sitting in front of it, with Harley and Doris on the floor playing with a kitten. But there was no fireplace. She wondered vaguely whether a stovepipe could be put out of the window, and so make possible a fire in a small cook-stove. She was sure she had seen stovepipes coming out of all sorts of odd places in the cities. But would the owners allow it? And would any fire at all perhaps make it dangerous and affect the fire-insurance? Oh, there were so many things to think about, and it was all so impossible, of course.

She turned with heavy heart, and let herself down the ladder. It was time she went home, for the afternoon was well on its way. She could hear the whir of the trolley-car going up. She must be out and down the road a little way to get the next one that passed it at the switch when it came back.

So with a wistful glance about the big dusty floor she turned away, and went down to the ground floor and out into the afternoon sunshine.

Just as she crossed the knoll and was stepping over the broken fence, she saw a clump of clover, and among the tiny stems one bearing four leaves. She was not superstititous, nor did the clover mean any special omen to her; but she stooped, smiling, and plucked it, tucking it into the buttonhole of her coat, and hurried down the road; for she could already hear the returning trolley-car, and she wished to be a little farther from the barn before it overtook her. Somehow she shrank from having people in the car know where she had been, for it seemed like exposing her audacious wish to the world.

Seated in the car, she turned her eyes back to the last glimpse of the stone gables and the sweeping branches of the budding tree as the car sped down the hill and curved away behind another slope.

After all, it was but half-past four when the car reached the city hall. Its route lay on half a mile nearer to the little brick house, and she could stay in it, and have a shorter walk if she chose. It was not in the least

17

likely anybody would be in any office at this hour of the day, anyway; that is, anybody with authority; but somehow Shirley had to signal that car and get out, long walk or not. A strong desire seized her to put her fate to the test, and either crush out this dream of hers forever, or find out at once whether it had a foundation to live.

She walked straight to the Ward Trust Building and searched the bulletin-board in the hallway carefully. Yes, there is was, "Graham-Walter—Fourth floor front."

With rapidly beating heart she entered the elevator and tried to steady her voice as she said, "Fourth"; but it shook in spite of her. What was she doing? How dared she? What should she say when they asked her what she wanted?

But Shirley's firm little lips were set, and her head had that tilt that her mother knew meant business. She had gone so far she would see the matter to the finish, even if it *was* ridiculous. For now that she was actually on the elevator and almost to the fourth floor it seemed the most extraordinary thing in the world for a girl to enter a great business office and demand that its head should stoop to rent her an old barn out in the country for the infinitesimal sum she could offer. He would perhaps think her crazy, and have her put out.

But she got out of the elevator calmly, and walked down the hall to where a ground-glass door proclaimed in gold letters the name she was hunting. Timidly she turned the knob, and entered a large room, spacious and high ceiled, with Turkish rugs on the inlaid floor, leather chairs, and mahogany desks.

There was no one in the office but a small office-boy, who lolled idly on one elbow on the table, reading the funny page of the afternoon paper. She paused, half frightened, and looked about her appealingly; and now she began to be afraid she was too late. It had taken longer than she had thought it would to get here. It was almost a quarter to five by the big clock on the wall. No head of a business firm was likely to stay in his office so late in the day as that, she knew. Yet she could hear the steady click of typewriter keys in an inner office; he might have remained to dictate a letter.

The office-boy looked up insolently.

"Is Mr. Graham in?" asked Shirley.

"Which Mr. Graham?"

"Why," hesitating and catching the name on the door, "Mr. Walter Graham."

"No, he isn't here. Never here after four o'clock." The boy dropped on his elbow again, and resumed his reading.

"Oh!" said Shirley, dismayed now, in spite of her fright, as she saw all hope fading from her. "Well, is there another—I mean is the other—Mr. Graham in?"

Someone stirred in the inner office, and came across to the door, looking out, someone with an overcoat and hat on. He looked at the girl, and then spoke sharply to the boy, who stood up straight as if he had been shot.

"Edward! See what the lady wants."

"Yes, sir!" said Edward with sudden respect.

Shirley caught her breath, and plunged in.

"I would like to see *some* Mr. Graham if possible for just a moment." There was something self-possessed and businesslike in her voice now that commanded the boy's attention. Her brief business training was upon her.

The figure from the inner room emerged, and took off his hat. He was a young man and strikingly handsome, with heavy dark hair that waved over his forehead and fine, strong features. His eyes were both keen and kind. There was something luminous in them that made Shirley think of Doris's eyes when she asked a question. Doris had wonderfully wise eyes.

"I am Mr. *Sidney* Graham," said the young man, advancing. "What can I do for you?"

"Oh, I wanted to ask you about a barn," began Shirley eagerly, then stopped abashed. How could she ask this immaculate son of luxury if he would rent a young girl his barn to live in during the summer? She could feel the color mounting in her cheeks, and would have turned and fled gladly if a way had been open. She was aware not only of the kind eyes of the man

19

upon her, but also of the gaping boy taking it all in, and her tongue was suddenly tied. She could say no more.

But the young man saw how it was, and he bowed as gracefully as if asking about barns was a common habit of young women coming into his office.

"Oh, certainly," he said; "won't you just step in here a moment and sit down? We can talk better. Edward, you may go. I shall not need you any longer this evening."

"But I am detaining you; you were just going out!" cried Shirley in a panic. "I will go away now and come again—perhaps." She would do anything to get away without telling her preposterous errand.

"Not at all!" said young Mr. Graham. "I am in no hurry whatever. Just step this way, and sit down." His tone was kindness itself. Somehow Shirley had to follow him. Her face was crimson now, and she felt ready to cry. What a fool she had been to get herself into a predicament like this! What would her mother say to her? How could she tell this strange young man what she had come for? But he was seated and looking at her with his nice eyes, taking in all the little pitiful attempts at neatness and style and beauty in her shabby little toilet. She was awfully conscious of a loose fluff of gold-glinted hair that had come down over one hot cheek and ear. How dishevelled she must look, and how dusty after climbing over that dirty barn! And then she plunged into her subject.

CHAPTER III

"I'M sure I don't know what you will think of my asking," said Shirley excitedly, "but I want very much to know whether there is any possibility that you would rent a beautiful big stone barn you own out on the old Glenside Road, near Allister Avenue. You do own it, don't you? I was told you did, or at least that Mr. Walter Graham did. They said it belonged to 'the estate.' "

"Well, now you've got one on me," said the young

man with a most engaging smile. "I'm sure I don't know whether I own it or not. I'm sorry. But if it belongs to grandfather's estate,—his name was Walter, too, you know,—why, I suppose I do own part of it. I'm sorry father isn't here. He of course knows all about it—or the attorney—of course he would know. But I think he has left the office. However, that doesn't matter. What was it you wanted? To rent it, you say?"

"Yes," said Shirley, feeling very small and very much an imposter; "that is, if I could afford it. I suppose perhaps it will be way ahead of my means, but I thought it wouldn't do any harm to ask." Her shy eyes were almost filled with tears, and the young man was deeply distressed.

"Not at all, not at all," he hastened to say. "I'm just stupid that I don't know about it. Where did you say it was? Out on the Glenside Road? A barn? Come to think of it, I remember one of my uncles lived out that way once, and I know there is a lot of land somewhere out there belonging to the estate. You say there is a barn on it?"

"Yes, a beautiful barn," said Shirley anxiously, her eyes dreamy and her cheeks like two glowing roses. "It is stone, and has a wide grassy road like a great staircase leading up to it, and a tall tree over it. There is a brook just below,—it is high up from the road on a little grassy hill."

"Oh, yes, yes," he said, nodding eagerly, "I see! It almost seems as if I remember. And you wanted to rent it for the summer, you say? You are—ah—in the agricultural business, I suppose?" He looked at her respectfully. He knew the new woman, and honored her. He did not seem at all startled that she wanted to rent a barn for the summer.

But Shirley did not in the least understand. She looked at him bewildered a moment.

"Oh, no! I am only a stenographer myself—but my mother—that is——" she paused in confusion.

"Oh, I see, your mother is the farmer, I suppose. Your home is near by—near to the barn you want to rent?"

Then she understood.

21

"No, oh, no!" she said desperately. "We don't want to use the barn for a barn at all. I want to use it for a house!"

It was out at last, the horrible truth; and she sat trembling to see his look of amazement.

"Use it for a house!" he exclaimed. "Why, how could you? To live in, do you mean? or just to take a tent and camp our there for a few days?"

"To *live in*," said Shirley doggedly, lifting her eyes in one swift defiant look and then dropping them to her shabby gloves and thin pocketbook, empty now even of the last precious nickel. If he said anything more, she was sure she should cry. If he patronized her the least little bit, or grew haughty, now that he saw how low she was reduced, she would turn and fly from the office and never look him in the face.

But he did neither. Instead, he just talked in a natural tone, as if it were the most common thing in the world for a girl to want to live in a barn, and nothing to be surprised over in the least.

"Oh, I see," he said pleasantly. "Well, now, that might be arranged, you know. Of course I don't know much about things, but I could find out. You see, I don't suppose we often have calls to rent the property that way——"

"No, of course not," said Shirley, gathering up her scattered confidence. "I know it's queer for me to ask, but we *have* to move—they are going to build an apartment-house where we are renting now, and mother is sick. I should like to get her out into the country, our house is so little and dark; and I thought, if she could be all summer where she could see the sky and hear the birds, she might get well. I want to get my little sisters and brothers out of the city, too. But we couldn't likely pay enough rent. I suppose it was silly of me to ask."

"Not at all!" said the young man courteously, as though she had been a queen whom he delighted to honor. "I don't see why we shouldn't be able to get together on some kind of a proposition—that is, unless father has other plans that I don't know about. A

22

barn ought not to be worth such a big price. How much would you feel like paying?"

He was studying the girl before him with interested eyes, noting the well-set head on the pretty shoulders, even in spite of the ill-fitting shabby blue coat; the delicate features; the glint of gold in the soft brown hair; the tilt of the firm little chin, and the wistfulness in the big blue eyes. This was a new kind of girl, and he was disposed to give her what she wanted if he could. And he *could*. He knew well that anything he willed mightily would not be denied him.

The frightened color came into the delicate cheeks again, and the blue eyes fluttered down ashamedly.

"We are only paying fifteen a month now," she said; "and I couldn't pay any more, for we haven't got it. I couldn't pay as *much,* for it would cost sixty cents a week apiece for George and me to come in to our work from there. I couldn't pay more than twelve! and I know that's ridiculous for such a great big, beautiful place, but—I *had* to ask."

She lifted her eyes swiftly in apology, and dropped them again; the young man felt a glow of sympathy for her, and a deep desire to help her have her wish.

"Why, certainly," he said heartily. "Of course you did. And it's not ridiculous at all for you to make a business proposition of any kind. You say what you can do, and we accept it or not as we like. That's our lookout. Now of course I can't answer about this until I've consulted father; and, not knowing the place well, I haven't the least idea what it's worth; it may not be worth even twelve dollars." (He made a mental reservation that it *should* not be if he could help it.) "Suppose I consult with father and let you know. Could I write or phone you, or will you be around this way any time to-morrow?"

Shirley's breath was fairly gone with the realization that he was actually considering her proposition in earnest. He had not laughed at her for wanting to live in a barn, and he had not turned down the price she offered as impossible! He was looking at her in a kindly way as if he liked her for being frank.

23

"Why, yes," she said, looking up shyly, "I can come in to-morrow at my noon hour—if that would not be too soon. I always have a little time to myself then, and it isn't far from the office."

"That will be perfectly all right for me," smiled young Graham. "I shall be here till half-past one, and you can ask the boy to show you to my office. I will consult with father the first thing in the morning and be ready to give you an answer. But I am wondering if you have seen this barn. I suppose you have, or you would not want to rent it; but I should suppose a barn would be an awfully unpleasant place to live, kind of almost impossible. Are you sure you realize what the proposition would be?"

"Yes, I think so," said Shirley, looking troubled and earnest. "It is a beautiful big place, and the outlook is wonderful. I was there to-day, and found a door open at the back, and went in to look around. The up-stairs middle floor is so big we could make several rooms out of it with screens and curtains. It would be lovely. We could live in picnic style. Yes, I'm sure mother would like it. I haven't told her about it yet, because if I couldn't afford it I didn't want to disappoint her; so I thought I would wait till I found out; but I'm just about certain she would be delighted. And anyhow we've *got* to go *some*where."

"I see," said this courteous young man, trying not to show his amazement and delight in the girl who so coolly discussed living in a barn with curtains and screens for partitions. He thought of his own luxurious home and his comfortable life, where every need had been supplied even before he realized it, and, wondering again, was refreshed in soul by this glimpse into the brave heart of the girl.

"Then I will expect you," he said pleasantly, and, opening the door, escorted her to the elevator, touching his hat to her as he left her.

Shirley would not have been a normal girl if she had not felt the least flutter in her heart at the attention he showed her and the pleasant tones of his voice. It was for all the world as if she had been a lady dressed in broadcloth and fur. She looked down at her shabby

24

little serge suit—that had done duty all winter with an old gray sweater under it—half in shame and half in pride in the man who had not let it hinder him from giving her honor. He was a *man*. He must be. She had bared her poverty-stricken life to his gaze, and he had not taken advantage of it. He had averted his eyes, and acted as if it were just like other lives and others' necessities; and he had made her feel that she was just as good as any one with whom he had to deal.

Well, it was probably only a manner, a kind of refined, courteous habit he had; but it was lovely, and she was going to enjoy the bit of it that had fallen at her feet.

On the whole, Shirley walked the ten blocks to her narrow little home feeling that she had had a good day. She was weary, but it was a healthy weariness. The problem which had been pressing on her brain for days, and nights too, did not seem so impossible now, and hope was in her heart that somehow she would find a way out. It had been good to get away from the office and the busy monotony and go out into the wide, open out-of-doors. It was good also to meet a real nobleman, even if it were only in passing, and on business.

She decided not to tell her mother and the children of her outing yet, not until she was sure there were to be results. Besides, it might only worry her mother the more and give her a sleepless night if she let out the secret about the barn.

One more little touch of pleasantness there came to make this day stand out from others as beautiful. It was when she turned into Chapel Street, and was swinging along rapidly in order to get home at her usual time and not alarm her mother, that a car rolled quickly past to the middle of the block, and stopped just under a street-light. In a moment more a lady came out of the door of a house, entered the car, and was driven away. As she closed the car-door, Shirley fancied she saw something drop from the lady's hand. When Shirley reached the place she found it was two great, luscious pink rosebuds that must have slipped from the lady's corsage and fallen on the pavement. Shirley picked them up almost reverently, inhaling their exotic breath, and taking in their delicate curves and texture. Then she looked after the limousine. It was three blocks away and just turning into another street. It would be impossible for her to overtake it, and there was little likelihood of the lady's returning for two roses. Probably she would never miss them. Shirley turned toward the house, thinking she ought to take them in, but discovered that it bore the name of a fashionable modiste, who would, of course, not have any right to the roses, and Shirley's conscience decided they were meant by Providence for her. So, happily, she hurried on to the little brick house, bearing the wonderful flowers to her mother.

She hurried so fast that she reached home ten minutes earlier than usual, and they all gathered around her eagerly as if it were some great event, the mother calling half fearfully from her bedroom up-stairs to know whether anything had happened. She was always expecting some new calamity like sickness, or the loss of their positions by one or the other of her children.

"Nothing at all the matter, mother dear!" called Shirley happily as she hung up her coat and hat, and hugged Doris. "I got off earlier than usual because Mr. Barnard had to go away. Just see what a beautiful thing I have brought you—found it on the street, dropped by a beautiful lady. You needn't be afraid of them, for she and her limousine looked perfectly hygienic; and it wasn't stealing, because I couldn't possibly have caught her. Aren't they lovely?"

By this time she was up in her mother's room, with Doris and Carol following close behind exclaiming in delight over the roses.

She kissed her mother, and put the flowers into a glass beside the bed.

"You're looking better to-night, I believe, dear," said the mother. "I've been worried about you all day. You were so white and tired this morning."

"Oh, I'm feeling fine, mother dear!" said Shirley

gayly, "and I'm going down to make your toast and poach you an egg while Carol finishes getting supper. George will be here in ten minutes now, and Harley ought to be in any minute. He always comes when he gets hungry. My! I'm hungry myself! Let's hurry, Carol. Doris, darling, you fix mother's little table all ready for her tray. Put on the white cloth, take away the books, set the glass with the roses in the middle very carefully. You won't spill it, will you, darling?"

Doris, all smiles at the responsibility accorded her, promised: "No, I yun't spill it. I'll move it tarefully."

There was something in Shirley's buoyant air that night that lifted them all above the cares that had oppressed them for weeks, and gave them new hope. She flew around, getting the supper things together, making her mother's tray pretty, and taking little extra pains for each one as she had not felt able to do before. Carol caught the contagion, and mashed the potatoes more carefully, so that there wasn't a single lump in them.

"Goodness! But it's been hot in this kitchen all day, Shirley," said Carol. "I had the back door open, but it just seemed stifling. I got the ironing all done except a tablecloth, and I guess I can finish that this evening. I haven't got much studying to do for to-morrow. Nellie Waite stopped and left me my books. I don't believe I'll have to stay at home another day this week. Mother says she can get along. I can leave her lunch all ready, and Doris can manage."

Shirley's conscience gave a sudden twinge. Here had she been sitting under a lovely tree by a brook, eating her lunch and dreaming foolish day-dreams about living in a barn, while Carol stayed at home from school and toiled in the kitchen! Perhaps she ought to have come home and sent Carol back to school. And yet perhaps that nice young Mr. Graham would be able to do something; she would not condemn herself until the morrow, anyway. She had tried to do her best. She had not gone off there selfishly just to have a good time by herself when her dear ones were suffering. It had been for their sake.

Then George came in whistling, and Harley banged in gayly a minute later, calling to know whether supper was ready.

"'Cause I gotta date with the fellas this evening, and I gotta beat it," he declared impatiently.

The shadow of anxiety passed over Shirley's face again at that, but she quieted her heart once more with her hopes for to-morrow. If her plan succeeded, Harley would be away from "the fellas," and wouldn't have so many questionable "dates" to worry them all.

George was in a hurry, too.

"Gee, Shirley, I gotta be at the store all evening," he said, bolting his food hurriedly. "I wouldn't 'a' come home, only I knew you'd worry, and mother gets so upset. Gee, Shirley, what we gonta do about a house? It's getting almost time to move. I went to all those places you suggested at noon to-day, but there wasn't a vacant spot anywhere. There's some rooms on Louden Street, but there's all sorts in the house. Mother wouldn't like it. It's dirty besides. I suppose if we look long enough we could find rooms; but we'd have to get along with only two or three, for they come awful high. We'd have to have three anyway, you girls and mother in one, us boys in the other, and one for parlor and kitchen together. Gee! Wouldn't that be fierce? I oughtta get a better job. We can't live that way."

"Don't worry, George; I think we'll find something better," said Shirley with a hopeful ring in her voice. "I've been thinking out a plan. I haven't got it all just arranged in my mind yet, but I'll tell you about it pretty soon. You don't have school to-morrow night, do you? No, I thought not. Well, maybe we can talk it over then. You and I will have to go out together and look up a place perhaps," and she smiled an encouraging smile, and sent him off to his school happily.

She extracted a promise from Harley that he would be in by nine o'clock, discovered that he was only going to a "movie" show around the corner with one of the fellows who was going to "stand treat" on account of a wonderful ball game they had won, found out where his lessons were for the morrow, promised to help him when he returned, and sent him away with a feeling of comfort and responsibility to return early. She washed the dishes and ironed the tablecloth so Carol could go to her lessons. Then she went up and put Doris to bed with a story about a little bird that built a nest in a tall, beautiful tree that grew beside the place where the little girl lived; a little bird that drank from a little running brook, and took a bath on its pebbly shore, and ate the crumbs and berries the little girl gave it, and sat all day on five little blue eggs.

Harley came in at five minutes after nine, and did his lessons with her help. George came home just as they finished. He was whistling, though he looked tired. He said "the prof." had been "the limit" all the evening. Shirley fixed her mother comfortably for the night, and went at last to her own bed, more tired than she had been for weeks, and yet more happy. For through it all she had been sustained by a hope; inspired by a cultured, pleasant voice, and eyes that wanted to help, and seemed to understand.

As she closed her eyes to sleep, somehow that pleasant voice and those kind eyes mingled with her dreams, and seemed to promise relief from her great anxieties.

It was with a feeling of excitement and anticipation that she dressed the next morning and hurried away. Something was coming, she felt sure, some help for their trying situation. She had felt it when she knelt for her usual prayer that morning, and it throbbed in her excited heart as she hurried through the streets to the office. It almost frightened her to feel so sure, for she knew how terrible would be the disappointment if she got her hopes too high.

There was plenty to be done at the office, a great many letters to answer, and a telegram with directions from Mr. Barnard. But she worked with more ease than for some time, and was done by half-past eleven. When she took the letters out to Mr. Clegg to be signed, he told her that she would not be needed the rest of the day, and might go at once if she chose.

She ate her bit of lunch hurriedly, and made herself as fresh and tidy as was possible in the office. Then she took her way to the fourth floor of the Ward Trust Building. With throbbing heart and glowing cheeks she entered the office of Walter Graham, and asked for Mr. Sidney Graham.

The office-boy had evidently received instructions, for he bowed most respectfully this time, and led her at once to the inner office.

CHAPTER IV

THE afternoon before, when Mr. Sidney Graham had returned to his office from seeing Shirley to the elevator, he stood several minutes looking thoughtfully at the chair where she had sat, while he carefully drew on his gloves.

There had been something interesting and appealing in the spirited face of the girl, with her delicate features and wistful eyes. He could not seem to get away from it. It had left an impression of character and a struggle with forces of which in his sheltered life he had had only a vague conception. It had left him with the feeling that she was stronger in some ways than himself, and he did not exactly like the sensation of it. He had always aimed to be a strong character himself; and for a young man who had inherited two hundred and fifty thousand dollars on coming of age, and double that amount two years later, with the prospect of another goodly sum with his paternal grandfather's estate was divided, he had done very well indeed. He had stuck to business ever since leaving college, where he had been by no means a nonentity either in studies or in athletics; and he had not been spoiled by the adulation that a young man of his good looks and wealth and position always receives in society. He had taken society as a sort of duty, but had never given it an undue proportion of his time and thoughts. Notably he was a young man of fine balance and strong self-control, not given to impulsive or erratic likes and dislikes; and he could not understand why a shabby little person with a lock of gold over one crimson cheek, and tired, discouraged lights in her eyes, had made so strong an impression upon him.

It had been his intention just before Shirley's arrival to leave the office at once and perhaps drop in on Miss Harriet Hale. If the hour seemed propitious, he would take her for a spin in his new racing-car that even now waited in the street below; but somehow suddenly his plan did not attract him deeply. He felt the need of being by himself. After a turn or two up and down his luxurious office he took the elevator down to the street floor, dismissed his chauffeur, and whirled off in his car, taking the opposite direction from that which would have taken him to the Hale residence. Harriet Hale was a very pretty girl with a brilliant mind and a royal fortune. She could entertain him and stimulate him tremendously, and sometimes he almost thought the attraction was strong enough to last him through life; but Harriet Hale would not be able to appreciate his present mood nor explain to him why the presence in his office for fifteen minutes of a nervy little stenographer who was willing to live in a barn should have made him so vaguely dissatisfied with himself. If he were to try to tell her about it, he felt sure he would meet with laughing taunts and brilliant sarcasm. She would never understand.

He took little notice of where he was going, threading his way skilfully through the congested portion of the city and out into the comparatively empty highways, until at last he found himself in the suburbs. The name of the street as he slowed up at a grade crossing gave him an idea. Why shouldn't he take a run out and hunt up that barn for himself? What had she said about it, where it was? He consulted the memorandum he had written down for his father's edification. "Glenside Road, near Allister Avenue." He further searched his memory. "Big stone barn, wide approach like a grand staircase, tall tree overhanging, brook." This surely ought to be enough to help him identify it. There surely were not a flock of stone barns in that neighborhood that would answer that description.

He turned into Glenside Road with satisfaction, and set a sharp watch for the names of the cross-avenues with a view to finding Allister Avenue, and once he stopped and asked a man in an empty milk-wagon whether he knew where Allister Avenue was, and was informed that it was "on a piece, about five miles."

There was something interesting in hunting up his own strange barn, and he began to look about him and try to see things with the eyes of the girl who had just called upon him.

Most of the fields were green with spring, and there was an air of things doing over them, as if growing were a business that one could watch, like house-cleaning and paper-hanging and painting. Graham had never noticed before that the great bare spring out-of-doors seemed to have a character all its own, and actually to have an attraction. A little later when the trees were out, and all the orchards in bloom, and the wild flowers blowing in the breeze, he could rave over spring; but he had never seen the charm of its beginnings before. He wondered curiously over the fact of his keen appreciation now.

The sky was all opalescent with lovely pastel colors along the horizon, and a few tall, lank trees had put on a soft gauze of green over their foreheads like frizzes, discernible only to a close observer. The air was getting chilly with approaching night, and the bees were no longer proclaiming with their hum the way to the skunk-cabbages; but a delicate perfume was in the air, and though perhaps Graham had never even heard of skunk-cabbages, he drew in long breaths of sweetness, and let out his car over the smooth road with a keen delight.

Behind a copse of fine old willows, age-tall and hoary with weather, their extremities just hinting of green, as they stood knee-deep in the brook on its way to a larger stream, he first caught sight of the old barn.

He knew it at once by something indefinable. Its substantial stone spaciousness, its mossy roof, its arching tree, and the brook that backed away from the wading willows, up the hillside, under the rail fence, and ran around its side, all were unmistakable. He could see it just as the girl had seen it, and something in him responded to her longing to live there and make it into a home. Perhaps he was a dreamer, even as she, although he passed in the world of business for a practical young man. But anyhow he slowed his car down and looked at the place intently as he passed by. He was convinced that this was the place. He did not need to go on and find Allister Avenue—though he did, and then turned back again, stopping by the roadside. He got out of the car, looking all the time at the barn and seeing it in the light of the girl's eyes. As he walked up the grassy slope to the front doors, he had some conception of what it must be to live so that this would seem grand as a home. And he showed he was not spoiled by his life in the lap of luxury, for he was able to get a glimpse of the grandeur of the spot and the dignity of the building with its long simple lines and rough old stones.

The sun was just going down as he stood there looking up. It touched the stones, and turned them into jewelled settings, glorifying the old structure into a palace. The evening was sweet with the voices of birds not far away. One above the rest, clear and occasional, high in the elm-tree over the barn, a wood-thrush spilling its silver notes down to the brook that echoed them back in a lilt. The young man took off his hat and stood in the evening air, listening and looking. He could see the poetry of it, and somehow he could see the girl's face as if she stood there beside him, her wonderful eyes lighted as they had been when she told him how beautiful it was there. She was right. It was beautiful, and it was a lovely soul that could see it and feel what a home this would make in spite of the ignominy of its being nothing but a barn. Some dim memory, some faint remembrance, of a stable long ago, and the glory of it, hovered on the horizon of his mind; but his education had not been along religious lines, and he did not put the thing into a definite thought. It was just a kind of sensing of a great fact of the universe which he perhaps might have understood in a former existence.

33

Then he turned to the building itself. He was practical, after all, even if he was a dreamer. He tried the big padlock. How did they get into this thing? How had the girl got in? Should he be obliged to break into his own barn?

He walked down the slope, around to the back, and found the entrance close to the ladder; but the place was quite dark within the great stone walls, and he peered into the gloomy basement with disgust at the dirt and murk. Only here and there, where a crack looked toward the setting sun, a bright needle of light sent a shaft through to let one see the inky shadows. He was half turning back, but reflected that the girl had said she went up a ladder to the middle floor. If she had gone, surely he could. Again that sense that she was stronger than he rebuked him. He got out his pocket flash-light and stepped within the gloom determinedly. Holding the flash-light above his head, he surveyed his property disapprovingly; then with the light in his hand he climbed in a gingerly way up the dusty rounds to the middle floor.

As he stood alone in the dusky shadows of the big barn, with the blackness of the hay-loft overhead, the darkness pierced only by the keen blade of the flash-light and a few feebler darts from the sinking sun, the poetry suddenly left the old barn, and a shudder ran through him. To think of trying to live here! How horrible!

Yet still that same feeling that the girl had more nerve than he had forced him to walk the length and breadth of the floor, peering carefully into the dark corners and acquainting himself fully with the bare, big place; and also to climb part way up the ladder to the loft and send his flash-light searching through its dusty hay-strewn recesses.

With a feeling utterly at variance with the place he turned away in disgust, and made his way down the ladders again, out into the sunset.

In that short time the evening had arrived. The sky had flung out banners and pennants, pencilled by a fringe of fine saplings like slender brown threads against the sky. The earth was sinking into dusk, and off by the brook the frogs were tinkling like tiny answering silver rattles. The smell of earth and growing stole upon his senses, and even as he gazed about him a single star burned into being in the clear ether above him. The birds were still now, and the frogs with the brook for accompaniment held the stage. Once more the charm of the place stole over him; and he stood with hat removed, and wondered no longer that the girl was willing to live here. A conviction grew within him that somehow he must make it possible for her to do so, that things would not be right and as they ought to be unless he did. In fact, he had a curiosity to have her do it and see whether it could be done.

He went slowly down to his car at last with lingering backward looks. The beauty of the situation was undoubted, and called for admiration. It was too bad that only a barn should occupy it. He would like to see a fine house reared upon it. But somehow in his heart he was glad that it was not a fine house standing there against the evening sky, and that it was possible for him to let the girl try her experiment of living there. Was it possible? Could there be any mistake? Could it be that he had not found the right barn, after all? He must make sure, of course,

But still he turned his car toward home, feeling reasonably sure that he had found the right spot; and, as he drove swiftly back along the way, he was thinking, and all his thoughts were woven with the softness of the spring evening and permeated with its sounds. He seemed to be in touch with nature as he had never been before.

At dinner that night he asked his father:

"Did Grandfather Graham ever live out on the old Glenside Road, father?"

A pleasant twinkle came in the elder Graham's eyes.

"Sure!" he said. "Lived there myself when I was five years old, before the old man got to speculating and made his pile, and we got too grand to stay in a farmhouse. I can remember rolling down a hill under a great big tree, and your Uncle Billy pushing me into the brook that ran at the foot. We boys used to wade in that brook, and build dams, and catch little minnows, and sail boats. It was great sport. I used to go back holidays now and then after I got old enough to go away to school. We were living in town then, but I used to like to go out and stay at the farmhouse. It was rented to a queer old dick; but his wife was a good sort, and made the bulliest apple turnovers for us boys —and doughnuts! The old farmhouse burned down a year or so ago. But the barn is still standing. I can remember how proud your grandfather was of that barn. It was finer than any barn around, and bigger. We boys used to go up in the loft, and tumble in the hay; and once when I was a little kid I got lost in the hay, and Billy had to dig me out. I can remember how scared I was when I thought I might have to stay there forever, and have nothing to eat."

"Say, father," said the son, leaning forward eagerly, "I've a notion I'd like to have that old place in my share. Do you think it could be arranged? The boys won't care, I'm sure; they're always more for the town than the country."

"Why, yes, I guess that could be fixed up. You just see Mr. Dalrymple about it. He'll fix it up. Billy's boy got that place up river, you know. Just see the lawyer, and he'll fix it up. No reason in the world why you shouldn't have the old place if you care for it. Not much in it for money, though, I guess. They tell me property's way down out that direction now."

The talk passed to other matters, and Sidney Graham said nothing about his caller of the afternoon, nor of the trip he had taken out to see the old barn. Instead, he took his father's advice, and saw the family lawyer, Mr. Dalrymple, the first thing in the morning.

It was all arranged in a few minutes. Mr. Dalrymple called up the other heirs and the children's guardian. An office-boy hurried out with some papers, and came back with the signatures of heirs and guardians, who happened all to be within reach; and presently the control of the old farm was formally put into the hands of Mr. Sidney Graham, he having signed certain papers agreeing to take this as such and such portion of his right in the whole estate.

It had been a simple matter; and yet, when at about

36

half-past eleven o'clock Mr. Dalrymple's stenographer laid a folded paper quietly on Sidney Graham's desk and silently left the room, he reached out and touched it with more satisfaction than he had felt in any acquisition in a long time, not excepting his last racing-car. It was not the value the paper represented, however, that pleased him, but the fact that he would now be able to do as he pleased concerning the prospective tenant for the place, and follow out a curious and interesting experiment. He wanted to study this girl and see whether she really had the nerve to go and live in a barn—a girl with a face like that to live in a barn! He wanted to see what manner of girl she was, and to have the right to watch her for a little space.

It is true that the morning light might present her in a very different aspect from that in which she had appeared the evening before, and he mentally reserved the right to turn her down completely if she showed the least sign of not being all that he had thought her. At the same time, he intended to be entirely sure. He would not turn her away without a thorough investigation.

Graham had been greatly interested in the study of social science when in college, and human nature interested him at all times. He could not but admit to himself that this girl had taken a most unusual hold upon his thoughts.

CHAPTER V

As the morning passed on and it drew near to the noon hour Sidney Graham found himself almost excited over the prospect of the girl's coming. Such foolish fancies as a fear lest she might have given up the idea and would not come at all presented themselves to his distraught brain, which refused to go on its well-ordered way, but kept reverting to the expected caller and what he should say to her. When at last she was announced, he drew back his chair from the desk and prepared to meet her with a strange tremor in his whole bearing. It annoyed him, and brought almost a frown of sternness to his fine features. It seemed not quite in keeping with his dignity as junior member of his father's firm that he should be so childish over a simple matter like this, and he began to doubt whether, after all, he might not be doing a most unwise and irregular thing in having anything at all to do with this girl's preposterous proposition. Then Shirley entered the office, looked eagerly into his eyes; and he straight-way forgot all his reasoning. He met her with a smile that seemed to reassure her, for she drew in her breath half relieved, and smiled shyly back.

She was wearing a little old crêpe de chine waist that she had dyed a real apple-blossom pink in the wash-bowl with a bit of pink crêpe-paper and a kettle of boiling water. The collar showed neatly over the shabby dark-blue coat, and seemed to reflect apple-blossom tints in her pale cheeks. There was something sky-like in the tint of her eyes that gave the young man a sense of spring fitness as he looked at her contentedly. He was conscious of gladness that she looked as good to him in the broad day as in the dusk of evening. There was still that spirited lift of her chin, that firm set of the sweet lips, that gave a conviction of strength and nerve. He reflected that he had seldom seen it in the girls of his acquaintance. Was it possible that poverty and privation and big responsibility made it, or was it just innate?

"You—you have found out?" she asked breathlessly as she sat down on the edge of the chair, her whole body tense with eagerness.

"Sure! It's all right," he said smilingly. "You can rent it if you wish."

"And the price?" It was evident the strain was intense.

"Why, the price will be all right, I'm sure. It really isn't worth what you mentioned at all. It's only a barn, you know. We couldn't think of taking more than ten dollars a month, if we took that. I must look it over again; but it won't be more than ten dollars, and it may be less."

Young Graham wore his most businesslike tone to say this, and his eyes were on the paper-knife wherewith he was mutilating his nice clean blotter pad on the desk.

"Oh!" breathed Shirley, the color almost leaving her face entirely with the relief of his words. "Oh, *really?*"

"And you haven't lost your nerve about living away out there in the country in a great empty barn?" he asked quickly to cover her embarrassment—and his own, too, perhaps.

"Oh, no!" said Shirley with a smile that showed a dimple in one cheek, and the star sparks in her eyes. "Oh, no! It is a lovely barn, and it won't be empty when we all get into it."

"Are there many of you?" he asked interestedly. Already the conversation was taking on a slightly personal tinge, but neither of them was at all aware of it.

"Two brothers and two sisters and mother," said the girl shyly. She was so full of delight over finding that she could rent the barn that she hardly knew what she was answering. She was unconscious of the fact that she had in a way taken this strange young man into her confidence by her shy, sweet tone and manner.

"Your mother approves of your plan?" he asked. "She doesn't object to the country?"

"Oh, I haven't told her yet," said Shirley. "I don't know that I shall; for she has been quite sick, and she trusts me entirely. She loves the country, and it will be wonderful to her to get out there. She might not like the idea of a barn beforehand; but she has never seen the barn, you know, and, besides, it won't look like a barn inside when I get it fixed up. I must talk it over with George and Carol, but I don't think I shall tell her at all till we take her out there and surprise her. I'll tell her I've found a place that I think she will like, and ask her if I may keep it a surprise. She'll be willing, and she'll be pleased, I know!" Her eyes were smiling happily, dreamily; the dreamer was uppermost in her face now, and made it lovely; then a sudden cloud came, and the strong look returned, with courage to meet a storm.

"But, anyhow," she finished after a pause, "we *have* to go there for the summer, for we've nowhere else to go that we can afford; and *anywhere* out of the city will be good, even if mother doesn't just choose it. I think perhaps it will be easier for her if she doesn't know about it until she's there. It won't seem so much like not going to live in a house."

"I see," said the young man interestedly. "I shouldn't wonder if you are right. And anyhow I think we can manage between us to make it pretty habitable for her." He was speaking eagerly and forgetting that he had no right, but a flush came into the sensitive girl's cheek.

"Oh, I wouldn't want to make you trouble," she said. "You have been very kind already, and you have made the rent so reasonable! I'm afraid it isn't right and fair; it is such a *lovely* barn!"

"Perfectly fair," said Graham glibly. "It will do the barn good to be lived in and taken care of again."

If he had been called upon to tell just what good it would do the barn to be lived in, he might have floundered out of the situation, perhaps; but he took care not to make that necessary. He went on talking.

"I will see that everything is in good order, the doors made all right, and the windows—I—that is, if I remember rightly there were a few little things needed doing to that barn that ought to be attended to before you go in. How soon did you want to take possession? I'll try to have it all ready for you."

"Oh, why, that is very kind," said Shirley. "I don't think it needs anything; that is, I didn't notice anything, but perhaps you know best. Why, we have to leave our house the last of this month. Do you suppose we could have the rent begin a few days before that, so we could get things moved gradually? I haven't much time, only at night, you know."

"We'll date the lease the first of next month," said the young man quickly; "and then you can put your things in any time you like from now on. I'll see that the locks are made safe, and there ought to be a partition put in—just a simple partition, you know—at one end of the up-stairs room, where you could lock up things. Then you could take them up there when you like. I'll attend to that partition at once. The barn needs it. This is as good a time as any to put it in. You wouldn't object to a partition? That wouldn't upset any of your plans?"

He spoke as if it would be a great detriment to the barn not to have a partition, but of course he wouldn't insist if she disliked it.

"Oh, why, no, of course not," said Shirley, bewildered. "It would be lovely. Mother could use that for her room, but I wouldn't want you to do anything on our account that you do not have to do anyway."

"Oh, no, certainly not, but it might as well be done now as any time, and you get the benefit of it, you know. I shouldn't want to rent the place without putting it in good order, and a partition is always needed in a barn, you know, if it's to be a really good barn."

It was well that no wise ones were listening to that conversation; else they might have laughed aloud at this point and betrayed the young man's strategy, but Shirley was all untutored in farm lore, and knew less about barns and their needs than she did of Sanskrit; so the remark passed without exciting her suspicion.

"Oh, it's going to be lovely!" said Shirley suddenly, like an eager child, "and I can't thank you enough for being so kind about it."

"Not at all," said the young man gracefully. "And now you will want to go out and look around again to make your plans. Were you planning to go soon? I should like to have you look the place over again and see if there is anything else that should be done."

"Oh, why," said Shirley, "I don't think there could be anything else; only I'd like to have a key to that big front door, for we couldn't carry things up the ladder very well. I was thinking I'd go out this afternoon, perhaps, if I could get George a leave of absence for a little while. There's been a death in our firm, and the office is working only half-time to-day, and I'm off again. I thought I'd like to have George see it if possible; he's very wise in his judgments, and mother trusts him a lot next to me; but I don't know whether they'll let him off on such short notice."

"Where does he work?"

"Farwell and Story's department store. They are pretty particular, but George is allowed a day off every three months if he takes it out of his vacation; so I thought I'd try."

"Here, let me fix that. Harry Farwell's a friend of mine." He caught up the telephone.

"Oh, you are very kind!" murmured Shirley, quite overcome at the blessings that were falling at her feet.

Graham already had the number, and was calling for Mr. Farwell, Junior.

"That you, Hal? Oh, good morning! Have a good time last night? Sorry I couldn't have been there, but I had three other engagements and couldn't get around. Say, I want to ask a favor of you. You have a boy there in the store I want to borrow for the afternoon if you don't mind. His name is George Hollister. Could you look him up and send him over to my office pretty soon? It will be a personal favor to me if you will let him off and not dock his pay. Thank you! I was sure you would. Return the favor sometime myself if opportunity comes my way. Yes, I'll hold the phone till you hunt him up. Thank you."

Graham looked up from the phone into the astonished, grateful girl's eyes, and caught her look of deep admiration, which quite confused Shirley for a moment, and put her in a terrible way trying to thank him again.

"Oh, that's all right. Farwell and I went to prep school together. It's nothing for him to arrange matters. He says it will be all right. Now, what are your plans? I wonder if I can help in any way. How were you planning to go out?"

"Oh, by the trolley, of course," said Shirley. How strange it must be to have other ways of travelling at one's command!

"I did think," she added, half thinking aloud, "that perhaps I would stop at the schoolhouse and get my sister. I don't know but it would be better to get her judgment about things. She is rather a wise little girl."

She looked up suddenly, and seeing the young man's eyes upon her, grew ashamed that she had brought her private affairs to his notice; yet it had seemed necessary to say something to fill in this embarrassing pause. But Sidney Graham did not let her continue to be embarrassed. He entered into her plans just as if they concerned himself also.

"Why, I think that would be a very good plan," he said. "It will be a great deal better to have a real family council before you decide about moving. Now I've thought of something. Why couldn't you all go out in the car with me and my kid sister? I've been promising to take her a spin in the country, and my chauffeur is to drive her down this afternoon for me. It's almost time for her to be here now. Your brother will be here by the time she comes. Why couldn't we just go around by the schoolhouse and pick up your sister, and all go out together? I want to go out myself, you know, and look things over, and it seems to me that would save time all around. Then, if there should be anything you want done, you know——"

"Oh, there is nothing I want done," gasped Shirley. "You have been most kind. I couldn't think of asking for anything at the price we shall be paying. And we mustn't impose upon you. We can go out in the trolley perfectly well, and not trouble you."

"Indeed, it is no trouble whatever when I am going anyway." Then to the telephone: "Hello! He's coming, you say? He's on his way? Good. Thank you very much, Harry. Good-by!"

"That's all right!" he said, turning to her, smiling. "Your brother is on his way, and now excuse me just a moment while I phone to my sister."

Shirley sat with glowing cheeks and apprehensive mind while the young man called up a girl whom he addressed as "Kid" and told her to hurry the car right down, that he wanted to start very soon, and to bring some extra wraps along for some friends he was going to take with him.

He left Shirley no opportunity to express her overwhelming thanks, but gave her some magazines, and hurried from the room to attend to some matters of business before he left.

SHIRLEY sat with shining eyes and glowing cheeks, turning over the leaves of the magazines with trembling fingers, but unable to read anything, for the joy of what was before her. A real automobile ride! The first she had ever had! And it was to include George and Carol! How wonderful! And how kind in him, how thoughtful, to take his own sister, and hers, and so make the trip perfectly conventional and proper! What a nice face he had! What fine eyes! He didn't seem in the least like the young society man she knew he must be from the frequent mention she had noticed of his name in the papers. He was a real gentleman, a real nobleman! There were such. It was nice to know of them now and then, even though they did move in a different orbit from the one where she had been set. It gave her a happier feeling about the universe just to have seen how nice a man could be to a poor little nobody when he didn't have to. For of course it couldn't be anything to him to rent that barn—at ten dollars a month! That was ridiculous! Could it be that he was thinking her an object of charity? That he felt sorry for her and made the price merely nominal? She couldn't have that. It wasn't right nor honest, and —it wasn't respectable! That was the way unprincipled men did when they wanted to humor foolish little dolls of girls. Could it be that he thought of her in any such way?

Her cheeks flamed hotly and her eyes flashed. She sat up very straight indeed, and began to tremble. How was it she had not thought of such a thing before? Her mother had warned her to be careful about having anything to do with strange men, except in the most distant business way; and here had she been telling him frankly all the private affairs of the family and letting him make plans for her. How had it happened? What must he think of her? This came of trying to keep a secret from mother. She might have known it was wrong, and yet the case was so desperate and mother so likely to worry about any new and unconventional suggestion. It had seemed right. But of course it wasn't right for her to fall in that way and allow him to take them all in his car. She must put a stop to it somehow. She must go in the trolley if she went at all. She wasn't sure but she had better call the whole thing off and tell him they couldn't live in a barn, that she had changed her mind. It would be so dreadful if he had taken her for one of those girls who wanted to attract the attention of a young man!

In the midst of her perturbed thoughts the door opened and Sidney Graham walked in again. His fine, clean-cut face and clear eyes instantly dispelled her fears again. His bearing was dignified and respectful, and there was something in the very tone of his voice as he spoke to her that restored her confidence in him and in his impression of her. Her half-formed intention of rising and declining to take the ride with him fled, and she sat quietly looking at the pictures in the magazine with unseeing eyes.

"I hope you will find something to interest you for a few minutes," young Graham said pleasantly. "It won't be long, but there are one or two matters I promised father I would attend to before I left this afternoon. There is an article in that other magazine under your hand there about beautifying country homes, bungalows, and the like. It may give you some ideas about the old barn. I shouldn't wonder if a few flowers and vines might do a whole lot."

He found the place in the magazine, and left her again; and strangely enough she became absorbed in the article because her imagination immediately set to work thinking how glorious it would be to have a few flowers growing where Doris could go out and water them and pick them. She grew so interested in the remarks about what flowers would grow best in the open and which were easiest to care for that she got out her little pencil and notebook that were in her coat-pocket, and began to copy some of the lists. Then suddenly the door opened again, and Graham returned with George.

The boy stopped short on the threshold, startled, a

45

white wave of apprehension passing over his face. He did not speak. The boy-habit of silence and self-control in a crisis was upon him. He looked with apprehension from one to the other.

Shirley jumped to her feet.

"Oh, George, I'm so glad you could come! This is Mr. Graham. He has been kind enough to offer to take us in his car to see a place we can rent for the summer, and it was through his suggestion that Mr. Farwell let you off for the afternoon."

There was a sudden relaxing of the tenseness in the young face and a sigh of relief in the tone as the boy answered:

"Aw, gee! That's great! Thanks awfully for the holiday. They don't come my way often. It'll be great to have a ride in a car, too. Some lark, eh, Shirley?"

The boy warmed to the subject with the friendly grasp the young man gave him, and Shirley could see her brother had made a good impression; for young Graham was smiling appreciatively, showing all his even white teeth just as if he enjoyed the boy's offhand way of talking.

"I'm going to leave you here for ten minutes more until I talk with a man out here in the office. Then we will go," said young Graham, and hurried away again.

"Gee, Shirley!" said the boy, flinging himself down luxuriously in a big leather chair. "Gee! You certainly did give me some start! I thought mother was worse, or you'd got arrested, or lost your job, or something, finding you here in a strange office. Some class to this, isn't there? Look at the thickness of that rug!" and he kicked the thick Turkish carpet happily. "Say, he must have some coin! Who is the guy, anyway? How'd ya get onto the tip? You don't think he's handing out Vanderbilt residences at fifteen a month, do you?"

"Listen, George. I must talk fast because he may come back any minute. Yesterday I got a half-holiday, and instead of going home I thought I'd go out and hunt a house. I took the Glenside trolley; and, when we got out past the city, I heard two men talking about a place we were passing. It was a great big, beautiful stone barn. They told who owned it, and

46

said a lot about its having such a splendid spring of water beside it. It was a beautiful place, George; and I couldn't help thinking what a thing it would be for mother to be out in the country this summer, and what a wonderful house that would make——"

"We couldn't live in a barn, Shirl!" said the boy, aghast.

"Wait, George. Listen. Just you don't say that till you see it. It's the biggest barn you ever saw, and I guess it hasn't been used for a barn in a long time. I got out of the trolley on the way back, and went in. It is just enormous, and we could screen off rooms and live like princes. It has a great big front door, and we could have a hammock under the tree; and there's a brook to fish in, and a big third story with hay in it. I guess it's what they call in books a hay-loft. It's great."

"Gee!" was all the electrified George could utter. "Oh, gee!"

"It is on a little hill with the loveliest tree in front of it, and right on the trolley line. We'd have to start a little earlier in the morning; but I wouldn't mind, would you?"

"Naw!" said George, "but could we walk that far?"

"No, we'd have to ride, but the rent is so much lower it would pay our carefare."

"Gee!" said George again, "isn't that great? And is this the guy that owns it?"

"Yes, or at least he and his father do. He's been very kind. He's taking all this trouble to take us out in his car to-day to make sure if there is anything that needs to be done for our comfort there. He certainly is an unusual man for a landlord."

"He sure is, Shirley. I guess mebbe he has a case on you the way he looks at you."

"George!" said Shirley severely, the red staining her cheeks and her eyes flashing angrily. "George! That was a *dreadful* thing for you to say. If you ever even *think* a thing like that again, I won't have anything to do with him or the place. We'll just stay in the city all summer. I suppose perhaps that would be better, anyway."

Shirley got up and began to button her coat haughtily, as if she were going out that minute.

"Aw, gee, Shirley! I was just kidding. Can't you take a joke? This thing must be getting on your nerves. I never saw you so touchy."

"It certainly is getting on my nerves to have you say a thing like that, George."

Shirley's tone was still severe.

"Aw, cut the grouch, Shirley. I tell you I was just kidding. 'Course he's a good guy. He probably thinks you're cross-eyed, knock-kneed——"

"George!" Shirley started for the door; but the irrepressible George saw it was time to stop, and he put out an arm with muscles that were iron-like from many wrestlings and ball-games with his fellow laborers at the store.

"Now, Shirley, cut the comedy. That guy'll be coming back next, and you don't want to have him ask what's the matter, do you? He certainly is some fine guy. I wouldn't like to embarrass him, would you? He's a peach of a looker. Say, Shirley, what do you figure mother's going to say about this?"

Shirley turned, half mollified.

"That's just what I want to ask you, George. I don't want to tell mother until it's all fixed up and we can show it to her. You know it will sound a great deal worse to talk about living in a barn than it will to go in and see it all fixed up with rugs and curtains and screens and the piano and a couch, and the supper-table set, and the sun setting outside the open door, and a bird singing in the tree."

"Gee! Shirley, wouldn't that be some class? Say, Shirley, don't let's tell her! Let's just make her say she'll trust the moving to us to surprise her. Can't you kid her along and make her willing for that?"

"Why, that was what I was thinking. If you think there's no danger she will be disappointed and sorry, and think we ought to have done something else."

"What else could we do? Say, Shirley, it would be great to sleep in the hay-loft!"

"We could just tell her we were coming out in the country for the summer to camp in a nice place where it was safe and comfortable, and then we would have plenty of time to look around for the right kind of a house for next winter."

"That's the dope, Shirley! You give her that. She'll fall for that, sure thing. She'll like the country. At least, if it's like what you say it is."

"Well, you wait till you see it."

"Have you told Carol?" asked George, suddenly sobering. Carol was his twin sister, inseparable chum, and companion when he was at home.

"No," said Shirley, "I haven't had a chance; but Mr. Graham suggested we drive around by the school and get her. Then she can see how she likes it, too; and, if Carol thinks so, we'll get mother not to ask any questions, but just trust to us."

"Gee! That guy's great. He's got a head on him. Some lark, what?"

"Yes, he's been very kind," said Shirley. "At first I told him I couldn't let him take so much trouble for us, but he said he was going to take his sister out for a ride——"

"A girl! Aw, gee! I'm going to beat it!" George stopped in his eager walk back and forth across the office, and seized his old faded cap.

"George, stop! You mustn't be impolite. Besides, I think she's only a very little girl, probably like Doris. He called her his 'kid sister.' "

"H'm! You can't tell. I ain't going to run any risks. I better beat it."

But George's further intentions were suddenly brought to a finish by the entrance of Mr. Sidney Graham.

"Well, Miss Hollister," he said with a smile, "we are ready at last. I'm sorry to have kept you waiting so long; but there was something wrong with one of my tires, and the chauffeur had to run around to the garage. Come on, George," he said to the boy, who hung shyly behind now, wary of any lurking female who might be haunting the path. "Guess you'll have to sit in the front seat with me, and help me drive. The chauffeur has to go back and drive for mother. She has to go to some tea or other."

George suddenly forgot the possible girl, and followed his new hero to the elevator with a swelling soul. What would the other fellows at the store think of him? A whole half-holiday, an automobile-ride, and a chance to sit in the front and learn to drive! But all he said was:

"Aw, gee! Yes, sure thing!"

The strange girl suddenly loomed on his consciousness again as they emerged from the elevator and came out on the street. She was sitting in the great back seat alone, arrayed in a big blue velvet coat the color of her eyes, and George felt at once all hands and feet. She was a slender wisp of a thing about Carol's age, with a lily complexion and a wealth of gold hair caught in a blue veil. She smiled very prettily when her brother introduced her as "Elizabeth." There was nothing snobbish or disagreeable about her, but that blue velvet coat suddenly made George conscious of his own common attire, and gave Shirley a pang of dismay at her own little shabby suit.

However, Sidney Graham soon covered all differences in the attire of his guests by insisting that they should don the two long blanket coats that he handed them; and somehow when George was seated in the big leather front seat, with that great handsome coat around his shoulders, he did not much mind the blue velvet girl behind him, and mentally resolved to earn enough to get Carol a coat like it some day; only Carol's should be pink or red to go with her black eyes and pink cheeks.

After all, it was Shirley, not George, who felt embarrassment over the strange girl and wished she had not come. She was vexed with herself for it, too. It was foolish to let a child no older than Carol fluster her so, but the thought of a long ride alone on that back seat with the dainty young girl actually frightened her.

But Elizabeth was not frightened. She had been brought up in the society atmosphere, and was at home with people always, everywhere. She tucked the robes about her guest, helped Shirley button the big, soft dark-blue coat about her, remarking that it got awfully chilly when they were going; and somehow before Shirley had been able to think of a single word to say in response the conversation seemed to be moving along easily without her aid.

"Sid says we're going to pick up your sister from her school. I'm so glad! How old is she? About my age? Won't that be delightful? I'm rather lonesome this spring because all my friends are in school. I've been away at boarding-school, and got the measles. Wasn't that too silly for a great big girl like me? And the doctor said I couldn't study any more this spring on account of my eyes. It's terribly lonesome. I've been home six weeks now, and I don't know what to do with myself. What's your sister's name? Carol? Carol Hollister? That's a pretty name! Is she the only sister you have? A baby sister? How sweet! What's her name? Oh, I think Doris is the cutest name ever. Doris Hollister. Why don't we go and get Doris? Wouldn't she like to ride, too? Oh, it's too bad your mother is ill; but of course she wouldn't want to stay all alone in the house without some of her family."

Elizabeth was tactful. She knew at a glance that trained nurses and servants could not be plentiful in a family where the young people wore such plain, old-style garments. She gave no hint of such a thought, however.

"That's your brother," she went on, nodding toward George. "I've got another brother, but he's seventeen and away at college, so I don't see much of him. Sid's very good to me when he has time, and often he takes me to ride. We're awfully jolly chums, Sid and I. Is this the school where your sister goes? She's in high school, then. The third year? My! She must be bright. I've only finished my second. Does she know she's going with us? What fun to be called out of school by a surprise! Oh, I just know I'm going to like her."

Shirley sat dumb with amazement, and listened to the eager gush of the lively girl, wondered what shy Carol would say, trying to rouse herself to answer the young questioner in the same spirit in which she asked questions.

51

George came out with Carol in a very short time, Carol struggling into her coat and trying to straighten her hat, while George mumbled in her ear as he helped her clumsily:

"Some baby doll out there! Kid, you better preen your feathers. She's been gassing with Shirley to beat the band. I couldn't hear all they said, but she asked a lot about you. You should worry! Hold up your head, and don't flicker an eyelash. You're as good as she is any day, if you don't look all dolled up like a new saloon. But she's some looker! Pretty as a red wagon! Her brother's a peach of a fellow. He's going to let me run the car when we get out of the city limit; and say! Shirley says for me to tell you we're going out to look at a barn where we're going to move this summer, and you're not to say a word about it's being a barn. *See?* Get onto that sky-blue-pink satin scarf she's got around her head? Ain't she some chicken, though?"

"Hush, George! She'll hear you!" murmured Carol in dismay. "What do you mean about a barn? How could we live in a barn?"

"You just shut up and saw wood, kid, and you'll see. Shirley thinks she's got onto something pretty good."

Then Carol was introduced to the beautiful blue-velvet girl and sat down beside her, wrapped in a soft furry cloak of garnet, to be whirled away into a fairy-land of wonder.

CHAPTER VII

CAROL and Elizabeth got on very well together. Shirley was amazed to see the ease with which her sister entered into this new relation, unawed by the garments of her hostess. Carol had more of the modern young America in her than Shirley, perhaps, whose early life had been more conventionally guarded. Carol was democratic, and, strange to say, felt slightly superior to Elizabeth on account of going to a public school. The high-school girls were in the habit of referring to a neighboring boarding-school as "Dummy's Retreat"; and therefore Carol was not at all awed by the other girl, who declared in a friendly manner that she had always been crazy to go to the public school, and asked rapid intelligent questions about the doings there. Before they were out of the city limits the two girls were talking a steady stream, and one could see from their eyes that they liked each other. Shirley, relieved, settled back on the comfortable cushions, and let herself rest and relax. She tried to think how it would feel to own a car like this and be able to ride around when she wanted to.

On the front seat George and Graham were already excellent friends, and George was gaining valuable information about running a car, which he had ample opportunity to put into practice as soon as they got outside the crowded thoroughfares.

They were perhaps half-way to the old barn and running smoothly on an open road, with no one in sight a long way ahead, when Graham turned back to Shirley, leaving George to run the car for a moment himself. The boy's heart swelled with gratitude and utmost devotion to be thus trusted. Of course there wasn't anything to do but keep things just as he had been told, but this man realized that he would do it and not perform any crazy, daring action to show off. George set himself to be worthy of this trust. To be sure, young Graham had a watchful eye upon things, and was taking no chances; but he let the boy feel free, and did not make him aware of his espionage, which is a course of action that will win any boy to give the best that is in him to any responsibility, if he has any best at all.

It was not the kind of conversation that one would expect between landlord and tenant that the young girl and the man carried on in these brief sentences now and then. He called her attention to the soft green tint that was spreading over the tree-tops more distinctly than the day before; to the lazy little clouds floating over the blue; to the tinting of the fields, now taking on every hour new colors; to the perfume in the air. So with pleasantness of passage they arrived at last at the old barn.

Like a pack of eager children they tumbled out of the car and hurried up to the barn, all talking at once, forgetting all difference in station. They were just young and out on a picnic.

Graham had brought a key for the big padlock; and clumsily the man and the boy, unused to such maneuvres, unlocked and shoved back the two great doors.

"These doors are too heavy. They should have ball bearings," remarked young Graham. "I'll attend to that at once. They should be made to move with a light touch. I declare it doesn't pay to let property lie idle without a tenant, there are so many little things that get neglected."

He walked around with a wise air as if he had been an active landowner for years, though indeed he was looking at everything with strange, ignorant eyes. His standard was a home where every detail was perfect, and where necessities came and vanished with the need. This was his first view into the possibilities of "being up against it," as he phrased it in his mind.

Elizabeth in her blue velvet cloak and blue cloudy veil stood like a sweet fairy in the wide doorway, and looked around with delight.

"Oh Sid, wouldn't this be just a dandy place for a party?" she exclaimed eagerly. "You could put the orchestra over in that corner behind a screen of palms, and decorate with gray Florida moss and asparagus vine with daffodils wired on in showers from the beams, and palms all around the walls, and colored electrics hidden everywhere. You could run a wire in from the street, couldn't you? the way they did at Uncle Andy's, and serve the supper out on the lawn with little individual rustic tables. Brower has them, and brings them out with rustic chairs to match. You could have the tree wired, too, and have colored electrics all over the place. Oh! wouldn't it be just heavenly? Say, Sid, Carol says they are coming out here to live, maybe; why couldn't we give them a party like that for a house-warming?"

Sidney Graham looked at his eager, impractical young sister and then at the faces of the three Hollisters, and tried not to laugh as the tremendous contrast of circumstances was presented to him. But his rare tact served him in good stead.

"Why, Elizabeth, that would doubtless be very delightful; but Miss Hollister tells me her mother has been quite ill, and I'm sure, while that might be the happiest thing imaginable for you young folks, it would be rather trying on an invalid. I guess you'll have to have your parties somewhere else for the present."

"Oh!" said Elizabeth with quick recollection, "of course! They told me about their mother. How thoughtless of me! But it would be lovely, wouldn't it, Miss Hollister? Can't you see it?"

She turned in wistful appeal to Shirley, and that young woman, being a dreamer herself, at once responded with a radiant smile:

"Indeed I can, and it would be lovely indeed, but I've been thinking what a lovely home it could be made, too."

"Yes?" said Elizabeth questioningly, and looking around with a dubious frown. "It would need a lot of changing, I should think. You would want hardwood floors, and lots of rugs, and some partitions and windows——"

"Oh, no," said Shirley, laughing. "We're not hardwood people, dear; we're just plain hard-working people; and all we need is a quiet, sweet place to rest in. It's going to be just heavenly here, with that tree outside to shade the doorway, and all this wide space to walk around in. We live in a little narrow city house now, and never have any place to get out except the street. We'll have the birds and the brook for orchestra, and we won't need palms, because the trees and vines will soon be in leaf and make a lovely screen for our orchestra. I imagine at night the stars will have almost as many colors as electrics."

Elizabeth looked at her with puzzled eyes, but half convinced.

"Well, yes, perhaps they would," she said, and smiled. "I've never thought of them that way, but it sounds very pretty, quite like some of Browning's poetry that I don't understand, or was it Mrs. Browning? I can't quite remember."

Sidney Graham, investigating the loft above them, stood a moment watching the tableau and listening to the conversation, though they could not see him; and he thought within himself that it might not be a bad thing for his little sister, with her boarding-school rearing, to get near to these true-hearted young working people, who yet were dreamers and poets, and get her standards somewhat modified by theirs. He was especially delighted with the gentle, womanly way in which Shirley answered the girl now when she thought herself alone with her.

George and Carol had grasped hold of hands and run wildly down the slope to the brook after a most casual glance at the interior of the barn. Elizabeth now turned her dainty high-heeled boots in the brook's direction, and Shirley was left alone to walk the length and breadth of her new abode and make some real plans.

The young man in the dim loft above watched her for a moment as she stood looking from one wall to the other, measuring distances with her eye, walking quickly over to the window and rubbing a clear space on the dusty pane with her handkerchief that she might look out. She was a goodly sight, and he could not help comparing her with the girls he knew, though their garments would have far outshone hers. Still, even in the shabby dark-blue serge suit she seemed lovely.

The young people returned as precipitately as they had gone, and both Carol and George of their own accord joined Shirley in a brief council of war. Graham thoughtfully called his sister away, ostensibly to watch a squirrel high in the big tree, but really to admonish her about making no further propositions like that for the party, as the young people to whom he had introduced her were not well off, and had no money or time for elaborate entertainments.

"But they're lovely, Sid, aren't they? Don't you like them just awfully? I know you do, or you wouldn't have taken the trouble to bring them out here in the car with us. Say, you'll bring me to see them often after they come here to live, won't you?"

"Perhaps," said her brother smilingly. "But hadn't you better wait until they ask you?"

"Oh, they'll ask me," said Elizabeth with a charming smile and a confident little toss of her head. "I'll make them ask me."

"Be careful, kid," he said, still smiling. "Remember, they won't have much money to offer you entertainment with, and probably their things are very plain and simple. You may embarrass them if you invite yourself out."

Elizabeth raised her azure eyes to her brother's face thoughtfully for a moment, then smiled back confidently once more.

"Don't you worry, Sid, dear; there's more than one way. I won't hurt their feelings, but they're going to ask me, and they're going to want me, and I'm going to come. Yes, and you're going to bring me!"

She turned with a laughing pirouette, and danced down the length of the barn to Carol, catching her hand and whirling her after her in a regular childish frolic.

"Well, do you think we ought to take it? Do you think I dare give my final word without consulting mother?" Shirley asked her brother when they were thus left alone for a minute.

"Sure thing! No mistake! It's simply *great*. You couldn't get a place like this if you went the length and breadth of the city and had a whole lot more money than you have to spend."

"But remember it's a barn!" said Shirley impressively. "Mother may mind that very much."

"Not when she sees it," said Carol, whirling back to the consultation. "She'll think it's the sensiblest thing we ever did. She isn't foolish like that. We'll tell her we've found a place to camp with a shanty attached, and she can't be disappointed. I think it'll be great. Just think how Doris can run in the grass!"

"Yes," put in George. "I was telling Carol down by the spring—before that *girl* came and stopped us—I think we might have some chickens and raise eggs.

Harley could do that, and Carol and I could raise flowers, and I could take 'em to town in the morning. I could work evenings."

Shirley smiled. She almost felt like shouting that they agreed with her. The place seemed so beautiful, so almost heavenly to her when she thought of the close, dark quarters at home and the summer with its heat coming on.

"We couldn't keep a lodger, and we'd have that much less," said Shirley thoughtfully.

"But we wouldn't have their laundry nor their room-work to do," said Carol, "and I could have that much more time for the garden and chickens."

"You mustn't count on being able to make much that way," said Shirley gravely. "You know nothing about gardening, and would probably make a lot of mistakes at first anyway."

"I can make fudge and sandwiches, and take them to school to sell," declared Carol stoutly; "and I'll find out how to raise flowers and parsley and little things people have to have. Besides, there's watercress down by that brook, and people like that. We could sell that."

"Well, we'll see," said Shirley thoughtfully, but you mustn't get up too many ideas yet. If we can only get moved and mother is satisfied, I guess we can get along. The rent is only ten dollars."

"Good *night!* That's cheap enough!" said George, and drew a long whistle. Then, seeing Elizabeth approaching, he put on an indifferent air, and sauntered to the dusty window at the other end of the barn.

Sidney Graham appeared now, and took Shirley over to the east end to ask her just where she thought would be a good place to put the partition, and did she think it would be a good thing to have another one at the other end just like it? And so they stood and planned, quite as if Shirley were ordering a ten-thousand-dollar alteration put into her ten-dollar barn. Then suddenly the girl remembered her fears; and, looking straight up into the interested face of the young man, she asked earnestly:

"You are sure you were going to put in these parti-

58

tions? You are not making any change on my account? Because I couldn't think of allowing you to go to any trouble or expense, you know."

Her straightforward look embarrassed him.

"Why, I——" he said, growing a little flushed. "Why, you see I hadn't been out to look things over before. I didn't realize how much better it would be to have those partitions in, you know. But now I intend to do it right away. Father put the whole thing in my hands to do as I pleased. In fact, the place is mine now, and I want to put it in good shape to rent. So don't worry yourself in the least. Things won't go to wrack and ruin so quickly, you know, if there is someone on the place."

He finished his sentence briskly. It seemed quite plausible even to himself now, and he searched about for a change of topic.

"You think you can get on here with the rough floor? You might put padding or something under your carpets, you know, but it will take pretty large carpets——" He looked at her dubiously. To his conventional mind every step of the way was blocked by some impassable barrier. He did not honestly see how she was going to do the thing at all.

"Oh, we don't need carpets!" laughed Shirley gayly. "We'll spread down a rug in front of mother's bed, and another one by the piano, and the rest will be just perfectly all right. We're not expecting to give receptions here, you know," she added mischievously. "We're only campers, and very grateful campers at that, too, to find a nice, clean, empty floor where we can live. The only thing that is troubling me is the cooking. I've been wondering if it will affect the insurance if we use an oil-stove to cook with, or would you rather we got a wood-stove and put the pipe out of one of the windows? I've seen people do that sometimes. Of course we could cook outdoors on a campfire if it was necessary, but it might be a little inconvenient rainy days."

Graham gasped at the coolness with which this slip of a girl discoursed about hardships as if they were necessities to be accepted pleasantly and without a murmur. She actually would not be daunted at the idea of cooking her meals on a fire out-of-doors! Cooking indeed! That was of course a question that people had to consider. It had never been a question that crossed his mind before. People cooked—how did they cook? By electricity, gas, coal and wood fires, of course. He had never considered it a matter to be called in any way serious. But now he perceived that it was one of the first main things to be looked out for in a home. He looked down at the waiting girl with a curious mixture of wonder, admiration, and dismay in his face.

"Why, of course you will need a fire and a kitchen," he said as if those things usually grew in houses without any help and it hadn't occurred to him before that they were not indigenous to barns. "Well, now, I hadn't thought of that. There isn't any chimney here, is there? H'm! There ought to be a chimney in every barn. It would be better for the—ah—for the hay, I should think; keep it dry, you know, and all that sort of thing. And then I should think it might be better for the animals. I must look into that matter."

"No, Mr. Graham," said Shirley decidedly. "There is no necessity for a chimney. We can perfectly well have the pipe go through a piece of tin set in the back window if you won't object, and we can use the little oil-stove when it's very hot if that doesn't affect the insurance. We have a gas stove, of course, that we could bring; but there isn't any gas in a barn."

Graham looked around blankly at the cobwebby walls as if expecting gas-jets to break forth simultaneously with his wish.

"No, I suppose not," he said, "although I should think there ought to be. In a *barn,* you know. But I'm sure there will be no objection whatever to your using any kind of a stove that will work here. This is a stone barn, you know, and I'm sure it won't affect the insurance. I'll find out and let you know."

Shirley felt a trifle uneasy yet about those partitions and the low price of the rent, but somehow the young man had managed to impress her with the fact that he was under no unpleasant delusions concerning herself and that he had the utmost respect for her. He stood looking down earnestly at her for a moment without saying a word, and then he began hesitatingly.

"I wish you'd let me tell you," he said frankly, "how awfully brave you are about all this, planning to come out here in this lonely place, and not being afraid of hard work, and rough floors, and a barn, and even a fire out-of-doors."

Shirley's laugh rang out, and her eyes sparkled.

"Why, it's the nicest thing that's happened to me in ages," she said joyously. "I can't hardly believe it's true that we can come here, that we can really *afford* to come to a great, heavenly country place like this. I suppose of course there'll be hard things. There always are, and some of them have been just about unbearable, but even the hard things can be made fun if you try. This is going to be grand!" and she looked around triumphantly on the dusty rafters and rough stone walls with a little air of possession.

"You are rather"—he paused—"unusual!" he finished thoughtfully as they walked toward the doorway and stood looking off at the distance.

But now Shirley had almost forgotten him in the excitement of the view.

"Just think of waking up to that every morning," she declared with a sweep of her little blue-clad arm toward the view in the distance. "Those purply hills, the fringe of brown and green against the horizon, that white spire nestling among those evergreens! Is that a church? Is it near enough for us to go to? Mother wouldn't want us to be too far from church."

"We'll go home that way and discover," said Graham decidedly. "You'll want to get acquainted with your new neighborhood. You'll need to know how near there is a store, and where your neighbors live. We'll reconnoitre a little. Are you ready to go?"

"Oh, yes. I'm afraid we have kept you too long already, and we must get home about the time Carol usually comes from school, or mother will be terribly worried. Carol is never later than half-past four."

"We've plenty of time," said the driver of the car,

looking at his watch and smiling assurance. "Call the children, and we'll take a little turn around the neighborhood before we go back."

And so the little eager company were reluctantly persuaded to climb into the car again and start on their way.

CHAPTER VIII

THE car leaped forward up the smooth white road, and the great barn as they looked back to it seemed to smile pleasantly to them in farewell. Shirley looked back, and tried to think how it would seem to come home every night and see Doris standing at the top of the grassy incline waiting to welcome her; tried to fancy her mother in a hammock under the big tree a little later when it grew warm and summery, and the boys working in their garden. It seemed too heavenly to be true.

The car swept around the corner of Allister Avenue, and curved down between tall trees. The white spire in the distance drew nearer now, and the purplish hills were off at one side. The way was fresh with smells of spring, and everywhere were sweet scents and droning bees and croaking frogs. The spirit of the day seemed to enter into the young people and make them glad. Somehow all at once they seemed to have known one another a long time, and to be intimately acquainted with one another's tastes and ecstasies. They exclaimed together over the distant view of the misty city with the river winding on its far way, and shouted simultaneously over a frightened rabbit that scurried across the road and hid in the brushwood; and then the car wound round a curve and the little white church swept into view below them.

"The little white church in the valley
    Is bright with the blossom of May,
And true is the heart of your lover
    Who waits for your coming to-day!"

chanted forth George in a favorite selection of the department-store victrola, and all the rest looked interested. It was a pretty church, and nestled under the hills as if it were part of the landscape, making a home-centre for the town.

"We can go to church and Sunday-school there," said Shirley eagerly. "How nice! That will please mother!"

Elizabeth looked at her curiously, and then speculatively toward the church.

"It looks awfully small and cheap," said Elizabeth.

"All the more chance for us to help!" said Shirley. "It will be good for us."

"What could you do to help a church?" asked the wondering Elizabeth. "Give money to paint it? The paint is all scaling off."

"We couldn't give much money," said Carol, "because we haven't got it. But there's lots of things to do in a church besides giving. You teach in Sunday-school, and you wait on table at suppers when they have Ladies' Aid."

"Maybe they'll ask you to play the organ, Shirley," suggested George.

"Oh George!" reproved Shirley. "They'll have plenty that can play better than I can. Remember I haven't had time to practise for ages."

"She's a crackerjack at the piano!" confided George to Graham in a low growl. "She hasn't had a lesson since father died, but before that she used to be at it all the time. She c'n sing too. You oughtta hear her."

"I'm sure I should like to," assented Graham heartily. "I wonder if you will help me get her to sing sometime if I come out to call after you are settled."

"Sure!" said George heartily, "but she mebbe won't do it. She's awful nutty about singing sometimes. She's not stuck on herself nor nothing."

But the little white church was left far behind, and the city swept on apace. They were nearing home now, and Graham insisted on knowing where they lived, that he might put them down at their door. Shirley would have pleaded an errand and had them set down in the business part of the town; but George airily gave the street and number, and Shirley could not prevail upon Graham to stop at his office and let them go their way.

And so the last few minutes of the drive were silent for Shirley, and her cheeks grew rosy with humiliation over the dark little narrow street where they would presently arrive. Perhaps when he saw it this cultured young man would think they were too poor and common to be good tenants even for a barn. But, when they stopped before the little two-story brick house, you would not have known from the expression on the young man's face as he glanced at the number but that the house was a marble front on the most exclusive avenue in the city. He handed down Shirley with all the grace that he would have used to wait upon a millionaire's daughter, and she liked the way he helped out Carol and spoke to George as if he were an old chum.

"I want you to come and see me next Saturday," called Elizabeth to Carol as the car glided away from the curb; "and I'm coming out to help you get settled, remember!"

The brother and two sisters stood in front of their little old dark house, and watched the elegant car glide away. They were filled with wonder at themselves that they had been all the afternoon a part of that elegant outfit. Was it a dream? They rubbed their eyes as the car disappeared around the corner, and turned to look up at the familiar windows and make sure where they were. Then they stood a moment to decide how they should explain to the waiting mother why they happened to be home so early.

It was finally decided that George should go to hunt up a drayman and find out what he would charge to move their things to the country, and Shirley should go to a neighbor's to inquire about a stove she heard they wanted to sell. Then Carol could go in alone, and there would be nothing to explain. There was no telling when either George or Shirley would have a holiday again, and it was as well to get these things arranged as soon as possible.

Meantime Elizabeth Graham was eagerly interviewing her brother, having taken the vacant front seat for the purpose.

"Sid, where did you find those perfectly dear people? I think they are just great! And are they really going to live in that barn? Won't that be dandy? I wish mother'd let me go out and spend a month with them. I mean to ask her. That Carol is the nicest girl ever. She's just a dear!"

"Now, look here, kid," said Graham, facing about to his sister. "I want you to understand a thing or two. I took you on this expedition because I thought I could trust you. See?"

Elizabeth nodded.

"Well, I don't want a lot of talk at home about this. Do you understand? I want you to wait a bit and go slow. If things seem to be all right a little later on, you can ask Carol to come and see you, perhaps; but you'll have to look out. She hasn't fine clothes to go visiting in, I imagine, and they're pretty proud. I guess they've lost their money. Their father died a couple of years ago, and they've been up against it. They do seem like awfully nice people, I'll admit; and, if it's all right later on, you can get to be friends, but you'll have to go slow. Mother wouldn't understand it, and she mustn't be annoyed, you know. I'll take you out to see them sometime when they get settled if it seems all right, but meantime can you keep your tongue still?"

Elizabeth's face fell, but she gave her word immediately. She and her brother were chums; it was easy to see that.

"But can't I have her out for a week-end, Sid? Can't I tell mother anything about her? I could lend her some dresses, you know."

"You go slow, kid, and leave the matter to me. I'll tell mother about them pretty soon when I've had a chance to see a little more of them and am sure mother wouldn't mind. Meantime, don't you fret. I'll take you out when I go on business, and you shall see her pretty soon again."

Elizabeth had to be content with that. She perceived

that for some reason her brother did not care to have the matter talked over in the family. She knew they would all guy him about his interest in a girl who wanted to rent his barn, and she felt herself that Shirley was too fine to be talked about in that way. The family wouldn't understand unless they saw her.

"I know what you mean, Sid," she said after a thoughtful pause. "You want the folks to see them before they judge what they are, don't you?"

"That's just exactly the point," said Sidney with a gleam of satisfaction in his eyes. "That's just what makes you such a good pal, kid. You always understand."

The smile dawned again in Elizabeth's eyes, and she patted her brother's sleeve.

"Good old Sid!" she murmured tenderly. "You're all right. And I just know you're going to take me out to that barn soon. Aren't you going to fix it up for them a little? They can't live there that way. It would be a dandy place to live if the windows were bigger and there were doors like a house, and a piazza, and some fireplaces. A great big stone fireplace in the middle there opposite that door! Wouldn't that be sweet? And they'll have to have electric lights and some bathrooms, of course."

Her brother tipped back his head, and laughed.

"I'm afraid you wouldn't make much of a hand to live in a barn, kid," he said. "You're too much of an aristocrat. How much do you want for your money? My dear, they don't expect tiled bathrooms, and electric lights, and inlaid floors when they rent a barn for the summer."

"But aren't you going to do anything, Sid?"

"Well, I can't do much, for Miss Hollister would suspect right away. She's very businesslike, and she has suspicions already because I said I was going to put in partitions. She isn't an object of charity, you know. I imagine they are all pretty proud."

Elizabeth sat thoughtful and still. It was the first time in her life she had contemplated what it would be to be very poor.

Her brother watched her with interest. He had a feeling that it was going to be very good for Elizabeth to know these Hollisters.

Suddenly he brought the car to a stop before the office of a big lumber-yard they were passing.

"I'm going in here, kid, for just a minute, to see if I can get a man to put in those partitions."

Elizabeth sat meditatively studying the office window through whose large dusty panes could be seen tall strips of moulding, unpainted window-frames, and a fluted column or two, evidently ready to fill an order. The sign over the door set forth that window-sashes, doors, and blinds were to be had. Suddenly Elizabeth sat up straight and read the sign again, strained her eyes to see through the window, and then opened the car door and sprang out. In a moment more she stood beside her brother, pointing mutely to a large window-frame that stood against the wall.

"What is it, kid?" he asked kindly.

"Sid, why can't you put on great big windows like that? They would never notice the windows, you know. It would be so nice to have plenty of light and air."

"That's so," he murmured. "I might change the windows some without its being noticed."

Then to the man at the desk:

"What's the price of that window? Got any more?"

"Yes," said the man, looking up interested; "got half a dozen, made especially for a party, and then he wasn't pleased. Claimed he ordered sash-winders 'stead of casement. If you can use these six, we'll make you a special price."

"Oh, take them, Sid! They're perfectly lovely," said Elizabeth eagerly. "They're casement windows with diamond panes. They'll just be so quaint and artistic in that stone!"

"Well, I don't know how they'll fit," said the young man doubtfully. "I don't want to make it seem as if I was trying to put on too much style."

"No, Sid, it won't seem that way, really. I tell you they'll never notice the windows are bigger, and casement windows aren't like a regular house, you know. See, they'll open wide like doors. I think it would be just grand!"

"All right, kid, we'll see! We'll take the man out with us; and, if he says it can be done, I'll take them."

Elizabeth was overjoyed.

"That's just what it needed!" she declared. "They couldn't live in the dark on rainy days. You must put two in the front on each side the door, and one on each end. The back windows will do well enough."

"Well, come on, kid. Mr. Jones is going out with me at once. Do you want to go with us, or shall I call a taxi and send you home?" asked her brother.

"I'm going with you, of course," said Elizabeth eagerly, hurrying out to the car as if she thought the thing would be done all wrong without her.

So Elizabeth sat in the back seat alone, while her brother and the contractor discoursed on the price of lumber and the relative values of wood and stone for building-purposes, and the big car went back over the way it had been before that afternoon.

They stopped on the way out, and picked up one of Mr. Jones's carpenters who was just leaving a job with his kit of tools, and who climbed stolidly into the back seat, and sat as far away from the little blue-velvet miss as possible, all the while taking furtive notes to tell his own little girl about her when he went home.

Elizabeth climbed out, and went about the barn with them, listening to all they had to say.

The two men took out pencils and foot rules, and went around measuring and figuring. Elizabeth watched them with bright, attentive eyes, putting a whispered suggestion now and then to her brother.

"They can't go up and down a ladder all the time," she whispered. "There ought to be some rough stairs with a railing, at least as good as our back stairs at home."

"How about it?" said Graham aloud to the contractor. "Can you put in some steps, just rough ones, to the left? I'm going to have a party out here camping for a while this summer, and I want it to be safe. Need a railing, you know, so nobody will get a fall."

The man measured the space up with his eye.

"Just want plain steps framed up with a handrail?" he said, squinting up again. "Guess we better start 'em up this way to the back wall and then turn back from a landing. That'll suit the overhead space best. Just pine, you want 'em, I s'pose?"

Elizabeth stood like a big blue bird alighted on the door-sill, watching and listening. She was a regular woman, and saw big possibilities in the building. She would have enjoyed ordering parquetry flooring and carved newel-posts and making a regular palace.

The sun was setting behind the purply hill and sending a glint from the weather-vane on the little white church spire when they started back to the city. Elizabeth looked wistfully toward it, and wondered about the rapt expression on Shirley's face when she spoke of "working" in the church. How could one get any pleasure out of that? She meant to find out. At present her life was rather monotonous, and she longed to have some new interests.

That night after she had gone to her luxurious little couch she lay in her downy nest, and tried to think how it would be to live in that big barn and go to sleep up in the loft, lying on that hay. Then suddenly the mystery of life was upon her with its big problems. Why, for instance, was she born into the Graham family with money and culture and all the good times, and that sweet, bright Carol-girl born into the Hollister family where they had a hard time to live at all?

CHAPTER IX

Quite early the next morning Sidney Graham was in his office at the telephone. He conferred with the carpenter, agreeing to meet him out at the barn and make final arrangements about the windows in a very short time. Then he called up the trolley company and the electric company, and made arrangements with them to have a wire run from the road to his barn, with a very satisfactory agreement whereby he could pay them a certain sum for the use of as much light as he needed.

This done, he called up an electrician, and arranged that he should send some men out that morning to wire the barn.

He hurried through his morning mail, giving his stenographer a free hand with answering some of the letters, and then speeded out to Glenside.

Three men were already there, two of them stonemasons, working away under the direction of the contractor. They had already begun working at the massive stone around the windows, striking musical blows from a light scaffolding that made the old barn look as if it had suddenly waked up and gone to house-cleaning. Sidney Graham surveyed it with satisfaction as he stopped his car by the roadside and got out. He did delight to have things done on time. He decided that if this contractor did well on the job he would see that he got bigger things to do. He liked it that his work had been begun at once.

The next car brought a quartette of carpenters, and before young Graham went back to the city a motortruck had arrived loaded with lumber and windowframes. It was all very fascinating to him, this new toy barn that had suddenly come into his possession, and he could hardly tear himself away from it and go back to business. One would not have supposed, perhaps, that it was so very necessary for him to do so, either, seeing that he was already so well off that he really could have gotten along quite comfortably the rest of his life without any more money; but he was a conscientious young man, who believed that no living being had a right to exist in idleness, and who had gone into business from a desire to do his best and keep up the honorable name of his father's firm. So after he had given careful directions for the electric men when they should come he rushed back to his office once more.

The next two days were filled with delightful novelties. He spent much time flying from office to barn and back to the office again, and before evening of the second day he had decided that a telephone in the barn was an absolute necessity, at least while the work was going on. So he called up the telephone company, and arranged that connection should be put in at once. That evening he wrote a short note to Miss Shirley Hollister, telling her that the partitions were under way and would soon be completed, and that in a few days he would send her the key so that she might begin to transport her belongings to the new home.

The next morning, when Graham went out to the stone barn, he found that the front windows were in, and gave a very inviting appearance to the edifice, both outside and in. As Elizabeth had surmised, the big latticed windows opening inwards like casement doors seemed quite in keeping with the rough stone structure. Graham began to wonder why all barns did not affect this style of window, they were so entirely attractive. He was thoroughly convinced that the new tenants would not be likely to remember or notice the difference in the windows; he was sure he shouldn't have unless his attention had been called to them in some way. Of course the sills and sashes were rather new-looking, but he gave orders that they should at once be painted an unobtrusive dark green which would well accord with the mossy roof, and he trusted his particular young tenant would not think that he had done anything pointed in changing the windows. If she did, he would have to think up some excuse.

But, as he stood at the top of the grassy slope and looked about, he noticed the great pile of stones under each window from the masonry that had been torn away to make room for the larger sashes, and an idea came to him.

"Mr. Jones!" he called to the contractor, who had just come over on the car to see how the work was progressing. "Wouldn't there be stones enough all together from all the windows to build some kind of a rude chimney and fireplace?" he asked.

Mr. Jones thought there would. There were stones enough down in the meadow to piece out with in case they needed more, anyway. Where would Mr. Graham want the fireplace? Directly opposite the front doors? He had thought of suggesting that himself, but didn't know as Mr. Graham wanted to go to any more expense.

"By all means make that fireplace!" said the young

71

owner delightedly. "This is going to be a jolly place when it gets done, isn't it? I declare I don't know but I'd like to come out here and live."

"It would make a fine old house, sir," said the contractor respectfully, looking up almost reverently at the barn. "I'd like to see it with verandys, and more winders, and a few such. You don't see many of these here old stone buildings around now. They knew how to build 'em substantial in those old times, so they did."

"H'm! Yes. It would make a fine site for a house, wouldn't it?" said the young man, looking about thoughtfully. "Well, now, we'll have to think about that sometime, perhaps. However, I think it looks very nice for the present"; and he walked about, looking at the improvements with great satisfaction.

At each end of the barn a good room, long and narrow, had been partitioned off, each of which by use of a curtain would make two very large rooms, and yet the main section of the floor looked as large as ever. A simple stairway of plain boards had been constructed a little to one side of the middle toward the back, going up to the loft, which had been made safe for the children by a plain rude railing consisting of a few uprights with strips across. The darkening slats at the small windows in the loft had been torn away and shutters substituted that would open wide and let in air and light. Rough spots in the floor had been mended, and around the great place both up-stairs and down, and even down in the basement underneath, electric wires ran with simple lights and switches conveniently arranged, so that if it became desirable the whole place could be made a blaze of light. The young man did not like to think of this family of unprotected women and children coming out into the country without all the arrangements possible to make them feel safe. For this reason also he had established the telephone. He had talked it over with the agent, paying a certain sum for its installation, and had a telephone put in that they could pay for whenever they desired to use it. This would make the young householder feel more comfortable about leaving her mother out in the country all day, and also prevent her pride from being hurt. The telephone was there. She need not use it unless necessity arose. He felt he could explain that to her. If she didn't like it, of course she could have it taken away.

There were a lot more things he would like to do to make the place more habitable, but he did not dare. Sometimes even now his conscience troubled him. What did he know about these people, anyway? and what kind of a flighty youth was he becoming that he let a strange girl's appealing face drive him to such lengths as he was going now? Telephone, and electric lights, and stairs, and a fireplace in a barn! It was all perfectly preposterous, and, if his family should hear of it, he would never hear the last of it; that he was certain.

At such times he would hunt up his young sister and carry her off for a long drive in the car, always ending up at Glenside Road, where she exclaimed and praised to his heart's satisfaction, and gave anew her word not to tell anybody a thing about it until he was ready.

Indeed, Elizabeth was wild with delight. She wanted to hunt up some of her mother's old Turkish rugs that were put away in dark closets, to decorate the walls with pictures and bric-à-brac from her own room, and to smother the place in flowering shrubs for the arrival of the tenants; but her brother firmly forbade anything more being done. He waited with fear and trembling for the time when the clear-eyed young tenant should look upon the changes he had already made; for something told him she would not stand charity, and there was a point beyond which he must not go if he wished ever to see her again.

At last one morning he ventured to call her up on the telephone at her office.

"My sister and I were thinking of going out to see how things are progressing at the Glenside place," he said after he had explained who he was. "I was wondering if you would care to come along and look things over. What time do you get through at your office this afternoon?"

"That is very kind of you, Mr. Graham," said Shirley, "but I'm afraid that won't be possible. I'm not usually done until half-past five. I might get through by five, but not much sooner, and that would be too late for you."

"Not at all, Miss Hollister. That would be a very agreeable time. I have matters that will keep me here quite late to-night, and that will be just right for me. Shall I call for you, then, at five? Or is that too soon?"

"Oh, no, I can be ready by then, I'm sure," said Shirley with suppressed excitement. "You are very kind——"

"Not at all. It will be a pleasure," came the answer. "Then I will call at your office at five," and the receiver clicked at the other end, leaving Shirley in a whirl of doubt and joy.

How perfectly delightful! And yet ought she to go? Would mother think it was all right? His little sister was going, but was it quite right for her to accept this much attention even in a business way? It wasn't at all customary or necessary, and both he and she knew it. He was just doing it to be nice.

And then there was mother. She must send a message somehow, or mother would be frightened when she did not come home at her usual time.

She finally succeeded in getting Carol at her school, and told her to tell mother she was kept late and might not be home till after seven. Then she flew at her work to get it out of the way before five o'clock.

But, when she came down at the appointed time, she found Carol sitting excitedly in the back seat with Elizabeth, fairly bursting with the double pleasure of the ride and of surprising her sister.

"They came to the school for me, and took me home; and I explained to mother that I was going with you to look at a place we were going to move to. I put on the potatoes, and put the meat in the oven, and mother is going to tell George just what to do to finish supper when he gets home," she exclaimed eagerly. "And, oh, isn't it lovely?"

"Indeed it is lovely," said Shirley, her face flushing with pleasure and her eyes speaking gratitude to the young man in the front seat who was opening the door for her to step in beside him.

That was a wonderful ride.

The spring had made tremendous advances in her work during the ten days since they went that way before. The flush of green that the willows had worn had become a soft, bright feather of foliage, and the maples had sent out crimson tassels to offset them. Down in the meadows and along the roadside the grass was thick and green, and the bare brown fields had disappeared. Little brooks sang tinklingly as they glided under bridges, and the birds darted here and there in busy, noisy pairs. Frail wavering blossoms starred the swampy places, and the air was sweet with scents of living things.

But, when they came in sight of the barn, Elizabeth and her brother grew silent from sheer desire to talk and not act as if there was anything different about it. Now that they had actually brought Shirley here, the new windows seemed fairly to flaunt themselves in their shining mossy paint and their vast extent of diamond panes, so that the two conspirators were deeply embarrassed, and dared not face what they had done.

It was Carol who broke the silence that had come upon them all.

"Oh! Oh! Oh!" she shouted. "Shirley, just look! New, great big windows! Isn't that *great?* Now you needn't worry whether it will be dark for mother days when she can't go out! Isn't that the best ever?"

But Shirley looked, and her cheeks grew pink as her eyes grew starry. She opened her lips to speak, and then closed them again, for the words would not come, and the tears came instead; but she drove them back, and then managed to say:

"Oh, Mr. Graham! Oh, you have gone to so much trouble!"

"No, no trouble at all," said he almost crossly; for he had wanted her not to notice those windows, at least not yet.

"You see it was this way. The windows were some that were left over from another order, and I got a chance to get them at a bargain. I thought they might

75

as well be put in now as any time and you get the benefit of them. The barn really needed more light. It was a very dark barn indeed. Hadn't you noticed it? I can't see how my grandfather thought it would do to have so little light and air. But you know in the old times they didn't use to have such advanced ideas about ventilation and germs and things——" He felt he was getting on rather famously until he looked down at the clear eyes of the girl, and knew she was seeing right straight through all his talk. However, she hadn't the face to tell him so; and so he boldly held on his way, making up fine stories about things that barns needed until he all but believed them himself; and, when he got through, he needed only to finish with "And, if it isn't so, it ought to be" to have a regular Water-Baby argument out of it. He managed to talk on in this vein until he could stop the car and help Shirley out, and together they all went up the now velvety green of the incline to the big door.

"It is beautiful! beautiful!" murmured Shirley in a daze of delight. She could not yet make it seem real that she was to come to this charmed spot to live in a few days.

Graham unlocked the big doors, and sent them rolling back with a touch, showing what ball bearings and careful workmanship can do. The group stepped inside, and stood to look again.

The setting sun was casting a red glow through the diamond panes and over the wide floor. The new partitions, guiltless of paint, for Graham had not dared to go further, were mellowed into ruby hangings. The stone fireplace rose at the opposite side of the room, and the new staircase was just at the side, all in the ruddy evening glow that carried rich dusky shadows into the corners, and hung a curtain of vagueness over blemishes.

Then all suddenly, before they had had time to take in the changes, more than the fact of the partitions which they expected, Graham stepped to the side of the door, and touched a button, and behold a myriad of lights burst forth about the place, making it bright like noontime.

"Oh! Oh! Oh!" breathed Carol in awe and wonder, and "Oh!" again, as if there were nothing else to say. But Shirley only looked and caught her breath. It seemed a palace too fine for their poor little means, and a sudden fear gripped hold upon her.

"Oh Mr. Graham! You have done too much!" she choked. "You shouldn't have done it! We can never afford to pay for all this!"

"Not at all!" said young Graham quickly. "This isn't anything. The electric people gave permission for this, and I thought it would be safer than lamps and candles, you know. It cost scarcely anything for the wiring. I had our regular man do it that attends to the wiring and lights at the office. It was a mere trifle, and will make things a lot more convenient for you. You see it's nothing to the company. They just gave permission for a wire to be run from the pole there. Of course they might not do it for every one, but I've some pretty good friends in the company; so it's all right."

"But the fireplace!" said Shirley, going over to look at it. "It's beautiful! It's like what you see in magazine pictures of beautiful houses."

"Why, it was just the stones that were left from cutting the windows larger. I thought they might as well be utilized, you know. It wasn't much more work to pile them up that way while the men were here than if we had had them carted away."

Here Carol interrupted.

"Shirley! There's a telephone! A real telephone!" Shirley's accusing eyes were upon her landlord.

"It was put in for our convenience while the workmen were here," he explained defensively. "It is a pay phone, you see, and is no expense except when in use. It can be taken out if you do not care to have it, of course; but it occurred to me since it was here your mother might feel more comfortable out here all day if she could call you when she needed to."

Shirley's face was a picture of varying emotions as she listened, but relief and gratitude conquered as she turned to him.

"I believe you have thought of everything," she said at last. "I have worried about that all this week. I have wondered if mother would be afraid out in the country with only the children, and the neighbors not quite near enough to call; but this solves the difficulty. You are sure it hasn't cost you a lot to have this put in?"

"Why, don't you know the telephone company is glad to have their phones wherever they can get them?" he evaded. "Now, don't worry about anything more. You'll find hardships enough living in a barn without fretting about the few conveniences we have been able to manage."

"But this is real luxury!" she said, sitting down on the steps and looking up where the lights blazed from the loft. "You have put lights up there, too, and a railing. I was so afraid Doris would fall down some time!"

"I'm glad to find you are human, after all, and have a few fears!" declared the owner, laughing. "I had begun to think you were Spartan through and through and weren't afraid of anything. Yes, I had the men put what lumber they had left into that railing. I thought it wasn't safe to have it all open like that, and I didn't want you to sue me for life or limb, you know. There's one thing I haven't managed yet, and that is piping water up from the spring. I haven't been able to get hold of the right man so far; but he's coming out to-morrow, and I hope it can be done. There is a spring on the hill back of us, and I believe it is high enough to get the water to this floor. If it is it will make your work much easier and be only the matter of a few rods of pipe."

"Oh, but, indeed, you mustn't do anything more!" pleaded Shirley. "I shall feel so ashamed paying such a little rent."

"But, my dear young lady," said Graham in his most dignified business manner, "you don't at all realize how much lower rents are in the country, isolated like this, than they are in the city; and you haven't as yet realized what a lot of inconveniences you have to put up with. When you go back to the city in the winter, you will be glad to get away from here."

"Never!" said Shirley fervently, and shuddered. "Oh, never! You don't know how dreadful it seems that we shall have to go back. But of course I suppose we shall. One couldn't live in a barn in the winter, even though it is a palace for the summer"; and she looked about wistfully. Then, her eyes lighting up, she said in a low tone, for the young man's benefit alone:

"I think God must have made you do all this for us!" She turned and walked swiftly over to one of the new casement windows, looking out at the red glow that the sun in sinking had left in the sky; and there against the fringes of the willows and maples shone out the bright weather-vane on the spire of the little white church in the valley.

"I think God must have sent you to teach me and my little sister a few things," said a low voice just behind Shirley as she struggled with tired, happy tears that would blur her eyes. But, when she turned to smile at the owner of the voice, he was walking over by the door and talking to Carol. They tumbled joyously into the car very soon, and sped on their way to the city again.

That night the Hollister children told their mother they had found a place in which to live.

CHAPTER X

THE crisis was precipitated by Shirley's finding her mother crying when she came up softly to see her.

"Now, little mother, *dear!* What can be the matter?" she cried aghast, sitting down on the bed and drawing her mother's head into her lap.

But it was some time before Mrs. Hollister could recover her calmness, and Shirley began to be frightened. At last, when she had kissed and petted her, she called down to the others to come up-stairs quickly.

They came with all haste, George and Harley with dish-towels over their shoulders, Carol with her arithmetic and pencil, little Doris trudging up breathless, one step at a time, and all crying excitedly, "What's the matter?"

"Why, here's our blessed little mother lying here all by herself, crying because she doesn't know where in the world we can find a house!" cried Shirley; "and I think it's time we told our beautiful secret, don't you?"

"Yes," chorused the children, although Harley and Doris had no idea until then that there was any beautiful secret. Beautiful secrets hadn't been coming their way.

"Well, I think we better tell it," said Shirley, looking at George and Carol questioningly. "Don't you? We don't want mother worrying." So they all clustered around her on the bed and the floor, and sat expectantly while Shirley told.

"You see, mother, it's this way. We've been looking around a good deal lately, George and I, and we haven't found a thing in the city that would do; so one day I took a trolley ride out of the city, and I've found something I think will do nicely for the summer, anyway, and that will give us time to look around and decide. Mother dear, would you mind camping so very much if we made you a nice, comfortable place?"

"Camping!" said Mrs. Hollister in dismay. "Dear child! In a tent?"

"No, mother, not in a tent. There's a—a—sort of a house—that is, there's a building, where we could sleep, and put our furniture, and all; but there's a lovely out-of-doors. Wouldn't you like that, for Doris and you?"

"Oh, yes," sighed the poor woman; "I'd like it; but, child, you haven't an idea what you are talking about. Any place in the country costs terribly, even a shanty ——"

"That's it, mother, call it a shanty!" put in Carol. "Mother, would you object to living in a shanty all summer if it was good and clean, and you had plenty of out-of-doors around it?"

"No, of course not, Carol, if it was perfectly respectable. I shouldn't want to take my children among a lot of low-down people——"

"Of course not, mother!" put in Shirley. "And there's nothing of that sort. It's all perfectly respectable, and the few neighbors are nice, respectable people. Now, mother, if you're willing to trust us, we'd like it if you'll just let us leave it at that and not tell you anything more about it till we take you there. George and Carol and I have all seen the place, and we think it will be just the thing. There's plenty of room, and sky, and a big tree, and birds; and it only costs ten dollars a month. Now, mother, will you trust us for the rest and not ask any questions?"

The mother looked in bewilderment from one to another, and, seeing their eager faces, she broke into a weary smile.

"Well, I suppose I'll have to," she said with a sigh of doubt; "but I can't understand how any place you could get would be only that price, and I'm afraid you haven't thought of a lot of things."

"Yes, mother, we've thought of everything—and then some," said Shirley, stooping down to kiss the thin cheek; "but we are sure you are going to like this when you see it. It isn't a palace, of course. You don't expect plate-glass windows, you know."

"Well, hardly," said Mrs. Hollister dryly, struggling with herself to be cheerful. She could see that her children were making a brave effort to make a jolly occasion out of their necessity, and she was never one to hang back; so, as she could do nothing else, she assented.

"You are sure," she began, looking at Shirley with troubled eyes. "There are so many things to think of, and you are so young."

"Trust me, mudder dearie," said Shirley joyously, remembering the fireplace and the electric lights. "It really isn't so bad; and there's a beautiful hill for Doris to run down, and a place to hang a hammock for you right under a big tree where a bird has built its nest."

"Oh-h?" echoed the wondering Doris. "And could I see de birdie?"

"Yes, darling, you can watch him every day, and see him fly through the blue sky."

"It's all right, mother," said George in a businesslike tone. "You'll think it's great after you get used to it. Carol and I are crazy over it."

"But will it be where you can get to your work, both of you? I shouldn't like you to take long, lonely walks, you know," said the troubled mother.

"Right on the trolley line, mother dear; and the difference in rent will more than pay our fare."

"Besides, I'm thinking of buying a bicycle from one of the fellows. He says he'll sell it for five dollars, and I can pay fifty cents a month. Then I could go in on my bike in good weather, and save that much." This from George.

"Oh, gee!" said Harley breathlessly. "Then I could ride it sometimes, too."

"Sure!" said George generously.

"Now," said Shirley with her commanding manner that the children called "brigadier-general," "now, mother dear, you're going to put all your worries out of your head right this minute, and go to sleep. Your business is to get strong enough to be moved out there. When you get there, you'll get well so quick you won't know yourself; but you've got to rest from now on every minute, or you won't be able to go when the time comes; and then what will happen? Will you promise?"

Amid the laughing and pleading of her children the mother promised, half smilingly, half tearfully, and succumbed to being prepared for the night. Then they all tiptoed away to the dining-room for a council of war.

It was still two weeks before they had to vacate the little brick house, plenty of time to get comfortably settled before they took their mother out there.

It was decided that George and Shirley should go out the next evening directly from their work, not waiting to return for supper, but eating a lunch down-town. Now that the place was lighted and they had been told to use the light as freely as they chose, with no charge, the question of getting settled was no longer a problem. They could do it evenings after their work was over. The first thing would be to clean house, and for that they needed a lot of things, pails, pans, brooms, mops and the like. It would be good to take a load of things out the next day if possible.

So George went out to interview the man with the moving-wagon, while Shirley and Carol made out a list of things that ought to go in that first load. George came back with the report that the man could come at half past four in the afternoon; and, if they could have the things that were to go all ready, he would have his son help to load them, and they could get out to Glenside by six o'clock or seven at the latest. Harley might go along if he liked, and help to unload at the other end.

Harley was greatly excited both at the responsibility placed upon him and at the prospect of seeing the new home. It almost made up for the thought of leaving "the fellows" and going to live in a strange place.

The young people were late getting to bed that night, for they had to get things together so that Carol would not have her hands too full the next day when she got home from school. Then they had to hunt up soap, scrubbing-pails, rags, brushes and brooms; and, when they went to bed at last, they were much too excited to sleep.

Of course there were many hindrances to their plans, and a lot of delay waiting for the cartman, who did not always keep his word; but the days passed, and every one saw some little progress toward making a home out of the big barn. Shirley would not let them stay later in the evenings than ten o'clock, for they must be ready to go to work the next morning; so of course the work of cleaning the barn progressed but slowly. After the first night they got a neighbor to sit with their mother and Doris, letting Carol and Harley come out on the car to help; and so with four willing workers the barn gradually took on a nice smell of soap and water.

The old furniture arrived little by little, and was put in place eagerly, until by the end of the first week the big middle room and the dining-room and kitchen began really to look like living.

It was Saturday evening of that first week, and Shirley was sitting on the old couch at the side of the fireplace, resting, watching George, who was reeling out a stormy version of chopsticks on the piano, and looking about on her growing home hopefully. Suddenly there came a gentle tapping at the big barn door, and George as the man of the house went to the door with his gruffest air on, but melted at once when he saw the landlord and his sister standing out in front in the moonlight.

"Are you ready for callers?" asked Graham, taking off his hat in greeting. "Elizabeth and I took a spin out this way, and we sighted the light, and thought we'd stop and see if we could help any. My, how homelike you've made it look! Say, this is great!"

Sidney Graham stood in the centre of the big room, looking about him with pleasure.

The young people had put things in apple-pie order as far as they had gone. A fire was laid in the big stone fireplace, all ready for touching off, and gave a homelike, cleared-up look to the whole place as if it were getting ready for some event. On each side of the chimney stood a simple set of bookshelves filled with well-worn volumes that had a look of being beloved and in daily intimate association with the family. On the top of the shelves Carol had placed some bits of bric-à-brac, and in the centre of each a tall vase. Beside them were a few photographs in simple frames, a strong-faced man with eyes that reminded one of Shirley and a brow like George's; a delicate-featured, refined woman with sweet, sensitive mouth and eyes like Carol's; a lovely little child with a cloud of fair curls.

The old couch was at one side of the fireplace, at a convenient angle to watch the firelight, and yet not hiding the bookshelves. On the other side, with its back toward the first landing of the rude staircase, stood an old upright piano with a pile of shabby music on the top and a book of songs open on the rack. On the floor in the space between was spread a worn and faded ingrain rug, its original colors and pattern long since blended into neutral grays and browns, which strangely harmonized with the rustic surroundings. A few comfortable but shabby chairs were scattered about in a homelike way, and a few pictures in plain frames were hung on the clean new partitions. Under one stood a small oak desk and a few writing-materials. A little further on a plain library table held a few magazines and papers and a cherished book or two. There had been no attempt to cover the wide bare floor spaces, save by a small dingy rug or two or a strip of carpet carefully brushed and flung here and there in front of a chair. There was no pretension and therefore no incongruity. The only luxurious thing in the place was the bright electric light, and yet it all looked pleasant and inviting.

"Say, now, this is great!" reiterated the young owner of the place, sinking into the nearest chair and looking about him with admiration. "Who would ever have imagined you could make a barn look like this? Why, you're a genius, Miss Hollister. You're a real artist."

Shirley, in an old gingham dress, with her sleeves rolled high and her hair fluffing wilfully in disorder about her hot cheeks, stood before him in dismay. She had been working hard, and was all too conscious of the brief time before they must be done; and to have company just now—and *such* company—put her to confusion; but the honest admiration in the young man's voice did much to restore her equilibrium. She began to pull down her sleeves and sit down to receive her callers properly; but he at once insisted that she should not delay on his account, and, seeing her shyness, immediately plunged into some questions about the water-pipes, which brought about a more businesslike footing and relieved her embarrassment. He was soon on his way to the partitioned corner which was to be the kitchen, telling Shirley how it was going to be no trouble to run a pipe from the spring and have a faucet put in, and that it should be done on the morrow. Then he called to Elizabeth.

"Kid, what did you do with those eats you brought along? I think it would be a good time to hand them out. I'm hungry. Suppose you take George out to the car to help you bring them in, and let's have a picnic!"

Then, turning to Shirley, he explained:

"Elizabeth and I are great ones to have something along to eat. It makes one hungry to ride, you know."

The children needed no second word, but all hurried out to the car, and came back with a great bag of most delicious oranges and several boxes of fancy cakes and crackers; and they all sat down to enjoy them, laughing and chattering, not at all like landlord and tenants.

"Now what's to do next?" demanded the landlord as soon as the repast was finished. "I'm going to help. We're not here to hinder, and we must make up for the time we have stopped you. What were you and George doing, Miss Carol, when we arrived?"

"Unpacking dishes," giggled Carol, looking askance at the frowning Shirley, who was shaking her head at Carol behind Graham's back. Shirley had no mind to have the elegant landlord see the dismal state of the Hollister crockery. But the young man was not to be so easily put off, and to Carol's secret delight insisted upon helping despite Shirley's most earnest protests that it was not necessary to do anything more than evening. He and Elizabeth repaired to the dining-room end of the barn, and helped unpack dishes, pans, kettles, knives, and forks, and arrange them on the shelves that George had improvised out of a large old bookcase that used to be his father's. After all, there was something in good breeding, thought Shirley, for from the way in which Mr. Graham handled the old cracked dishes, and set them up so nicely, you never would have known but they were Haviland china. He never seemed to see them at all when they were cracked. One might have thought he had been a member of the family for years, he made things seem so nice and comfortable and sociable.

Merrily they worked, and accomplished wonders that night, for Shirley let them stay until nearly eleven o'clock "just for once"; and then they all piled into the car, Shirley and Carol and Elizabeth in the back seat, George and the happy Harley with Graham in the front. If there had been seven more of them, they would have all happily squeezed in. The young Hollisters were having the time of their lives, and as for the Grahams it wasn't quite certain but that they were also. Certainly society had never seen on Sidney Graham's face that happy, enthusiastic look of intense satisfaction that the moon looked down upon that night. And, after all, they got home almost as soon as if they had gone on the ten-o'clock trolley.

After that on one pretext or another those Grahams were always dropping in on the Hollisters at their work and managing to "help," and presently even Shirley ceased to be annoyed or to apologize.

The east end of the barn had been selected for bedrooms. A pair of cretonne curtains was stretched across the long, narrow room from wall to partition, leaving the front room for their mother's bed and Doris's crib, and the back room for Shirley and Carol. The boys had taken possession of the loft with many shouts and elaborate preparations, and had spread out their treasures with deep delight, knowing that at last there was room enough for their proper display and they need feel no fear that they would be thrown out because their place was wanted for something more necessary. Little by little the Hollisters were getting settled. It was not so hard, after all, because there was that glorious big "attic" in which to put away things that were not needed below, and there was the whole basement for tubs and things, and a lovely faucet down there, too, so that a lot of work could be done below the living-floor. It seemed just ideal to the girls, who had been for several years accustomed to the cramped quarters of a tiny city house.

At last even the beds were made up, and everything had been moved but the bed and a few necessities in their mother's room, which were to come the next day while they were moving their mother.

That moving of mother had been a great problem to Shirley until Graham anticipated her necessity, and said in a matter-of-fact way that he hoped Mrs. Hollister would let him take her to her new home in his car. Then Shirley's eyes filled with tears of gratitude. She knew her mother was not yet able to travel comfortably in a trolley-car, and the price of a taxicab was more than she felt they ought to afford; yet in her secret heart she had been intending to get one; but now there would be no necessity.

Shirley's words of gratitude were few and simple, but there was something in her eyes as she lifted them to Graham's face that made a glow in his heart and fully repaid him for his trouble.

The last thing they did when they left the barn that night before they were coming to stay was to set the table, and it really looked very cozy and inviting with a white cloth on it and the dishes set out to look their best. Shirley looked back at it with a sweeping glance that took in the great, comfortable living-room, the open door into the dining-room on one hand and the vista of a white bed on the other side through the bed-room door. She smiled happily, and then switched off the electric light, and stepped out into the sweet spring night. Graham, who had stood watching her as one might watch the opening of some strange, unknown flower, closed and locked the door behind them, and followed her down the grassy slope to the car.

"Do you know," he said earnestly, "it's been a great thing to me to watch you make a real home out of this bare barn? It's wonderful! It's like a miracle. I wouldn't have believed it could be done. And you have done it so wonderfully! I can just see what kind of a delightful home it is going to be."

There was something in his tone that made Shirley forget he was rich and a stranger and her landlord. She lifted her face to the stars, and spoke her thoughts.

"You can't possibly know how much like heaven it is going to be to us after coming from that other awful little house," she said; "and you are the one who has made it possible. If it hadn't been for you I know I never could have done it."

"Oh, nonsense, Miss Hollister! You mustn't think of it. I haven't done anything at all, just the simplest things that were absolutely necessary."

"Oh, I understand," said Shirley; "and I can't ever repay you, but I think God will. That is the kind of thing the kingdom of heaven is made of."

"Oh, really, now," said Graham, deeply embarrassed; he was not much accustomed to being connected with the kingdom of heaven in any way. "Oh, really, you—you overestimate it. And as for pay, I don't ask any better than the fun my sister and I have had helping you get settled. It has been a great play for us. We never really moved, you see. We've always gone off and had some one do it for us. I've learned a lot since I've known you."

That night as she prepared to lie down on the mattress and blanket that had been left behind for herself and Carol to camp out on, Shirley remembered her first worries about Mr. Graham, and wondered whether it could be possible that he thought she had been forward in any way, and what her mother would think when she heard the whole story of the new landlord; for up to this time the secret had been beautifully kept from mother, all the children joining to clap their hands over wayward mouths that started to utter telltale sentences, and the mystery grew, and became almost like Christmas-time for little Doris and her mother. It must, however, be stated that Mrs. Hollister, that last night, as she lay wakeful on her bed in the little bare room in the tiny house, had many misgivings, and wondered whether perchance she would not be sighing to be back even here twenty-four hours later. She was holding her peace wonderfully, because there really was nothing she could do about it even if she was going out of the frying-pan into the fire; but the tumult and worry in her heart had been by no means bliss. So the midnight drew on, and the weary family slept for the last night in the cramped old house where they had lived since trouble and poverty had come upon them.

CHAPTER XI

SHIRLEY was awake early that morning, almost too excited to sleep but fitfully even through the night. Now that the thing was done and they were actually moved into a barn she began to have all sorts of fears and compunctions concerning it. She seemed to see her delicate mother shrink as from a blow when she first learned that they had come to this. Try as she would to bring back all the sensible philosophy that had caused her to enter into this affair in the first place, she simply could not feel anything but trouble. She longed to rush into her mother's room, tell her all about it, and get the dreaded episode over. But anyhow it was inevitable now. They were moved. They had barely enough money to pay the cartage and get things started before next pay-day. There was nothing for it but to take her mother there, even if she did shrink from the idea.

Of course mother always had been sensible, and all that; but somehow the burden of the great responsibility of decision rested so heavily upon her young shoulders that morning that it seemed as if she could no longer bear the strain.

They still had a good fire in the kitchen range, and Shirley hastened to the kitchen, prepared a delicate piece of toast, a poached egg, a cup of tea, and took it to her mother's room, tiptoeing lightly lest she still slept.

But the mother was awake and glad to see her. She had been awake since the first streak of dawn had crept into the little back window. She had the look of one who was girded for the worst. But, when she saw her daughter's face, the mother in her triumphed over the woman.

"What's the trouble, little girl? Has something happened?"

The tenderness in her voice was the last straw that broke Shirley's self-control. The tears suddenly sprang into her eyes, and her lip trembled.

"Oh mother!" she wailed, setting the tray down quickly on a box and fumbling for her handkerchief. "I'm so worried! I'm so afraid you won't like what we've done, and then what shall we do?"

"I *shall* like it!" said the mother with instant determination. "Don't for a minute think of anything else. Having done something irrevocably, never look back and think you might have done something better. You did the best you could, or you thought you did, anyway; and there didn't seem to be anything else at the time. So now just consider it *was* the very best thing in the world, and don't go to fretting about it. There'll be *something* nice about it, I'm sure, and goodness knows we've had enough unpleasant things here; so we needn't expect beds of roses. We are just going to *make* it nice, little girl. Remember that! We are going to like it. There's a tree there, you say; so, when we find things we don't like, we'll just go out and look up at our tree, and say 'We've got *you*, anyway, and *we're glad of it!*'"

"You blessed little mother!" laughed Shirley, wiping

her tears away. "I just believe you will like it, maybe, after all, though I've had a lot of compunctions all night. I wondered if maybe I oughtn't to have told you all about it; only I knew you couldn't really judge at all until you had seen it yourself, and we wanted to surprise you."

"Well, I'm determined to be surprised," said the brave little woman; "so don't you worry. We're going to have a grand good time to-day. Now run along. It's almost time for your car, and you haven't had any breakfast yet."

Shirley kissed her mother, and went smiling down to eat her breakfast and hurry away to the office.

There was a big rush of work at the office, or Shirley would have asked for a half-holiday; but she did not dare endanger her position by making a request at so busy a season. She was glad that the next day was Sunday and they would have a whole day to themselves in the new home before she would have to hurry away to the office again. It would serve to make it seem less lonely for her mother, having them all home that first day. She meant to work fast to-day and get all the letters written before five if possible. Then she would have time to get home a few minutes before Graham arrived with his car, and see that her mother was all comfortably ready. It was a good deal to put upon Carol to look after everything. It wasn't as if they had neighbors to help out a little, for they were the very last tenants in the doomed block to leave. All the others had gone two or three weeks before.

Thinking over again all the many details for the day, Shirley walked down to the office through the sunshine. It was growing warm weather, and her coat felt oppressive already. She was so thankful that mother would not have to sleep in those breathless rooms after the heat began. The doctor had said that her mother needed rest and air and plenty of sunshine more than anything else. She would at least have those at the barn, and what did other things matter, after all? Mother was game. Mother wouldn't let herself feel badly over such a silly thing. They certainly were going to be more comfortable than they had been for several years.

Think of that wonderful electric light. And clear cold water from the spring! Oh, it was great! And a little thrill of ecstasy passed over her, the first she had let herself feel since she had taken the great responsibility of transplanting her family to a barn.

After all, the day passed very quickly; and, when at half-past four the telephone-bell rang and Graham's voice announced that he would be down at the street door waiting for her in half an hour, that she needn't hurry, he would wait till she was ready, her heart gave a little jump of joy. It was as if school was out and she was going on a real picnic like other girls. How nice of him! How perfectly lovely of him! And yet there hadn't been anything but the nicest friendliness in his voice, such as any kindly disposed landlord might use if he chose, nothing that she need feel uncomfortable about. At least, there was the relief that after to-night mother would know all about it; and, if she didn't approve, Shirley could decline any further kindness, of course. And now she was just going to take mother's advice and forget everything but the pleasant part.

At home Carol and Harley bustled about in the empty house like two excited bumble-bees, washing up the few dishes, putting in an open box everything that had been left out for their last night's sleeping, getting lunch, and making mother take a nap. Doris, vibrating between her mother's room and down-stairs, kept singing over to herself: "We goin' to tuntry! We goin' to tuntry! See birdies an' twees and walk on gween gwass!"

After lunch was over and the dishes were put carefully into the big box between comfortables and blankets Carol helped her mother to dress, and then made her lie down and take a good long nap, with Doris asleep by her side. After that Carol and Harley tiptoed down to the bare kitchen, and sat on a box side by side to converse.

"Gee! Ain't you tired, Carol?" said the boy, pushing his hair back from his hot face. "Gee! Don't it seem funny we aren't coming back here any more? It kind of gets my goat I sha'n't see the fellows so often, but it'll be great to ask 'em to see us sometimes. Say, do you suppose we really can keep chickens?"

"Sure!" said Carol convincingly. "I asked Mr. Graham if we might,—George said we ought to, he was such a good scout you'd want to be sure he'd like it, and he said, 'Sure, it would be great.' He'd like to come out and see them sometimes. He said he used to keep chickens himself when he was a kid, and he shouldn't wonder if they had a few too many at their place they could spare to start with. He told me he'd look it up and see soon's we got settled."

"Gee! He's a peach, isn't he? Say, has he got a case on Shirl?"

"I don't know," said the girl thoughtfully; "maybe he has, but he doesn't know it yet, I guess. But anyhow you must promise me you will never breathe such a word. Why, Shirley would just bust right up if you did. I said a little something to her like that once; it wasn't much, only just that he was awfully nice and I guessed he liked her by the way he looked at her, and she just fairly froze. You know the way her eyes get when she is sore at us? And she said I must never, *never* even *think* anything like that, or she would give the place right up, and get a few rooms down on South Street, and stay in the city all summer! She said Mr. Graham was a gentleman, and she was only a working girl, and it would be a disgrace for her to accept any favors from him except what she could pay for, and an insult for him to offer them, because she was only a working girl and he was a gentleman, you know."

"H'm!" growled Harley. "I guess our sister's as good as he is any day."

"Of course!" snapped Carol; "but then he might not think so."

"Well, if he don't, he can go to thunder!" bristled Harley wrathfully. "I'm not going to have him looking down on Shirley. She's as good as his baby-doll sister with her pink cheeks, and her little white hands, and her high heels and airs, any day! She's a nut, she is."

"Harley! You stop!" declared Carol, getting wrathful.

93

"Elizabeth's a dear, and you're not going to talk about her that way. Just because she is pretty and doesn't have to work."

"Well, you said her brother looked down on our sister," declared Harley.

"I did not! I only said he *might!* I only meant that was the way *some* gentlemen would. I only said people kind of expect gentlemen to do that."

"Not if they're real gentlemen, they won't. And anyhow, *he* won't. If I find him looking down on my sister Shirley, I'll punch his face for him. Yes, I will! I'm not afraid. George and I could beat the stuffing out of him, and we will if he does any looking-down stunts, and don't you forget it!"

"Well, I'm sure he doesn't," said Carol pacifically, trying to put a soothing sound into her voice as wise elder sisters learn to do. "You see if he did look down on her, Shirley would know it; right away she'd know it. Nobody would have to tell *her!* She'd see it in his voice and smile and everything. And, if he had, she wouldn't have gone out there to live in the place he owns, you know. So I guess you can trust Shirley. *I* think he's been just dandy, fixing up that fireplace and stairs and lights and water and everything."

"Well, mebbe!" said Harley grudgingly. "Say, this is slow. I'm going out to meet the fellows when they come from school, and see what the score of the game is. Gee! I wish I could play to-day!"

"You'll be sure to come back in time?" asked Carol anxiously.

"Sure! You don't suppose I'd miss going out in that car, do you?" said the brother contemptuously. "Not on your tintype!"

"Well, maybe there won't be room for you. Maybe Elizabeth'll come along, and you'll have to go in the trolley with George."

"No chance!" declared the boy. "Mr. Graham said I should ride with him in the front seat, and he looks like a man that kept his word."

"You see! *You* know he's a gentleman!" triumphed Carol. "Well, I think you'd better stay here with me.

94

You'll forget and be late, and make a mess waiting for you."

"No, I won't!" said the restless boy. "I can't be bothered sticking round this dump all afternoon"; and Harley seized his cap, and disappeared with a whoop around the corner. After he was gone Carol found she was tired out herself, and, curling up on a mattress that was lying ready for the cartman, was soon asleep. It was so that Harley found her when he hurried back an hour later, a trifle anxious, it must be confessed, lest he had stayed too long. He stirred up the small household noisily, and in no time had Carol in a panic brewing the cup of tea that was to give her mother strength to take the journey, dressing Doris, smoothing her own hair, putting the last things into bags and baskets and boxes, and directing the cartman, who arrived half an hour sooner than he promised. Carol was quite a little woman, going from one thing to another and taking the place of everybody.

Meantime Elizabeth Graham and her brother had been spending the afternoon in business of their own. It was Elizabeth who had suggested it, and her brother saw no reason why she should not carry out her plan and why he should not help her.

She came down in the car after lunch, the chauffeur driving her, a great basket of cut and potted flowers from the home conservatory in the tonneau beside her, carefully wrapped in wax-paper. She stopped at the office for her brother, and together they went about to several shops giving orders and making purchases. When they had finished they drove out to Glenside to unpack their bundles and baskets. Graham left Elizabeth with the old servant to help her, and drove rapidly back to his office, where he telephoned to Shirley.

Certainly Elizabeth had never had such fun in her life. She scarcely knew which delightful thing to do first, and she had only about two hours to complete her arrangements before the family would arrive.

She decided to decorate first, and the great hamper of flowers was forthwith brought into the barn, and the chauffeur set to work twining ropes and sprays of smilax and asparagus fern over doorways and pictures, and training it like a vine about the stone chimney. Then came the flowers. Pots of tall starry lilies, great, heavy-headed, exquisite-breathed roses, pink, white, yellow, and crimson; daffodils and sweet peas, with quantities of sweet violets in the bottom of the basket. Elizabeth with deft fingers selected the flowers skilfully, putting pots of lilies on the window-sills, massing a quantity of pink roses in a dull gray jar she found among the kitchen things, that looked to the initiated amazingly as though it might once have been part of a water-filter, but it suited the pink roses wonderfully. The tall vases on the bookcases each side of the fireplace held daffodils. Sweet peas were glowing in small vases and glasses and bowls, and violets in saucers filled the air with fragrance. White and yellow roses were on the dining-table, and three exquisite tall crimson rosebuds glowed in a slender glass vase Elizabeth had brought with her. This she placed in Mrs. Hollister's room on the little stand that she judged would be placed beside the bed when the bed arrived. The flowers certainly did give an atmosphere to the place in more senses than one; and the girl was delighted, and fluttered from one spot to another, changing the position of a vase or bowl, and then standing off to get the effect.

"Now bring me the big bundle, Jenkins, please," she said at length when she was satisfied with the effect. "Oh, and the little long box. Be careful. It is broken at one end, and the screws may fall out."

Jenkins was soon back with the things.

"Now, you get the rods put up at the windows, Jenkins, while I get out the curtains," and she untied the big bundle with eager fingers.

Jenkins was adaptable, and the rods were simple affairs. He was soon at work, and Elizabeth ran the rods into the curtains.

They were not elegant curtains. Graham had insisted that she should get nothing elaborate, nothing that would be out of keeping with the simplicity. They were soft and straight and creamy, with a frost-like pattern rambling over them in threads of the same, illuminated here and there with a single rose and a leaf in color. There was something cheerful and spring-like to them, and yet they looked exceedingly plain and suitable, no ruffles or trimming of any kind, just hems. To Elizabeth's mind they had been very cheap. Shirley would have exclaimed over their beauty wistfully and turned from them with a gasp when she heard their price. They were one of those quiet fitting things that cost without flaunting it. They transformed the room into a dream.

"Oh, isn't it *beautiful!*" exclaimed Elizabeth, standing back to look as the first curtain went up.

"Yes, Miss, it's very stunning, Miss," said the man, working away with good will in his face.

When the curtains were all up, Elizabeth pinned one of her cards to the curtain nearest the front door, inscribed, "With love from Elizabeth."

Then in a panic she looked at her watch.

"Oh Jenkins! It's almost six o'clock," she cried in dismay. "They might get here by half-past, perhaps. We must hurry! Bring the other things in quick now, please."

So Jenkins brought them in, bundles and bags and boxes, an ice-cream freezer, and last of all the cooking-outfit belonging to their touring-car.

"Now you get the hot things ready, Jenkins, while I fix the table," directed the girl.

Jenkins, well trained in such things, went to work, opening cans and starting his chafing-dish fire. Elizabeth with eager fingers opened her parcels.

A great platter of delicious triangular chicken sandwiches, a dish of fruit and nut salad surrounded by crisp lettuce leaves, a plate of delicate rolls, cream puffs, chocolate éclairs, macaroons, a cocoanut pie, things she liked herself; and then because she knew no feast without them there were olives, salted almonds, and bonbons as a matter of course.

Delicious odors from the kitchen end of the room began to fill the air. Jenkins was heating a pail of rich soup—chicken with rice and gumbo—from one of the best caterers in the city. He was making rich cocoa

97

to be eaten with whipped cream that Elizabeth was pouring into a glass pitcher; the pitcher came from the ten-cent store if she had only known it. Jenkins was cooking canned peas and heating lovely little brown potato croquettes. The ice-cream freezer was out in full sight, where they could never miss it. Everything was ready now.

"Jenkins, you better light up that queer stove of theirs now if you're sure you know how,—she said it was just like a lamp the way it worked,—and put those things in the oven to keep warm. Then we'll pack up our things, and hide them out in the grass where they can't see, and get them in the car when they get out. Hurry, for they'll be here very soon now, I think."

Elizabeth stuck a card in the middle of the rose-bowl that said in pretty letters, "Welcome Home," stood back a minute to see how everything looked, and then fluttered to the door to watch for the car.

CHAPTER XII

WHEN Shirley came down to the street at five o'clock, Graham was waiting for her as he promised, and swung the car door open for her with as much eagerness as if he were taking the girl of his choice on a picnic instead of just doing a poor little stenographer a kindness.

"I telephoned to the store and sent a message to George. We're going to pick him up on our way," he said as the car wended its way skilfully through the traffic.

She was sitting beside him, and he looked down at her as if they were partners in a pleasant scheme. A strange sense of companionship with him thrilled through her, and was properly rebuked and fled at once, without really rippling the surface of her joy much. She had determined to have the pleasure out of this one evening ride at least, and would not let her thoughts play truant to suggest what wider, sweeter realms might be for other girls. She was having this good time. It was for her and no one else, and she would just enjoy it as much as she could, and keep it the sweet, sane, innocent pleasure that it really was. If she was not a fool, everything would be all right.

George was waiting in a quiver of pride and eagerness for them as they swept up to the employees' entrance, and a line of admiring fellow-laborers stood gaping on the sidewalk to watch his departure.

"Oh, gee! Isn't this great?" shouted George, climbing into the back seat hilariously. "Got a whole omnibus of a car this time, haven't you?"

"Yes, I thought we'd have plenty of room for your mother, so she could lie down if she liked."

"That was very kind of you," murmured Shirley. "You think of everything, don't you? I'm sure I don't see how we ever could have managed without your help. I should have been frightened a dozen times and been ready to give up."

"Not you!" said Graham fervently. "You're the kind that never gives up. You've taught me several valuable lessons."

As they turned the corner into the old street where the little brick house stood, Shirley suddenly began to have a vivid realization that she had told her mother nothing whatever about Mr. Graham. What would she think, and how could she explain his presence? She had expected to get there before Graham arrived and have time enough to make her mother understand, but now she began to realize that her real reason for leaving the matter yet unexplained was that she did not know just what to say without telling the whole story from beginning to end.

"I'll hurry in and see if mother is all ready," she said, as the car stopped in front of the house, and the children rushed out eagerly, Doris just behind the others, to see the "booful tar."

"Mother," said Shirley, slipping softly into the house and going over to the bed where she lay with hat and coat on, fully ready. "Mother, I sha'n't have time to explain all about it, but it's all right; so don't think anything. Mr. Graham, the man who owns the place where we are going, has been kind enough to offer to take you in his car. He thinks it will be easier for you than the trolley, and he is out at the door now waiting. It's perfectly all right. He has been very kind about it——"

"Oh daughter, I couldn't think of troubling any one like that!" said the mother, shrinking from the thought of a stranger; but, looking up, she saw him standing, hat in hand, just in the doorway. The children had led him to the door when he offered to help their mother out to the car.

"Mother, this is Mr. Graham," said Shirley.

Mrs. Hollister, a little pink spot on each cheek, tried to rise, but the young man came forward instantly and stooped over her.

"Don't try to get up, Mrs. Hollister. Your daughter tells me you haven't been walking about for several weeks. You must reserve all your strength for the journey. Just trust me. I'm perfectly strong, and I can lift you and put you into the car almost without your knowing it. I often carry my own mother up-stairs just for fun, and she's quite a lot larger and heavier than you. Just let me put my hand under your back so, and now this hand here. Now if you'll put your arms around my neck—yes, that way—no, don't be a bit afraid. I'm perfectly strong, and I won't drop you."

Little Mrs. Hollister cast a frightened look at her daughter and another at the fine, strong face bent above her, felt herself lifted like thistle-down before she had had time to protest, and found herself obediently putting her weak arms around his neck and resting her frightened head against a strong shoulder. A second more, and she was lying on the soft cushions of the car, and the young man was piling pillows about her and tucking her up with soft, furry robes.

"Are you perfectly comfortable?" he asked anxiously. "I didn't strain your back or tire you, did I?"

"Oh, no, indeed!" said the bewildered woman. "You are very kind, and I hardly knew what you were doing till I was here. I never dreamed of anything like this. Shirley didn't tell me about it."

"No," said the young man, smiling, "she said she

wanted to surprise you; and I believe she thought you might worry a little if you heard the details of the journey. Now, kitten, are you ready to get in?" He turned a smiling face to Doris, who stood solemnly waiting her turn, with an expression of one who at last sees the gates of the kingdom of heaven opening before her happy eyes.

"Soor!" said Doris in a tone as like Harley's as possible. She lifted one little shabby shoe, and tried to reach the step, but failed, and then surrendered her trusting hands to the young man; and he lifted her in beside her mother.

"Sit there, kitten, till your sister comes out," he said, looking at her flower face admiringly.

Doris giggled.

"I ain't a kitty," she declared; "I'se a 'ittle gurrul!"

"Well, little girl, do you like to go riding?"

"Soor! I do 'ike to go widin'!" said Doris. "Oh! There goes muvver's bed!" as the drayman came out carrying the headboard.

Shirley meanwhile was working rapidly, putting the last things from her mother's bed into the box, tossing things into the empty clothes-basket that had been left for this purpose, and directing the man who was taking down the bed and carrying out the boxes and baskets. At last all the things were out of the house, and she was free to go. She turned for one swift moment, and caught a sob in her throat. There had not been time for it before. It had come when she saw the young man stoop and lift her mother so tenderly and bear her out to the car.

But the children were calling her loudly to come. She gave one happy dab at her eyes with her handkerchief to make sure no tears had escaped, and went out of the little brick house forever.

A little middle seat had been turned down for Carol, and Doris was in her lap. Graham turned the other middle seat down for Shirley; the boys piled into the front seat with him; and they were off. Mrs. Hollister in her wonder over it all completely forgot to look back into what she had been wont to call in the stifling days of summer her "frying-pan," or to wonder whether she were about to jump into the fire. She just lay back on her soft cushions, softer than any she had ever rested upon before, and felt herself glide along away from the hated little dark house forever! It was a wonderful experience. It almost seemed as if a chariot of fire had swooped down and gathered all her little flock with her, and was carrying them to some kind of gracious heaven where comfort would be found at last. A bit of hope sprang up within her, utterly unpremeditated and unreasonable, and persisted so that she could not help feeling happy. As yet it had not come to her to wonder who this handsome young man was that presumed to lift her and carry her like a baby, and move her on beds of down to utterly unknown regions. She was too much taken up with the wonder of it all. If Doris hadn't been prattling, asking questions of her, and the light breeze hadn't flapped a lock of hair into her eyes and tickled her nose, she might have thought she was dreaming, so utterly unreal did it all seem to her.

And now they passed out from the narrow streets, through crowded thoroughfares for a brief space, then out beyond, and free, into the wider reaches. Fair houses and glimpses of green were appearing. The car was gliding smoothly, for the sake of the invalid not going at high speed; and she could see on every side. The trees were in full leaf; the sky was large and blue; the air was filled with freshness. She drew a long breath; and closed her eyes to pray, "Oh, my Father!" and then opened them again to see whether it was all true. Shirley, sensitive for her to the slightest breath, turned and drew the robes closer about her mother, and asked whether she were perfectly warm and whether she wanted another pillow under her head.

Graham did not intrude himself upon the family behind him. He was absorbed in the two boys, who were entirely willing to be monopolized. He told them all about the car, and discoursed on the mysteries of the different makes with a freedom that gave George the impression that he was himself almost a man to be honored by such talk.

It was nearly seven o'clock when they reached Glenside and the big stone barn came in sight, for they had travelled slowly to make it easier for the invalid.

Elizabeth had sighted the car far down the road below the curve; and, switching on every electric light in the place, she fled down the ladder to the basement, dragging the willing Jenkins after her. Here they waited with bated breath until the family had gone inside, when they made their stealthy way out the east end, across the little brook under the fence, and down the road, to be picked up by the car according to previous arrangement.

As the car came in sight of the barn a deep silence suddenly fell upon the little company. Even Doris felt it, and ceased her prattle to look from one to another. "Whatzie mattah?" she asked Shirley shyly, putting out her hand to pat Shirley's face in a way she had when she was uneasy or troubled. *"Whatzie mattah, Surly?"*

But Shirley only squeezed her hand reassuringly, and smiled.

As they drew near, the young people noticed that the bars of the fence in front of the barn had been taken down and the ditch filled in smoothly. Then they saw that the car was turning in and going straight up the grassy incline to the door.

Mrs. Hollister, lying comfortably among her cushions, was looking at the evening sky, hearing a bird that reminded her of long ago, and scarcely noticed they had turned until the car stopped. Then in silent joy the children swarmed out of the car, and with one consent stood back and watched mother, as the strong young man came to the open door and gathered her in his arms once more.

"Now we're almost home, Mrs. Hollister," he said pleasantly. "Just put your arms around my neck once more, and we'll soon have you beside your own fire." He lifted her and bore her in to the wide couch before the crackling fire that Elizabeth had started just before she went to look out the door the last time.

Then into the blazing light of the transformed barn they all stepped, and every one stood back and stared, blinking. What was this? What wondrous perfume met their senses? What luxury! What flowers! What hangings!

They stood and stared, and could not understand; and between them they forgot to wonder what their mother was thinking, or to do a thing but stupidly stare and say, "Why!" and "Oh!" and "Ah!" half under their breath.

"Just phone me if you need anything, Miss Hollister, please. I shall be glad to serve you," said Graham, stepping quickly over to the door. "Mrs. Hollister, I hope you'll be none the worse for your ride"; and he slipped out the door, and was gone.

The sound of the car softly purring its way backward down the slope brought Shirley out of her daze; but, when she turned and understood that he was gone, the car was just backing into the road, turning with a quick whirl, and was away before she could make him hear.

"Oh! He is *gone!*" she cried out, turning in dismay to the children. "He is gone, and we never thanked him!"

George was out down the road like a shot; and the rest, forgetful for the moment of the invalid who had been the great anxiety all day, crowded at the door to watch him. They could hear the throbbing of the machine; they heard it stop down the road and start again almost immediately, growing fainter with every whir as it went farther from them. In a moment more George came running back.

"He's gone. He meant to, I guess, so we could have it all to ourselves right at first. Elizabeth and the man were down the road waiting for him. They've been dolling the place up to surprise us."

"Oh!" said Shirley, turning to look around, her cheeks growing rosy. "Oh! Isn't it beautiful?" Then, turning swiftly to the couch and kneeling, she said, "Oh, *mother!*"

"What does it all mean, daughter?" asked the bewildered mother, looking about on the great room that seemed a palace to her sad eyes.

But they all began to clamor at once, and she could make nothing of it.

"Oh Shirley, look at the curtains! Aren't they perfectly dear?" cried Carol ecstatically.

"Perf'ly deah!" echoed Doris, dancing up and down gleefully.

"And here's a card, 'With love from Elizabeth'! Isn't it sweet of her? Isn't she a perfect *darling?*"

"Who is Elizabeth?" asked Mrs. Hollister, rising to her elbow and looking around.

"Gee! Look at the flowers!" broke in George. "It's like our store at Easter! I say! Those lilies are pretty keen, aren't they, Shirl?"

"Wait'll you see the dining-room!" called Harley, who was investigating with the help of his nose. *"Some* supper-table! Come on quick; I'm starved. Hello! Hustle here quick. Here's another sign-board!"

They followed to the dining-room. Harley, still following his nose, pursued his investigations to the kitchen, discovered the source of the savory odors that were pervading the place, and raised another cry so appreciative that the entire family, with the exception of the invalid, followed him and found the supper steaming hot and crying to be eaten.

After the excitement was somewhat quieted Shirley took command.

"Now, children, you're getting mother all excited, and this won't do. And, besides, we must eat this supper right away before it spoils. Quiet down, and bring the hot things to the table while I get mother's things off. Then we will tell her all about it. There's plenty of time, you know. We're going to stay right here all summer."

"Aw, gee! Can't we bring mother out to the table?" pleaded George. "Harley and I could lift that couch just as easy."

"Why, I don't know," said Shirley, hesitating. "You know she isn't strong, and she will worry about your lifting her."

"Oh Shirley, let her come," pleaded Carol. "We could all take hold and wheel the couch out here; you know the floor is real smooth since those new boards were put in, and there are good castors on the couch."

"Mother! Mother!" You're coming out to supper!"

they chorused, rushing back to the living-room; and before the invalid realized what was happening her couch was being wheeled carefully, gleefully into the brilliantly lighted dining-room, with Doris like a fairy sprite dancing attendance, and shouting joyously:

"Mudder's tumin' to suppy! Mudder's tumin' to suppy adin!"

The mother gazed in amazement at the royally spread table, so smothered in flowers that she failed to recognize the cracked old blue dishes.

"Children, I insist," she raised her voice above the happy din. "I insist on knowing immediately what all this means. Where are we, and what is this? A hotel? And who was the person who brought us here? I cannot eat anything nor stay here another minute until I know. People can't rent houses like this for ten dollars a month anywhere, and I didn't suppose we had come to charity, even if I am laid up for a few days."

Shirley could see the hurt in her mother's eyes and the quick alarm in her voice, and came around to her couch, smiling.

"Now, mother dear, we'll tell you the whole thing. It isn't a hotel we're in, and it isn't a house at all. It's only an old barn!"

"A barn!" Mrs. Hollister sat up on her couch alertly, and looked at the big bowl of roses in the middle of the table, at the soft, flowing curtains at the window and the great pot of Easter lilies on the little stand in front, and exclaimed, "Impossible!"

"But it is, really, mother, just a grand old stone barn! Look at the walls. See, those two over there are just rough stones, and this one back of you is a partition made of common boards. That's only an old brown denim curtain over there to hide the kitchen, and we've got the old red chenille curtains up to partition off the bedrooms. The boys are going to sleep up in the hayloft, and it's going to be just great!"

Mrs. Hollister looked wildly at the stone walls, back at the new partition, recognized one by one the ancient chairs, the old bookcase now converted into a china-closet, the brown denim curtain that had once been a cover for the dining-room floor in the little brick house.

Now it was washed and mended, and was doing its faded part to look like a wall and fit into the scheme of things. She darted questioning glances at the wealth of flowers, and the abundantly set table, then settled back on her pillow but half satisfied.

"They don't have curtains in a barn!" she remarked dryly.

"Those are a present from Elizabeth, the little sister of the landlord. She was out here with him when he came to see about things, and she got acquainted with Carol. She has put up those curtains, and brought the flowers, and fixed the table, for a surprise. See, mother!" and Shirley brought the card on which Elizabeth had printed her crude welcome.

Mrs. Hollister took the card as if it were some sort of a life-preserver, and smiled with relief.

"But this is a great deal to do for strangers," she said tremblingly, and tears began to glitter in her eyes. "They must be wealthy people."

"Yes, mother, I think they are," said Shirley, "and they have been most kind."

"But, daughter, wealthy people do not usually take the trouble to do things like that for nothing. And ten dollars a month for a barn could be nothing to them."

"I know, mother, but he seems very well satisfied with the price," said Shirley with a troubled brow. "I——"

"Something's burning!" yelled Harley at the top of his lungs from the kitchen, and immediately they all rushed out to rescue the supper, which took that moment to assert itself.

"Now, mother," said Shirley, coming in with a big tureen of soup, "we've got to eat this supper or it will spoil. You're not to ask another question till we are through."

They all settled expectantly down at the table, Doris climbing joyously into her high chair, calling:

"Suppy! Suppy! Oh goody!"

Such a clatter and a clamor, such shoutings over the sandwiches and such jumpings up and down to carry something to mother! Such lingering over the delicious ice-cream and fresh strawberries that were found in the freezer! Think of it! Real strawberries for *them* that time of year!

Then, when they had eaten all they could, and began to realize that it was time to get mother to bed, they pushed the chairs back, and all fell to clearing off the table and putting things away. It was Carol who discovered the big roasted fowl and the bowl of salad set away in the tiny ice-box ready for to-morrow. How had Elizabeth, who never kept house in her life, known just what would be nice for a family that were all tired out with moving, and needed to lie back and rest before starting on with living?

The dishes were almost washed when the cart arrived with the last load of things, and the drayman helped George to put up mother's bed.

They wheeled the couch into the living-room after the big doors were closed and safely fastened for the night. Before the glowing fire Shirley helped mother to undress, then rolled her couch into the bedroom and got her to bed.

"Do you mind very much that it is only a barn, mother dear?" questioned Shirley, bending anxiously over her mother after she was settled.

"I can't make it seem like a barn, dear; it seems a palace!" said the mother with a tremble in her voice. "I'm glad it's a barn, because we could never afford a house with space like this, and air!" She threw out her hands as if to express her delight in the wide rooms, and drew in a breath of the delicious country air, so different from air of the dusty little brick house in the city.

"Daughter!" she drew Shirley down where she could whisper to her. "You're sure he is not looking on us as objects of charity, and you're sure he understands that you are a self-respecting girl earning her honorable living and paying her way? You know this is a wicked, deceitful world we live in, and there are all sorts of people in it."

"Mother dear! I'm sure. Sure as anybody could be. He has been a perfect gentleman. You didn't think he looked like one of those—those people—that go around misunderstanding girls, did you mother?"

The mother remembered the gentle, manly way in which the young man had lifted her and carried her to and from the car, and her heart warmed to him. Yet her fears lingered as she watched her sweet-eyed girl.

"No-o-o," she answered slowly; "but then, you can't always judge. He certainly was a gentleman, and he was very nice-looking." Then she looked sharply at Shirley.

"You won't go to getting any notions in your head, dear child?" Her eyes were wistful and sad as she searched the sweet, weary face of the girl. "You know rich young men follow whims sometimes for a few days. They don't mean anything. I wouldn't want your heart broken. I wish he was an old man with white hair."

"Oh mother dear!" laughed Shirley with heart-free ring to her voice, "did you think you had a young fool for a daughter? He was only being nice because he is a perfect gentleman; but I know he is not in the same universe as I am, so far as anything more than pleasant kindliness is concerned. We shall probably never see him again now that we are settled. But don't you think I ought to go and telephone thanks to his little sister? They will be home by this time, and it seems as if we ought to make some acknowledgment of her great kindness."

"By all means, dear; but how can you? Is there a pay-station near here? I thought you said this was out in the country."

"Why, we have a telephone of our own, muddy dear! Just think of the luxury of it! Us with a telephone! Mr. Graham had it put into the barn when he was making some repairs, so he could communicate with his workmen; and he said if we would like it we might keep it. It is one of those 'pay-as-you-go' phones, with a place to drop nickels and dimes in; so we are perfectly independent. Mr. Graham thought it would be a comfort to you when George or I had to stay late in town."

"How thoughtful of him! He must be a *wonderful* rich man! By all means telephone at once, and tell the little girl to say to her brother from me that I shall esteem it a privilege to thank him personally for all that he has done for my children, sometime when he is out this way. Think. A real rose by my bed!" She reached out a frail hand, and touched the exquisite petals lovingly. "It is wonderful!"

So Shirley went into the living-room to telephone, while all the children stood about to watch and comment and tell her what to say. Doris sat on a little cushion at her feet in awe, and listened, asking Carol with large eyes: "Is Shirley tautin to Dod? Vy doesn't see sut her yeyes?" for Shirley's conversation over the telephone sounded to the little sister much like a prayer of thanksgiving; only she was not accustomed to hearing that joyous laughter in the voice when people prayed.

Then Doris was put to bed in her own little crib, and the light in mother's room was switched off amid Doris's flood of questions.

"Vat makes it light? Vy did it do avay? Will it tum adin?"

At last she was asleep, and the other children tiptoed excitedly about preparing for bed, going up and downstairs softly, whispering back and forth for this or that they could not find, till quiet settled down upon the tired, happy household, and the bullfrogs in the distant creek droned out the nightly chorus.

CHAPTER XIII

IT was beautiful to wake the next morning with the birds singing a matin in the trees, and a wonderful Sabbath quiet over everything. Tired out as she was and worn with excitement and care, Shirley was the first to waken, and she lay there quiet beside Carol for a little while with her eyes closed, listening, and saying a prayer of thanksgiving for the peace of the place, and the wonder that it had come into her life. Then suddenly a strange luminousness about her simply forced her to open her eyes.

The eastern window was across the room from her bed, and the sky was rosy, with the dawn, and flooding the room. It was the first time in years she had watched the sun rise. She had almost forgotten, in the little dark city house, that there was a sun to rise and make things glorious. The sun had seemed an enemy to burn and wilt and stifle.

But now here was a friend, a radiant new friend, to be waited for and enjoyed, to give glory to all their lives. She raised herself on one elbow and watched until the red ball had risen and burst into the brightness of day. Then she lay down softly again and listened to the birds. They seemed to be mad with joy over the new day. Presently the chorus grew less and less. The birds had gone about their morning tasks, and only a single bright song now and then from some soloist in the big tree overhead marked the sweet-scented silence of the morning.

In the quiet Shirley lay and went over events since she had first seen this spot and taken the idea of living in the barn. Her heart gave thanks anew that her mother had not disliked it as she had feared. There was no sense that it was a stable, no odor of living creatures having occupied it before, only sweet dusty clover like a lingering of past things put away carefully. It was like a great camping expedition. And then all those flowers! The scent of the lilies was on the air. How lovely of the young girl out of her luxury to think to pass on some of the sweet things of life! And the gracious, chivalrous man, her brother! She must not let him think she would presume upon his kindness. She must not let even her thoughts cross the line and dwell on the ground of social equality. She knew where he belonged, and there he should stay for all her. She was heart-free and happy, and only too glad to have such a kind landlord.

She drifted off to sleep again, and it was late when she awoke the next time. A silvery bell from the little white church in the valley was ringing and echoing distantly. Sabbath, real Sabbath, seemed brooding happily in the very air. Shirley got up and dressed hastily. She felt as if she had already lost too much of this first wonderful day in the country.

A thrush was spilling his liquid notes in the tree

111

overhead when she tiptoed softly into her mother's room. Doris opened her eyes and looked in wonder, then whispered softly:

"Vat is dat, Sirley? Vat *is* dat pitty sound?"

"A birdie in the tree, dearie!" whispered Shirley.

"A *weel budie!* I yantta see it! Take Doris up, Sirley!"

So Shirley lifted the little maiden, wrapped a shawl about her, and carried her softly to the window, where she looked up in wonder and joy.

The boys came tumbling down from their loft in a few minutes, and there was no more sleep to be had. Carol was up and out, and the voice of one or the other of them was continually raised in a shout of triumph over some new delight.

"I saw a fish in the brook!" shouted Harley under his mother's window. "It was only a little fellow, but maybe it'll grow bigger some day, and then we can fish!"

"You silly!" cried George. "It was a minnow. Minnows don't grow to be big. They're only good for bait!"

"Hush, George, there's a nest in the big tree. I've been watching and the mother bird is sitting on it. That was the father bird singing a while ago." This from Carol.

George, Harley, and Carol declared their intention of going to church. That had likely been the first bell that rang, their mother told them, and they would have plenty of time to get there if they hurried. It was only half-past nine. Country churches rang a bell then, and another at ten, and the final bell at half-past ten, probably. Possibly they had Sunday-school at ten. Anyhow, they could go and find out. It wouldn't matter if they were a little late the first time.

So they ate some breakfast in a hurry, took each a sandwich left from the night before, crossed the road, climbed the fence, and went joyously over the green fields to church, thinking how much nicer it was than walking down a brick-paved street, past the same old grimy houses to a dim, artificially lighted church.

Shirley took a survey of the larder, decided that roast

112

chicken, potato croquettes, and peas would all warm up quickly, and, as there was plenty of ice cream left and some cakes, they would fare royally without any work; so she sat beside her mother and told the whole story of her ride, the finding of the barn, her visit to the Graham office, and all that transpired until the present time.

The mother listened, watching her child, but said no word of her inner thoughts. If it occurred to her that her oldest daughter was fair to look upon, and that her winning ways, sweet, unspoiled face, and wistful eyes had somewhat to do with the price of their summer's abode, it would be no wonder. But she did not mean to trouble her child further. She would investigate for herself when opportunity offered. So she quieted all anxieties Shirley might have had about her sanction of their selection of a home, kissed Shirley, and told her she felt it in her bones she was going to get well right away.

And, indeed, there was much in the fact of the lifting of the burden of anxiety concerning where they should live that went to brighten the eyes of the invalid and strengthen her heart.

When the children came home from church Shirley was putting dinner on the table, and her mother was arrayed in a pretty kimono, a relic of their better days, and ready to be helped to the couch and wheeled out to the dining-room. It had been pleasant to see the children coming across the green meadow in the distance, and get things all ready for them when they rushed in hungry. Shirley was so happy she felt like crying.

After the dinner things were washed they shoved the couch into the living-room among the flowers, where George had built up a beautiful fire, for it was still chilly. The children gathered around their mother and talked, making plans for the summer, telling about the service they had attended, chattering like so many magpies. The mother lay and watched them and was content. Sometimes her eyes would search the dim, mellow rafters overhead, and glance along the stone walls, and she would say to herself: "This is a barn! I am living in a barn! My husband's children have come to this, that they have no place to live but a barn!" She was testing herself to see if the thought hurt her. But, looking on their happy faces, somehow she could not feel sad.

"Children," she said suddenly in one of the little lulls of conversation, "do you realize that Christ was born in a stable? It isn't so bad to live in a barn. We ought to be very thankful for this great splendid one!"

"Oh mother, dear! It is so beautiful of you to take it that way!" cried Shirley with tears in her eyes.

"Doris, you sing your little song about Jesus in the stable," said Carol. "I'll play it for you."

Doris, nothing loath, got a little stool, stood up beside her mother's couch, folded her small hands demurely, and began to sing without waiting for accompaniment:

"Away in a manger,
    No trib for His head,
The litta Lord Jesus
    Lay down His sveet head.
The tars in the haaven
    Look down vhere 'e lay—
The litta Lord Jesus
    As'eep in the hay.

"The catta are lowing,
    The poor baby wates;
But the litta Lord Jesus
    No cwyin' He mates.
I love Thee, Lord Jesus;
    Look down fum the sky,
An' stay by my trib,
    Watching my lul-la-by!"

Shirley kissed Doris, and then they began to sing other things, all standing around the piano. By and by that distant bell from the valley called again.

"There's a vesper service at five o'clock. Why don't you go, Shirley? You and George and Harley," said Carol.

"Me 'ant do too!" declared Doris earnestly, and it was finally decided that the walk would not be too long; so the boys, Shirley and the baby started off across the fields, while Carol stayed with her mother. And this time Mrs. Hollister heard all about Elizabeth and how she wanted Carol to come and see her sometime. Heard, too, about the proposed dance, and its quiet squelching by the brother. Heard, and looked thoughtful, and wondered more.

"Mother is afraid they are not quite our kind of people, dear!" she said gently. "You mustn't get your heart bound up in that girl. She may be very nice, but she's a society girl, and you are not, you know. It stands to reason she will have other interests pretty soon, and then you will be disappointed when she forgets all about you."

"She won't forget, mother, I know she won't!" declared Carol stoutly. "She's not that kind. She loves me; she told me so. She wanted to put one of her rings on my finger to 'bind our friendship,' only I wouldn't let her till I had asked you, because I didn't have any but grandmother's to give her, and I couldn't give her that."

"That was right, dear. You can't begin things like that. You would find a great many of them, and we haven't the money to keep up with a little girl who has been used to everything."

Carol's face went down. Tears began to come in her eyes.

"Can't we have even *friends?*" she said, turning her face away to hide the quiver in her lip, and the tears that were rolling down her cheeks.

"Yes, dear," said the mother sorrowfully, "but don't choose them from among another people. People who can't possibly have much in common with us. It is sure to hurt hard when there are differences in station like that."

"But I didn't choose them. They chose us!" declared Carol. "Elizabeth just went wild over us the first time she saw us, and her brother told Shirley he was glad, that it would do Elizabeth a lot of good to know us. He said, 'We've learned a lot of things from you already'; just like that, he said it! I was coming down the stairs behind them when they stood here talking one day, and I couldn't help hearing them."

"Yes?" said Mrs. Hollister thoughtfully. "Well, perhaps, but, dear, go slow and don't pin your heart to a friendship like that, for it will most likely be disappointing. Just be happy in what she has done for us already, and don't expect anything more. She may never come again. It may just have been a passing whim. And I don't want you to be always looking for her and always disappointed."

"I shall not be disappointed, mamma," said Carol decidedly. "You'll see!" and her face brightened.

Then as if to make good her words a big car came whirring up the road and stopped in front of the barn, and almost before she could get to the window to look out Carol heard Elizabeth's voice calling softly:

"Carol! Car-*roll!* Are you there?" and she flung the door open and rushed into her new friend's arms.

Graham came more slowly up the incline, smiling apologetically and hoping he didn't intrude, coming so soon.

Carol led them over to the invalid and introduced her friend, and the young man came after them.

"I'm afraid this is rather soon to obey your summons, Mrs. Hollister," he said engagingly, "but Elizabeth couldn't stand it without coming over to see if you really found the ice-cream freezer, so I thought we'd just drop in for a minute and see whether you were quite comfortable."

Somehow, suddenly, Mrs. Hollister's fears and conclusions concerning these two young people began to vanish, and in spite of her she felt just as Shirley had done, that they were genuine in their kindliness and friendship. Carol, watching her, was satisfied, and a glow of triumph shone in her eyes. Nevertheless, Mrs. Hollister gathered her caution about her as a garment, and in dignified and pleasant phrases thanked the two in such a way that they must see that neither she nor her children would ever presume upon what had been done for them, nor take it for more than a passing kindliness.

But to her surprise the young man did not seem to be more than half listening to her words. He seemed to be studying her face with deep intention that was almost embarrassing. The soft color stole into her thin cheeks, and she stopped speaking and looked at him in dismay.

"I beg your pardon," he said, seeing her bewilderment, "but you can't understand perhaps how interested I am in you. I am afraid I have been guilty of staring. You see it is simply amazing to me to find a woman of your refinement and evident culture and education who is content—I might even say joyful—to live in a *barn!* I don't know another woman who would be satisfied. And you seem to have brought up all your children with just such happy, adaptable natures, that it is a great puzzle to me. I—I—why, I feel sort of rebuked! I feel that you and your children are among the great of the earth. Don't thank Elizabeth and me for the little we have been able to do toward making this barn habitable. It was a sort of—I might say homage, due to you, that we were rendering. And now please don't think anything more about it. Let's just talk as if we were friends—that is, if you are willing to accept a couple of humble strangers among your list of friends."

"Why, surely, if you put it that way!" smiled the little woman. "Although I'm sure I don't know what else we could do but be glad and happy over it that we had a barn like this to come to under a sweet blue sky, with a bird and a tree thrown in, when we literally didn't know where we could afford to lay our heads. You know beggars shouldn't be choosers, but I'm sure one would choose a spacious place like this any day in preference to most of the ordinary city houses, with their tiny dark rooms, and small breathless windows."

"Even if 'twas called a barn?"

"Even if 'twas called a barn!" said the woman with a flitting dance in her eyes that reminded him of the girl Shirley.

"Well, I'm learning a lot, I tell you!" said the young man. "The more I see of you all, the more I learn.

It's opened my eyes to a number of things in my life that I'm going to set right. By the way, is Miss Hollister here? I brought over a book I was telling her about the other day. I thought she might like to see it."

"She went over to the vesper service at the little church across the fields. They'll be coming home soon, I think. It must be nearly over."

He looked at his watch.

"Suppose I take the car and bring them back. You stay here, Elizabeth. I'll soon be back. I think I can catch them around by the road if I put on speed."

He was off, and the mother lay on the couch watching the two girls and wishing with all her heart that it were so that her children might have these two fine young people for friends. But of course such things could not very well be in this world of stern realities and multitudinous conventionalities. What, for instance, would be said in the social set to which the Grahams belonged if it were known that some of their intimate friends lived in a barn? No, such things did not happen even in books, and the mother lay still and sighed. She heard the chatter of the two girls.

"You're coming home with me to stay over Sunday pretty soon. Sidney said he would fix it all up with your mother pretty soon. We'll sleep together and have the grandest times. Mother likes me to have friends stay with me, but most of the girls I know are off at boarding-school now, and I'm dreadfully lonesome. We have tennis-courts and golf links and a bowling-alley. Do you play tennis? And we can go out in the car whenever we like. It's going to be grand. I'll show you my dog and my pony I used to ride. He's getting old now, and I'm too big for him, but I love him just the same. I have a saddle-horse, but I don't ride much. I'd rather go motoring with Sid——"

And so she rattled on, and the mother sighed for her little girl who was being tempted by a new and beautiful world, and had not the wherewithal to enter it, even if it were possible for her to do so.

Out in the sunset the car was speeding back again with the seats full, Doris chirping gleefully at the ride, for her fat legs had grown very weary with the long walk through the meadow and Shirley had been almost sorry she had taken her along.

The boys were shouting all sorts of questions about dogs and chickens and cars and a garden, and Graham was answering them all good-humoredly, now and then turning around to throw back a pleasant sentence and a smile at the quiet girl with the happy eyes sitting in the back seat with her arm around her little sister.

There was nothing notable about the ride to remember. It was just one of those beautiful bits of pleasantness that fit into the mosaic of any growing friendship, a bit of color without which the whole is not perfect. Shirley's part in it was small. She said little and sat listening happily to the boys' conversation with Graham. She had settled it with her heart that morning that she and the young man on that front seat had nothing in future to do with each other, but it was pleasant to see him sitting there talking with her brothers. There was no reason why she should not be glad for that, and glad he was not a snob. For every time she looked on his clean, frank face, and saw his nice gray eyes upon her, she was surer that he was not a snob.

The guests stayed a little while after they all got back, and accepted quite as a matter of course the dainty little lunch that Carol and Elizabeth, slipping away unobserved, prepared and brought in on trays, —some of the salad left from dinner, some round rolls that Shirley had brought out with her Saturday, cut in two and crisply toasted, cups of delicious cocoa, and little cakes. That was all, but it tasted fine, and the two self-invited guests enjoyed it hugely. Then they all ranged themselves around the piano and sang hymns, and it is safe to say that the guests at least had not spent as "Sabbathy" a Sabbath in all their lives. Elizabeth was quite astonished when she suggested that they sing a popular song to have Carol answer in a polite but gently reproving tone, "Oh, not to-day, you know."

"Why not? Doesn't your mother like it?" whispered Elizabeth.

"Why, we don't any of us usually sing things like that on Sunday, you know. It doesn't seem like Sunday. It doesn't seem quite respectful to God." Carol was terribly embarrassed and was struggling to make her idea plain.

"Oh!" Elizabeth said, and stood looking wistfully, wonderingly at her friend, and finally stole out a soft hand and slipped it into Carol's, pressing her fingers as if to make her know she understood. Then they lifted up their voices again over the same hymn-book:

"Thine earthly Sabbaths, Lord, we love,
But there's a nobler rest above;
To that our longing souls aspire
With cheerful hope and strong desire."

Graham looked about on the group as they sang, his own fine tenor joining in the words, his eyes lingering on the earnest face of his little sister as she stood arm in arm with the other girl, and was suddenly thrilled with the thought of what a Sabbath might be, kept in this way. It had never appealed to him quite like that before. Sabbath-keeping had seemed a dry, thankless task for a few fanatics; now a new possibility loomed vaguely in his mind. He could see that people like this could really make the Sabbath something to love, not just a day to loll through and pass the time away.

When they finally went away there was just a streak of dull red left in the western horizon where the day had disappeared, and all the air was seething with sweet night sounds and odors, the dampness of the swamps striking coolly in their faces as the car sped along.

"Sidney," said Elizabeth after a long time, "did you ever feel as if God were real?"

"Why, how do you mean, kid?" asked the brother, rather embarrassed. These subjects were not discussed at all in the Graham household.

"Did you ever feel as if there really was a God somewhere, like a person, that could see and hear you and know what you did and how you felt to Him? Because *they* do. Carol said they didn't sing 'Tipperary' on Sunday because it didn't seem quite respectful to

120

God, and I could see she really meant it. It wasn't just because her mother said she had to or anything like that. She thought so *herself*."

"H'm!" said Graham thoughtfully. "Well, they're rather remarkable people, I think."

"Well, I think so too, and I think it's about time you fixed it up with mamma to let Carol come and visit me."

"I'm going to get mother to go out there and call this week if I can," said Graham after another longer pause, and then added: "I think she will go and I think she will like them. After that we'll see, kid. Don't you worry. They're nice, all right." He was thinking of the look on Shirley's face as she sat at the piano playing for them all to sing.

CHAPTER XIV

THE first few days in the new home were filled with wonder and delight for them all. They just could not get used to having plenty of room indoors, with all outdoors for a playground. Doris's cheeks took on a lovely pink, and her eyes began to sparkle. She and Harley spent all day out-of-doors. They were making a garden. Not that they had any experience or any utensils. There was an old hoe and a broken spade down in the basement of the barn, and with these Harley managed to remove a few square feet of young turf, and mellow up an inch or two of soil depth. In this they planted violet roots and buttercups and daisies which they found in the meadows. Doris had a corner all her own, with neat rows of tiny stones from the brook laid in elaborate baby-patterns around the edge, and in this she stuck twigs and weeds of all descriptions, and was never daunted, only pained and surprised when they drooped and died in a day or two and had to be supplanted by others.

It had been decided that Harley was to stop school and stay at home with mother and Doris, which indeed he was quite willing to do under the glamour of the new life. The school itself never had much attraction for him, and "the fellows" were almost forgotten in searching for angleworms and building dams in the creek.

Carol went to high school every morning with Shirley and George on the trolley. There were only six more weeks till the term was over, and it was better for Carol to finish out her year and get her credits. Shirley thought they could afford the extra carfare for just that little while, and so all day long mother and Doris and Harley kept quiet home in the old barn, and the meadows rang with Doris's shouts and Harley's answers.

One day the doctor came out in his machine to see Mrs. Hollister as he had promised to do, and found her so much better that he told her she might get up and go around a little while every day if she was very careful not to get over-tired. He prophesied a speedy return to health if she kept on looking happy and breathing this good air. He praised the good sense that brought her out into the country to live, in preference to any little tucked-up house in town, and said if she could only get well enough to work outdoors in the ground and have a flower-bed it would be the making of her. Her eyes brightened at that, for she loved flowers, and in the days of her youth had been extremely successful at making things grow.

The doctor was deeply interested in the barn. He walked about with his hands in his pockets, looking the rooms over, as delighted as a child at seeing a new mechanical toy.

"Well, now this is great!" he said heartily. "This is simply great! I admire you people for having the nerve to go against conventionality and come out here. If I had a few more patients who could be persuaded to go out into the country and take some of the unused old barns and fix them up to live in, I'd have to change my occupation. It's a great idea, and I mean to recommend it to others if you don't mind. Only I doubt if I find two others who have the nerve to follow your example."

The invalid laughed.

"Why, doctor, I can't see the nerve. We really hadn't

any choice. We couldn't find a decent place that we could afford, and this was big and healthful and cost less than the worst little tenement that would have done in town. Anyone would be a fool not to have come here."

"Mrs. Hollister, do you know that most people would rather starve and swelter, yes—and *die* in a conventional house, than to do such an unheard-of thing as to live in a barn, no matter how delightful that barn might be? You are a great little woman, Mrs. Hollister, and you deserve to get well, and to see your children prosper. And they will. They have the right spirit."

After his visit Mrs. Hollister began to get up a little while every day, and her improvement in health was rapid. She even ventured out to see Doris's garden and watch the "budie" in his nest in the tree.

One day a drayman stopped at the place and left several great rolls of chicken-wire, and a couple of big crates. One crate was bigger than the other and contained half a dozen big yellow hens and a beautiful rooster. The small crate held two lovely white rabbits.

The children hovered joyfully over the crates.

"Mine wabbits!" declared Doris solemnly. "Nice Mistah Dwaham give Doris wabbits."

"Did Mr. Graham say he was going to send you some rabbits?" questioned her mother.

" 'Es. He did say he was goin' to sen' me some wabbits. On 'e way fum chutch in big oughtymobeel. He did say he would give me wabbits. Oh, mine wabbits!" Doris was in ecstasy.

Mrs. Hollister looked at the big rolls of wire questioningly:

"George and I told him we wanted some chickens. I guess that's why he sent 'em," announced Harley excitedly.

"I hope you boys didn't hint. That's very bad manners. You know I can't have Mr. Graham giving you such expensive presents; it won't do, dear."

"No, mother, we didn't hint. George just asked him if he minded if we kept chickens here, and he said no, indeed, he'd like to go into the business himself. He said he used to have a lot of his own when he was a boy, and he guessed there was a lot of wire from the old chicken-run around at his place yet. If there was, there wasn't any reason why it shouldn't be in use, and he'd look it up. He said, if it was, he and we'd go into business. He'd furnish the tools and we could do the work, and maybe some day we could sell eggs and make it pay."

"That's very kind of him, I'm sure. But, Harley, that looks like new wire. It isn't the least bit rusted."

"It's galvanized, mother. Galvanized wire doesn't rust, don't you know that?" said Harley in a superior, man's voice.

Harley and Doris were wild over their pets, and could do nothing all that day but hover about them, and the minute George arrived the boys went out to see about putting up some of the wire and making a temporary abode for the creatures until they could get time to plan an elaborate chicken-run.

Before dark Graham arrived. He had brought a book on chicken-raising and had a good many suggestions to offer. With him in the front seat of the car rode a great golden-brown dog with a white-starred face, great affectionate eyes, and a plumy white tail. He bounded floppily out after Graham and came affably up to the door as if he understood everything; and at sight of him the children went wild.

"I brought this fellow along, thinking perhaps you'd like him to help look after things here. He's only a puppy, but he's a good breed, and I think you'll find him a splendid watch-dog. You don't need to keep him, of course, if you don't want him, Mrs. Hollister, but I thought out in the country this way it might be as well for you to have him on guard, at night especially. He'll be good company for the children. We've got so many of them that we want to give this one away."

And what was there to do but accept him with thanks, a dog like that begging for a home, and a home like that really needing a dog?

So the dog was promptly accepted as a member of the family, was named Star, and accepted the overtures of his devoted worshippers in many amiable waggings of tail and a wide puppy laugh on his face. He stayed behind most contentedly when Graham departed after a long conference with George and Harley over the "chicken" book, and a long discussion in the back yard as to the best place for the chicken-run. He seemed to know from the start that he had come to stay, that this was his "job" and he was on it for life.

It must be admitted that Mrs. Hollister went to sleep that night with more content, knowing that big, floppy, deep-voiced dog was lying across the door out in the living-room. The hillside had seemed a bit lonely at night, though she had never admitted it even to herself before, and she was glad the dog had come. That night in the little prayer that she said every night with all her children gathered about her couch in front of the fire, she added, "We thank Thee, oh, Lord, for sending us such good kind friends to make the world so much happier for us."

A few days later Mrs. Graham came to call.

Her son did not explain to her anything about the Hollisters, nor say a word about the place where they were living. He merely remarked casually: "Mother, there are some people I'd like you to call on if you don't mind. They live out Glenside way, and I'll take you any afternoon you have time."

"I really haven't much time now before we go to the shore, Sidney," she said. "Couldn't they wait till the fall when we return?"

"No, mother, I'd like you to call now. It needn't take you long, and I think you'll like them—her— Mrs. Hollister, I mean. Can't you go this afternoon? I'll call for you with the car anywhere you say, along about half-past four or five o'clock. It will be a pleasant little drive and rest you."

"Shall I have to be much dressed?" asked the mother thoughtfully, "because I shouldn't have time for an elaborate toilet. I have to go to Madame's for a fitting, meet with the Red Cross committee, drop in at the hospital for a few minutes, and see Mrs. Sheppard and Mrs. Follette about our Alumni Anniversary banquet."

"Just wear something simple, mother. They are not society people. It's you I want to show them, not your clothes."

"You ridiculous boy! You're as unsophisticated as your father. Well, I'll be ready at half-past four. You may call for me then at the Century Building."

Elizabeth had been loyal to her brother's commands and had said nothing about her new-found friend, awaiting his permission. Graham earnestly discussed the pros and cons of woman's suffrage with his mother during the drive out, so that she was utterly unprejudiced by any former ideas concerning the Hollisters, which was exactly what her son desired her to be. He knew that his mother was a woman of the world, and hedged about by conventions of all sorts, but he also knew her to be fair in her judgments when once she saw a thing right, and a keen reader of character. He wanted her to see the Hollisters without the least bit of a chance to judge them beforehand.

So when the car drew up in front of the old barn Mrs. Graham was quite unprepared to have her son get out and open the car door and say, "Mother, this is the place; may I help you out?" She had been talking earnestly, and had thought he was getting out to look after something wrong about the car. Now she looked up startled.

"Why, Sidney! Why, you must have made a mistake! This isn't a house; it is a barn!"

"This is the place, mother. Just come right up this way."

Mrs. Graham picked her way over the short green turf up to the door and stood astonished while her son knocked. What in the world did he mean? Was this one of his jokes? Had he brought her out to see a new riding-horse? That must be it, of course. He was always taking a fancy to a horse or a dog. She really hadn't the time to spare for nonsense this afternoon, but one must humor one's son once in a while. She stepped back absent-mindedly, her eyes resting on the soft greens and purples of the foliage across the meadows, her thoughts on the next paper she intended to write

126

for the club. This incident would soon be over, and then she might pursue the even tenor of her busy way.

Then the door slid back and she became aware of something unusual in the tenseness of the moment. Looking up quickly she saw a beautiful girl of about Elizabeth's age, with a wealth of dark wavy hair, lovely dark eyes, and vivid coloring, and by her side one of the loveliest golden-haired, blue-eyed babies she had ever seen in her life. In the wonder of the moment she forgot that the outside of the building had been a barn, for the curtain had risen on a new setting, and here on the very threshold there opened before her amazed eyes a charming, homelike room.

At first she did not take in any of the details of furnishings. Everything was tastefully arranged, and the dull tones of wall and floor and ceiling in the late afternoon light mellowed the old furniture into its background so perfectly that the imperfections and make-shifts did not appear. It was just a place of comfort and beauty, even though the details might show shabby poverty.

But her son was speaking.

"Mother, this is Miss Carol Hollister, and this little girl is her sister Doris——"

Doris put out a fat hand and gravely laid it in the lady's kid glove, saying carefully, with shy lashes drooped sideways, and blue eyes furtively searching the stranger's face,

"How oo do?"

Then as if she had performed her duty, she turned on her smiles and dimples with a flash, and grasping Graham's hand said,

"Now, Mistah Dwa'm, oo tum out an' see my wab bits!"

It was evident to the mother that her son had been here before. She looked at him for an explanation, but he only said to Carol,

"Is your mother able to see callers for a few minutes?"

"Oh, yes," said Carol with a glad little ring in her voice. "Mother is up in a *chair* this afternoon. See!

127

The doctor says she may get up now, she is so much better!" and she turned and flung out her arm toward the big easy chair where her mother sat.

Mrs. Hollister arose and came forward to meet them.

She was dressed in a plain little gown of cheap gray challis, much washed and mended, but looking somehow very nice; and Carol had just finished fastening one of Shirley's sheer white fluffy collars around her neck, with a bit of a pink ribbon looped in a pretty knot. Her hair was tastefully arranged, and she looked every inch a lady as she stood to receive her unexpected guests. Graham had never seen her in any but invalid's garb before, and he stood amazed for a moment at the likeness between her and Shirley. He introduced his mother with a few words, and then yielded to Doris's eager, pulling hand and went out to see the bunnies.

The situation was a trifle trying for both ladies, but to the woman of the world perhaps the more embarrassing. She hadn't a clew as to who this was she had been brought to see. She was entirely used to dominating any situation, but for a moment she was almost confused.

Mrs. Hollister, however, tactfully relieved the situation, with a gentle, "Won't you sit here by the fire? It is getting a little cool this evening, don't you think?" and put her at once at her ease. Only her family would have guessed from the soft pink spots in her cheeks that she was at all excited over her grand guest. She took the initiative at once, leading the talk into natural channels, about the spring and its wonderful unfolding in the country, exhibited a vase with jack-in-the-pulpits, and a glass bowl of hepaticas blushing blue and pink, told of the thrush that had built a nest in the elm over the door, and pointed out the view over the valley where the sinking sun was flashing crimson from the weather-vane on the little white spire of the church. She said how much they had enjoyed the sunsets since coming out here to live, taking it for granted that her visitor knew all about their circumstances, and making no apologies or comments; and the visitor, being what her son called "a good sport," showed no hint that she had never heard of the Hollisters before, but smiled and said the right thing at the right moment. And somehow, neither knew just how, they got to the subject of Browning and Ibsen, and from there to woman's suffrage, and when Graham returned with Carol and Harley, Doris chattering beside him and the dog bounding in ahead, they were deep in future politics. Graham sat and listened for a while, interested to note that the quiet little woman who had spent the last few years of her life working in a narrow dark city kitchen could talk as thoughtfully and sensibly as his cultured, versatile mother.

The next trolley brought Shirley and George, and again the mother was amazed to find how altogether free and easy seemed to be the relation between all these young people.

She gave a keen look at Shirley, and then another at her son, but saw nothing which gave her uneasiness. The girl was unconscious as a rose, and sweet and gracious to the stranger guests as if she had been in society all her life. She slipped away at once to remove her hat, and when she came back her hair was brushed, and she looked as fresh as a flower in her clean white ruffled blouse. The older woman could not take her eyes from her face. What a charming girl to be set among all this shabbiness! For by this time her discriminating eyes had discovered that everything—literally *every*thing was shabby. Who were these people, and how did they happen to get put here? The baby was ravishingly beautiful, the girls were charming, and the boys looked like splendid, manly fellows. The mother was a product of culture and refinement. Not one word or action had shown that she knew her surroundings were shabby. She might have been mistress of a palace for aught she showed of consciousness of the pitiful poverty about her. It was as if she were just dropped down for the day in a stray barn and making a palace out of it while she stayed.

Unconsciously the woman of the world lingered

longer than was her wont in making calls. She liked the atmosphere, and was strangely interested by them all.

"I wish you would come and see me," she said cordially as she rose at last to go, and she said it as if she meant it,—as if she lived right around the corner and not twenty-two miles away,—as if she really wanted her to come, and not as if this other woman lived in a barn at all.

"Good old sport!" commented her son in his heart as he listened. He had known she must see their worth, and yet he had been strangely afraid.

Mrs. Hollister received the invitation with a flush of pleasure.

"Thank you," she answered graciously, "I'm afraid not. I seldom go anywhere any more. But I've been very glad to have had this call from you. It will be a pleasure to think about. Come sometime again when you are out this way. Your son has been most kind. I cannot find words to express my thanks."

"Has he?" and his mother looked questioningly at her son. "Well, I'm very glad——"

"Yes, and Elizabeth! She is a dear sweet girl, and we all love her!"

Revelations!

"Oh, has Elizabeth been here too? Well, I'm glad. I hope she has not been a nuisance. She's such an impulsive, erratic child. Elizabeth is quite a problem just now. She's out of school on account of her eyes, and her girl friends, most of them, being away at school, she is perfectly forlorn. I am delighted to have her with your children. I am sure they are charming associates for her." And her eyes rested approvingly on the sparkling Carol in her simple school dress of brown linen with its white collar and cuffs. There was nothing countrified about Carol. She looked dainty in the commonest raiment, and she smiled radiantly at Elizabeth's mother and won her heart.

"Would you let Elizabeth stay overnight with us here sometime?" she asked shyly.

"Why, surely! I presume she would be delighted. She does about as she pleases these days. I really don't

130

see very much of her, I'm so busy this time of year, just at the end of the season, you know, and lots of committee meetings and teas and things."

They stopped at the doorway to look up into the big tree, in response to the earnest solicitations of Doris, who pulled at the lady's gloved hand insistently, murmuring sweetly:

"Budie! Budie! See mine budie in the twee!"

The Hollisters stood grouped at the doorway when at last the visitors got into their car and went away. Mrs. Graham looked back at them wistfully.

"What a lovely group they make!" she murmured. "Now, Sidney, tell me at once who they are and why they live in a barn, and why you brought me out here. I know you had some special object. I knew the minute I saw that charming woman."

"Mother, you certainly are great! I thought you'd have the good sense to see what they are."

"Why, I haven't spent a more delightful hour in a long time than I spent talking with her. She has very original ideas, and she expresses herself well. As for the children, they are lovely. That oldest girl has a great deal of character in her face. But what are they doing in a barn, Sidney, and how did you come to know them?"

And so, as they speeded out the smooth turnpike to their lovely home Sidney Graham told his mother as much of the story of Shirley Hollister and the old barn as he thought she would care to know, and his mother sat thoughtfully watching his handsome, enthusiastic face while he talked, and wondering.

One comment she made as they swept up the beautiful drive to their luxurious country home:

"Sidney dear, they are delightful and all that, and I'm sure I'm glad to have that little girl come to see Elizabeth, but if I were you I wouldn't go out there too often when that handsome oldest girl is at home. She's not exactly in your set, you know, charming as she is, and you wouldn't want to give her any ideas. A gentleman looks out for things like that, you know."

"What has being in our set got to do with it, mother dear? Do you know any girl in our set that is better-looking or has nicer manners, or a finer appreciation of nature and books? You ought to hear her talk!"

"Yes, but, Sidney, that isn't everything! She isn't exactly——"

"Mother, were you and father, when you used to have good times together? Now, mother, you know you are just talking twaddle when you let that idea about 'our set' rule your mind. Be a good sport, mother dear, and look the facts in the face. That girl is as good as any other girl I know, and you know it. She's better than most. Please admit the facts. Yet you never warned me to be careful about calling on any of the girls in our set. Do please be consistent. However, don't worry about me. I've no idea at present of paying any special attention to anybody," and he swung the car door open and jumped down to help her out.

CHAPTER XV

A MAN arrived one morning with a horse and a plough and several other implements of farm life of which Harley didn't know the name, and announced that Mr. Graham had sent him to plough the garden. Would Mrs. Hollister please tell him where she wanted the ground broken, and how much? He volunteered the information that he was her next neighbor, and that if he was in her place he'd plough the south slope of the meadow, and if she wanted flower-beds a strip along the front near the road; the soil was best in those spots, and she wouldn't need so much fertilizer.

Mrs. Hollister asked him how much he would charge to do it, and he said a little job like that wasn't worth talking about; that he used to rent the barn himself, and he always did a little turn for Mr. Graham whenever he needed it. He did it for Mr. Graham, and it wouldn't cost her "nothin'."

Mrs. Hollister asked him how much he would charge to see where it would be best to have the ploughing done, and when she came in a few minutes later and dropped down on the couch to rest from her unusual fatigue a new thought was racing through her mind.

They could have a garden, a real garden, with lettuce and green peas and lima beans and corn! She knew all about making them grow. She had been brought up in a little village home, where a garden was a part of every one's necessary equipment for living. She used to help her father every spring and all summer. Her own little patch always took the prize of the family. But for years she had been in the city without an inch of space. Now, however, the old fever of delight in gardening took possession of her. If she could get out and work in the ground, as the doctor had suggested, she would get well right away. And why, with Harley to help, and George and Carol to work a little every evening, couldn't they raise enough on all that ground to sell some? George could take things into town early in the morning, or they could find some private families who would buy all they had to sell. It was worth thinking about, anyway. She could raise flowers for sale, too. She had always been a success with flowers. She had always wanted a hothouse and a chance to experiment. She heard the children say there were some old window-sashes down under the barn. She would get George to bring them out, and see what she could do with a coldframe or two. Violets would grow under a coldframe, and a lot of other things. Oh, if they could only just live here always, and not have to go back to the city in the fall! But of course there was no way to heat the barn in winter, and that was out of the question. Nevertheless, the idea of making some money with growing things had seized hold of her mind and would not be entirely put by. She thought of it much, and talked of it now and then to Shirley and the other children.

Shirley brought home some packages of seeds she got at the ten-cent store, and there was great excitement planting them. Then Mr. Graham sent over a lot of seeds, of both vegetables and flowers, and some shrubs, cuttings and bulbs which he said were "leftovers" at their country house that he thought perhaps the children could use; and so before the Hollisters knew it they were possessed of a garden, which almost in a breath lifted up its green head and began to grow.

Life was very full for the Hollisters in those days, and those who went to the city for the day could hardly bear to tear themselves away from the many delights of the country. The puppy was getting bigger and wiser every day, tagging Doris and Harley wherever they went, or sitting adoringly at Mrs. Hollister's feet; always bounding out to meet the evening trolley on which George and Shirley came, and always attending them to the trolley in the morning.

Out behind the barn a tiny coop held a white hen and her seven little downy balls of chickens. Another hen was happily ensconced in a barrel of hay with ten big blue duck-eggs under her happy wings, and a little further down toward the creek a fine chicken-run ended in a trig little roosting-place for the poultry, which George had manufactured out of a packing-box and some boards. The feathered family had been increased by two white Leghorns and three bantams. George and Harley spent their evenings watching them and discussing the price of eggs and chickens per pound. They were all very happy.

Elizabeth came out to spend Sunday as she had promised. She got up early to see the sun rise and watch the birds. She helped get breakfast and wash the dishes. Then she went with the others across the fields to the little white church in the valley to Sunday-school and church. She was as hungry and eager as any of them when she came home, and joyfully helped to do the work, taking great pride in the potatoes she was allowed to warm up under careful tutelage. In the afternoon there was no more eager listener among them to the Bible story Shirley told to Doris and the book she read aloud to them all afterward; her voice was sweetest and clearest of them all in the hymns they sang together; and she was most eager to go with Shirley to the Christian Endeavor.

"I shouldn't wonder if Sidney wishes he was here too," she remarked dreamily that evening, as she sat before the fire on a little cushion, her chin in her hands, her eyes on the fantastic shadows in the ashes.

She went to school with Carol the next morning, came home with her in the afternoon, and when her brother came for her in the evening she was most reluctant to go home to the big, lonely, elegant house again, and begged that Carol might soon come and see her.

Friday afternoon Elizabeth called up Mrs. Hollister.

"Please, Mrs. Hollister, let Carol come and stay with me till Monday. I'm so lonesome, and mamma says she will be so glad if you will let her come."

"Oh, my dear, that would be impossible. Carol isn't suitably dressed to make a visit, you know," answered the mother quickly, glad that she had so good an excuse for keeping her child from this venture into an alien world about which she had many grave doubts.

But the young voice at the other end of the telephone was insistent.

"Dear Mrs. Hollister, please! She doesn't need any other clothes. I've got lots of things that would fit her. She loaned me her gingham dress to make garden in, and why shouldn't I loan her a dress to wear on Sunday? I've got plenty of clean middy blouses and skirts and can fix her all out fresh for school, too, Monday morning, and if you'll just let her stay Sidney will take us both down to her school when he goes to the office. You've got all those children there at home, and I've only myself. Sidney doesn't count, you know, for he's grown up."

So, with a sigh, the mother gave her consent, and Carol found the Graham car waiting for her when she came out of school. Thus she started on her first venture into the world.

It was all like fairy-land that wonderful week-end to the little girl whose memories were full of burdens and sacrifices: the palatial home of many rooms and rich furnishings, the swarm of servants, the anticipation of every want, the wide, beautiful grounds with all that heart could wish in the way of beauty and amusement, the music-room with grand piano, harp, and violin lying mute most of the time, the great library with its walls lined with rare books, mostly unread. Everything there to satisfy any whim, reasonable or unreasonable, and nobody using any of it much.

"Not a room in the whole place as dear and cozy

and homey as this!" sighed Carol happily, sinking into the old denim-covered couch before the fireplace in the barn-living-room that Monday night after she got home. "I declare, mother, I don't see how Elizabeth stands it. Her mother is nice, but she's hardly ever there, unless she has a swarm of people dinnering or teaing or lunching. She hardly ever has time to speak to Elizabeth, and Elizabeth doesn't seem to care much, either. She almost seems to think more of that old nurse Susan that took care of her when she was a baby than she does of her mother. I'm so glad I was sent to you instead of to her!" And Carol suddenly slipped across the room and buried her face in her mother's neck, hugging and kissing her, leaving a few bright tears on her mother's happy face.

It was a wonderful relief to Mrs. Hollister to find her child unspoiled by her first experience of the world and glad to get back to her home, after all the anxiety her mother heart had felt. Carol presently sat up and told them minutely all about her visit. The grand concert that Sidney had taken them to Friday evening in the Academy of Music, where a world-renowned pianist was the soloist with the great symphony orchestra; the tennis and riding Saturday morning; the luncheon at a neighboring estate, where there were three girls and a brother who were "snobs" and hadn't at all good manners; the party in the evening that lasted so late that they didn't get to bed till long after midnight; the beautiful room they slept in, with every imaginable article for the toilet done in sterling silver with monograms; the strange Sabbath, with no service in the morning because they woke up too late, and no suggestion of anything but a holiday,—except the vesper service in a cold, formal chapel that Carol had begged to go to; just a lot of worldly music and entertaining, with a multitude of visitors for the end of it. Carol told of the beautiful dresses that Elizabeth had loaned her, coral crêpe de chine accordian-plaited for the concert, white with an orange sash for the luncheon, pale yellow with a black velvet girdle for the party, a little blue silk affair and another lovely white organdie for Sunday, and all with their accompanying silk stockings and slippers and gloves, and necklaces and bands for her hair. It was most wonderful to her, and as they listened they marvelled that their Carol had come back to them so gladly, and rejoiced to see her nestling in her brown linen skirt and middy blouse close beside her mother's chair. She declared herself satisfied with her flight into the world. She might like to go again for a glimpse now and then, but she thought she would rather have Elizabeth out to Glenside. She hated to lose any of the time out here, it was so pretty. Besides, it was lonesome without them all.

About that time Shirley picked up the morning paper in her office one day to look up a matter for Mr. Barnard. Her eye happened to fall on the society column and catch the name of Sidney Graham. She glanced down the column. It was an account of a wedding in high circles in which Graham had taken the part of best man, with Miss Harriet Hale—in blue tulle and white orchids as maid of honor—for his partner down the aisle. She read the column hurriedly, hungrily, getting every detail, white spats, gardenia, and all, until in those few printed sentences a picture was printed indelibly upon her vision, of Graham walking down the lily-garlanded aisle with the maid in blue tulle and white orchids on his arm. To make it more vivid the lady's picture was in the paper along with Graham's, just under those of the bride and groom, and her face was both handsome and haughty. One could tell that by the tilt of chin, the short upper lip, the cynical curve of mouth and sweep of long eyelash, the extreme effect of her dress and the arrangement of her hair. Only a beauty could have stood that hair and not been positively ugly.

Shirley suddenly realized what she was doing and turned over the page of the paper with a jerk that tore the sheet from top to bottom, going on with her search for the real-estate column and the item she was after. All that morning her typewriter keys clicked with mad rapidity, yet her work was strangely correct and perfect. She was working under a tense strain.

By noon she had herself in hand, realized what she had been doing with her vagrant thoughts, and was able to laugh at Miss Harriet Hale—whoever or whatever she was. What mattered it, Miss Harriet Hale or somebody else? What was that to Shirley Hollister? Mr. Graham was her landlord and a kindly gentleman. He would probably continue to be that to her to the end of her tenancy, without regard to Miss Hale or any other intruding Miss, and what did anything else matter? She wanted nothing else of Mr. Graham but to be a kindly gentleman whenever it was her necessity to come in his way.

But although her philosophy was on hand and her pride was aroused, she realized just where her heart might have been tending if it had not been for this little jolt it got; and she resolved to keep out of the gentleman's way whenever it was possible, and also, as far as she was able, to think no more about him.

Keeping out of Sidney Graham's way was one thing, but making him keep out of her way was quite another matter, and Shirley realized it every time he came out to Glenside, which he did quite frequently. She could not say to him that she wished he would not come. She could not be rude to him when he came. There was no way of showing him pointedly that she was not thinking of him in any way but as her landlord, because he never showed in any way that he was expecting her to. He just happened in evening after evening, in his frank, jolly way, on one pretext or other, never staying very long, never showing her any more attention than he did her mother or Carol or the boys, not so much as he did to Doris. How was she to do anything but sit quietly and take the whole thing as a matter of course? It really was a matter to deal with in her own heart alone. And there the battle must be fought if ever battle there was to be. Meantime, she could not but own that this frank, smiling, merry young man did bring a lot of life and pleasure into their lives, dropping in that way, and why should she not enjoy it when it came, seeing it in no wise interfered with Miss Harriet Hale's rights and prerogatives? Nevertheless, Shirley withdrew more and more into quietness whenever he came, and often slipped into the kitchen on some household pretext, until one day he boldly came out into the kitchen after her with a book he wanted her to read, and was so frank and companionable that she led the way back to the living-room, and concluded it would be better in future to stay with the rest of the family.

Shirley had no intention whatever of letting her heart stray out after any impossible society man. She had her work in the world, and to it she meant to stick. If there were dreams she kept them well under lock and key, and only took them out now and then at night when she was very tired and discouraged and life looked hard and long and lonely on ahead. Shirley had no intention that Sidney Graham should ever have reason to think, when he married Miss Harriet Hale or some one equivalent to her, that any poor little stenographer living in a barn had at one time fancied him fond of her. No, indeed! Shirley tilted her firm little chin at the thought, and declined to ride with Graham and Elizabeth the next time they called at the office for her, on the plea that she had promised to go home in the trolley with one of the office girls. And yet the next time she saw him he was just as pleasant, and showed no sign that she had declined his invitation. In fact, the whole basis of their acquaintance was such that she felt free to go her own way and yet know he would be just as pleasant a friend whenever she needed one.

Matters stood in this way when Graham was suddenly obliged to go West on a trip for the office, to be gone three or four weeks. Mrs. Graham and Elizabeth went to the Adirondacks for a short trip, and the people at Glenside settled down to quiet country life, broken only by a few visits from their farm neighbors, and a call from the cheery, shabby pastor of the little white church in the valley.

CHAPTER XVI

GRAHAM did not seem to forget his friends entirely while he was gone. The boys received a number of post-cards from time to time, and a lot of fine views of California, Yellowstone Park, the Grand Cañon, and other spots of interest. A wonderful picture-book came for Doris, with Chinese pictures, and rhymes printed on crêpe paper. The next morning a tiny sandalwood fan arrived for Carol with Graham's compliments, and a few days later a big box of oranges for Mrs. Hollister with no clew whatever as to their sender. Shirley began to wonder what her part would be and what she should do about it, and presently received—a letter! And then, after all, it was only a pleasant request that she would not pay the rent, about which she had always been so punctual, until his return, as no one else understood about his affairs. He added a few words about his pleasant trip and a wish that they were all prospering,—and that was all.

Shirley was disappointed, of course, and yet, if he had said more, or if he had ventured to send her even a mere trifle of a gift, it would have made her uncomfortable and set her questioning how she should treat him and it. It was the perfection of his behavior that he had not overstepped a single bound that the most particular might set for a landlord and his respected tenant. She drew a deep sigh and put the letter back into the envelope, and as she did so she spied a small card, smaller than the envelope, on which was an exquisite bit of scenery, a colored photograph, apparently, and underneath had been pencilled, "One of the many beautiful spots in California that I am sure you would appreciate."

Her heart gave an unforbidden leap, and was promptly taken to task for it. Yet when Shirley went back to her typewriter the bit of a picture was pinned to the wall back of her desk, and her eyes rested on it many times that day when she lifted them from her work. It is questionable whether Shirley remembered Miss Harriet Hale at all that day.

The garden was growing beautifully now. There would soon be lettuce and radishes ready to eat. George had secured a number of customers through people at the store, and was planning to take early trips to town, when his produce was ripe, to deliver it. They watched every night and looked again every morning for signs of the first pea blossoms, and the little green spires of onion tops, like sparse hairs, beginning to shoot up. Every day brought some new wonder. They almost forgot they had ever lived in the little old brick house, until George rode by there on his bicycle one noon and reported that it had been half pulled down, and you could now see the outline of where the stairs and closets had been, done in plaster, on the side of the next house. They were all very silent for a minute thinking after he told that, and Mrs. Hollister looked around the great airy place in which they were sitting, and then out the open door where the faint stain of sunset was still lingering against the horizon, and said:

"We ought all to be very thankful, children. George, get the Bible and read the thirty-fourth psalm." Wonderingly George obeyed, and they all sat listening as the words sank into their souls.

"Now," said the mother when the psalm was finished and those last words, "The Lord redeemeth the soul of his servants, and none of them that trust in him shall be desolate"; "now let us kneel down and thank Him."

And they all knelt while she prayed a few earnest, simple words of thanksgiving and commended them to God's keeping.

By this time Mrs. Hollister was so well that she went every day for a little while into the garden and worked, and was able to do a great deal in the house. The children were overjoyed, and lived in a continual trance of delight over the wild, free life they were living. Carol's school had closed and Carol was at home all day. This made one more to help in the garden. George was talking about building a little pigeon-house and raising squabs for sale. The man who did the ploughing had given him a couple to start with and told him there was money in squabs if one only went about it right. George and Harley pored over a book that told all about it, and talked much on the subject.

The weather was growing warm, and Shirley was wishing her vacation came in July or August instead

141

of the first two weeks in September. Somehow she felt so used up these hot days, and the hours dragged by so slowly. At night the trolleys were crowded until they were half-way out to Glenside. She often had to stand, and her head ached a great deal. Yet she was very happy and thankful—only there *was* so much to be done in this world, and she seemed to have so little strength to do it all. The burden of next fall came occasionally to mar the beauty of the summer, and rested heavily upon her young shoulders. If only there wouldn't be any winter for just one year, and they could stay in the barn and get rested and get a little money ahead somehow for moving. It was going to be so hard to leave that wide, beautiful abiding-place, barn though it was.

One morning nearly four weeks after Graham left for California Shirley was called from her desk to the outer office to take some dictation for Mr. Clegg. While she was there two men entered the outer office and asked for Mr. Barnard. One of them was a short, thick-set man with a pretentious wide gray mustache parted in the middle and combed elaborately out on his cheeks. He had a red face, little cunning eyes, and a cruel set to his jaw, which somehow seemed ridiculously at variance with his loud, checked suit, sporty necktie of soft bright blue satin, set with a scarf-pin of two magnificent stones, a diamond and a sapphire, and with the three showy jewelled rings which he wore on his fat, pudgy hand. The other man was sly, quiet, gray, unobtrusive, obviously the henchman of the first.

Mr. Clegg told the men they might go into the inner office and wait for Mr. Barnard, who would probably be in shortly, and Shirley watched them as they passed out of her view, wondering idly why those exquisite stones had to be wasted in such an out-of-place spot as in that coarse-looking man's necktie, and if a man like that really cared for beautiful things, else why should he wear them? It was only a passing thought, and then she took up her pencil and took down the closing sentences of the letter Mr. Clegg was dictating. It was but a moment more and she was free to go back to her own little alcove just behind Mr. Barnard's office and connecting with it. There was an entrance to it from the tiny cloak-room, which she always used when Mr. Barnard had visitors in his office, and through this way she now went, having a strange repugnance toward being seen by the two men. She had an innate sense that the man with the gaudy garments would not be one who would treat a young girl in her position with any respect, and she did not care to come under his coarse gaze, so she slipped in quietly through the cloak-room, and passed like a shadow the open door into Mr. Barnard's office, where they sat with their backs toward her, having evidently just settled down and begun to talk. She could hear a low-breathed comment on the furnishings of the office as indicating a good bank-account of the owner, and a coarse jest about a photograph of Mr. Barnard's wife which stood on his desk. It made her wish that the door between the rooms was closed; yet she did not care to rise and close it lest she should call attention to herself, and of course it might be but a minute or two before Mr. Barnard returned. A pile of envelopes to be addressed lay on her desk, and this work she could do without any noise, so she slipped softly into her seat and began to work.

"Well, we got them Grahams good and fast now!" a coarse voice, that she knew for that of the man with the loud clothing, spoke. "The young feller bit all right! I thought he would. He's that kind." He stopped for a laugh of contempt, and Shirley's heart stood still with apprehension. What could it mean? Was it something about her Grahams? Some danger threatening them? Some game being played on them? He looked like the kind of man who lived on the blindnesses of others. What was it they called such? A parasite? Instinctively she was on the alert at once, and automatically she reached for the pad on which she took dictation and began to write down in shorthand what she had just heard. The voice in the other room went on and her fountain pen kept eager pace, her breath coming quick and short now, and her face white with excitement.

"He went out to see the place, you know, examine the mines and all that. Oh, he's awful cautious! Thought he took a government expert with him to test the ore. We fixed that up all right—had the very man on tap at the right minute, government papers all O.K.—you couldn't have told 'em from the real thing. It was Casey; you know him; he's a crackerjack on a job like that,—could fool the devil himself. Well, he swore it was the finest kind of ore and all that kind of dope, and led that Graham kid around as sweetly as a blue-eyed baby. We had a gang out there all bribed, you know, to swear to things, and took particular pains so Graham would go around and ask the right ones questions,—Casey tended to that,—and now he's come home with the biggest kind of a tale and ready to boost the thing to the skies. I've got his word for it, and his daddy is to sign the papers this morning. When he wakes up one of these fine days he'll find himself minus a hundred thousand or so, and nobody to blame for it, because how could anybody be expected to know that those are only pockets? He'll recommend it right and left too, and we'll clean out a lot of other fellers before we get done. Teddy, my boy, pat yourself on the back! We'll have a tidy little sum between us when we pull out of this deal, and take a foreign trip for our health till the fracas blows over. Now mind you, not a word of this to Barnard when he comes in. We're only going to pave the way this morning. The real tip comes from Graham himself. See?"

Shirley was faint and dizzy with excitement as she finished writing, and her brain was in a whirl. She felt as if she would scream in a minute if this strain kept up. The papers were to be signed that morning! Even now the deed might be done and it would be too late, perhaps, to stop it. And yet she must make no sign, must not have the men know that she was there and that they had been heard. She must sit here breathless until they were gone, so they would not know she had overheard them, or they might manage to prevent her getting word to Graham. How long would they stay? Would they talk on and reveal more? The other man had only grunted something unintelligible in reply, and then before more could be said an office boy opened the outer door and told them that Mr. Barnard had just phoned that he would not be back before two o'clock.

The men swore and went out grumbling. Suddenly Shirley knew her time had come to do something. Stepping quickly to the door she scanned the room carefully to make sure they were gone, then closing her own door she took up the telephone on her desk and called up the Graham number. She did not know just what she meant to say, nor what she would do if Sidney Graham were not in the office,—and it was hardly probable he would be there yet if he had only arrived home the day before. He would be likely to take a day off before getting back to work. Her throbbing heart beat out these questions to her brain while she waited for the number. Would she dare to ask for Mr. Walter Graham? And if she did, what would she say to him? How explain? He did not know her, and probably never heard of her. He might think her crazy. Then there was always the possibility that there was some mistake—and yet it seemed a coincidence that two men of the same name should both be going West at that time. It must be these Grahams that the plot was against. But how explain enough over the phone to do any good? Of course she must give them a copy of what she had taken down in shorthand, but first she must stop the signing of those papers, whatever they were, at all costs.

Then all at once, into the midst of her whirling confusion of thoughts, came a voice at the other end of the phone, "Hello!" and her frantic senses realized that it was a familiar one.

"Oh, is this,—this *is* Mr. Sidney Graham, isn't it? This is Shirley Hollister."

There was a catch in her voice that sounded almost like a sob as she drew in her breath with relief to know that he was there, and his answer came in swift alarm:

"Yes? Is there anything the matter, Miss Shirley? You are not ill, are you?"

145

There was a sharp note of anxiety in the young man's voice, and even in her excitement it made Shirley's heart leap to hear it.

"No, there is nothing the matter with me," she said, trying to steady her voice, "but something has happened that I think you ought to know at *once*. I don't know whether I ought to tell it over the phone. I'm not sure but I may be overheard."

"I will come to you immediately. Where can I find you?"

Her heart leaped again at his willingness to trust her and to obey her call.

"In Mr. Barnard's private office. If you ask for me they will let you come right in. There is one thing more. If there is anything important your father was to decide this morning, could you get him to wait till you return, or till you phone him?"

There was a second's hesitation, and the reply was politely puzzled but courteous:

"He is not in the office at present and will not be for an hour."

"Oh, I'm so glad! Then *please hurry!*"

"I will get there as soon as I can," and the phone clicked into place.

Shirley sat back in her chair and pressed her hands over her eyes to concentrate all her powers. Then she turned to her typewriter and began to copy off the shorthand, her fingers flying over the keys with more than their usual swiftness. As she wrote she prayed, prayed that nothing might have been signed, and that her warning might not come too late; prayed, too, that Mr. Barnard might not return until Mr. Graham had been and gone, and that Mr. Graham might not think her an utter fool in case this proved to have nothing whatever to do with his affairs.

CHAPTER XVII

WHEN Graham entered the office Shirley came to meet him quietly, without a word of greeting other than to put her little cold hand into his that he held out to her. She began to speak in a low voice full of suppressed excitement. She had a vague fear lest the two men might be still lingering about the outer office, waiting for Mr. Barnard, and a momentary dread lest Mr. Barnard might enter the room at any minute. She must get the telling over before he came.

"Mr. Graham, two men were sitting in this room waiting for Mr. Barnard a few minutes ago, and I was in my little room just back there. I could not help hearing what they said, and when I caught the name of Graham in connection with what sounded like an evil plot I took down their words in shorthand. It may not have anything to do with your firm, but I thought I ought to let you know. I called you on the phone as soon as they left the office and would not hear me, and I have made this copy of their conversation. Read it quickly, please, because if it does have anything to do with you, you will want to phone your father at once, before those men can get there."

Her tone was very cool, and her hand was steady as she handed him the typewritten paper, but her heart was beating wildly, because there had been a look in his eyes as he greeted her that made her feel that he was glad to see her, and it touched an answering gladness in her heart and filled her both with delight and with apprehension. What a fool she was!

She turned sharply away and busied herself with arranging some papers on Mr. Barnard's desk while he read. She must still this excitement and get control of herself before he was through. She *must* be the cool, impersonal stenographer, and not let him suspect for a moment that she was so excited about seeing him again.

The young man stood still, reading rapidly, his face growing graver as he read. The girl snatched a furtive glance at him, and felt convinced that the matter was a serious one and had to do with him.

Suddenly he looked up.

"Do you know who those men were, Miss Shirley?" he asked, and she saw his eyes were full of anxiety.

"No," said Shirley. "But I saw them as they passed through the outer office, and stopped to speak to Mr.

Clegg. I was taking dictation from Mr. Clegg at the time. I came back to my desk through the cloak-room, so they did not know I was within hearing."

"What kind of looking men were they? Do you remember?"

She described them.

Certainty grew in his face as she talked, and grave concern.

"May I use your phone a minute?" he asked after an instant's thought.

She led him to her own desk and handed him the receiver, then stepped back into the office and waited.

"Hello! Is that you, Edward?" she heard him say. "Has father come yet? Give me his phone, please. Hello, father; this is Sidney. Father, has Kremnitz come in yet? He has? You say he's waiting in the office to see you? Well, don't see him, father, till I get there. Something has turned up that I'm afraid is going to alter matters entirely. Yes, pretty serious, I'm afraid. Don't see him. Keep him waiting. I'll be there in five minutes, and come in from the back way directly to your office. Don't talk with him on any account till I can get there. Good-by."

He hung up the receiver and turned to Shirley.

"Miss Shirley, you were just in time to save us. I haven't time now to tell you how grateful I am for this. I must hurry right over. Do you suppose if we should need you it would be possible for you to come over and identify those men? Thank you. I'll speak to Mr. Clegg about it as I go out, and if we find it necessary we'll phone you. In case you have to come I'll have an office-boy in the hall to take your hat, and you can come right into the office as if you were one of our employees—just walk over to the bookcase as if you were looking for a book—any book. Select one and look through it, meanwhile glancing around the room, and see if you find those men. Then walk through into my office. I'll be waiting there. Good-by, and thank you so much!"

He gave her hand one quick clasp and was gone, and Shirley found she was trembling from head to foot. She walked quickly into her own room and sat down, burying her face in her hands and trying to get control of herself, but the tears would come to her eyes in spite of all she could do. It was not the excitement of getting the men and stopping their evil plans before they could do any damage, although that had something to do with her nervous state, of course; and it was not just that she had been able to do a little thing in return for all he had done for her; nor even his gratitude; it was—she could not deny it to herself —it was a certain quality in his voice, a something in the look he gave her, that made her whole soul glow, and seemed to fill the hungry longing that had been in her heart.

It frightened her and made her ashamed, and as she sat with bowed head she prayed that she might be given strength to act like a sensible girl, and crush out such foolish thoughts before they dared lift their heads and be recognized even by her own heart. Then strengthened, she resolved to think no more about the matter, but just get her work done and be ready to enter into that other business if it became necessary. Mr. Barnard would be coming soon, and she must have his work finished. She had lost almost an hour by this matter.

She went at her typewriter pell-mell, and soon had Mr. Clegg's letters done. She was nearly through with the addressing that Mr. Barnard left for her to do when the telephone called her to Graham's office.

She slipped on her hat and hurried out.

"Will it be all right for me to take my noontime now, Mr. Clegg?" she said, stopping by his desk. "Mr. Graham said he spoke to you."

"Yes, he wants you to help him identify some one. That's all right. I'll explain to Mr. Barnard when he comes. There's nothing important you have to finish, is there? All done but those envelopes? Well, you needn't return until one o'clock, anyway. The envelopes can wait till the four-o'clock mail, and if Mr. Barnard needs anything in a hurry Miss Dwight can attend to it this time. Just take your time, Miss Hollister."

Shirley went out bewildered by the unusual generosity of Mr. Clegg, who was usually taciturn and abrupt. She realized, however, that his warmth must be due to Graham's visit, and not to any special desire to give her a holiday. She smiled to think what a difference wealth and position made in the eyes of the world.

The same office-boy she had met on her first visit to Graham's office was waiting most respectfully for her now in the hall when she got out of the elevator, and she gave him her hat and walked into the office according to programme, going straight to the big glass bookcase full of calf-bound volumes, and selecting one after running her finger over two rows of them. She was as cool as though her part had been rehearsed many times, although her heart was pounding most unmercifully, and it seemed as though the people in the next room must hear it. She stood and opened her book, casting a casual glance about the room.

There, sure enough, quite near to her, sat the two men, fairly bursting with impatience. The once immaculate hair of the loudly dressed one was rumpled as if he had run his fingers through it many times, and he played nervously with his heavy rings, and caressed half viciously his elaborate mustache, working his thick, sensuous lips impatiently all the while. Shirley took a good look at him, necktie, scarf-pin, and all; looked keenly into the face of the gray one also; then coolly closed the door of the bookcase and carried the book she had selected into Sidney Graham's office.

Graham was there, standing to receive her, and just back of him stood a kindly-faced elderly man with merry blue eyes, gray hair, and a stylishly cut beard. By their attitude and manner Shirley somehow sensed that they had both been watching her. Then Graham introduced her.

"This is my father, Miss Hollister."

The elder man took her hand and shook it heartily, speaking in a gruff, hearty way that won her from the first:

"I'm glad to know you, Miss Hollister. I certainly am! My son has been telling me what you've done for us, and I think you're a great little girl! That was bully work you did, and I appreciate it. I was watching you out there in the office. You were as cool as a cucumber. You ought to be a detective. You found your men all right, did you?"

"Yes, sir," said Shirley, much abashed, and feeling the return of that foolish trembling in her limbs. "Yes, they are both out there, and the short one with the rings and the blue necktie is the one that did the talking."

"Exactly what I thought," drawled the father, with a keen twinkle in his kindly eyes. "I couldn't somehow trust that chap from the start. That's why I sent my son out to investigate. Well, now, will you just step into my private office, Miss Hollister, and take your seat by the typewriter as if you were my stenographer? You'll find paper there in the drawer, and you can just be writing—write anything, you choose, so it looks natural when the men come in. When we get to talking I'd like you to take down in shorthand all that is said by all of us. You're pretty good at that, I judge. Sid, will you phone for those officers now? I think it's about time for the curtain to rise." And he led the way into his own office.

Shirley sat down at the typewriter as she had been directed and began to write mechanically. Mr. Graham touched the bell on his desk, and told the office boy who answered to send in Mr. Kremnitz and his companion.

Shirley was so seated that she could get occasional glimpses of the men without being noticed, and she was especially interested in the twinkle that shone in the bright blue eyes of the elder Graham as he surveyed the men who thought he was their dupe. Her heart warmed to him. His kindly, merry face, his hearty, unconventional speech, all showed him to be a big, warm-hearted man without a bit of snobbishness about him.

The son came in, and talk began just as if the matter of the mine were going on. Mr. Kremnitz produced some papers which he evidently expected to be signed at once, and sat complacently answering questions; keen questions Shirley saw they were afterwards, and in the light of the revelation she had overheard in Mr. Barnard's office Kremnitz perjured himself hopelessly by his answers. Presently the office-boy announced the arrival of some one in the next room. Shirley had taken down minutely a great deal of valuable information which the Grahams had together drawn from their victim. She was surprised at the list of wealthy business men who were to have been involved in the scheme.

Then suddenly the quiet scene changed. The elder Graham gave a signal to his office-boy, which looked merely like waving him away, and the door was flung open, revealing four officers of the law, who stepped into the room without further word. Graham arose and faced his two startled callers, his hand firmly planted on the papers on his desk which he had been supposed to sign.

"Mr. Kremnitz," he said, and even in the midst of this serious business Shirley fancied there was a half-comic drawl to his words. He simply could not help letting his sense of humor come on top. "Mr. Kremnitz, it is not going to be possible for me to sign these papers this morning, as you expected. I do not feel satisfied that all things are as you have represented. In fact, I have the best evidence to the contrary. Officer, these are the gentlemen you have come to arrest," and he stepped back and waved his hand toward the two conspirators, who sat with startled eyes and blanched faces, appalled at the sudden developments where they had thought all was moving happily toward their desired end.

"Arrest! Who? On what charge?" flashed the little gaudy Kremnitz, angrily springing to his feet and making a dash toward the door, while his companion slid furtively toward the other end of the room, evidently hoping to gain young Graham's office before he was noticed. But two officers blocked their way and the handcuffs clanked in the hands of the other two policemen.

"Why, arrest *you*, my friend," said Graham senior, as if he rather enjoyed the little man's discomfiture. "And for trying to perpetrate the biggest swindle that has been attempted for ten years. I must say for you that you've worked hard, and done the trick rather neatly, but you made one unfortunate slip that saved all us poor rich men. It seems a pity that so much elaborate lying should have brought you two nothing but those bracelets you're wearing,—they don't seem to match well with your other jewels,—but that's the way things go in this world. Now, take them away, officer. I've no more time to waste on them this morning!" and he turned and walked over by Shirley's desk, while the curtain fell over the brief drama.

"Do you know how much money you've saved for us, little girl,—just plain *saved*? I'll tell you. A clean hundred thousand! That's what I was going to put into this affair! And as for other men, I expected to influence a lot of other men to put in a good deal also. Now, little girl, I don't know what you think about it, but I want to shake hands." He put out his hand and Shirley laid her own timid one in it, smiling and blushing rosily, and saying softly with what excited breath she had, "Oh, I'm so glad I got you in time!" Then she was aware that the man had gone on talking. "I don't know what you think about it," he repeated, "but I feel that you saved me a clean hundred thousand dollars, and I say that a good percentage of that belongs to you as a reward of your quickness and keenness."

But Shirley drew away her hand and stepped back, her face white, her head up, her chin tilted proudly, her eyes very dark with excitement and determination. She spoke clearly and earnestly.

"No, Mr. Graham, nothing whatever belongs to me. I don't want any reward. I couldn't think of taking it. It is utterly out of the question!"

"Well, well, well!" said the elder Graham, sitting down on the edge of his desk, watching her in undisguised admiration. "Now that's a new kind of girl that won't take what she's earned,—what rightly belongs to her."

"Mr. Graham, it was a very little thing I did,—anybody would have done it,—and it was just in the way of simple duty. Please don't say anything more about it. I am only too glad to have had opportunity to give a

153

little help to people who have helped me so much. I feel that I am under deep obligation to your son for making it possible for us to live in the country, where my mother is getting well."

"Well, now I shall have to inquire into this business. I haven't heard anything about obligations, and for my part I feel a big one just now. Perhaps you think it was a very little thing you did, but suppose you *hadn't* done it. Suppose you'd been too busy, or it hadn't occurred to you to take down that conversation until it was too late; or suppose you hadn't had the brains to see what it would mean to us. Why, then it would have become a very big thing indeed, and we should have been willing, if we had known, to pay a mighty big sum to get that evidence. You see a hundred thousand dollars isn't exactly a very little thing when you're swindled out of it. It's the *swindling* that hurts more than the loss of the money. And you saved us from that. Now, young lady, I consider myself under obligation to you, and I intend to discharge it somehow. If I can't do it one way I shall another, but in the meantime I'm deeply grateful, and please accept our thanks. If you are willing to add one more to your kindness, I shall be glad if you will make a carbon copy of those shorthand notes you took. I may need them for evidence. And, by the way, you will probably be called upon to testify in court. I'm sorry. That may be unpleasant, but I guess it can't be helped, so you see before you get through you may not think you did so very small a thing after all. Sid, I think you better escort this young lady back to her office and explain to Barnard. He's probably been on the verge of being buncoed also. You said Kremnitz was waiting for him when the conversation took place? I guess you better go with Miss Hollister and clear the whole thing up. Say, child, have you had your lunch yet? No, of course not. Sidney, you take her to get some lunch before she goes back to the office. She'd had an exciting morning. Now, good-by, little girl. I sha'n't forget what you've done for us, and I'm coming to see you pretty soon and get things squared up."

So that was how it came about that in spite of her

protests Mr. Sidney Graham escorted Shirley Hollister into one of the most exclusive tea-rooms of the city, and seated her at a little round table set for two, while off at a short distance Miss Harriet Hale sat with her mother, eating her lunch and trying in vain to "place" the pretty girl she did not recognize.

It never occurred to her for a moment that Sidney Graham's companion might be a stenographer, for Shirley had a knack about her clothes that made her always seem well dressed. That hat she wore had seen service for three summers, and was now a wholly different shape and color from what it had been when it began life. A scrub in hot water had removed the dust of toil, some judiciously applied dye had settled the matter of color, and a trifling manipulation on her head while the hat was still wet had made the shape not only exceedingly stylish but becoming. The chic little rosette and strictly tailored band which were its sole trimming were made from a much-soiled waist-ribbon, washed and stretched around a bottle of hot water to dry it, and teased into the latest thing in rosettes by Shirley's witching fingers. The simple linen dress she wore fitted well and at a distance could not have been told from something better, and neither were gloves and shoes near enough to be inspected critically, so Miss Hale was puzzled, and jealously watched the pretty color come and go in Shirley's cheek, and the simple grace of her movements.

Fortunately, Shirley did not see Miss Hale, and would not have recognized her if she had from that one brief glimpse she had of her picture on the society page of the newspaper. So she ate her delectable lunch, ordered by Graham, in terms that she knew not, about dishes that she had never seen before. She ate and enjoyed herself so intensely that it seemed to her she would never be able to make the rest of her life measure up to the privileges of the hour.

For Shirley was a normal girl. She could not help being pleased to be doing just for once exactly as other more favored girls did constantly. To be lunching at Blanco's with one of the most-sought-after men in the upper set, to be treated like a queen, and to be talking

155

beautiful things about travels and pictures and books, it was all too beautiful to be real. Shirley began to feel that if it didn't get over pretty soon and find her back in the office addressing the rest of those envelopes she would think she had died in the midst of a dream and gone to heaven.

There was something else too that brought an undertone of beauty, which she was not acknowledging even to her inmost self. That was the way Graham looked at her, as if she were some fine beautiful angel dropped down from above that he loved to look at; as if he really cared what she thought and did; as if there were somehow a soul-harmony between them that set them apart this day from others, and put them into tune with one another; as if he were glad, *glad* to see her once more after the absence! All through her being it thrilled like a song that brings tears to the throat and gladness to the eyes, and makes one feel strong and pure. That was how it seemed when she thought about it afterward. At the time she was just living it in wonder and thanksgiving.

At another time her sordid worldliness and pride might have risen and swelled with haughtiness of spirit over the number of people who eyed her enviously as they went out together; over the many bows and salutations her escort received from people of evident consequence, for she had the normal human pride somewhere in her nature as we all have. But just then her heart was too humble with a new, strange happiness to feel it or take it in, and she walked with unconscious grace beside him, feeling only the joy of being there.

Later, in the quiet of her chamber, her mother's warning came to her, and her cheeks burned with shame in the dark that her heart had dared make so much of a common little luncheon, just a mere courtesy after she had been able to do a favor. Yet through it all Shirley knew there was something fine and true there that belonged just to her, and presently she would rise above everything and grasp it and keep it hers forever.

She felt the distinction of her escort anew when she

156

entered Barnard and Clegg's in his company, and saw Mr. Clegg spring to open the door and to set a chair for his young guest, saw even Mr. Barnard rise and greet him with almost reverence. And this honor she knew was being paid to money, the great demagogue. It was not the man that she admired to whom they were paying deference, it was to his money! She smiled to herself. It was the *man* she admired, not his money.

All that afternoon she worked with flying fingers, turning off the work at marvellous speed, amused when she heard the new note of respect in Mr. Barnard's voice as he gave her a direction. Mr. Barnard had been greatly impressed with the story Graham had told him, and was also deeply grateful on his own account that Shirley had acted as she had, for he had been on the verge of investing a large trust fund that was in his keeping in the new mining operation, and it would have meant absolute failure for him.

When Shirley left the office that night she was almost too tired to see which trolley was coming, but some one touched her on the arm, and there was Sidney Graham waiting for her beside his car,—a little two-passenger affair that she had never seen before and that went like the wind. They took a road they had not travelled together before, and Shirley got in joyously, her heart all in a tumult of doubts and joys and questions.

CHAPTER XVIII

WHAT that ride was to Shirley she hardly dared let herself think afterwards. Sitting cozily beside Graham in the little racing car, gliding through the better part of town where all the tall, imposing houses slept with drawn blinds, and dust-covered shutters proclaimed that their owners were far away from heat and toil Out through wide roads and green-hedged lanes, where stately mansions set in flowers and mimic landscapes loomed far back from road in dignified seclusion Passing now and then a car of people who recognized Graham and bowed in the same deferential way as they had done in the tea-room. And all the time his eyes were upon her, admiring, delighting; and his care about her, solicitous for her comfort.

Once he halted the car and pointed off against the sunset, where wide gables and battlemented towers stood gray amidst a setting of green shrubbery and trees, and velvety lawns reached far, to high, trim hedges arched in places for an entrance to the beautiful estate.

"That is my home over there," he said, and watched her widening eyes. "I wish I had time to take you over to-night, but I know you are tired and ought to get home and rest. Another time we'll go around that way " And her heart leaped up as the car went forward again. There was to be another time, then! Ah! But she must not allow it. Her heart was far too foolish already. Yet she would enjoy this ride, now she was started.

They talked about the sunset and a poem he had lately read. He told her bits about his journey, referring to his experience at the mines, touching on some amusing incidents, sketching some of the queer characters he had met. Once he asked her quite abruptly if she thought her mother would be disturbed if he had a cement floor put in the basement of the barn some time soon. He wanted to have it done before cold weather set in, and it would dry better now in the hot days. Of course, if it would be in the least disturb ing to any of them it could wait, but he wanted to store a few things there that were being taken out of the office buildings, and he thought they would keep drier if there was a cement floor. When she said it would not disturb any one in the least, would on the contrary be quite interesting for the children to watch, she was sure, he went easily back to California scenery and never referred to it again.

All through the ride, which was across a country she had never seen before, and ended at Glenside approaching from a new direction, there was a subtle something between them, a sympathy and quick understanding as if they were comrades, almost partners in a lot of common interests. Shirley chided herself for it every time she looked up and caught his glance, and felt the thrill of pleasure in this close companionship. Of course it was wholly in her own imagination. and due entirely to the nervous strain through which she had passed that day, she told herself. Of course, he had nothing in his mind but the most ordinary kindly desire to give her a good time out of gratitude for what she had done for him. But nevertheless it was sweet, and Shirley was loath to surrender the joy of it while it lasted, dream though it might be.

It lasted all the way, even up to the very stop in front of the barn when he took her hand to help her out, and his fingers lingered on hers with just an instant's pressure, sending a thrill to her heart again, and almost bringing tears to her eyes. Foolishness! She was overwrought. It was a shame that human beings were so made that they had to become weak like that in a time of pleasant rejoicing.

The family came forth noisily to meet them, rejoicing openly at Graham's return, George and Harley vying with each other to shout the news about the garden and the chickens and the dove-cote; Carol demanding to know where was Elizabeth; and Doris earnestly looking in his face and repeating:

"Ickle budie fy away, Mistah Gwaham. All gone! All ickle budies fy away!"

Even Mrs. Hollister came smiling to the door to meet him, and the young man had a warm word of hearty greeting and a hand-shake for each one. It was as if he had just got home to a place where he loved to be, and he could not show his joy enough. Shirley stood back for the moment watching him, admiring the way his hair waved away from his temples, thinking how handsome he looked when he smiled, wondering that he could so easily fit himself into this group, which must in the nature of things be utterly different from his native element, rejoicing over the deference he paid to her plain, quiet mother, thrilling over the kiss he gave her sweet little sister.

Then Mrs. Hollister did something perfectly unexpected and dreadful—she invited him to stay to dinner! Shirley stood back and gasped. Of course he would decline, but think of the temerity of inviting the wealthy and cultured Mr. Graham to take dinner in his own *barn!*

Oh! But he wasn't going to decline at all. He was accepting as if it were a great pleasure Mrs. Hollister was conferring upon him. *Sure,* he would stay! He had been wishing all the way out they would ask him. He had wondered whether he dared invite himself.

Shirley with her cheeks very red hurried in to see that the table-cloth was put on straight, and look after one or two little things; but behold, he followed her out, and, gently insisting and assisting, literally compelled her to come and lie down on the couch while he told the family what she had been through that day. Shirley was so happy she almost cried right there before them all. It was so wonderful to have some one take care of her that way. Of course it was only gratitude—but she had been taking care of other people so long that it completely broke her down to have some one take care of her.

The dinner went much more easily than she had supposed it could with those cracked plates, and the forks from which the silver was all worn off. Doris insisted that the guest sit next to her and butter her bread for her, and she occasionally caressed his coat-sleeve with a sticky little hand, but he didn't seem to mind it in the least, and smiled down on her in quite a brotherly way, arranging her bib when it got tangled in her curls, and seeing that she had plenty of jelly on her bread.

It was a beautiful dinner. Mother Hollister had known what she was about when she selected that particular night to invite unexpected company. There was stewed chicken on little round biscuits, with plenty of gravy and currant jelly, mashed potatoes, green peas, little new beets, and the most delicious custard pie for dessert, all rich, velvety yellow with a golden-brown top. The guest ate as if he enjoyed it, and asked for a second piece of pie, just as if he were one of them. It was unbelievable!

He helped clear off the table too, and insisted on

Carol's giving him a wiping-towel to help with the dishes. It was just like a dream.

The young man tore himself reluctantly away about nine o'clock and went home, but before he left he took Shirley's hand and looked into her eyes with another of those deep understanding glances, and Shirley watched him whirling away in the moonlight, and wondered if there ever would be another day as beautiful and exciting and wonderful as this had been, and whether she could come down to sensible, every-day living again by morning.

Then there was the story of the day to tell all over again after he was gone, and put in the little family touches that had been left out when the guest was there, and there was: "Oh, did you notice how admiring he looked when he told mother Shirley had a remarkably keen mind?" and "He said his father thought Shirley was the most unspoiled-looking girl he had ever seen!" and a lot of other things that Shirley hadn't heard before.

Shirley told her mother what the senior Mr. Graham had said about giving her a reward, and her mother agreed that she had done just right in declining anything for so simple a service, but she looked after Shirley with a sigh as she went to put Doris to bed, and wondered if for this service the poor child was to get a broken heart. It could hardly be possible that a girl could be given much attention such as Shirley had received that day, from as attractive a young man as Graham, without feeling it keenly not to have it continue. And of *course* it was out of the question that it should continue. Mrs. Hollister decided that she had done wrong to invite the young man to stay to supper, and resolved never to offend in that way again. It was a wrong to Shirley to put him on so intimate a footing in the household, and it could not but bring her sadness. He was a most unusual young man to have even wanted to stay, but one must not take that for more than a passing whim, and Shirley must be protected at all hazards.

"Now," said the elder Graham the next morning,

when the business of the day was well under way and he had time to send for his son to come into his office, *"now,* I want you to tell me all about that little girl, and what you think we ought to give her. What did she mean by 'obligations' yesterday? Have you been doing anything for her, son? I meant to ask you last night, but you came home so late I couldn't sit up."

And then Sidney Graham told his father the whole story. It was different from telling his mother. He knew no barn would have the power to prejudice his father.

"And you say that girl lives in the old barn!" exclaimed the father when the story was finished. "Why, the nervy little kid! And she looks as if she came out of a bandbox! Well, she's a bully little girl and no mistake! Well, now, son, what can we do for her? We ought to do something pretty nice. You see it wasn't just the money we might have lost. That would have been a mere trifle beside getting all those other folks balled up in the mess. Why, I'd have given every cent I own before I'd have had Fuller and Browning and Barnard and Wilts get entangled. I tell you, son, it was a great escape!"

"Yes, father, and it was a great lesson for me. I'll never be buncoed as easily again. But about Miss Hollister, I don't know what to say. She's very proud and sensitive. I had an awful time doing the little things I just *had* to do to that barn without her suspecting I was doing it especially for her. Father, you ought to go out there and meet the family; then you'd understand. They're not ordinary people. Their father was a college professor and wrote things. They're cultured people."

"Well, I want to meet them. Why don't we go out there and call to-day? I think they must be worth knowing."

So late that afternoon the father and son rode out to Glenside, and when Shirley and George reached home they found the car standing in front of their place, and the Grahams comfortably seated in the great open doorway, enjoying the late afternoon breeze, and seemingly perfectly at home in their own barn.

"I'm not going to swarm here every day, Miss Shirley," said the son, rising and coming out to meet her. "You see father hadn't heard about the transformation of the old barn, and the minute I told him about it he had to come right out and see it."

"Yes," said the father, smiling contentedly, "I had to come and see what you'd done out here. I've played in the hay up in that loft many a day in my time, and I love the old barn. It's great to see it all fixed up so cozy. But we're going home now and let you have your dinner. We just waited to say 'Howdy' to you before we left."

They stayed a few minutes longer, however, and the senior Graham talked with Shirley while he held Doris on his knee and stroked her silky hair, and she nestled in his arms quite content.

Then, although young Graham was quite loath to leave so soon, they went, for he could not in conscience, expect an invitation to dinner two days in succession.

They rode away into the sunset, going across country to their home without going back to town, and Doris, as she stood with the others watching them away, murmured softly:

"Nice favver-man! Nice Gwaham favver man!"

The "nice-Graham-father-man" was at that moment remarking to his son in very decided tones, as he turned to get a last glimpse of the old barn:

"That old barn door ought to come down right away, Sid, and a nice big old-fashioned door with glass around the sides made to fill the space. That door is an eyesore on the place, and they need a piazza. People like those can't live with a great door like that to open and shut every day."

"Yes, father, I've thought of that, but I don't just know how to manage it. You see they're not objects of charity. I've been thinking about some way to fix up a heating arrangement without hurting their feelings, so they could stay there all winter. I know they hate to go back to the city, and they're only paying ten dollars a month. It's all they can afford. What could they get in the city for that?"

"Great Scott! A girl like that living in a house she

could get for ten dollars, when some of these feather-brained baby-dolls we know can't get on with less than three or four houses that cost from fifty to a hundred thousand dollars apiece! Say, son, that's a peach of a girl, do you know it? A peach of a girl! I've been talking with her, and she has a very superior mind."

"I know she has, father," answered the son humbly.

"I say, Sid, why don't you marry her? That would solve the whole problem. Then you could fix up the old barn into a regular house for her folks."

"Well, father, that's just what I've made up my mind to do—if she'll have me," said the son with a gleam of triumph in his eyes.

"Bully for you, Sid! Bully for you!" and the father gave his son's broad shoulder a resounding slap. "Why, Sid, I didn't think you had that much sense. Your mother gave me to understand that you were philandering around with that dolly-faced Harriet Hale, and I couldn't see what you saw in her. But if you mean it, son, I'm with you every time. That girl's a peach, and you couldn't get a finer if you searched the world over."

"Yes, I'm afraid mother's got her heart set on Harriet Hale," said the son dubiously, "but I can't see it that way."

"H'm! Your mother likes show," sighed the father comically, "but she's got a good heart, and she'll bowl over all right and make the best of it. You know neither your mother nor I were such high and mighties when we were young, and *we* married for *love*. But now, if you really mean business, I don't see why we can't do something right away. When does that girl have her vacation? Of course she gets one sometime. Why couldn't your mother just invite the whole family to occupy the shore cottage for a little while,—get up some excuse or other,—ask 'em to take care of it? You know it's lying idle all this summer, and two servants down there growing fat with nothing to do. We might ship Elizabeth down there and let 'em be company for her. They seem like a fine set of children. It would do Elizabeth good to know them."

"Oh, she's crazy about them. She's been out a number of times with me, and don't you remember she had Carol out to stay with her?"

"Was that the black-eyed, sensible girl? Well, I declare! I didn't recognize her. She was all dolled up out at our house. I suppose Elizabeth loaned 'em to her, eh? Well, I'm glad. She's got sense, too. That's the kind of people I like my children to know. Now if that vacation could only be arranged to come when your mother and I take that Western trip, why, it would be just the thing for Elizabeth, work right all around. Now, the thing for you to do is to find out about that vacation, and begin to work things. Then you could have everything all planned, and rush the work so it would be done by the time they came back."

So the two conspirators plotted, while all unconscious of their interest Shirley was trying to get herself in hand and not think how Graham's eyes had looked when he said good-night to her.

CHAPTER XIX

SINCE the pastor from the village had called upon them, the young people of the stone barn had been identified with the little white church in the valley. Shirley had taken a class of boys in the Sunday-school and was playing the organ, as George had once predicted. Carol was helping the primary teacher, George was assistant librarian and secretary, Harley was in Shirley's class, and Doris was one of the primaries.

Shirley had at once identified herself with the struggling little Christian Endeavor society and was putting new life into it, with her enthusiasm, her new ideas about getting hold of the young people of the community, and her wonderful knack of getting the silent ones to take part in the meetings. She had suggested new committees, had invited the music committee to meet her at her home some evening to plan out special music, and no coöperate with the social committee in planning for music at the socials. She always carried a few appropriate clippings or neatly written verses or other quotations to meeting to slip into the hands of some who had not prepared to speak, and she saw to it that her brothers and sisters were always ready to say something. Withal, she did her part so unobtrusively that none of the old members could think she was trying to usurp power or make herself prominent. She became a quiet power behind the powers, to whom the president and all the other officers came for advice, and who seemed always ready to help in any work, or to find a way out of any difficulty. Christian Endeavor in the little white church at once took great strides after the advent of the Hollisters, and even the idlers on the street corners were moved with curiosity to drop into the twilight service of the young people and see what went on, and why everybody seemed so interested. But the secret of it all, Shirley thought, was the little five-minute prayer service that the prayer-meeting committee held in the tiny primary room just before the regular meeting. Shirley as chairman of the prayer-meeting committee had started this little meeting, and she always came into the larger room with an exalted look upon her face and a feeling of strength in her heart from this brief speaking with her Master.

Shirley was somewhat aghast the next Sabbath to have Sidney Graham arrive and ask her to take a ride with him.

"Why, I was just going to church," she said, half hesitating, and then smiling bravely up at him; "besides, I have a Sunday-school class. I couldn't very well leave them, you know."

He looked at her for a moment thoughtfully, trying to bridge in his thoughts this difference between them. Then he said quite humbly,

"Will you take me with you?"

"To church?" she asked, and there was a glad ring in her voice. Would he really go to church with her?

"Yes, and to Sunday School if I may. I haven't been to Sunday School in years. I'd like to go if you'll only let me."

Her cheeks grew rosy. She had a quick mental picture of putting him in Deacon Pettigrew's Bible class.

"I'm afraid there isn't any class you would enjoy," she began with a troubled look. "It's only a little country church, you know. They don't have all the modern system, and very few teachers."

"I should enjoy going into your class very much if I might."

"Oh, mine are just boys, just little boys like Harley!" said Shirley, aghast.

"I've been a little boy once, you know. I should enjoy it very much," said the applicant with satisfaction.

"Oh, but—I couldn't teach *you!*" There was dismay in her voice.

"Couldn't you, though? You've taught me more in the few months I've known you than I've learned in that many years from others. Try me. I'll be very good. I'll be a boy with the rest of them, and you can just forget I'm there and go ahead. I really am serious about it. I want to hear what you have to say to them."

"Oh, I couldn't teach with you there!" exclaimed Shirley, putting her hands on her hot cheeks and looking like a frightened little child. "Indeed I couldn't, really. I'm not much of a teacher. I'm only a beginner. I shouldn't know how to talk before any but children."

He watched her silently for a minute, his face grave with wistfulness.

"Why do you teach them?" he asked rather irrelevantly.

"Because—why, because I want to help them to live right lives; I want to teach them how to know God."

"Why?"

"So that they will be saved. Because it was Christ's command that His disciples should give the message. I am His disciple, so I have to tell the message."

"Was there any special stipulation as to whom that message should be given?" asked the young man thoughtfully. "Did he say you were just to give it to those boys?"

"Why, no; it was to be given to—all the world, every creature." Shirley spoke the words hesitatingly, a dimple beginning to show in her cheek as her eyelids drooped over her shy eyes.

"And don't I come in on that?" asked Graham, with a twinkle that reminded Shirley of his father.

Shirley had to laugh shamefacedly then.

"But I couldn't!" said Shirley. "I'd be so scared I couldn't think of a thing to say."

"You're not afraid of me, Miss Shirley? You wouldn't be scared if you thought I really needed to know the message, would you? Well, I really do, as much as any of those kids."

Shirley looked steadily into his earnest eyes and saw something there that steadied her nerve. The laughter died out of her own eyes, and a beautiful light of longing came into them.

"All right," she said, with a little lift of her chin as if girding up her strength to the task. "You may come, and I'll do the best I can, but I'm afraid it will be a poor best. I've only a little story to tell them this morning."

"Please give them just what you had intended. I want the real thing, just as a boy would get it from you. Will the rest of them come in the car with us?"

Shirley was very quiet during the ride to church. She let the rest do all the talking, and she sat looking off at the woods and praying for help, trying to calm the flutter of her frightened heart, trying to steady her nerves and brace herself to teach the lesson just as she had intended to teach it.

She watched him furtively during the opening exercises, the untrained singing, the monotonous prayer of an old farmer-elder, the dry platitudes of the illiterate superintendent; but he sat respectfully listening, taking it all for what it was worth, the best service these people knew how to render to their Maker.

Somehow her heart had gained the strength she needed from the prayers she breathed continually, and when the time for teaching the lesson arrived she came to her class with quietness.

There was a little awe upon the boys because of the stranger in their midst. They did not fling the hymnbooks down with a noisy thud, nor send the lesson leaves flying like winged darts across the room quite so much as they were wont to do. They looked askance at Harley, who sat proudly by the visitor, supplying him with Bibles, hymn-books, lesson leaves, and finding the place for him officiously. But Graham sat among the boys without ostentation, and made as little of his own presence as possible. He smiled at them now and then, put a handful of silver into the collection envelope when they would have passed him by, and promised a ride to one fellow who ventured to ask him hoarsely if that was his car outside the church.

Shirley had made up her mind to forget as far as she could the presence of the visitor in the class, and to this end she fixed her eyes upon the worst little boy present, the boy who got up all the disturbances, and made all the noises, and was the most adorable, homely, sturdy young imp the Valley Church could produce. He sat straight across from her, while Graham was at the side, and she could see in Jack's eye that he meant mischief if he could overcome his awe of the stranger. So before Jack could possible get started she began her story, and told it straight to Jack, never taking her eyes from his face from start to finish, and before she was half-way through she had her little audience enthralled. It was a story of the Bible told in modern setting, and told straight to the heart of a boy who was the counter-part in his own soul of the man whom Christ cured and forgave. What Graham was thinking or looking Shirley did not know. She had literally forgotten his existence after the first few minutes. She had seen the gleam of interest in the eyes of the boy Jack; she knew that her message was going home to a convicted young soul, and that he saw himself and his own childish sins in the sinful life of the hero of her tale. Her whole soul was bent on making him see the Saviour who could make that young life over. Not until the story was almost finished did any one of the listeners, unless perhaps Harley, who was used to such story-recitals, have a suspicion that the story was just a plain, ordinary chapter out of the Bible. Then suddenly one of the elder boys broke forth: "Aw! Gee! That's just the man in the Bible let down through the roof!" There was a slight stir in the class at the discovery as it dawned upon them that the teacher had "put one over on them" again, but the interest for the most part was sustained breathlessly until the superintendent's bell rang, and the heads drew together in an absorbed group around her for the last few sentences, spoken in a lower tone because the general hum of teaching in the room had ceased.

Graham's face was very grave and thoughtful as she finished and slipped away from them to take her place at the little organ. One could see that it was not in the teacher alone, but in her message as well, that he was interested. The boys all had that subdued, half-ashamed, half-defiant look that boys have when they have been caught looking serious. Each boy frowned and studied his toes, or hunted assiduously in his hymn-book to hide his confusion, and the class in various keys lifted up assertive young voices vigorously in the last hymn.

Graham sat beside Shirley in the little crowded church during the rather monotonous service. The regular pastor, who was a good, spiritual man if not a brilliant one, and gave his congregation solid, practical sermons, was on his vacation, and the pulpit was supplied by a young theologue who was new to his work that his sermon was a rather involved effort. But so strong was the power of the Sunday-school lesson to which he had just listened that Graham felt as if he were sitting in some hallowed atmosphere. He did not see the red-faced, embarrassed young preacher, nor notice his struggles to bring forth his message bravely; he saw only the earnest-faced young teacher as she spoke the words of life to her boys; saw the young imp-faces of her boys softened and touched by the story she told; saw that she really believed and felt every word she spoke; and knew that there was something in it all that he wanted.

The seat was crowded and the day was warm, but the two who looked over the same hymn-book did not notice it. The soft air came in from the open window beside them, breathing sweet clover and wild honeysuckle, and the meadow-larks sang their songs, and made it seem just like a little bit of heaven.

Shirley's muslin frills trembled against Graham's hand as she reached to catch a fluttering leaf of the hymn-book that the wind had caught; once her hand brushed the coat-sleeve beside her as they turned the page, and she felt the soft texture of the fine dark blue goods with a pleasant sense of the beautiful and fitting. It thrilled her to think he was standing thus beside her in her own little church, yielding himself to the same worship with her in the little common country congregation. It was wonderful, beautiful! And to have come to her! She glanced shyly up at him, so handsome, standing there singing, his hand almost touching hers holding the book. He felt her glance and answered it with a look and smile, their eyes holding each other for just the fraction of a second in which some inner thought was interchanged, some question asked and answered by the invisible flash of heart-beats, a mutual joining in the spiritual service, and then half-frightened Shirley dropped her eyes to the page and the soft roses stole into her cheeks again. She felt as if she had seen something in his eyes and acknowledged it in her own, as if she had inadvertently shown him her heart in that glance, and that heart of hers was leaping and bounding with an uncontrollable joy, while her conscience sought by every effort to get it in control. What nonsense, it said, what utter folly, to make so much of his coming to church with her once! To allow her soul to get into such a flutter over a man who had no more idea of noticing her or caring for her than he had for a bird on the tree.

And with all the tumult in her heart she did not even see the envious glances of the village maidens who stared and stared with all their might at the handsome man who came to church in an expensive car and brought the girl who lived in a barn! Shirley's social position went up several notches, and she never even knew it. In fact, she was becoming a great puzzle to the residents of Glenside.

It was good to know that for once the shabby collection-box of the little church was borne back to the altar laden with a goodly bill, put in with so little ostentation that one might have judged it but a penny, looking on, though even a penny would have made more noise in the unlined wooden box.

After the service was over Graham went out with the children, while Shirley lingered to play over an accompaniment for a girl who was going to sing at the vesper service that afternoon. He piled all the children in the back seat of the car, put the boy he had promised a ride in the seat beside him, took a spin around the streets, and was back in front of the church by the time Shirley came out. Then that foolish heart of hers had to leap again at the thought that he had saved the front seat for her. The boy descended as if he had been caught up into heaven for a brief space, and would never forget it the rest of his life.

There was that same steady look of trust and understanding in Graham's eyes whenever he looked at her on the way home, and once while the children were talking together in the back seat he leaned toward her and said in a low tone:

"I wonder if you will let me take you away for a little while this afternoon to a quiet place I know where there is a beautiful view, and let us sit and talk. There are some things I want to ask you, about what you said this morning. I was very much interested in it all, and I'm deeply grateful that you let me go. Now, will you go with me? I'll bring you back in time for the Christian Endeavor service, and you see in the mean time I'm inviting myself to dinner. Do you think your mother will object?"

What was there for Shirley to do but accept this alluring invitation? She did not believe in going off on pleasure excursions on the Sabbath, but this request that she ride to a quiet place out-of-doors for a religious talk could not offend her strongest sense of what was right on the Sabbath day. And surely, if the Lord had a message for her to bear, she must bear it to whomsoever He sent. This, then, was this man's interest in her, that she had been able to make him think of God. A glad elation filled her heart, something deep and true stirred within her and lifted her above the thought of self, like a blessing from on high. To be asked to bring light to a soul like this one, this was honor indeed. This was an answer to her prayer of the morning, that she might fulfil God's pleasure with the lesson of the day. The message then had reached his soul. It was enough. She would think no more of self.

Yet whenever she looked at him and met that smile again she was thrilled with joy in spite of herself. At least there was a friendliness here beyond the common acquaintance, a something that was true, deep, lasting, even though worlds should separate them in the future; a something built on a deep understanding, sympathy and common interests. Well, so be it. She would rejoice that it had been given her to know one man of the world in this beautiful way; and her foolish little human heart should understand what a high, true thing this was that must not be misunderstood.

So she reasoned with herself, and watched him during the dinner, among the children, out in the yard among the flowers and animals, everywhere, he seemed so fine and splendid, so far above all other men that she had ever met. And her mother, watching, trembled for her when she saw her happy face.

"Do you think you ought to go with him, daughter?" she asked with troubled eyes, when they were left alone for a moment after dinner. "You know it is the Sabbath, and you know his life is very different from ours."

"Mother, he wants to talk about the Sunday School lesson this morning," said Shirley shyly. "I guess he is troubled, perhaps, and wants me to help him. I guess he has never thought much about religious things."

"Well, daughter dear, be careful. Do all you can for him, of course, but remember, don't let your heart stray out of your keeping. He is very attractive, dear, and very unconventional for a wealthy man. I think he is true and wouldn't mean to trifle, but he wouldn't realize."

"I know, mother; don't you be afraid for me!" said Shirley with a lofty look, half of exultation, half of proud self-command.

He took her to a mossy place beside a little stream, where the light filtered down through the lacy leaves flecking the bank, and braided golden currents in the water; with green and purple hazy hills in the distance, and just enough seclusion for a talk without being too far away from the world.

"My little sister says that you people have a 'real' God," he said, when she was comfortably fixed with cushions from the car at her back against a tall tree-trunk. "She says you seem to realize His presence—I don't know just how to say it, but I'd like to know if this is so. I'd like to know what makes you different from other girls, and your home different from most of the homes I know. I'd like to know if I may have it too."

That was the beginning.

Shirley, shy as a bird at first, having never spoken on such subjects except to children, yet being well versed in the Scriptures, and feeling her faith with every atom of her being, drew out her little Bible that she had slipped into her pocket when they started, and plunged into the great subject.

Never had preacher more earnest listener, or more lovely temple in which to preach. And if sometimes the young man's thoughts for a few moments strayed from the subject to rest his eyes in tenderness upon the lovely face of the young teacher, and long to draw her into his arms and claim her for his own, he might well have been forgiven. For Shirley was very fair, with the light of other worlds in her face, her eyes all sparkling with her eagerness, her lips aglow with words that seemed to be given her for the occasion. She taught him simply, not trying to go into deep arguments, but urging the only way she knew, the way of taking Christ's promise on its face value, the way of being willing to do His will, trusting it to Him to reveal Himself, and the truth of the doctrine, and make the believer sure.

They talked until the sun sunk low, and the calling of the wood-birds warned them that the Endeavor hour was near. Before they left the place he asked her for the little Bible, and she laid it in his hand with joy that he wanted it, that she was chosen to give him a gift so precious.

"It is all marked up," she said apologetically. "I always mark the verses I love, or have had some special experience with."

"It will be that much more precious to me," he said gently, fingering the leaves reverently, and then he looked up and gave her one of those deep looks that seemed to say so much to her heart. And all at once she realized that she was on earth once more, and that his presence and his look were very precious to her. Her cheeks grew pink with the joy of it, and she looked down in confusion and could not answer, so she rose to her feet. But he, springing at once to help her up, kept her hand for just an instant with earnest pressure, and said in deeply moved tones:

"You don't know what you have done for me this afternoon, my—*friend!*" He waited with her hand in his an instant as if he were going to say more, but had decided it were better not. The silence was so compelling that she looked up into his eyes, meeting his smile, and that said so many things her heart went into a tumult again and could not quite come to itself all through the Christian Endeavor service.

On the way home from the church he talked a little about her vacation: when it came, how long it lasted, what she would do with it. Just as they reached home he said,

"I hope you will pray for me, *my friend!*"

There was something wonderful in the way he said that word "friend." It thrilled her through and through as she stood beside the road and watched him speed away into the evening.

"My friend! I hope you will pray for me, *my friend!*" It sang a glory-song down in her heart as she turned to go in with the vivid glory of the sunset on her face.

CHAPTER XX

THE cement floor had been down a week and was as hard as a rock, when one day two or three wagon-loads of things arrived with a note from Graham to Mrs. Hollister to say that he would be glad if these might be stored in one corner of the basement floor, where they would be out of her way and not take up too much room.

Harley and George went down to look them over that evening.

"He said something about some things being taken from the office building," said Harley, kicking a pile of iron pipes with his toe.

"These don't look like any old things that have been used," said George thoughtfully. "They look perfectly new." Then he studied them a few minutes more from another angle, and shut his lips judiciously. He belonged to the boy species that has learned to "shut up and saw wood," whatever that expression may mean. If anything was to come out of that pile of iron in the future, he did not mean to break confidence with anybody's secrets. He walked away whistling and said nothing further about them.

The next day Mrs. Graham came down upon the Hollisters in her limousine, and an exquisite toilet of organdie and ribbons. She was attended by Elizabeth, wild with delight over getting home again. She begged Mrs. Hollister very charmingly and sincerely to take care of Elizabeth for three or four weeks, while she and her husband were away, and to take her entire family down to the shore and occupy their cottage, which had been closed all summer and needed opening and airing. She said that nothing would please Elizabeth so much as to have them all her guests during September. The maids were there, with nothing to do but look after them, and would just love to serve them; it really would be a great favor to her if she could know that Elizabeth was getting a little salt air under such favorable conditions. She was so genuine in her request and suggested so earnestly that Shirley and George needed the change during their vacation, and could just as well come down every night and go up every morning for a week or two more after the vacations were over, that Mrs. Hollister actually promised to consider it and talk it over with Shirley when she came home. Elizabeth and Carol nearly went into spasms of joy over the thought of all they could do down at the shore together.

When Shirley came home she found the whole family quite upset discussing the matter. Carol had brought out all the family wardrobe and was showing how she could wash this, and dye that, and turn this skirt upside down, and put a piece from the old waist in there to make the lower part flare; and Harley was telling how he could get the man next door to look after the hens and pigeons, and there was nothing needing much attention in the garden now, for the corn was about over except the last picking, which wasn't ripe yet.

Mrs. Hollister was saying that they ought really to stay at home and look up another place to live during the winter, and Carol was pleading that another place would be easier found when the weather was cooler anyway, and that Shirley was just awfully tired and needed a change.

Shirley's cheeks grew pink in spite of the headache which she had been fighting all day, when she heard of the invitation, and sat down to think it out. Was this, then, another of the kind schemes of her kind friend to make the way easier for her? What right had she to take all this? Why was he doing it? Why were the rest of the family? Did they really need some one to take care of Elizabeth? But of course it was a wonderful opportunity, and one that her mother at least should not let slip by. And Doris! Think of Doris playing in the sand at the seaside!

Supper was flung onto the table that night any way it happened, for they were all too excited to know what they were about. Carol got butter twice and forgot to cut the bread, and Harley poured milk into the already filled water-pitcher. They were even too excited to eat.

Graham arrived with Elizabeth early in the evening to add his pleading to his mother's, and before he left he had about succeeded in getting Mrs. Hollister's promise that she would go.

Shirley's vacation began the first of September, and George had asked for his at the same time so that they could enjoy it together. Each had two weeks. Graham said that the cost of going back and forth to the city for the two would be very little. By the next morning they had begun to say what they would take along, and to plan what they would do with the dog. It was very exciting. There was only a week to get ready, and Carol wanted to make bathing-suits for everybody.

Graham came again that night with more suggestions. There were plenty of bathing-suits down at the cottage, of all sizes and kinds. No need to make bathing-suits. The dog, of course, was to go along. He needed the change as much as anybody, and they needed him there. That breed of dog was a great swimmer. He would take care of the children when they went in bathing. How would Mrs. Hollister like to have one of the old Graham servants come over to sleep at the barn and look after things while they were gone? The man had really nothing to do at home while everybody was away, as the whole corps of servants would be there, and this one would enjoy coming out to the country. He had a brother living on a place about a mile away. As for the trip down there, Graham would love to take them all in the big touring-car with Elizabeth. He had been intending to take her down that way, and there was no reason in the world why they should not all go along. They would start Saturday afternoon as soon as Shirley and George were free, and be down before bedtime. It would be cool and delightful journeying at that hour, and a great deal pleasanter than the train.

So one by one the obstructions and hindrances were removed from their path, and it was decided that the Hollisters were to go to the seashore.

At last the day came.

Shirley and George went off in the morning shouting last directions about things. They were always having to go to their work whatever was happening. It was sometimes hard on them, particularly this day when everything was so delightfully exciting.

The old Graham servant arrived about three o'clock in the afternoon, and proved himself invaluable in doing the little last things without being told. Mrs. Hollister had her first gleam of an idea of what it must be to have plenty of perfectly trained servants about to anticipate one's needs. He entered the barn as if barns were his native heath, and moved about with the ease and unobtrusiveness that marks a perfect servant, but with none of the hauteur and disdain that many of those individuals entertain toward all whom they consider poor or beneath them in any way. He had a kindly face, and seemed to understand just exactly what was to be done. Things somehow moved more smoothly after he arrived.

At four o'clock came Graham with the car and a load of long linen dust-cloaks and veils. The Hollisters donned them and bestowed themselves where they were told. The servant stowed away the wraps and suitcases; Star mounted the seat beside Harley, and they were ready.

They turned to look back at the barn as the car started. The old servant was having a little trouble with the big door, trying to shut it. "That door is a nuisance," said Graham as they swept away from the curb. "It must be fixed. It is no fit door for a barn anyway." Then they curved up around Allister Avenue and left the barn far out of sight.

They were going across country to the Graham home to pick up Elizabeth. It was a wonderful experience for them, that beautiful ride in the late afternoon; and when they swept into the great gates, and up the broad drive to the Graham mansion, and stopped under the porte-cochère, Mrs. Hollister was quite overcome with the idea of being beholden to people who lived in such grandeur as this. To think she had actually invited their son to dine in a barn with her!

Elizabeth came rushing out eagerly, all ready to start, and climbed in beside Carol. Even George, who was usually silent when she was about, gave her a grin of welcome. The father and mother came out to say good-by, gave them good wishes, and declared they were perfectly happy to leave their daughter in such good hands. Then the car curved about the great house, among tennis courts, green-houses, garage, stable, and what not, and back to the pike again, leaping out upon the perfect road as if it were as excited as the children.

Two more stops to pick up George, who was getting off early, and Shirley, who was through at five o'clock, and then they threaded their way out of the city, across the ferry, through another city, and out into the open country, dotted all along the way with clean, pretty little towns.

They reached a lovely grove at sundown and stopped by the way to have supper. Graham got down and made George help him get out the big hamper.

There was a most delectable lunch; sandwiches of delicate and unknown condiments, salad as bewildering, soup that had been kept hot in a thermos bottle, served in tiny white cups, iced tea and ice-cream meringues from another thermos compartment, and plenty of delicious little cakes, olives, nuts, bonbons, and fruit. It seemed a wonderful supper to them all, eaten out there under the trees, with the birds beginning their vesper songs and the stars peeping out slyly. Then they packed up their dishes and hurried on their beautiful way, a silver thread of a moon coming out to make the scene more lovely.

Doris was almost asleep when at last they began to hear the booming of the sea and smell the salt breeze as it swept back inland; but she roused up and opened wide, mysterious eyes, peering into the new darkness, and murmuring softly: "I yant to see ze osun! I yant to see the gate bid watter!"

Stiff, bewildered, filled with ecstasy, they finally unloaded in front of a big white building that looked like a hotel. They tried to see into the deep, mysterious darkness across the road, where boomed a great voice that called them, and where dashing spray loomed high like a waving phantom hand to beckon them now and again, and far-moving lights told of ships and a world beyond the one they knew,—a wide, limitless thing like eternity, universe, chaos.

With half-reluctant feet they turned away from the mysterious unseen lure and let themselves be led across an unbelievably wide veranda into the bright light of a hall, where everything was clean and shining, and a great fireplace filled with friendly flames gave cheer and welcome. The children stood bewildered in the brightness while two strange serving-maids unfastened their wraps and dust-cloaks and helped them take off their hats. Then they all sat around the fire, for Graham had come in by this time, and the maids brought trays of some delicious drink with little cakes and crackers, and tinkling ice, and straws to drink with. Doris almost fell asleep again, and was carried upstairs by Shirley and put to bed in a pretty white crib she was too sleepy to look at, while Carol, Elizabeth, George, and Harley went with Graham across the road to look at the black, yawning cavern they called ocean, and to have the shore light-houses pointed out to them and named one by one.

They were all asleep at last, a little before midnight, in spite of the excitement over the spacious rooms, and who should have which. Think of it! Thirty rooms in the house, and every one as pretty as every other one! What luxury! And nobody to occupy them but themselves! Carol could hardly get to sleep. She felt as if she had dropped into a novel and was living it.

When Graham came out of his room the next morning the salt breeze swept invitingly through the hall and showed him the big front door of the upper piazza open and some one standing in the sunlight, with light, glowing garments, gazing at the sea in rapt enjoyment. Coming out softly, he saw that it was Shirley dressed in white, with a ribbon of blue at her waist and a soft pink color in her cheeks, looking off to sea.

He stood for a moment to enjoy the picture, and said in his heart that sometime, if he got his wish, he would have her painted so by some great artist, with just that little simple white dress and blue ribbon, her round white arm lifted, her small hand shading her eyes, the sunlight burnishing her brown hair into gold. He could scarcely refrain from going to her and telling her how beautiful she was. But when he stepped quietly up beside her only his eyes spoke, and brought the color deeper into her cheeks; and so they stood for some minutes, looking together and drawing in the wonder of God's sea.

"This is the first time I've ever seen it, you know," spoke Shirley at last, "and I'm so glad it was on Sunday morning. It will always make the day seem more holy and the sea more wonderful to think about. I like best things to happen on Sunday, don't you, because that is the best day of all?"

Graham looked at the sparkling sea all azure and pearls, realized the Sabbath quiet, and marvelled at the beauty of the soul of the girl, even as her feeling about it all seemed to enter into and become a part of himself.

"Yes, I do," said he. "I never did before, but I do now,—and always shall," he added under his breath.

That was almost as wonderful a Sabbath as the one they had spent in the woods a couple of weeks before. They walked and talked by the sea, and they went to a little Episcopal chapel, where the windows stood open for the chanting of the waves and the salt of the breeze to come in freely, and then they went out and walked by the sea again. Wherever they went, whether resting in some of the many big rockers on the broad verandas or walking on the hard smooth sand, or sitting in some cozy nook by the waves, they felt the same deep sympathy, the same conviction that their thoughts were one, the same wonderful thrill of the day and each other's nearness.

Somehow in the new environment Shirley forgot for a little that this young man was not of her world, that he was probably going back soon to the city to enter into a whirl of the winter's season in society, that other girls would claim his smiles and attentions, and she would likely be forgotten. She lost the sense of it entirely and companioned with him as joyously as if there had never been anything to separate them. Her mother, looking on, sighed, feared, smiled, and sighed again.

They walked together in the sweet darkness beside the waves that evening, and he told her how when he was a little boy he wanted to climb up to the stars and find God, but later how he thought the stars and God were myths like Santa Claus, and that the stars were only electric lights put up by men and lighted from a great switch every night, and when they didn't shine somebody had forgotten to light them. He told her many things about himself that he had never told to any one before, and she opened her shy heart to him, too.

Then they planned what they would do next week when he came back. He told her he must go back to the city in the morning to see his father and mother off and attend to a few matters of business at the office. It might be two or three days before he could return, but after that he was coming down to take a little vacation himself if she didn't mind, and they would do a lot of delightful things together: row, fish, go crabbing, and he would teach her to swim and show her all the walks and favorite places where he used to go as a boy. Reluctantly they went in, his fingers lingering about hers for just a second at the door, vibrating those mysterious heart-strings of hers again, sweeping dearest music from them, and frightening her with joy that took her half the night to put down.

CHAPTER XXI

SIDNEY GRAHAM went back to the city the next morning. They all stood out on the piazza to watch the big car glide away. Doris stood on the railing of the piazza with Shirley's arm securely about her and waved a little fat hand; then with a pucker of her lip she demanded:

"Fy does mine Mister Dwaham do way? I don't yant him to do way. I yant him to stay wif me *aw*ways, don't oo, Sirley?"

Shirley with glowing cheeks turned from watching the retreating car and put her little sister down on the floor suddenly.

"Run get your hat, Doris, and we'll take a walk on the sand!" she said, smiling alluringly at the child, till the baby forgot her grievance and beamed out with answering smiles.

That was a wonderful day.

They all took a walk on the sand first, George pushing his mother in a big wheeled chair belonging to the cottage. Elizabeth was guide and pointed out all the beauties of the place, telling eager bits of reminiscence from her childhood memories to which even George listened attentively. From having been only tolerant of her George had now come to look upon Elizabeth as "a good scout."

When Mrs. Hollister grew tired they took her back to the cottage and established her in a big chair with a book. Then they all rushed off to the bath-houses and presently emerged in bathing-suits, Doris looking like a little sprite in her scarlet flannel scrap of a suit, her bright hair streaming, and her beautiful baby arms and legs flashing white like a cherub's in the sunlight.

They came back from their dip in the waves, hungry and eager, to the wonderful dinner that was served so exquisitely in the great cool dining-room, from the windows of which they could watch the lazy ships sailing in the offing.

Doris fell asleep over her dessert and was tumbled into the hammock to finish her nap. Carol and Elizabeth and the boys started off crabbing, and Shirley settled herself in another hammock with a pile of new magazines about her and prepared to enjoy a whole afternoon of laziness. It was so wonderful to lie still, at leisure and unhurried, with all those lovely magazines to read, and nothing to disturb her. She leaned her head back and closed her eyes for a minute just to listen to the sea, and realize how good it was to be here. Back in her mind there was a pleasant consciousness of the beautiful yesterday, and the beautiful to-morrows that might come when Sidney Graham returned, but she would not let her heart dwell upon them; that would be humoring herself too much, and perhaps give her a false idea of things. She simply would not let this wonderful holiday be spoiled by the thought that it would have to end some day and that she would be back at the old routine of care and worry once more.

She was roused from her reverie by the step of the postman bringing a single letter, for her!

It was addressed in an unknown hand and was in a fat long envelope. Wonderingly she opened it and found inside a bank book and blank check book with a little note on which was written:

DEAR LITTLE GIRL:

This is just a trifle of that present we were talking about the other day that belongs to you. It isn't all by any means, but we'll see to the rest later. Spend this on chocolates or chewing-gum or frills or whatever you like and have a good time down at the shore. You're a bully little girl and deserve everything nice that's going. Don't be too serious, Miss Shirley. Play a little more.

Your elderly friend,

Walter K. Graham

In the bank book was an entry of five thousand dollars, on check account. Shirley held her breath and stared at the figures with wide eyes, then slipped away and locked herself in the big white room that was hers. Kneeling down by the bed she cried and prayed and smiled all in one, and thanked the Lord for making people so kind to her. After that she went to find her mother.

Mrs. Hollister was sitting on the wide upper piazza in a steamer chair looking off to sea and drawing in new life at every breath. Her book was open on her lap, but she had forgotten to read in the joy of all that was about her. To tell the truth she was wondering if the dear father who was gone from them knew of their happy estate, and thinking how glad he would be for them if he did.

She read the letter twice before she looked at the bank book with its astonishing figures, and heard again Shirley's tale of the happening in the office the morning of the arrest. Then she read the letter once more.

"I'm not just sure, daughter," she said at last with a smile, "what we ought to do about this. Are you?"

"No," said Shirley, smiling; "I suppose I'll give it back, but wasn't it wonderful of him to do it? Isn't it grand that there are such men in the world?"

"It certainly is, dear, and I'm glad my little girl was able to do something that was of assistance to him; and that she has won her way into his good graces so simply and sweetly. But I'm not so sure what you ought to do. Hadn't we better pray about it a bit before you decide? How soon ought you to write to him? It's too late to reach him before he leaves for California, isn't it?"

"Oh, yes, he's just about starting now," said the girl. "Don't you suppose he planned it so that I couldn't answer right away? I don't know his address. I can't do a thing till I find out where to write. I wouldn't like to send it to the office because they would probably think it was business and his secretary might open it."

"Of course. Then we'll just pray about it, shall we, dear? I'm not just sure in my mind whether it's a well-meant bit of charity that we ought to hand back with sincere thanks, or whether it's God's way of reward-ing my little girl for her faithfulness and quickness of action. Our Father knows we have been—and still are —in a hard place. He knows that we have need of all these things that money has to buy. You really did a good thing and saved Mr. Graham from great loss, you know, and perhaps he is the kind of man who would feel a great deal happier if he shared a little of it with you, was able to make some return for what you did for him. However, five thousand dollars is a great deal of money for a brief service. What do you think, dear?"

"I don't know, mother dear. I'm all muddled just as you say, but I guess it will come right if we pray about it. Anyhow, I'm going to be happy over his thinking of me, whether I keep it or not."

Shirley went thoughtfully back to her hammock and her magazines, a smile on her lips, a dream in her eyes. She found herself wondering whether Sidney Gra-ham knew about this money and what he would wish her to do about it. Then suddenly she cast the whole question from her and plunged into her magazine, wondering why it was that almost any question that came into her mind promptly got around and entangled itself with Mr. Sidney Graham. What did he have to do with it, anyway?

The magazine story was very interesting and Shirley soon forgot everything else in the pleasure of surrender-ing herself to the printed page. An hour went by, an-other passed, and Shirley was still oblivious to all about her. Suddenly she became aware of a boy on a bicycle, riding almost up to the very steps, and whis-tling vigorously.

"Miss Shirley Hollister here?" he demanded as he alighted on one foot on the lower step, the other foot poised for flight as soon as his errand should have been performed.

"Why, yes," said Shirley, startled, struggling to her feet and letting a shower of magazines fall all about her.

"Long distance wants yer," he announced, looking her over apathetically. "Mr. Barnard, of Philadelphia, wants to talk to yer!" and with the final word chanted nasally he alighted upon his obedient steed and spun away down the walk again.

"But, wait! Where shall I go? Where is the telephone?"

"Pay station!" shouted the impervious child, turning his head over his shoulder, "Drug store! Two blocks from the post office!"

Without waiting to go upstairs Shirley, whose training had been to answer the telephone at once, caught up Elizabeth's parasol that lay on a settee by the door, rumpled her fingers through her hair by way of toilet and hurried down the steps in the direction the boy had disappeared, wondering what in the world Mr. Bernard could want of her? Was he going to call her back from her vacation? Was this perhaps the only day she would have, this and yesterday? There would always be yesterday! With a sigh she looked wistfully at the sea. If she had only known a summons was to come so soon she would not have wasted a second on magazines. She would have sat and gazed all the afternoon at the sea. If Mr. Barnard wanted her, of course she would have to go. Business was business and she couldn't afford to lose her job even with that fairy dream of five thousand to her credit in the bank. She knew, of course, she meant to give that back. It was hers for the day, but it could not become tangible. It was beautiful, but it was right that it must go back, and if her employer felt he must cut short her vacation why of course she must acquiesce and just be glad she had had this much. Perhaps it was just as well, anyway, for if Sidney Graham came down and spent a few days there was no knowing what foolish notions her heart

187

would take, jumping and careening the way it had been doing lately when he just looked at her. Yes, she would go back if Mr. Barnard wanted her. It was the best thing she could do. Though perhaps he would only be calling her to ask where she had left something for which they were searching. That stupid Ashton girl who took her place might not have remembered all her directions.

Breathless, with possibilities crowding upon her mind, she hurried into the drug store and sought the telephone booth. It seemed ages before the connection was made and she heard Mr. Barnard's dry familiar tones over the phone:

"That you, Miss Hollister? This is Mr. Barnard. I'm sorry to disturb you right in the midst of your holiday, but a matter has come up that is rather serious and I'm wondering if you could help us out for a day or two. If you would we'd be glad to give you fifty dollars for the extra time, and let you extend your vacation to a month instead of two weeks. Do you think you could spare a day or two to help us right away?"

"Oh! Why, yes, of course!" faltered Shirley, her eyes dancing at the thought of the extra vacation and money.

"Thank you! I was sure you would," said Mr. Barnard, with relief in his voice. You see we have got that Government contract. The news just came in the afternoon mail. It's rather particular business because it has to do with matters that the Government wishes to keep secret. I am to go down to-morrow morning to Washington to receive instructions, and I have permission to bring a trusted private secretary with me. Now you know, of course, that I couldn't take Miss Ashton. She wouldn't be able to do what I want done even if she were one I could trust not to say a word about the matter. I would take Jim Thorpe, but his father has just died and I can't very well ask him to leave. Neither can I delay longer than to-morrow. Now the question is, would you be willing to go to Washington in the morning? I have looked up the trains and I find you can leave the shore at 8:10 and meet me in Baltimore at ten o'clock. I will be waiting for you at the train gate, but in case we miss each other wait in the station, close to the telephone booths, till I find you. We will take the next train for Washington and be there a little before noon. If all goes well we ought to be through our business in plenty of time to make a four o'clock train home. Of course there may be delays, and it is quite possible you might have to remain in Washington over night, though I hardly think so. But in case you do I will see that you are safe and comfortable in a quiet hotel near the station where my wife's sister is staying this summer.

"Of course your expenses will all be paid. I will telegraph and have a mileage book put at your disposal that you can call for right there in your station in the morning. Are you willing to undertake this for us? I assure you we shall not forget the service."

When Shirley finally hung up the receiver and looked about the little country drug store in wonder at herself the very bottles on the shelves seemed to be whirling and dancing about before her eyes. What strange exciting things were happening to her all in such breathless haste! Only one day at the shore and a piece of another, and here she was with a trip to Washington on her hands! It certainly was bewildering to have things come in such rapid succession. She wished it had come at another time, and not just now when she had not yet got used to the great sea and the wonder of the beautiful place where they were staying. She did not want to be interrupted just yet. It would not be quite the same when she got back to it she was afraid. But of course she could not refuse. It never entered her head to refuse. She knew enough about the office to realize that Mr. Barnard must have her. Jimmie Thorpe would have been the one to go if he were available, because he was a man and had been with Barnard and Clegg for ten years and knew all their most confidential business, but of course Jimmie could not go with his father lying dead and his mother and invalid sister needing him; and there was no one else but herself.

She thought it all out on the way back to the cottage, with a little pang at the thought of losing the next day and of having perhaps to stay over in Washington a day and maybe miss the arrival of Sidney Graham, if he should come in a day or two, as he had promised. He might even come and go back again before she was able to return, and perhaps he would think her ungrateful to leave when he had been so kind to plan all this lovely vacation for her pleasure. Then she brought herself up smartly and told herself decidedly that it was nothing to him whether she was there or not, and it certainly had no right to be anything to her. It was a good thing she was going, and would probably be a good thing for all concerned if she stayed until he went back to the city again.

With this firm determination she hurried up to the veranda where her mother sat with Doris, and told her story.

Mrs. Hollister looked troubled.

"I'm sorry you gave him an answer, Shirley, without waiting to talk it over with me. I don't believe I like the idea of your going to a strange city, all alone that way. Of course Mr. Barnard will look after you in a way, but still he's a good deal of a stranger. I do wish he had let you alone for your vacation. It seems as if he might have found somebody else to go. I wish Mr. Graham was here. I shouldn't wonder if he would suggest some way out of it for you."

But Shirley stiffened into dignity at once.

"Really, mother dear, I'm sure I don't see what Mr. Graham would have to say about it if he were here. I shouldn't ask his advice. You see, mother, really, there isn't anybody else that could do this but Jimmie Thorpe, and he's out of the question. It would be unthinkable that I should refuse in this emergency. And you know Mr. Barnard has been very kind. Besides, think of the ducky vacation I'll have afterward, a whole month! And all that extra money! That shall go to the rent of a better house for winter! Think of it! Don't you worry, mother dear! There isn't a thing in the world could happen to me. I'll be the very most-discreetest person you ever heard of. I'll even glance shyly at the White House and Capitol! Come, let's go up and get dolled up for supper! Won't the children be surprised when they hear I'm really to go to Washington! I'm so excited I don't know what to do!"

Mrs. Hollister said no more, and entered pleasantly into the merry talk at the table, telling Shirley what she must be sure to see at the nation's capital. But the next morning just as Shirley was about to leave for the station, escorted by all the children, Mrs. Hollister came with a package of addressed postal cards which she had made George get for her the night before, and put them in Shirley's bag.

"Just drop us a line as you go along, dear," she said. "I'll feel happier about it to be hearing from you. Mail one whenever you have a chance."

Shirley laughed as she looked at the fat package.

"All those, mother dear? You must expect I am going to stay a month! You know I won't have much time for writing, and I fully expect to be back to-night or to-morrow at the latest."

"Well, that's all right," said her mother. "You can use them another time, then; but you can just put a line on one whenever it is convenient. I shall enjoy getting them even after you get back. You know this is your first journey out into the world alone."

Shirley stooped to kiss the little mother.

"All right, dear! I'll write you a serial story. Each one continued in our next. Good-by! Don't take too long a walk to-day. I want you rested to hear all I'll have to tell when I get back to-night!"

Shirley wrote the first postal card as soon as she was settled in the train, describing the other occupants of the car, and making a vivid picture of the landscape that was slipping by her windows. She wrote the second in the Baltimore station, after she had met Mr. Barnard, while he went to get seats in the parlor car, and she mailed them both at Baltimore.

The third was written as they neared Washington, with the dim vision of the great monument dawning on her wondering sight in the distance. Her last sentence gave her first impression of the nation's capital.

They had eaten lunch in the dining car, a wonderful experience to the girl, and she promised herself another

191

postal devoted to that, but there was no time to write more after they reached Washington. She was put into a taxi and whirled away to an office where her work began. She caught glimpses of great buildings on the way, and gazed with awe at the dome of the Capitol building. Mr. Barnard was kind and pointed out this and that, but it was plain his mind was on the coming interview. When Shirley sat at last in a quiet corner of a big dark office, her pen poised, her note-book ready for work, and looked at the serious faces of the men in the room, she felt as if she had been rushed through a treasure vault of glorious jewels and thrust into the darkness of a tomb. But presently the talk about her interested her. Things were being said about the vital interests of the country, scraps of sentences that reminded her of the trend of talk in the daily papers, and the headings of front columns. She looked about her with interest and noted the familiarity with which these men quoted the words of those high up in authority in the government. With awe she began her work, taking down whatever Mr. Barnard dictated, her fingers flying over the tiny pages of the note-book, in small neat characters, keeping pace with the voices going on about her. The detail work she was setting down was not of especial interest to her, save that it was concerned with Government work, for its phraseology was familiar and a part of her daily routine office work at home; but she set every sense on the alert to get the tiniest detail and not to make the smallest mistake, understanding from the voices of the men about her that it was of vital interest to the country that this order should be filled quickly and accurately. As she capped her fountain pen, and slipped the rubber band on her note-book when it was over, she heard one of the men just behind her say in a low tone to Mr. Barnard:

"You're sure of your secretary of course? I just want to give you the tip that this thing is being very closely watched. We have reason to believe there's some spying planned. Keep your notes carefully and don't let too many in on this. We know pretty well what's going on, but it's not desirable just now to make any arrests until we can watch a little longer and round up the whole party. So keep your eyes peeled, and don't talk."

"Oh, certainly! I quite understand," said Mr. Barnard, "and I have a most discreet secretary," and he glanced with a significant smile toward Shirley as she rose.

"Of course!" said the other. "She looks it," and he bowed deferentially to Shirley as she passed.

She did not think of it at the time, but afterwards she recalled how in acknowledging his courtesy she had stepped back a little and almost stumbled over a page, a boy about George's age, who had been standing withdrawn into the shadow of the deep window. She remembered he had a keen intelligent look, and had apologized and vanished immediately. A moment later it seemed to be the same boy in blue clothes and gilt buttons who held the outer door open for them to pass out—or was this a taller one? She glanced again at his side face with a lingering thought of George as she paused to fasten her glove and slip her note-book into her hand-bag.

"I think I will put you into the taxi and let you go right back to the station while I attend to another errand over at the War Department. It won't take me long. We can easily catch that four-o'clock train back. I suppose you are anxious to get back to-night?"

"Oh, yes," said Shirley earnestly, "I must, if possible. Mother isn't well and she worries so easily."

"Well, I don't know why we can't. Then perhaps you can come up to town to-morrow and type those notes for us. By the way, I guess it would be better for me to take them and lock them in the safe to-night. No, don't stop to get them out now"—as Shirley began to unfasten her bag and get the note-book out—"We haven't much time if we want to catch that train. Just look after them carefully and I'll get them when we are on the train."

He helped her into the taxi, gave the order, "To the station," and touching his hat, went rapidly over to the War Department Building. No one saw a boy with a blue cap and brass buttons steal forth on a bicycle from the court just below the office, and circling about the asphalt uncertainly for a moment, shoot off across the park.

Shirley sat up very straight and kept her eyes about her. She was glad they were taking another way to the station so that she might see more. When she got there she would write another postal and perhaps it would go on the same train with her.

It was all too short, that ride up Pennsylvania Avenue and around by the Capitol. Shirley gathered up her bag and prepared to get out reluctantly. She wished she might have just one more hour to go about, but of course that would be impossible if she wished to reach home to-night.

But before the driver of the car could get down and open the door for her to get out a boy with a bicycle slid up to the curb and touching his gilt-buttoned cap respectfully said:

"Excuse me, Miss, but Mr. Barnard sent me after you. He says there's been some mistake and you'll have to come back and get it corrected."

"Oh!" said Shirley, too surprised to think for a minute. "Oh! Then please hurry, for Mr. Barnard wants to get back in time to get that four-o'clock train."

The driver frowned, but the boy stepped up and handed him something, saying:

"That's all right, Joe, he sent you this." The driver's face cleared and he started his machine again. The boy vanished into the throng. It was another of Shirley's after-memories that she had caught a glimpse of a scrap of paper along with the money the boy had handed the driver, and that he had stuffed it in his pocket after looking intently at it; but at the time she thought nothing of it. She was only glad that they were skimming along rapidly.

CHAPTER XXII

SHIRLEY's sense of direction had always been keen. Even as a child she could tell her way home when others were lost. It was some minutes, however, before she suddenly became aware that the car was being driven in an entirely different direction from the place she had just left Mr. Barnard. For a moment she looked around puzzled, thinking the man was merely taking another way around, but a glance back where the white dome of the Capitol loomed, palace-like, above the city, made her sure that something was wrong. She looked at the buildings they were passing, at the names of the streets—F Street—they had not been on that before! These stores and tall buildings were all new to her eyes. Down there at the end of the vista was a great building all columns. Was that the Treasury and were they merely seeing it from another angle? It was all very confusing, but the time was short, why had the man not taken the shorter way?

She looked at her small wrist watch anxiously and watched eagerly for the end of the street. But before the great building was reached the car suddenly curved around a corner to the right,—one block,—a turn to the left,—another turn,—a confusion of new names and streets! New York Avenue! Connecticut Avenue! Thomas Circle! The names spun by so fast she could read but few of them, and those she saw she wanted to remember that she might weave them into her next postal. She opened her bag, fumbled for her little silver pencil in the pocket of her coat and scribbled down the names she could read as she passed, on the back of the bundle of postal cards, and without looking at her writing. She did not wish to miss a single sight. Here were rows of homes, pleasant and palatial, some of them even cozy. The broad avenues were enchanting, the park spaces, the lavish scattering of noble statues. But the time was hastening by and they were going farther and farther from the station and from the direction of the offices where she had been. She twisted her neck once more and the Capitol dome loomed soft and blended in the distance. A thought of alarm leaped into her mind. She leaned forward and spoke to the driver:

"You understood, didn't you, that I am to return to the office where you took me with the gentleman?"

The man nodded.

"All right, lady. Yes, lady!" And the car rushed on, leaping out upon the beautiful way and disclosing new beauties ahead. For a few minutes more Shirley was distracted from her anxiety in wondering whether the great buildings on her right belonged to any of the embassies or not. And then as the car swerved and plunged into another street and darted into a less thickly populated district, with trees and vacant lots almost like the country, alarm arose once more and she looked wildly back and tried to see the signs, but they were going faster still now upon a wide empty road past stretches of park, with winding drives and charming views, and a great stone bridge to the right, arching over a deep ravine below, a railroad crossing it. There were deer parks fenced with high wire, and filled with the pretty creatures. Everything went by so fast that Shirley hardly realized that something really must be wrong before she seemed to be in the midst of a strange world aloof.

"I am sure you have made a mistake!" The girl's clear voice cut through the driving wind as they rushed along. "I must go back right away to that office from which you brought me. I must go *at once* or I shall be too late for my train! The gentleman will be very angry!" She spoke in the tone that always brought instant obedience from the employees around the office building at home.

But the driver was stolid. He scarcely stirred in his seat to turn toward her. His thick voice was brought back to her on the breeze:

"No, lady, it's all right, lady! I had my orders, lady! You needn't to worry. I get you there plenty time."

A wild fear seized Shirley, and her heart lifted itself as was its habit, to God. "Oh, my Father! Take care of me! Help me! Show me what to do!" she cried.

Thoughts rushed through her brain as fast as the car rushed over the ground. What was she up against? Was this man crazy or bad? Was he perhaps trying to kidnap her? What for? She shuddered to look the thought in the face. Or was it the notes? She remembered the men in the office and what they had said

196

about keeping still and "spying-enemies." But perhaps she was mistaken. Maybe this man was only stupid, and it would all come out right in a few minutes. But no, she must not wait for anything like that. She must take no chance. The notes were in her keeping. She must put them where they would be safe. No telling how soon she would be overpowered and searched if that was what they were after. She must hide them, and she must think of some way to send word to Mr. Barnard before it was too late. No telling what moment they would turn from the main road and she be hidden far from human habitation. She must work fast. What could she do? Scream to the next passer-by? No, for the car was going too fast for that to do any good, and the houses up this way seemed all to be isolated, and few people about. There were houses on ahead beyond the park. She must have something ready to throw out when they came to them. "Oh God! Help me think what to do!" she prayed again, and then looking down at her bag she saw the postal cards. Just the thing! Quickly she scribbled, still holding her hand within the bag so that her movements were not noticeable:

"Help! Quick! Being carried off! Auto! Connecticut Ave.! Park. Deer. Stone bridge. Phone Mr. Clegg. Don't tell mother! Shirley."

She turned the card over, drew a line through her mother's name and wrote Carol's in its place. Stealthily she slipped the card up her sleeve, dropped her hand carelessly over the side of the car for a moment, let the card flutter from her fingers, and wrote another.

She had written three cards and dropped them in front of houses before it suddenly occurred to her that even if these cards should be picked up and mailed it would be sometime before they reached their destination and far too late for help to reach her in time. Her heart suddenly went down in a swooning sickness and her breath almost went from her. Her head was reeling, and all the time she was trying to tell herself that she was exaggerating this thing, that probably the man would slow up or something and it would all be explained. Yes, he was slowing up, but for what? It was in another lonely spot, and out from the bushes there appeared, as if by magic, another man, a queer-looking man with a heavy mustache that looked as if it didn't belong to him. He stood alertly waiting for the car and sprang into the front seat without waiting for it to stop, or even glancing back at her, and the car shot forward again with great leaps.

Shirley dropped out the two cards together that she had just written and leaned forward, touching the newcomer on the arm.

"Won't you please make this driver understand that he is taking me to the wrong place?" she said with a pleasant smile. "I must get back to an office two or three blocks away from the Treasury Building somewhere. I must turn back at once or I shall miss my appointment and be late for my train. It is quite important. Tell him, please, I will pay him well if he will get me back at once."

The stranger turned with an oily smile.

"That's all right, Miss. He isn't making any mistake. We're taking you right to Secretary Baker's country home. He sent for your man, Mr. —— What's his name? I forget. Barnard? Oh, yes. He sent for Mr. Barnard to come out there, sent his private car down for him; and Mr. Barnard, he left orders we should go after you and bring you along. It's something they want to change in those notes you was taking. There was a mistake, and the Secretary he wanted to look after the matter himself."

Shirley sat back with a sudden feeling of weakness and a fear she might faint, although she had never done such a thing in her life. She was not deceived for an instant now, although she saw at once that she must not let the man know it. The idea that Secretary Baker would pause in the midst of his multiplicity of duties to look into the details of a small article of manufacture was ridiculous! It was equally impossible that Mr. Barnard would have sent strangers after her and let her be carried off in this queer way. He had been most particular that she should be looked after carefully. She was horribly to blame that she had allowed herself to be carried back at all until Mr. Barnard himself appeared; and yet, was she? That surely had been the page from the office who came with the message? Well, never mind, she was in for it now, and she must do her best while there was any chance to do anything. She must drop all those postals somehow, and she must hide those notes somewhere, and perhaps write some others,—fake ones. What should she do first?

"Father, help me! Show me! Oh, don't let me lose the notes! Please take care of me!" Again and again her heart prayed as her hand worked stealthily in her bag, while she tried to put a pleasant smile upon her face and pretend she was still deceived, leaning forward and speaking to the strange man once more:

"Is Secretary Baker's home much farther from here?" she asked, feeling her lips draw stiffly in the frozen smile she forced. "Will it take long?"

" 'Bout ten minutes!" the man answered graciously, with a peculiar look toward the driver. "Nice view 'round here!" he added affably with a leering look of admiration toward her.

Shirley's heart stood still with new fear, but she managed to make her white lips smile again and murmur, "Charming!"

Then she leaned back again and fussed around in her bag, ostentatiously bringing out a clean handkerchief, though she really had been detaching the pages which contained the notes from her loose-leaf notebook. There were not many of them, for she always wrote closely in small characters. But where should she hide them? Pull the lining away from the edge of her bag and slip them inside? No, for the bag would be the first place they would likely search, and she could not poke the lining back smoothly so it would not show. If she should try to drop the tiny pages down her neck inside her blouse, the men would very likely see her. Dared she try to slip the leaves down under the linen robe that lay over her lap and put them inside her shoe? She was wearing plain little black pumps, and the pages would easily go in the soles, three or four in each. Once in they would be well hidden, and they would not rattle and give notice of their presence; but *oh,* what a terrible risk if anything should happen to knock off her shoe, or if they should try to search her! Still she must take some risk and this was the safest risk at hand. She must try it and then write out some fake notes, giving false numbers and sizes, and other phraseology. Or stay! Wasn't there already something written in that book that would answer? Some specifications she had written down for the Tillman-Brooks Company. Yes, she was sure. It wasn't at all for the same articles, nor the same measurements, but only an expert would know that. She leaned down quite naturally to pick up her handkerchief and deftly managed to get five small leaves slipped into her right shoe. It occurred to her that she must keep her keepers deceived, so she asked once more in gracious tones:

"Would it trouble you any to mail a card for me as soon as possible after we arrive? I am afraid my mother will be worried about my delay and she isn't well. I suppose they have a post office out this way."

"Sure, Miss!" said the man again, with another leering smile that made her resolve to have no further conversation than was absolutely necessary. She took out her fountain pen and hurriedly wrote:

"Detained longer than I expected. May not get back to-night. S. H.," and handed the card to the man. He took it and turned it over, all too evidently reading it, and put it in his pocket. Shirley felt that she had made an impression of innocence by the move which so far was good. She put away her fountain pen deliberately, and managed in so doing to manipulate the rest of the leaves of notes into her left shoe. Somehow that gave her a little confidence and she sat back and began to wonder if there was anything more she could do. Those dropped postals were worse than useless, of course. Why had she not written an appeal to whoever picked them up? Suiting the action to the thought she wrote another postal card—her stock was getting low, there were but two more left.

"For Christ's sake send the police to help me! I am being carried off by two strange men! Shirley Hollister."

She marked out the address on the other side and wrote: "To whoever picks this up." She fluttered it to the breeze cautiously; but her heart sank as she realized how little likelihood there was of its being picked up for days perhaps. For who would stop in a car to notice a bit of paper on the road? And there seemed to be but few pedestrians. If she only had something larger, more attractive. She glanced at her belongings and suddenly remembered the book she had brought with her to read, one of the new novels from the cottage, a goodly sized volume in a bright red cover. The very thing!

With a cautious glance at her keepers she took up the book as if to read, and opening it at the flyleaf began to write surreptitiously much the same message that had been on her last postal, signing her name and home address and giving her employers' address. Her heart was beating wildly when she had finished. She was trying to think just how she should use this last bit of ammunition to the best advantage. Should she just drop it in the road quietly? If only there were some way to fasten the pages open so her message would be read! Her handkerchief! Of course! She folded it cornerwise and slipped it in across the pages so that the book would fall open at the fly leaf, knotting the ends on the back of the cover. Every moment had to be cautious, and she must remember to keep her attitude of reading with the printed pages covering the handkerchief. It seemed hours that it took her, her fingers trembled so. If it had not been for the rushing noise of wind and car she would not have dared so much undiscovered, but apparently her captors were satisfied that she still believed their story about going to Secretary Baker's country house, for they seemed mainly occupied in watching to see if they were pursued, casting anxious glances back now and then, but scarcely noticing her at all.

Shirley had noticed two or three times when a car had passed them that the men both leaned down to do something at their feet to the machinery of the car. Were they afraid of being recognized? Would this perhaps give her a chance to fling her book out where it would be seen by people in an oncoming car? Oh, if she but had the strength and skill to fling it *into* a car. But of course that was impossible without attracting the attention of the two men. Nevertheless, she must try what she could do.

She lifted her eyes to the road ahead and lo, a big car was bearing down upon them! She had almost despaired of meeting any more, for the road was growing more and more lonely and they must have come many miles. As soon as the two men in front of her sighted the car, they seemed to settle in their seats and draw their hats down a little farther over their eyes. The same trouble seemed to develop with the machinery at their feet that Shirley had noticed before, and they bobbed and ducked and seemed to be wholly engrossed with their own affairs.

Shirley's heart was beating so fast that it seemed as though it would suffocate her, and her hand seemed powerless as it lay innocently holding the closed book with the knotted handkerchief turned down out of sight; but she was girding herself, nerving herself for one great last effort, and praying to be guided.

The big car came on swiftly and was about to pass, when Shirley half rose and hurled her book straight at it and then sank back in her seat with a fearful terror upon her, closing her eyes for one brief second, not daring to watch the results of her act,—if there were to be any results.

The men in the front seat suddenly straightened up and looked around.

"What's the matter?" growled the man who had got in last in quite a different tone from any he had used before. "What you tryin' to put over on us?"

Shirley gasped and caught at her self-control.

"I've dropped my book," she stammered out wildly. "Could you stop long enough to pick it up? It was borrowed!" she ended sweetly as if by inspiration, and wondering at the steadiness of her tone when blood was pounding so in her throat and ears, and everything was black before her. Perhaps—oh, perhaps they would stop and she could cry out to the people for help.

The man rose up in his seat and looked back. Shirley cast one frightened glance back, too, and saw in that brief second that the other car had stopped and someone was standing up and looking back.

"Hell! No!" said her captor briefly, ducking down in his seat. *"Let her out!"* he howled to the driver, and the car broke into a galloping streak, the wheels hardly seeming to touch the ground, the tonneau bounding and swaying this way and that. Shirley had all she could do to keep in her seat. At one moment she thought how easy it would be to spring from the car and lie in a little still heap at the roadside. But there were the notes! She must not abandon her trust even for so fearful an escape from her captors. Suddenly, without warning, they turned a sharp curve and struck into a rough, almost unbroken road into the woods, and the thick growth seemed to close in behind them and shut them out from the world.

Shirley shut her eyes and prayed.

CHAPTER XXIII

THE next trolley that passed the old barn after the Hollisters had left brought a maid servant and a man servant from the Graham place. The other old servant met them, and together the three went to work. They had brought with them a lot of large dust-covers and floor-spreads such as are used by housemaids in cleaning a room, and with these they now proceeded to cover all the large pieces of furniture in the place. In a very short space of time the rugs and bits of carpet were carefully rolled up, the furniture piled in small compass in the middle of the rooms, and everything enveloped in thick coverings. The curtains, bric-à-brac, and even the dishes were put away carefully, and the whole big, inviting home was suddenly denuded. The clothes from the calico-curtained clothes-presses were folded and laid in drawers, and everything made perfectly safe for a lot of workmen to come into the house. Even the hay-loft bedrooms shared in this process. Only a cot was left for the old servant and a few necessary things for him to use, and most of these he transported to the basement out of the way. When the work was done the man and maid took the trolley back home again and the other old man servant arranged to make

his Sabbath as pleasant as possible in the company of
his brother from the near-by farm.

Monday morning promptly at eight o'clock the trolley landed a bevy of workmen, carpenters, plasterers, plumbers, and furnace men, with a foreman who
set them all at work as if it were a puzzle he had
studied out and memorized the solution. In a short time
the quiet spot was full of sound, the symphony of in-
dustry, the rhythm of toil. Some men were working
away with the furnace that had been stored in the cellar; others were measuring, fitting, cutting holes for
lead pipes; still others were sawing away at the roof,
making great gashes in its mossy extent; and two men
were busy taking down the old barn door. Out in
front more men were building a vat for mortar, and
opening bags of lime and sand that began to arrive.
Three men with curious aprons made of ticking, filled
with thin wire nails, were frantically putting laths on
the uprights that the carpenters had already set up, and
stabbing them with nails from a seemingly inexhaus-
tible supply in their mouths. It was as if they had all
engaged to build the tower of Babel in a day, and
meant to win a prize at it. Such sounds! Such shoutings,
such bangings, thumpings, and harsh, raucous noises!
The bird in the tall tree looked and shivered, thankful
that her brood were well away on their wings before
all this cataclysm came to pass.

Presently arrived a load of sashes, doors, and wood-
en frames, and another load of lumber. Things can be
done in a hurry if you have money and influence and
the will to insist upon what you want. Before night
there was a good start made toward big changes in
the old barn.

Plumbers and gas-fitters and men who were putting
in the hot-water heat chased one another around the
place, each man seeking to get his pipes in place before the lathers got to that spot; and the contractor
was everywhere, proving his right to be selected for
this rush job. As soon as the lathers had finished with a
room the plasterers took possession, and the old door
was rapidly being replaced with a great glazed door set

in a frame of more sashes, so that the old darkness was gone entirely.

In the roof big dormer windows were taking the place of the two or three little eyebrow affairs that had given air to the hay heretofore, and the loft was fast becoming pleasanter than the floor below.

Outside laborers were busy building up a terrace, where a wide cement-floor piazza with stone foundations and low stone walls was to run across the entire front. Another chimney was rising from the region of the kitchen. A white enamel sink with a wide drainshelf attached appeared next, with signs of a butler's pantry between kitchen and dining-room. A delightful set of china-closet doors with little diamond panes that matched the windows was put in one corner of the dining-room, and some bookcases with sliding doors began to develop along the walls of the living-room. Down in the basement a man was fitting stationary tubs for a laundry, and on both the first floor and the second bathrooms were being made. If the place hadn't been so big, the workmen would have got in one another's way. Closets big and little were being put in, and parts of a handsome staircase were lying about, until you wouldn't know the place at all. Every evening the old servant and the neighbor next door, who used to rent the old barn before he built his own new one, came together to look over what had been accomplished during the day, and to discourse upon this changing world and the wonders of it. The farmer, in fact, learned a great deal about modern improvements, and at once set about bringing some of them to bear upon his own modest farmhouse. He had money in the bank, and why shouldn't he "have things convenient for Sally"?

When Sidney Graham reached the city on Monday morning he scarcely took time to read his mail in the office and give the necessary attention to the day's work before he was up and off again, flying along the Glenside Road as fast as his car would carry him. His mind certainly was not on business that morning. He was as eager as a child to see how work at the old barn was

205

progressing, and the workmen stood small chance of lying down on their job that week, for he meant to make every minute count, no matter how much it cost. He spent a large part of Monday hovering about the old barn, gloating over each new sign of progress, using his imagination on more things than the barn. But when Tuesday arrived an accumulation of work at the office in connection with a large order that had just come in kept him close to his desk. He had hoped to get away in time to reach Glenside before the workmen left in the afternoon, but four o'clock arrived with still a great pile of letters for him to sign, before his work would be done for the day.

He had just signed his name for the forty-ninth time and laid his pen down with an impatient sigh of relief when the telephone on his desk rang. He hesitated. Should he answer it and be hindered again, or call his secretary and let her attend to it while he slipped away to his well-earned respite? A second insistent ring, however, brought him back to duty and he reached out and took up the receiver.

"Is this Mr. Sidney Graham? Long distance is calling!"

The young man frowned impatiently and wished he had sent for his secretary. It was probably another tiresome confab on that Chicago matter, and it really wasn't worth the trouble, anyway. Then a small scared voice at the other end of the wire spoke:

"Is that you, Mr. Graham? Well, this is Carol. Say, Mr. Graham, I'm afraid something awful has happened to Shirley! I don't know what to do, and I thought I'd better ask you." Her voice broke off in a gasp like a sob.

A cold chill struck at the young man's heart, and a vision of Shirley battling with the ocean waves was instantly conjured up.

"Shirley! Where is she? Tell me, quick!" he managed to say, though the words seemed to stick in his throat.

"She's down at Washington," answered Carol. "Mr. Barnard phoned her last night. There was something special nobody else could take notes about, because it was for a Government contract, and has to be secret. Mr. Barnard asked her to please go and she went this morning. Mother didn't like her to go, but she addressed a lot of postal cards for her to write back, and one came postmarked Baltimore in this afternoon's mail, saying she was having a nice time. But just now a call came for mother to go to the telephone. She was asleep and George was crabbing so I had to come. It was a strange man in Washington. He said he had just found three postal cards on the road addressed to mother, that all said 'Help! Quick! Two men were carrying off Shirley and please to phone to the police.' He took the postals to the police station, but he thought he ought to phone us. And oh, Mr. Graham, *what shall I do?* I can't tell mother. It will kill her, and how can we help Shirley?"

"Don't tell mother," said Graham quickly, trying to speak calmly out of his horror. "Be a brave girl, Carol. A great deal depends on you just now. Have you phoned Mr. Barnard? Oh, you say he's in Washington? He was to meet your sister in Baltimore? He *did* meet her you say? The postal card said she had met him? Well, the next thing is to phone Mr. Clegg and find out if he knows anything. I'll do that at once, and unless he has heard that she is all right I will start for Washington on the next train. Suppose you stay right where you are till half-past five. I may want to call you up again and need you in a hurry. Then you go back to the cottage as fast as you can and talk cheerfully. Say you went to take a walk. Isn't Elizabeth with you? Well, tell her to help keep your mother from suspecting anything. Above all things don't cry! It won't do any good and it may do lots of harm. Get George off by himself and tell him everything, and tell him I said he was to make some excuse to go down town after supper and stay at the telephone office till ten o'clock. I may want to call him up from Washington. Now be a brave little girl. I suspect your sister Shirley would tell you to pray. Good-by."

"I will!" gasped Carol. "Good-by!"

Graham pressed his foot on the bell under his desk and reached out to slam his desk drawers shut and put away his papers. His secretary appeared at the door.

"Get me Barnard and Clegg on the phone! Ask for Mr. Barnard or, if he isn't in, Mr. Clegg. Then go out to the other phone and call up the station. Find out what's the next express to Washington. Tell Bromwell to be ready to drive me to the station and bring my car back to the garage."

He was working rapidly as he talked; putting papers in the safe, jotting down a few notes for the next day's work, trying to think of everything at once. The secretary handed him the phone, quietly saying, "Mr. Clegg on the phone," and went out of the room.

Excited conference with Mr. Clegg brought out the fact that he was but just in receipt of a telegram from Police Headquarters in Washington saying that a book with Barnard and Clegg's address and an appeal from a young woman named Shirley Hollister who was apparently being kidnapped by two strange men in an auto, had been flung into a passing car and brought to them. They had sent forces in search of the girl at once and would do all in their power to find her. Meantime they would like any information that would be helpful in the search.

Mr. Clegg was much excited. He appeared to have lost his head. He seemed glad to have another cooler mind at work on the case. He spluttered a good deal about the importance of the case and the necessity for secrecy. He said he hoped it wouldn't get into the papers, and that it would be Barnard and Clegg's undoing if it did. He seemed more concerned about that and the notes that Shirley probably had, than about the girl's situation. When Graham brought him up rather sharply he admitted that there had been a message from Barnard that he would be detained over night probably, but he had attached no significance to that. He knew Barnard's usual hotel address in Washington but hadn't thought to phone him about the telegram from police headquarters. Graham hung up at last in a panic of fury and dismay, ringing violently for his secretary again.

"The next train leaves at five o'clock," she said

capably, as she entered. "Bromwell has gone after the car. I told him to buy you a mileage book and save your time at this end. You have forty minutes and he will be back in plenty of time."

"Good!" said Graham. "Now call up long distance and get me Police Headquarters in Washington. No! Use the phone in father's office please, I'll have to use this while you're getting them."

As soon as she had left the room he called up the shore again and was fortunate in getting Carol almost immediately, the poor child being close at hand all in a tremble, with Elizabeth in no less a state of nervousness, brave and white, waiting for orders.

"Can you give me an exact description of your sister's dress, and everything that she had with her when she started this morning?" asked Graham, prepared with pen and paper to write it down.

Carol summoned her wits and described Shirley's simple outfit exactly, even down to the little black pumps on her feet, and went mentally through the small hand-bag she had carried.

"Oh, yes!" she added, "and she had a book to read! One she found here in the cottage. It had a red cover and was called, "From the Car Behind.""

Graham wrote them all down carefully, asked a few more details of Shirley's plans, and bade Carol again to be brave and go home with a message to George to be at the phone from half-past eight to ten.

He was all ready to go to his train when the Washington call came in, and as he hurried to his father's office to answer it he found his heart crying out to an Unseen Power to help in this trying hour and protect the sweet girl in awful peril.

"Oh, God, I love her!" he found his heart saying over and over again, as if it had started out to be an individual by itself without his will or volition.

There was no comfort from Washington Police Headquarters. Nothing more had been discovered save another crumpled postal lying along the roadside. They received with alacrity, however, Mr. Barnard's Washington hotel address, and the description of the young woman and her belongings. When Graham had finished the hasty conversation he had to fly to make his train, and when at last he lay back in his seat in the parlor car and let the waves of his anxiety and trouble roll over him he was almost overwhelmed. He had led a comparatively tranquil life for a young man who had never tried to steer clear of trouble, and this was the first great calamity that had ever come his way. Calamity? No, he would not own yet that it was a calamity. He was hurrying to her! He would find her! He would not allow himself to think that anything had befallen her. But wherever she was, if she was still alive, no matter how great her peril, he was sure she was praying now, and he would pray too! Yes, pray as she had taught him. Oh, God! If he only knew how to pray better! What was it she had said so often? "Whatsoever ye ask in my name"—yes, that was it—"I will do it." What *was* that talismanic Name? Ah! Christ! "Oh, God, in the name of Christ—" But when he came to the thought of her she was too exquisite and dear to be put into words, so his petition went up in spirit form, unframed by words to weight it down, wafted up by the pain of a soul in torture.

At Baltimore it occurred to Graham to send a telegram to Barnard to meet him at the train, and when he got out at Union Station the first person he saw was Barnard, white and haggard, looking for him through the bars of the train gate. He grasped the young man's hand as if it were a last straw for a drowning man to cling to, and demanded in a shaking voice to know if he had heard anything from Miss Hollister.

One of the first questions that Graham asked was whether Barnard had been back to the office where Miss Hollister had taken the dictation, to report her disappearance.

"Well, no, I hadn't thought of that," said Barnard blankly. "What would they know about it? The fact is I was rather anxious to keep the facts from getting to them. You see they warned me that there were parties anxious to get hold of those specifications. It's Government work, you know."

"They should know at once," said Graham sternly. "They may have inside information which would give us a clew to follow. The secret service men are onto a lot of things that we common mortals don't suspect."

Mr. Barnard looked mortified and convinced.

"Well, what *have* you done so far? We would better understand each other thoroughly so as to save time and not go over old ground. You have been in communication with Police Headquarters, of course?" asked Graham.

"Why, no," said the older man apologetically. "You see, I got here just in time for the train, and failing to find the young lady in the station where we had agreed to meet, I took it for granted that she had used the extra time in driving about to see a few sights in the city, as I suggested, and had somehow failed to get back in time. I couldn't understand it because she had been quite anxious to get home to-night. I could have caught the train myself, but didn't exactly like to leave her alone in a strange city, though, of course, it's perfectly safe for a steady girl like that. Afterward it occurred to me that she might have gotten on the train and perhaps I should have done so too, but there was really very little time to decide, for the train pulled out two minutes after I reached the station. I waited about here for a time, and then went over to the Continental, where my sister is stopping, thinking I would ask her to stay in the station and watch for the young lady and I would go home; but I found my sister had run down to the shore for a few days; so I had something to eat and while I was in the dining-room your telegram came. I was hoping somehow you had seen Miss Hollister, or had word from her, and it was all right."

One could see the poor man had no conception of what was due to a lady in his care, and Graham looked at him for a moment with rage, wishing he could take him by the throat and shake some sense into him.

"Then you don't know that she's been kidnapped and the police are out on track for her?" said Graham dryly.

"No! You don't say!" exclaimed Barnard, turning white and showing he had some real feeling after all. "Kidnapped! Why—why—how *could* she? And she's got *those notes!* Why, Graham! You're fooling! Why, how came you to know?"

Graham told him tersely as he walked the man over to the telephone booths, and finished with:

"Now, you go in that booth and phone your Government man, and I'll call up police headquarters and see what's doing. We've got to work fast, for there's no telling what may have happened in the last three hours. It's up to us to find that girl before anything worse happens to her."

White and trembling Barnard tottered into the booth. When he came out again the slouth-hounds of the Secret Service were on the trail of Shirley Hollister's captors.

CHAPTER XXIV

THE car that was bearing Shirley Hollister through the lonely wooded road at a breathless speed suddenly came to a halt in the rear of an old house whose front faced on another road equally lonely. During the brief time that they had been in the woods, the sky seemed to have perceptibly darkened with the coming evening.

Shirley looked about her with increased fright. It was almost night and here was her prison, far from town or human dwelling place. Even the road was at some distance in front of the house, and there were more woods on either side.

"This here is Secretary Baker's summer home," announced the man who had done the talking, as he climbed out of the car and opened the door for her. "You can just step in the back door and go through to the parlor; the help's all out this afternoon. The Secretary'll be down presently. He always takes a nap afternoons about this time. I'll tell him you've come."

There seemed nothing to do but obey, and Shirley chose to let the farce continue. Surely the man must know she was not a fool, but it was better than open hostility. There was nothing to be gained by informing him that she knew he was guying her.

"Oh, Jesus Christ, I trust myself to you!" she breathed in her heart as she stepped across the leaf-strewn grass and looked about her, wondering whether she should ever walk the earth again after she had stepped into the dim tree-shrouded house. But why go in?

"I think I will remain out here," she said calmly, albeit her heart was pounding away like a trip-hammer. "Please tell Mr. Baker to come to me here. It is much pleasanter than in the house a day like this."

"Aw no! You won't neither! The Secretary don't receive in the open air even in summer," drawled the man and she noticed that he and the driver straightened up and stepped closer to her, one on either side. She gave one wild glance toward the open space. There was simply no chance at all to run away even if she succeeded in eluding them at the start by a quick, unexpected dash. They were alert athletic men, and no telling how many more were hidden in the house.

"Oh, very well, of course, if it's a matter of etiquette!" said Shirley pleasantly, determined to keep up the farce as long as possible.

A cold, dark air met the girl as she stepped within the creaking door and looked about her. At her left was an old-fashioned kitchen, dusty and cobwebby. A long, narrow hall led to the front of the house and her guide pointed her toward a room on the right. There was something hollow and eerie in the sound of their footsteps on the old oaken floor. The room into which she was ushered was musty and dusty as the rest. The floor was covered with an ancient ingrain carpet. The table was covered with a magenta felt cover stamped with a vine of black leaves and riddled with moth holes. The walls were hung with old prints and steel engravings suspended by woollen cords and tassels. The furniture was dilapidated. Everything was covered with dust, but there were finger marks in the dust here and there that showed the place had been recently visited. Through an open doorway an old square piano was visible in what must be the parlor. The place seemed to Shirley fairly teeming with memories of some family now departed. She leaped to the quick conclusion that the house had been long deserted and had only recently been entered and used as a rendezvous for illegal conferences. It occurred to her that there might be an opportunity for her to hide her precious papers somewhere safely if it came to it that she must be searched. How about that piano? Could she slip some of them between the keys? But it was hardly likely that there would be opportunity for anything like that.

She felt strangely calm as she looked about upon her prison.

"H'm! He ain't come yet!" remarked her guide as he glanced into the front room. "Well, you can set down. He won't be long now. Joe, you jest look about a bit and see if you can find the Secretary, and tell him the young lady is here."

The man flung himself full length on the carpet-covered couch and looked at her with satisfaction.

"What train was that you said you must make? I'm afraid now you might be going to be just a trifle late if he don't get a hustle on, but you can't hurry a great man like that you know."

"Oh, it's no matter!" said Shirley coolly, looking around her with the utmost innocence. "What a quaint old house! Has it been in the family a long time?"

The man looked at her amusedly.

"You're a cute one!" he remarked affably. "I believe you're a pretty good sport! You know perfectly well you're in my power and can't do a turn to help yourself, yet you sail around here as calm as a queen! You're some looker, too! Blamed if I'm not enjoying myself. I wouldn't mind a kiss or two from those pretty lips——"

But Shirley had melted through the doorway into the other room and her voice floated back with charming indifference as if she had not heard, though she was ready to scream with loathing and fear of the man:

"Why, isn't this a delightful old piano? The keys are actually mother-of-pearl. Isn't it odd? Would Mr. Baker mind if I played on it?"

And before her astonished captor could get himself to the doorway she had sat down on the rickety old hair-cloth stool and swept the keys lightly. The old chords trembled and shivered as if awaking from a tomb, and uttered forth a quavering, sweet sound like ancient memories.

The man was too much astonished to stop her, amused too, perhaps, and interested. Her white fingers over the dusty pearls in the growing dusk had a strange charm for the hardened reprobate, like the wonder of a flower dropped into the foulness of a prison. Before he could recover, he was startled again by her voice soaring out in the empty echoing house:

> "Rock of ages, cleft for me,
>   Let me hide myself in Thee;
> Let the water and the blood
>   From Thy riven side which flowed,
> Be of sin the double cure,
>   Save me Lord and make me pure!"

Perhaps those dim, gloomy walls had echoed before to the grand old tune, but never could it have been sung in direr strait, or with more earnest cry from a soul in distress. She had chosen the first words that seemed to fit the chords she had struck, but every syllable was a prayer to the God in whom she trusted. It may be the man felt the power of her appeal as he stood rooted in the doorway and listened while she sang through all the verses she could remember. But the last trembling note was broken harshly by Joe's voice at the kitchen door in sharp, rasping orders:

"Hist, there! Can that noise! Do you want to raise hell here? Wake up, Sam! Get onto your job. Hennie's comin'."

"That's all right, Joe! Dry up! This is good Sunday School dope! This won't rouse no suspicions. Go to the devil and mind your business! I know what I'm about!"

Shirley was almost ready to cry, but she drew a deep breath and started on another song:

"Jesus, Lover of my soul,
  Let me to Thy bosom fly,
While the nearer waters roll,
  While the tempest still is high!
Hide me, oh, my Saviour hide,
  Till the storm of life is past."

On through the time-worn words she sang, while the sin-hardened man stood silently and listened. His eyes had gradually lost their leer and grown soft and tender, as if some childhood memories of home and mother and a time when he was innocent and good were looking out his eyes, reminding him of what he once intended to be before he ate the apple of wisdom and became as the gods and devils. Shirley gradually became aware that she was holding her strange audience; and a power beyond herself steadied her voice, and kept her fingers from trembling on the old pearl keys, as she wandered on from song to song; perhaps happening on the very ones,—who knows?—that this man, standing in the dying twilight of the old gloomy house, had sung beside his mother's hearth or in church during his childhood? Certain it is that he stood there silent and listened for at least half an hour without an interruption, while the light in the big room grew dimmer and dimmer and all about the house seemed still as death in the intervals between her voice.

She was just beginning:

"Abide with me,
  Fast falls the eventide,
The darkness deepens,
  Lord, with me abide!"

when the man put his hand in his pocket and brought out a candle. Scratching a match on his trousers, he lit the candle and set it carefully on the piano, where its light fell flickering, wavering over her worn young face; and who shall say that she was not a messenger from another world to this man who had long trodden the downward path?

They were interrupted, however, before this song was finished by a newcomer who entered like a shadow and stood at the end of the piano looking wonderingly from Shirley to the man, when she glanced up. She stopped, startled, for although he wore no brass buttons nor blue clothes she was quite sure those were the same gray eyes that had looked at her from the recess of the window in the Government office that afternoon, perhaps the same boy who had come after her car and sent her off on this long way into the wilderness.

The man Sam straightened up suddenly and looked about him half-ashamed with an apologetic grin:

"Oh, you've come, have you, Hennie? Well, you been a long time about it! But now I guess we'll get to work. Where's Joe? Out on the watch? All right then, Miss, if you've no objection, we'll just take a little vacation on the psalm singin' and turn our attention to worldly things. I calculate you're sharp enough to know what we brought you out here for? I acknowledge you can sing real well, and you sorta got my goat for a while there with all that mourning bench tra-la, for you certainly have got that holy dope down fine; but now the time's come for business, and you needn't to think that because I can enjoy a little sentiment now and then in a leisure moment that you can put anything over on me, for it can't be did! I mean business and I've got you in my power! We're ten miles from any settlement, and no neighbors anywhere's about. Everybody moved away. So it won't do any good to work any funny business on us. You can't get away. We're all armed, and no one knows where you are! If you behave yourself and do as you're told there won't be any trouble. We'll just transact our business and then we'll have a bit of supper, and mebbe a few more tunes— got any rag-time in your repitwar?—and then sometime after midnight, when the moon's good and dark, we'll get you back to civilization where you won't have no trouble in gettin' home. But if you act up and get funny, why you know what to expect. There was a young girl murdered once in this house and buried in

217

the cellar and ever since folks say it's hanted and they won't come near it. That's the kind of a place we're in! So, now are you ready?"

Shirley sat cold and still. It seemed as if her life blood had suddenly congealed in her veins and for a second she felt as if her senses were going to desert her. Then the echo of her own song: "Hide me, oh, my Saviour hide!" seemed to cry out from her soul silently and she rallied once more and gained her self-control.

"Well, Miss," went on the man impressively, "I see you're ready for the question, and you've got your nerve with you, too, I'll hand you that! But I warn you it won't do no good! We brung you out here to get a hold of that note-book you wrote in this morning, and we're goin' to have it. We know that Mr. Barnard left it in your care. Hennie here heard him say for you to keep it. So it won't be of any use for you to lie about it."

"Of course!" said Shirley, standing up and reaching over for her hand-bag, which she had laid on the piano beside her while she played. "I understand perfectly. But I'd like to ask you a question, Mr. ——?"

"Smith, or Jones, whichever you like to call it. Spit it out!"

"I suppose you are paid to bring me out here, Mr. Smith, and get my property away from me?" she said gravely.

"Well, yes, we don't calculate to do it just for sweet charity."

"And *I* am paid to look after my note-book, you see. It's a trust that has been given me! I just *have* to look after it. It's out of the question for me to desert it!" Shirley spoke coolly and held her little bag close in the firm grasp of her two hands. The man stared at her and laughed. The boy Hennie fairly gaped in his astonishment. "A girl with all that nerve!"

"Of course, I understand perfectly that you can murder me and bury me down in the cellar beside that other girl that was murdered, and perhaps no one will find it out for a while, and you can go on having a good time on the money you will get for it. But the day will come when you will have to answer for it! You know I didn't come here alone to-day——!"

Both men looked startled and glanced uneasily into the shadows, as if there might be someone lurking there.

"*God* came with me and *He* knows! He'll *make you remember* some day!"

The boy laughed out a nervous ha! ha! of relief, but the man seemed held, fascinated by her look and words. There was silence for a second while the girl held off the ruffian in the man by sheer force of her strong personality. Then the boy laughed again, with a sneer in the end of it, and the spell was broken. The leer came into the eyes of the man again. The sneer of the boy had brought him to himself,—to the self he had come to be.

"Nix on the sob-stuff, girlie!" he said gruffly. "It won't go down with me! We're here for business and we've been delayed too long already. Come now, will you hand out that note-book or will we have to search you?" He took one stride across to where she stood and wrenched the hand-bag from her grasp before she was aware of his intention. She had not meant to give it up without a struggle, much as she loathed the thought of one. She must make the matter last as long as possible, if perchance God was sending help to her, and must contest every inch of the way as far as lay in her power. Oh, had anyone picked up her cards? Had the book with its message reached any friendly eye?

Frail and white and stern she stood with folded arms while they turned out the contents of the little bag and scattered it over the piano, searching with clumsy fingers among her dainty things.

The note-book she had rolled within her handkerchiefs and made it hard to find. She feared lest her ruse would be discovered when they looked it over. The boy was the one who clutched for the little book, recognizing it as the one he had seen in the office that morning. The man hung over his shoulder and peered in the candlelight, watching the boy anxiously. It meant a good deal of money if they put this thing through.

"Here it is!" said the boy, fluttering through the leaves and carefully scrutinizing the short-hand characters. "Yes, that's the dope!"

He ran his eye down the pages, caught a word here and there, technicalities of manufacture, the very items, of course, that he wanted, if this had been the specifications for the Government order. Shirley remembered with relief that none of the details were identical, however, with the notes she carried in her shoes. The book-notes were in fact descriptive of an entirely different article from that demanded by the Government. The question was, would these people be wise enough to discover that fact before she was out of their power or not?

Furtively she studied the boy. There was something keen and cunning about his youthful face. He was thick-set, with blond hair and blue eyes. He might be of German origin, though there was not a sign of accent about his speech. He had the bull-dog chin, retreating forehead and eagle nose of the Kaiser in embryo. Shirley saw all this as she studied him furtively. That he was an expert in short-hand was proved by the ease with which he read some of her obscure sentences, translating rapidly here and there as he examined the book. Was he well enough informed about the Government contract to realize that these were not the notes she had taken in the office that morning? And should he fail to recognize it, was there perhaps some one higher in authority to whom they would be shown before she was released? She shivered and set her weary toes tight with determination over the little crinkling papers in her shoes. Somehow she would protect those notes from being taken, even if she had to swallow them. There surely would be a way to hide them if the need came.

Suddenly the tense strain under which she was holding herself was broken by the man. He looked up with a grin, rubbing his hands with evident self-gratulation and relief:

"That's all right, Girlie! That's the dope we want. Now we won't trouble you any longer. We'll have supper. Hennie, you go get some of that wood out in the shed and we'll have a fire on the hearth and make some coffee!"

But Shirley, standing white and tense in the dim shadow of the room, suddenly felt the place whirling about her, and the candle dancing afar off. Her knees gave way beneath her and she dropped back to the piano stool weakly, and covered her face with her hands, pressing hard on her eyeballs; trying to keep her senses and stop this black dizziness that threatened to submerge her consciousness. She must not faint—if this was fainting. She must keep her senses and guard her precious shoes. If one of those should fall off while she was unconscious all would be undone.

CHAPTER XXV

THE man looked up from the paper he was twisting for a fire and saw Shirley's attitude of despair.

"Say, kid," he said, with a kind of gruff tenderness, "you don't need to take it that a-way. I know it's tough luck to lose out when you been so nervy and all, but you knew we had it over you from the start. You hadn't a show. And say! Girlie! I tell you what! I'll make Hennie sit down right now and copy 'em off for you, and you can put 'em in your book again when you get back and nobody be the wiser. We'll just take out the leaves. We gotta keep the original o' course, but that won't make any beans for you. It won't take you no time to write 'em over again if he gives you a copy."

Somehow it penetrated through Shirley's tired consciousness that the man was trying to be kind to her. He was pitying her and offering her a way out of her supposed dilemma, offering to assist her in some of his own kind of deception. The girl was touched even through all her other crowding emotions and weariness. She lifted up her head with a faint little smile.

"Thank you," she said, wearily, "but that wouldn't do me any good."

"Why not?" asked the man sharply. "Your boss would never know it got out through you."

"But *I* should know I had failed!" she said sadly. "If you had my notes I should know that I had failed in my trust."

"It wouldn't be your fault. You couldn't have helped it!"

"Oh, yes, I could, and I ought. I shouldn't have let the driver turn around. I should have got out of that car and waited at the station as Mr. Barnard told me to do till he came. I had been warned and I ought to have been on my guard. So you see it *was* my fault."

She drooped her head forward and rested her chin dejectedly on the palm of her hand, her elbow on her knee. The man stood looking at her for a second in half-indignant astonishment.

"By golly!" he said at last. "You certainly are some nut! Well, anyhow, buck up, and let's have some tea. Sorry I can't see my way clear to help you out any further, being as we're sort of partners in this job and you certainly have got some nerve for a girl, but you know how it is. I guess I can't do no more'n I said. I got my honor to think about, too. See? Hennie! Get a move on you. We ain't waitin' all night fer eats. Bring in them things from the cupboard and let's get to work."

Shirley declined to come to the table when at last the repast was ready. She said she was not hungry. In fact, the smell of the crackers and cheese and pickles and dried beef sickened her. She felt too hysterical to try to eat, and besides she had a lingering feeling that she must keep near that piano. If anything happened she had a vague idea that she might somehow hide the precious notes within the big old instrument.

The man frowned when she declined to come to supper, but a moment later stumbled awkwardly across the room with a slopping cup of coffee and set it down beside her.

"Buck up, girlie!" he growled. "Drink that and you'll feel better."

Shirley thanked him and tried to drink a few mouthfuls. Then the thought occurred to her that it might be drugged, and she swallowed no more. But she tried to look a bit brighter. If she must pass this strange evening in the company of these rough men, it would not help matters for her to give way to despair. So after toying with the teaspoon a moment, she put the cup down and began to play soft airs on the old piano again while the men ate and took a stealthy taste now and then from a black bottle. She watched them furtively as she played, marvelling at their softened expressions, remembering the old line:

"Music hath charms to soothe the savage breast," and wondering if perhaps there were not really something in it. If she had not been in such a terrifying situation she would really have enjoyed the character study that this view of those two faces afforded her, as she sat in the shadow playing softly while they ate with the flaring candle between them.

"I like music with my meals!" suddenly chanted out the boy in an interval. But the man growled in a low tone:

"Shut up! Ain't you got no manners?"

Shirley prolonged that meal as much as music could do it, for she had no relish for a more intimate tête-à-tête with either of her companions. When she saw them grow restless she began to sing again, light little airs this time with catchy words; or old tender melodies of home and mother and childhood. They were songs she had sung that last night in the dear old barn when Sidney Graham and Elizabeth were with them, and unconsciously her voice took on the wail of her heart for all that dear past so far away from her now.

Suddenly, as the last tender note of a song died away Joe stumbled breathlessly into the room. The boy Hennie slithered out of the room like a serpent at his first word.

"Beat it!" he cried in a hoarse whisper. "Get a move on! All hell's out after us! I bet they heard her singin'! Take her an' beat it! I'll douse the fire an' out the candle."

He seized a full bucket of water and dashed it over the dying fire. Shirley felt the other man grasp her arm in a fierce grip. Then Joe snuffed out the candle with his broad thumb and finger and all was pitch dark. She felt herself dragged across the floor regardless of furniture in the way, stumbling, choking with fear, her one thought that whatever happened she must not let her slippers get knocked off; holding her feet in a tense strain with every muscle extended to keep the shoes fastened on like a vise. She was haunted with a wild thought of how she might have slipped under the piano and eluded her captor if only the light had gone out one second sooner before he reached her side. But it was too late to think of that now, and she was being dragged along breathlessly, out the front door, perhaps, and down a walk; no, it was amongst trees, for she almost ran into one. The man swore at her, grasped her arm till he hurt her and she cried out.

"You shut up or I'll shoot you!" he said with an oath. He had lost all his suavity and there was desperation in his voice. He kept turning his head to look back and urging her on.

She tripped on a root and stumbled to her knees, bruising them painfully, but her only thought was one of joy that her shoes had not come off.

The man swore a fearful oath under his breath, then snatched her up and began to run with her in his arms. It was then she heard Graham's voice calling:

"Shirley! Where are you? I'm coming!"

She thought she was swooning or dreaming and that it was not really he, for how could he possibly be here? But she cried out with a voice as clear as a bell: "I'm here, Sidney, come quick!" In his efforts to hush her voice, the man stumbled and fell with her in his arms. There came other voices and forms through the night. She was gathered up in strong, kind arms and held. The last thought she had before she sank into unconsciousness was that God had not forgotten. He had been remembering all the time and sent His help before it was too late; just as she had known all along He must do, because He had promised to care for His own, and she was one of His little ones.

When she came to herself again she was lying in Sidney Graham's arms with her head against his shoulder feeling oh, so comfortable and tired. There were two automobiles with powerful headlights standing between the trees, and a lot of policemen in the shadowy background. Her captor stood sullen against a tree with his hands and feet shackled. Joe stood between two policemen with a rope bound about his body spirally, and the boy Hennie, also bound, beside his fallen bicycle, turned his ferret eyes from side to side as if he hoped even yet to escape. Two other men with hawk-like faces that she had not seen before were there also, manacled, and with eyes of smouldering fires. Climbing excitedly out of one of the big cars came Mr. Barnard, his usually immaculate pink face smutty and weary; his sparse white hair rumpled giddily, and a worried pucker on his kind, prim face.

"Oh, my dear Miss Hollister! How unfortunate!" he exclaimed. "I do hope you haven't suffered too much inconvenience!"

Shirley smiled up at him from her shoulder of refuge as from a dream. It was all so amusing and impossible after what she had been through. It couldn't be real.

"I assure you I am very much distressed on your account," went on Mr. Barnard, politely and hurriedly, "and I hate to mention it at such a time, but could you tell me whether the notes are safe? Did those horrid men get anything away from you?"

A sudden flicker of triumph passed over the faces of the fettered man and the boy, like a ripple over still water and died away into unintelligence.

But Shirley's voice rippled forth in a glad, clear laugh, as she answered joyously:

"Yes, Mr. Barnard, they got my note-book, but not the notes! They thought the Tilman-Brooks notes were what they were after, but the real notes are in my shoes. Won't you please get them out, for I'm afraid I can't hold them on any longer, my feet ache so!"

It is a pity that Shirley was not in a position to see the look of astonishment, followed by a twinkle of actual appreciation that came over the face of the shackled man beside the tree as he listened. One could almost fancy he was saying to himself: "The nervy little nut! She put one over on me after all!"

It was also a pity that Shirley could not have got the full view of the altogether precise and conventional

Mr. Barnard kneeling before her on the ground, removing carefully, with deep embarrassment and concern, first one, then the other, of her little black pumps, extracting the precious notes, counting over the pages and putting them ecstatically into his pocket. No one of that group but Shirley could fully appreciate the ludicrous picture he made.

"You are entirely sure that no one but yourself has seen these notes?" he asked anxiously as if he hardly dared to believe the blessed truth.

"Entirely sure, Mr. Barnard!" said Shirley happily, "and now if you wouldn't mind putting on my shoes again I can relieve Mr. Graham of the necessity of carrying me any further."

"Oh, surely, surely!" said Mr. Barnard, quite fussed and getting down laboriously again, his white forelock all tossed, and his forehead perplexed over the unusual task. How did women get into such a little trinket of a shoe, anyway?

"I assure you, Miss Hollister, our firm appreciates what you have done! We shall not forget it. You will see, we shall not forget it!" he puffed as he rose with beads of perspiration on his brow. "You have done a great thing for Barnard and Clegg to-day!"

"She's done more than that!" said a burly policeman significantly glancing around the group of sullen prisoners, as Graham put her upon her feet beside him. "She's rounded up the whole gang for us, and that's more than anybody else has been able to do yet! She oughtta get a medal of some kind fer that!"

Then, with a dare-devil lift of his head and a gleam of something like fun in his sullen eyes, the manacled man by the tree spoke out, looking straight at Shirley, real admiration in his voice:

"I say, pard! I guess you're the winner! I'll hand you what's comin' to you if I do lose. You certainly had your nerve!"

Shirley looked at him with a kind of compassion in her eyes.

"I'm sorry you have to be—there," she finished. "You were—as fine as you could be to me under the circumstances, I suppose! I thank you for that."

The man met her gaze for an instant, a flippant reply upon his lips, but checked it and dropping his eyes, was silent. The whole little company under the trees were hushed into silence before the miracle of a girl's pure spirit, leaving its impress on a blackened soul.

Then, quietly, Graham led her away to his car with Barnard and the detectives following. The prisoners were loaded into the other cars, and hurried on the way to judgment.

CHAPTER XXVI

THE ride back to the city was like a dream to Shirley afterward. To see the staid Mr. Barnard so excited, babbling away about her bravery and exulting like a child over the recovery of the precious notes, was wonder enough. But to feel the quiet protection and tender interest of Sidney Graham filled her with ecstasy. Of course it was only kindly interest and friendly anxiety, and by to-morrow she would have put it into order with all his other kindlinesses, but to-night, weary and excited as she was, with the sense of horror over her recent experience still upon her, it was sweet to feel his attention, and to let his voice thrill through her tired heart, without stopping to analyze it and be sure she was not too glad over it. What if he would be merely a friend to-morrow again! To-night he was her rescuer, and she would rest back upon that and be happy.

"I feel that I was much to blame for leaving you alone to go to the station with a bait like these notes in your possession," said Mr. Barnard humbly. "Though of course I did not dream that there was any such possibility as your being in danger."

"It is just as well not to run any risks in these days when the country is so unsettled," said the detective dryly.

"Especially where a lady is concerned!" remarked Graham significantly.

"I suppose I should have taken Miss Hollister with

227

me and left her in the cab while I transacted my business at the War Department!" said Barnard with self-reproach in his tones.

"They would have only done the same thing in front of the War Department," said the detective convincingly. "They had it all planned to get those notes somehow. You only made it a trifle easier for them by letting the lady go alone. If they hadn't succeeded here, they would have followed you to your home and got into your office or your safe. They are determined, desperate men. We've been watching them for some time, letting them work till we could find out who was behind them. To-night we caught the whole bunch red-handed, thanks to the lady's cleverness. But you had better not risk her alone again when there's anything like this on hand. She might not come out so easy next time!"

Graham muttered a fervent applause in a low tone to this advice, tucking the lap robes closer about the girl. Barnard gave little shudders of apology as he humbly shouldered the blame:

"Oh, no, of course not! I certainly am so sorry!" But Shirley suddenly roused herself to explain:

"Indeed, you mustn't any of you blame Mr. Barnard. He did the perfectly right and natural thing. He always trusts me to look after my notes, even in the most important cases; and I heard the warning as much as he did. It was my business to be on the lookout! I'm old enough and have read enough in the papers about spies and ruffians. I ought to have known there was something wrong when that boy ordered me back and said Mr. Barnard had sent me word. I ought to have known Mr. Barnard would never do that. I did know just as soon as I stopped to think. The trouble was I was giving half my attention to looking at the strange sights out of the window and thinking what I would tell the folks at home about Washington, or I would not have got into such a position. I insist that you shall not blame yourself, Mr. Barnard. It is a secretary's business to be on her job and not be out having a good time when she is on a business trip. I hadn't got

228

beyond the city limits before I knew exactly what I ought to have done. I should have asked that boy more questions, and I should have got right out of that car and told him to tell you I would wait in the station till you came for me. It troubled me from the start that you had sent for me that way. It wasn't like you."

Then they turned their questions upon her, and she had to tell the whole story of her capture, Graham and Barnard exclaiming indignantly as she went on, the detective sitting grim and serious, nodding his approval now and then. Graham's attitude toward her grew more tender and protective. Once or twice as she told of her situation in the old house, or spoke of how the man dragged her along in the dark, he set his teeth and drew his breath hard, saying in an undertone: "The villain!" And there was that in the way that he looked at her that made Shirley hasten through the story, because of the wild, joyous clamor of her heart.

As soon as the city limits were reached, Graham stopped the car to telephone. It was after eleven o'clock, and there was little chance that George would have stayed at the phone so long, but he would leave a message for the early morning at least. George, however, had stuck to his post.

"Sure! I'm here yet! What'd ya think? Couldn't sleep, could I, with *my sister* off alone with a fella somewhere *being kidnapped?* What'd ya say? Found her? She's all right? Oh, gee! That's good! I told Carol you would! I told her not to worry! What'd ya say? Oh, Shirley's going to talk? Oh, hello, Shirley! How's Washington? Some speed, eh? Say, when ya coming home? To-morrow? That's good. No, mother doesn't know a thing. She thinks I went to bed early 'cause I planned to go fishing at sunrise. She went to bed herself early. Say, Mister Graham's a prince, isn't he? Well, I guess I'll go to bed now. I might make the fishing in the morning yet, if I don't sleep too late. I sure am glad you're all right! Well, so long, Shirley!"

Shirley turned from the phone with tears in her eyes. It wasn't what George said that made her smile tenderly through them, but the gruff tenderness in his boy tones that touched her so. She hadn't realized before what she meant to him.

They drove straight to the station, got something to eat, and took the midnight train back to their home city. Graham had protested that Shirley should go to a hotel and get a good rest before attempting the journey, but she laughingly told him she could rest anywhere, and would sleep like a top in the train. When Graham found that it was possible to secure berths in the sleeper for them all, and that they would not have to get out until seven in the morning he withdrew his protests; and his further activities took the form of supplementing her supper with fruit and bonbons. His lingering hand-clasp as he bade her good-night told her how glad he was that she was safe; as if his eyes had not told her the same story every time there had been light enough for them to be seen!

Locked at last into her safe little stateroom, with a soft bed to lie on and no bothersome notes to be guarded, one would have thought she might have slept, but her brain kept time to the wheels, and her heart with her brain. She was going over and over the scenes of the eventful day, and living through each experience again, until she came to the moment when she looked up to find herself in Sidney Graham's arms, with her face against his shoulder. Her face glowed in the dark at the remembrance, and her heart thrilled wildly sweet with the memory of his look and tone, and all his carefulness for her. How wonderful that he should have come so many miles to find her! That *he* should have been the one to find her first, with all those other men on the hunt. He had forged ahead and picked her up before any of the others had reached her. He had not been afraid to rush up to an armed villain and snatch her from her perilous position! He was a man among men! Never mind if he wasn't her own personal property! Never mind if there were others in his own world who might claim him later, he was hers for to-night! She would never forget it!

She slept at last, profoundly, with a smile upon her lips. No dream of villians nor wild automobile rides came to trouble her thoughts. And when she woke in the home station with familiar sounds outside, and realized that a new day was before her, her heart was flooded with a happiness that her common sense found it hard to justify. She tried to steady herself while she made her toilet, but the face that was reflected rosily from the mirror in her little dressing room would smile contagiously back at her.

"Well, then, have it your own way for just one more day!" she said aloud to her face in the glass. "But to-morrow you must get back to common sense again!" Then she turned, fresh as a rose, and went out to meet her fellow travellers.

She went to breakfast with Sidney Graham, a wonderful breakfast in a wonderful place with fountains and palms and quiet, perfect service. Mr. Barnard had excused himself and hurried away to his home, promising to meet Shirley at the office at half-past nine. And so these two sat at a little round table by themselves and had sweet converse over their coffee. Shirley utterly forgot for the time that she was only a poor little stenographer working for her bread and living in a barn. Sidney Graham's eyes were upon her, in deep and unveiled admiration, his spirit speaking to hers through the quiet little commonplaces to which he must confine himself in this public place. It was not till the meal was over and he was settling his bill that Shirley suddenly came to herself and the color flooded her sweet face. What was she better than any other poor fool of a girl who let a rich man amuse himself for a few hours in her company and then let him carry her heart away with him to toss with his collection? She drew her dignity about her and tried to be distant as they went out to the street, but he simply did not recognize it at all. He just kept his tender, deferential manner, and smiled down at her with that wonderful, exalted look that made her dignity seem cheap; so there was nothing to do but look up as a flower would to the sun and be true to the best that was in her heart.

She was surprised to find his own car at the door

when they came out on the street. He must have phoned for it before they left the station. He was so kind and thoughtful. It was so wonderful to her to be cared for in this way. "Just as if I were a rich girl in his own social set," she thought to herself.

He gave his chauffeur the orders and sat beside her in the back seat, continuing his rôle of admirer and protector.

"It certainly is great to think you're here beside me," he said in a low tone as they threaded their way in and out of the crowded thoroughfare toward the office. "I didn't have a very pleasant afternoon and evening yesterday, I can tell you! I don't think we'll let you go off on any more such errands. You're too precious to risk in peril like that, you know!"

Shirley's cheeks were beautiful to behold as she tried to lift her eyes easily to his glance and take his words as if they had been a mere commonplace. But there was something deep down in the tone of his voice, and something intent and personal in his glance that made her drop her eyes swiftly and covered her with a sweet confusion.

They were at the office almost immediately and Graham was helping her out.

"Now, when will you be through here?" he asked, glancing at his watch. "What train were you planning to take down to the shore? I suppose you'll want to get back as soon as possible?"

"Yes," said Shirley, doubtfully, "I do. But I don't know whether I oughtn't to run out home first and get mother's big old shawl, and two or three other little things we ought to have brought along."

"No," said Graham, quickly, with a flash of anxiety in his face, "I wouldn't if I were you. They'll be anxious to see you, and if it's necessary you can run up again sometime. I think you'll find there are lots of shawls down at the cottage. I'm anxious to have you safely landed with your family once more. I promised Carol you'd be down the first train after you got your work done. How long is it going to take you to fix Mr. Barnard up so he can run things without you?"

"Oh, not more than two hours I should think, unless he wants something more than I know."

"Well, two hours. It is half-past nine now. We'll say two hours and a half. That ought to give you time. I think there's a train about then. I'll phone to the station and find out and let you know the exact time. The car will be here waiting for you."

"Oh, Mr. Graham, that's not a bit necessary! You have taken trouble enough for me already!" protested Shirley.

"No trouble at all!" declared Graham. "My chauffeur hasn't a thing to do but hang around with the car this morning and you might as well ride as walk. I'll phone you in plenty of time."

He lifted his hat and gave her a last look that kept the glow in her cheeks. She turned and went with swift steps in to her elevator.

Sidney Graham dropped his chauffeur at the station to enquire about trains and get tickets, with orders to report at his office within an hour, and himself took the wheel. Quickly working his way out of the city's traffic he put on all possible speed toward Glenside. He must get a glimpse of things and see that all was going well before he went to the office. What would Shirley have said if she had carried out her plan of coming out for her mother's shawl? He must put a stop to that at all costs. She simply must not see the old barn till the work was done, or the whole thing would be spoiled. Strange it had not occurred to him that she might want to come back after something! Well, he would just have to be on the continual lookout. For one thing he would stop at a store on the way back and purchase a couple of big steamer rugs and a long warm cloak. He could smuggle them into the cottage somehow and have the servants bring them out for common use as if they belonged to the house.

He was as eager as a child over every little thing that had been started during his absence, and walked about with the boss carpenter, settling two or three questions that had come up the day before. In ten minutes he was back in his car, whirling toward the city again, planning how he could best get those rugs and cloaks into the hands of the housekeeper at the shore without anybody suspecting that they were new. Then it occurred to him to take them down to Elizabeth and let her engineer the matter. There must be two cloaks, one for Shirley, for he wanted to take her out in the car sometimes and her little scrap of a coat was entirely too thin even for summer breezes at the shore.

Shirley met with a great ovation when she entered the office. It was evident that her fame had gone before her. Mr. Barnard was already there, smiling benevolently, and Mr. Clegg frowning approvingly over his spectacles at her. The other office clerks came to shake hands or called congratulations, till Shirley was quite overwhelmed at her reception. Clegg and Barnard both followed her into the inner office and continued to congratulate her on the bravery she had shown and to express their appreciation of her loyalty and courage in behalf of the firm. Mr. Barnard handed her a check for a hundred dollars as a slight token of their appreciation of her work, telling her that beginning with the first of the month her salary was to be raised.

When at last she sat down to her typewriter and began to click out the wonderful notes that had made so much trouble, and put them in shape for practical use, her head was in a whirl and her heart was beating with a childish ecstasy. She felt as if she were living a real fairy tale, and would not ever be able to get back to common every-day life again.

At half-past eleven Graham called her up to tell her there was a train a little after twelve if she could be ready, and the car would be waiting for her in fifteen minutes.

When she finally tore herself away from the smiles and effusive thanks of Barnard and Clegg and took the elevator down to the street she found Sidney Graham himself awaiting her eagerly. This was a delightful surprise, for he had not said anything about coming himself or mentioned when he would be coming back to the shore, so she had been feeling that it might be some time before she would see him again.

He had just slammed the door of the car and taken his seat beside her when a large gray limousine slowed down beside them and a radiant, well-groomed, much-tailored young woman leaned out of the car, smiling at Graham, and passing over Shirley with one of those unseeing stares wherewith some girls know so well how to erase other girls.

"Oh, Sidney! I'm so glad I met you!" she cried. "Mother has been phoning everywhere to find you. We are out at our country place for a couple of weeks, and she wants to ask you to come over this afternoon for a little tennis tournament we are having, with a dance on the lawn afterward."

"That's very kind of you, Harriet," said Graham pleasantly, "but I can't possibly be there. I have an engagement out of town for this afternoon and evening. Give my regards to your mother, please, and thank her for the invitation. I know you'll have a lovely time, you always do at your house."

"Oh, that's too bad, Sidney!" pouted the girl. "Why will you be so busy! and in the summer-time, too! You ought to take a vacation! Well, if you can't come to-night, you'll run down over the week-end, won't you? We are having the Foresters and the Harveys. You like them, and we simply can't do without you."

"Sorry," said Graham, smilingly, "but I've got all my week-ends filled up just now. Harriet, let me introduce you to Miss Hollister. Miss Hale, Miss Hollister!"

Then did Harriet Hale have to take over her unseeing stare and acknowledge the introduction; somewhat stiffly, it must be acknowledged, for Harriet Hale did not enjoy having her invitations declined, and she could not quite place this girl with the lovely face and the half-shabby garments, that yet had somehow an air of having been made by a French artist.

"I'm sorry, Harriet, but we'll have to hurry away. We're going to catch a train at twelve-fifteen. Hope you have a beautiful time this afternoon. Remember me to Tom Harvey and the Foresters. Sorry to disappoint you, Harriet, but you see I've got my time just full up at present. Hope to see you soon again."

They were off, Shirley with the impression of Harriet Hale's smile of vinegar and roses; the roses for Graham, the vinegar for her. Shirley's heart was beating wildly underneath her quiet demeanor. She had at last met the wonderful Harriet Hale, and Graham had not been ashamed to introduce her! There had been protection and enthronement in his tone as he spoke her name! It had not been possible for Miss Hale to patronize her after that. Shirley was still in a daze of happiness. She did not think ahead. She had all she could do to register new occurrences and emotions, and realize that her joy was not merely momentary. It had not occurred to her to wonder where Graham was going out of town. It was enough that he was here now.

When they reached the station Graham took two large packages out of the car, and gave some directions to the chauffeur.

"Sorry we couldn't have gone down in the car again," he said as they walked into the station, "but it needs some repairs and I don't want to take as long a run as that until it has been thoroughly overhauled."

Then he was going down too! He had declined Harriet Hale's invitation to go back to the cottage with her! Shirley's breath came in little happy gasps as she walked beside her companion down the platform to the train.

She found herself presently being seated in a big green velvet chair in the parlor car while the porter stowed away the two big packages in the rack overhead.

CHAPTER XXVII

THERE was only one other passenger in the car, an old man nodding behind a newspaper, with his chair facing in the other direction. Graham took a swift survey of him and turned happily back with a smile to Shirley:

"At last I have you to myself!" he said with a sigh of

satisfaction that made Shirley's cheeks bloom out rosily again.

He whirled her chair and his quite away from the vision of the old man, so that they were at the nearest possible angle to each other, and facing the windows. Then he sat down and leaned toward her.

"Shirley," he said in a tone of proprietorship that was tender and beautiful, "I've waited just as long as I'm going to wait to tell you something. I know it's lunch time, and I'm going to take you into the dining-car pretty soon and get you some lunch, but I must have a little chance to talk with you first, please."

Shirley's eyes gave glad permission and he hurried on.

"Shirley, I love you. I guess you've been seeing that for some time. I knew I ought to hide it till you knew me better, but I simply couldn't do it. I never saw a girl like you, and I knew the minute I looked at you that you were of finer clay than other girls, anyway. I knew that if I couldn't win you and marry you I would never love anybody else. But yesterday when I heard you were in peril away off down in Washington and I away up here helpless to save you, and not even having the right to organize a search for you, I nearly went wild! All the way down on the train I kept shutting my eyes and trying to pray the way you told your Sunday School boys how to pray. But all I could get out was, 'Oh, God, I love her! Save her! I love her!' Shirley, I know I'm not one-half worthy enough for you, but I love you with all my heart and I want you for my wife. Will you marry me, Shirley?"

When she had recovered a little from her wonder and astonishment, and realized that he had asked her to marry him, and was waiting for his answer, she lifted her wondering eyes to his face, and tried to speak as her conscience and reason bade her.

"But I'm not like the other girls you know," she said bravely. Then he broke in upon her fervently.

"No, you're not like any other girl I know in the whole wide world. Thank God for that! You are one among a thousand! No, you're one among the whole earthful of women! You're the *only* one I could ever love!"

"But listen, please; you haven't thought. I'm not a society girl. I don't belong in your circle. I couldn't grace your position the way your wife ought to do. Remember, we're nobodies. We're poor! We live in a *barn!*"

"What do you suppose I care about that?" he answered eagerly. "You may live in a barn all your days if you like, and I'll love you just the same. I'll come and live in the barn with you if you want me to. My position! My circle! What's that? You'll grace my home and my life as no other girl could do. You heart of my heart! You strong, sweet spirit! The only question I'm going to ask of you is, Can you love me? If you can, I know I can make you happy, for I love you better than my life. Answer, please. Do you love me?"

She lifted her eyes, and their spirits broke through their glances. If the old man at the other end of the car was looking they did not know it.

They came back to the cottage at the shore with a manner so blissful and so unmistakable that even the children noticed. Elizabeth whispered to Carol at table: "My brother likes your sister a lot, doesn't he? I hope she likes him, too."

"I guess she does," responded Carol philosophically. "She oughtta. He's been awfully good to her, and to all of us."

"People don't like people just for that," said wise Elizabeth.

Harley, out on the veranda after dinner, drew near to Carol to confide.

"Say, kid, I guess he *has* got a case on her all right now. Gee! Wouldn't that be great? Think of all those cars!"

But Carol giggled.

"Good night! Harley! How could we ever have a wedding in a barn? And they're such particular people, too!"

"Aw, gee!" said Harley, disgusted. "You girls are always thinking of things like that! As if that mattered. You can get married in a chicken-run if you really

238

have a case like that on each other! *You make me tired!"* and he stalked away in offended male dignity.

Meantime the unconscious subjects of this discussion had gone to Mrs. Hollister to confess, and the sea was forgotten by all three for that one evening at least, even though the moon was wide and bright and gave a golden pathway across the dark water. For a great burden had rolled from Mrs. Hollister's shoulders when she found her beloved eldest daughter was really loved by this young man, and he was not just amusing himself for a little while at her expense.

The days that followed were like one blissful fleeting dream to Shirley. She just could not get used to the fact that she was engaged to such a prince among men! It seemed as if she were dreaming, and that presently she would wake up and find herself in the office with a great pile of letters to write, and the perplexing problem before her of where they were going to live next winter. She had broached that subject once to Graham shyly, saying that she must begin to look around as soon as she got back to town, and he put her aside, asking her to leave that question till they all went back, as he had a plan he thought she might think well of, but he couldn't tell her about it just yet. He also began to urge her to write at once to Mr. Barnard and resign her position, but that she would not hear of.

"No," she said decidedly. "We couldn't live without my salary, and there are a lot of things to be thought out and planned before I can be married. Besides, we need to get to know each other and to grow into each other's lives a little bit. You haven't any idea even now how far I am from being fitted to be the wife of a man in your position. You may be sorry yet. If you are ever going to find it out, I want you to do it beforehand."

He looked adoringly into her eyes.

"I know perfectly now, dear heart!" he said, "and I'm not going to be satisfied to wait a long time for you to find out that you don't really care for me after all. If you've got to find that out, I believe I'd rather it would be after I have you close and fast and you'll *have* to like me anyway."

And then the wonder and thrill of it all would roll over her again and she would look into his eyes and be satisfied.

Still she continued quite decided that nothing could be done about prolonging her vacation, for she meant to go back to Barnard and Clegg's on the day set.

"You know I'm the man of the house," she said archly. "I can't quite see it at all myself—how I'm ever going to give up."

"But I thought I was going to be the man of the house," pleaded Sidney. "I'm sure I'm quite capable and eager to look out for the interests of my wife's family."

"But you see I'm not the kind of a girl that has been looking around for a man who will support my family."

"No, you surely are not!" said the young man, laughing. "If you had been, young lady, I expect you'd have been looking yet so far as I am concerned. It is because you are what you are that I love you. Now that's all right about being independent, but it's about time to fight this thing to a finish. I don't see why we all have to be made miserable just because there are a lot of unpleasant precedents and conventions and crochets in the world. Why may I not have the pleasure of helping to take care of your perfectly good family if I want to? It is one of the greatest pleasures to which I am looking forward, to try and make them just as happy as I can, so that you will be the happier. I've got plenty to do it with. God has been very good to me in that way, and why should you try to hinder me?"

And then the discussion would end in a bewildering look of worshipful admiration on Shirley's part and a joyous taking possession of her and carrying her off on some ride or walk or other on the part of Graham.

He did not care just now that she was slow to make plans. He was enjoying each day, each hour, to the full. He wanted to keep her from thinking about the future, and especially about the winter, till she got home, and so he humored her and led her to other topics.

One night, as they sat on the dark veranda alone, Graham said to George:

240

"If you were going to college, where would you want to prepare?"

He wondered what the boy would say, for the subject of college had never been mentioned with relation to George. He did not know whether the boy had ever thought of it. But the answer came promptly in a ringing voice:

"Central High! They've got the best football team in the city."

"Then you wouldn't want to go away to some preparatory school?"

"No, *sir!*" was the decided answer. "I believe in the public school every time! When I was a little kid I can remember my father taking me to walk and pointing out the Central High School, and telling me that some day I would go there to school. I used to always call that 'my school.' I used to think I'd get there yet, some day, but I guess that's out of the question."

"Well, George, if that's your choice you can get ready to enter as soon as you go back to the city."

"What?" George's feet came down from the veranda railing with a thud, and he sat upright in the darkness and stared wildly at his prospective brother-in-law. Then he slowly relaxed and his young face grew grim and stern.

"No chance!" he said laconically.

"Why not?"

"Because I've got my mother and the children to support. I can't waste time going to school. I've got to be a *man*."

Something sudden like a choke came in the young man's throat, and a great love for the brave boy who was so courageous in his self-denial.

"George, you're not a man yet, and you'll shoulder the burden twice as well when you're equipped with a college education. I mean you shall have it. Do you suppose I'm going to let my new brother slave away before his time? No, sir; you're going to get ready to make the best man that's in you. And as for your mother and the family, isn't she going to be my mother, and aren't they to be my family? We'll just shoulder the

241

job together, George, till you're older—and then we'll see."

"But I couldn't take charity from anybody."

"Not even from a brother?"

"Not even from a brother."

"Well, suppose we put it in another way. Suppose you borrow the money from me to keep things going, and when you are ready to pay it back we'll talk about it then. Or, better still, suppose you agree to pass it on to some other brother when you are able."

They talked a long time in the dark, and Graham had quite a hard time breaking down the boy's reserve and independence, and getting a real brotherly confidence. But at last George yielded, saw the common sense and right of the thing, and laid an awkward hand in the man's, growling out:

"You're a pippin and no mistake, Mr. Graham. I can't ever thank you enough! I never thought anything like this would happen to me!"

"Don't try thanks, George. We're brothers now, you know. Just you do your best at school, and it's all I ask. Shirley and I are going to be wonderfully proud of you. But please don't call me Mr. Graham any more. Sid, or Sidney, or anything you like, but no more mistering."

He flung a brotherly arm across the boy's shoulders and together they went into the house.

Meantime the beautiful days went by in one long, golden dream of wonder. The children were having the time of their lives, and Elizabeth was never so happy. Shirley sat on the wide verandas and read the wealth of books and magazines which the house contained, or roamed the beach with the children and Star, or played in the waves with Doris, and wondered if it were really Shirley Hollister who was having all this good time.

CHAPTER XXVIII

THE morning they all started back to the city was a memorable one. Graham had insisted that Shirley ask for a holiday until Tuesday morning so that she might go up with them in the car, and have the whole day to be at home and help her mother get settled. She had consented, and found to her surprise that Mr. Barnard was most kind about it. He had even added that he intended to raise her salary, and she might consider that hereafter she was to have ten dollars more per month for her services, which they valued very highly.

George had sent his resignation to the store and was not to go back at all. Graham had arranged that, for school began the day after his return and he would need to be free at once.

Elizabeth, to her great delight, was to go with the Hollisters and remain a few days until her parents returned. Mrs. Graham had written from the West making a proposition to Mrs. Hollister that Carol be allowed to go to school with Elizabeth the next winter, because Mrs. Graham felt it would be so good for Elizabeth to have a friend like that. Mrs. Hollister, however, answered that she felt it better for her little girl to remain with her mother a little longer; and that she did not feel it would be a good thing for her child, who would be likely to have a simple life before her with very few luxuries, to go to a fashionable finishing-school where the standards must all necessarily be so different from those of her own station in life, and, kind as the offer had been, she must decline it. She did not say that Carol had fairly bristled at the idea of leaving her beloved high school now when she was a senior and only one year before her graduation. That bit of horror and hysterics on Carol's part had been carefully suppressed within the four walls of her mother's room; but Elizabeth, deeply disappointed, had wept her heart out over the matter, and finally been comforted by the promise that Mrs. Hollister would write and ask Mrs. Graham to allow Elizabeth to go to school with Carol the coming winter. That proposition was now on its way West, together with an announcement of Sidney's engagement to Shirley. Sidney was confidently expecting congratulatory telegrams that morning when he reached the city. He had written his father in detail all about their plans for returning, and how the work at the old barn was progressing, and Mr. Graham, Senior, was too good a manager not to plan to greet the occasion properly. Therefore Graham stopped at his office for a few minutes before taking the family out to Glenside, and, sure enough, came down with his hands full of letters and telegrams, and one long white envelope which he put carefully in his breast pocket. They had a great time reading the telegrams and letters.

The way out to Glenside seemed very short now, watching as they did for each landmark. The children were as eager to get back as they had been to leave, and Star snuggled in between Harley's feet, held his head high, and smiled benevolently on everybody, as if he knew he was going home and was glad. They began to wonder about the chickens, and if the garden was all dried up, and whether the doves were all right. There was an undertone of sadness and suppressed excitement, for it was in the minds of all the Hollisters that the time in the old barn must of necessity be growing brief. The fall would soon be upon them, and a need for warmth. They must go hunting for a house at once. And yet they all wanted this one day of delight before they faced that question.

At last they reached the final curve and could see the tall old tree in the distance, and the clump of willows knee-deep in the brook. By common consent they all grew silent, watching for the first glimpse of the dear old barn.

Then they came around the curve, and there it was! But what was the matter?

Nobody spoke. It seemed as if they could not get their breath.

Shirley rubbed her eyes, and looked again. Mrs. Hollister gave a startled look from her daughter to Graham and back to the barn again. Elizabeth and Carol were utterly silent, grasping each other's hands in violent ecstasy. The boys murmured inarticulately, of which the only audible words were: "Good night! Some class!" Doris looked for a long second, puckered her lips as if she were going to cry, and inquired pitifully: "I yant my dear barn house home! I yant to doh home!" and Star uttered a sharp, bewildered bark and bounded from the car as if this were something he ought to attend to.

But before anybody could say anything more, Graham brought out the long white envelope and handed it to Shirley.

"Before you get out and go in I just want to say a word," he began. "Father and I both want Shirley to have the old barn for her very own, to do with as she pleases. This envelope contains the deed for the property made out in her name. We have tried to put it in thorough repair before handing it over to her, and if there is anything more she can think of that it needs we'll do that too. And now, welcome home to the old barn! Mother, may I help you out?"

"But there isn't any barn any more," burst forth the irrepressible Elizabeth. "The barn's gone! It's just a house!"

And, sure enough, there stood a stately stone mansion on a wide green terrace, where shrubs and small trees were grouped fittingly about, erasing all signs of the old pasture-land; and the old grassy incline to the door now rolled away in velvety lawn on either side of a smooth cement walk bordered with vivid scarlet geraniums. Trailing vines and autumn flowers were blossoming in jars on the wide stone railing. The old barn door had been replaced by glass which gave a glimpse of strange new rooms beyond, and the roof had broken forth in charming colonial dormer windows like a new French hat on a head that had worn the same old poke bonnet for years. No wonder Doris didn't recognize the dear old barn. It did seem as though a wizard had worked magic upon it. How was one to know that only a brief half-hour before the old gardener from the Graham estate set the last geranium in the row along the walk, and trailed the last vine over the stone wall; or that even now the corps of men who had been hastily laying and patting the turf in place over the terrace were in hiding down in the basement, with their wheelbarrows and picks and spades, having beat a hasty retreat at the sound of the car coming, and were only waiting till they could get away unobserved? For orders were orders, and the orders were that the work was to be *done* and every man out of sight by the time they arrived. A bonus to every man if the orders were obeyed. That is what money and influence can do in a month!

In due time they got themselves out of that car in a sort of bewildered daze and walked up the new cement path, feeling strangely like intruders as they met the bright stare of the geraniums.

They walked the length of the new piazza in delight. They exclaimed and started and smiled and almost wept in one another's arms. Graham stood and watched Shirley's happy face and was satisfied.

The first thing Doris did when she got inside the lovely glass door was to start to run for her own little willow chair and her own little old rag doll that had been left behind, and down she went on the slippery floor. And there, behold, the old barn floors too had disappeared under a coating of simple matched hardwood flooring, oiled and polished smoothly, and Doris was not expecting it.

She got up quickly, half ashamed, and looked around laughing.

"I vas skating!" she declared with a ringing laugh. "I skated yite down on mine nose."

Then she hurried more cautiously to the haven of her own chair, and with her old doll hugged to her breast she reiterated over and over as if to reassure herself: "Mine! Doris! Mine! Doris!"

Words would fail to describe all they said about the wonderful rooms, the walls all shining in a soft rough-finish plaster, tinted creamy on the upper half and gray below, and finished in dark chestnut trimmings; of the beautiful staircase and the wide bay window opening from the first landing like a little half-way room, with seats to rest upon. It was standing in this bay window that Graham first called Mrs. Hollister's attention to something strange and new outside behind the house. It was a long, low glass building with green things gleaming through its shining roof:

"There, mother," he said, coming up softly behind her. "There is your plaything. You said you had always wanted a hot-house, so we made you one. It is heated from a coil in the furnace, and you can try all the experiments with flowers you want to. We put in a few things to start with, and you can get more at your leisure."

Mrs. Hollister gave one look, and then turned and put her arms around the tall young man, reaching up on her tiptoes to do so, brought his handsome face down to hers, and kissed him.

"My dear son!" she said. That was all, but he knew that she had accepted him and given him a loving place with her own children in her heart.

There were shoutings and runnings up stairs and down by first one and then another. The bathrooms were discovered one by one, and then they had to all rush down into the basement by the new stairs to see the new laundry and the new furnace, and the entrance to the hot-house; and the hot-house itself, with its wealth of bloom transplanted from the Graham greenhouses.

They almost forgot the chickens and the doves, and the garden was a past Eden not to be remembered till long hours afterward.

The sunset was dying away in the sky, and the stars were large and few and piercing in the twilight night when Shirley and Sidney came walking up the terrace arm in arm, and found Doris sitting in the doorway cuddling her old rag doll and a new little gray kitten the farmer next door had brought her, and singing an evening song to herself.

Shirley and Sidney turned and looked off at the sky where a rosy stain was blending softly into the gray of evening.

"Do you remember the first night we stood here together?" Sidney said in a low tone, as he drew her fingers within his own. "I loved you then, Shirley, that first night——"

And then Doris's little shrill voice chimed above their murmurings:

"Oh, mine nice dear home! Mine kitty an' mine dolly! and mine piazza! and mine bafwoom wif a place to swim boats! an' mine f'owers an' pitty house! No more barn! Barn *all dawn!* Never tum bat any moh! Oh, mine nice, pitty dear home!"

Novels of Enduring Romance and Inspiration by

GRACE LIVINGSTON HILL

☐	14505	**THE BEST MAN #7**	$1.95
☐	23500	**IN TUNE WITH WEDDING BELLS #13**	$2.50
☐	23805	**MARIGOLD #15**	$2.50
☐	23317	**WHITE ORCHIDS #28**	$2.50
☐	23810	**COMING THROUGH THE RYE #32**	$2.50
☐	14173	**PARTNERS #35**	$1.95
☐	23361	**DAWN IN THE MORNING #43**	$2.50
☐	23429	**THE STREET OF THE CITY #47**	$2.50
☐	12167	**THE OBSESSION OF VICTORIA GRACEN #54**	$1.75
☐	23856	**THE HONOR GIRL #57**	$2.50
☐	24124	**THE PRODIGAL GIRL #56**	$2.50
☐	24238	**MIRANDA #60**	$2.50
☐	22903	**MYSTERY FLOWERS #61**	$2.50
☐	23558	**CHRISTMAS BRIDE #62**	$2.50
☐	20286	**MAN OF THE DESERT #63**	$2.25
☐	20911	**MISS LAVINIA'S CALL #64**	$2.50

<u>Prices and availability subject to change without notice.</u>

Buy them at your local bookstore or use this handy coupon for ordering:

GOLD, THE COLOR O... g in firelight.

By the hearth, a ... raps from her shoulders ...

A young man, hi... steps toward her, crossing a magic carpet that floats two inches above the floor. Beneath his bare feet, its intricate pattern shifts and reforms until it becomes a map of all the world's possibilities.

The room is a cage made of windows. Ocean waves batter the glass.

In the corner someone moves—a shadow, silent and dark.

Bam! Bam!

The woman spreads her arms like angel's wings. A red corsage blooms on her breast, and she falls. A bolt of lightning spins the young man in a circle and drops him to the floor.

The shadow circles the room, once, twice, three times. Waiting. Outside a storm rages.

The gale blows down the door and a man appears, wearing a shirt woven from discarded blueprints. Screaming louder than the wind, he rushes to embrace the fallen angel.

Behind him comes a girl, her face hidden behind a velvet mask. She rips off her mask and flings it away as she runs toward the storm. She looks back over her shoulder. Her face is a mirror and her brown eyes are imprinted with words: *Help me!*

Bam! Bam!

The mask hits the floor, turning into a tombstone carved of ice. The ocean shatters the glass and the room is engulfed in a tide of blood.

The shadow smiles and vanishes.

Claire wakes up screaming . . .

HOUSE OF WHISPERS
Book One of the Supernatural Properties

HOUSE OF WHISPERS
Book One of the Supernatural Properties

Margaret Locke

JUNO

House of Whispers
Copyright © 2008 by Margaret Lucke

Cover art copyright © 2008 by Timothy Lantz
www.stygiandarkness.com

ISBN: 978-0-8095-7158-1

Juno Books
Rockville, MD
www.juno-books.com
info@juno-books.com

To Charlie,
always there with
inspiration and encouragement.

CHAPTER 1

*C*old. So cold . . .

I haven't been warm since that night—that fiery night of blood and rage, when heat seared through us all and left us frozen. How long ago did it happen? Weeks? Months? I can't tell. Time has no meaning any more. Its definitions have been lost, its edges blurred.

I can't stand this cold. No matter how hard I try, I never thaw out. Some days the sun beats in through a glass wall that faces the ocean, and I know the temperature is rising in the room. I move into the middle of the bright glare, begging to feel the heat. But I remain ice.

Empty . . .

The house is empty now. I feel empty too.

The explosive sounds still echoed in the rooms and the blood was not yet dry when the first people arrived. Police in uniforms, detectives in plain clothes. They roamed everywhere, asking questions, taking photographs and measurements, and scattering dust as they hunted for clues and searched out answers. They churned the air, tied all the energy in the house into knots. Then they went away.

Just when the air had settled, more people came and stirred it again. They carted away our possessions—the furnishings, the artwork, the jewels, all of the private, personal things we had cherished, the things that

revealed our stories and hid our secrets. These people
left nothing behind but dirt from their shoes and the
memories we imprinted on the walls. That's how I
occupy myself in this empty house, reading the walls,
over and over.

I am trapped here. What else is there for me to do?

I despaired when the next group appeared. They
carried buckets and brushes and brought machines to
scrub away every trace of us. If the memories were
erased, would we cease to exist altogether? Imagine
my relief when I saw they still glowed, even after the
walls were washed and covered with coat upon coat of
fresh paint.

Once in awhile—I'm not sure how often—a lone man
comes and walks through the hollow rooms. He seems
familiar, someone I knew Before, but I can't recall his
name. I hear the thump of his footsteps, followed by an
echo as the thump bounces against the bare surfaces.
Occasionally I hear a sound that might be a sob. If I
move in close, I might taste tears on his cheek.

Recently strangers have shown up, arriving in twos
and threes. They stay just a short time—only minutes,
I'm guessing, not hours, not days, though I can't tell for
sure. They move hastily through the cavernous spaces,
peering into corners and closets, and they shudder
as they depart. I don't think they know how to read
the walls. Perhaps they can't even see the memories
there.

I miss having things around that have a shape or
make a sound or cast a shadow. People do all that, yet
when they're here, the house seems emptier than ever.

Lonely . . .

I can't recall when I was last with the ones like me,
the ones who were turned to ice that night. At first,

we huddled together, shocked and grieving. But after awhile we drifted into separate spaces. First one and then the next floated into the place called Forever, abandoning me to the cold and silence.

I miss them so much.

Just one of them remains stuck here with me, unable to move on. He's wrapped in chains, their stout links forged from the anger and scorn of the people we left behind, the people who've suffered because of what happened that night and have had to deal with its consequences. He's mute, blind, impervious to every effort I make to connect with him.

Having him here is worse than being alone.

I have no one. That's the hardest thing of all.

Whenever people come here, I try to make contact, but I've had no success. I feel such a bitter pang when I fail to reach them. I touch their hands, I breathe in their faces, I whisper in their ears, but they remain oblivious, unaware. They start to fidget and they leave as quickly as they can. They know only that they are uncomfortable; they never realize why. How can I tell them I'm here? If only they would acknowledge me, we would all feel release from the pain.

I want to follow the other ones like me, to join them in the place called Forever. I miss them so much. But I cannot leave yet. I promised I would unbind the chains and bring him with me. I promised I would let people know what really happened.

Until I do, the trouble will not be over.

CHAPTER 2

Late!

Claire slammed the door of her Volkswagen and dashed across the parking lot, juggling a purse, a briefcase, and a travel mug full of hot coffee. Her first Monday Meeting as an agent for Golden Gate Properties and she was late. Not the best way to make a favorable impression on her new colleagues. Not to mention the boss.

She pushed through big glass doors into the redwood-lined lobby of the office building and punched the elevator button. Fifteen seconds passed. Thirty. The door didn't open. Claire turned and ran up the stairs to the third and top floor.

Should have set two alarms, she thought as she arrived at the entrance to the conference room. Should have allowed more time to negotiate the miserable morning traffic. Should have skipped making coffee. Should have . . .

". . . had this listing," said the cool voice of Tess McMillan, owner and head broker of Golden Gate Properties. "It's Claire's turn to get the next cold-call client. But since she's not here, the listing goes to the next in line. That's you, Avery."

"I'm here," Claire said as she rushed in the door. "I'm sorry I'm late." She wished she weren't out of breath and panting. The only vacant chair left was at the far end of the long oval table. So much for slipping inconspicuously into a seat.

Half a dozen pairs of eyes stared at her as she set her purse and briefcase on the floor, placed the mug on the table, and sat down at the empty place. Two men, four women. All were strangers except Tess, who had impressed upon Claire her expectation that good real estate agents did not spend their time hanging around the office; they were out showing properties. The Monday Meeting was the only time in the week that the whole staff got together.

Claire smiled at them, hoping to convey the message that she was calm and capable. Which she knew herself to be. Except for this morning, when it counted.

She glanced down and was dismayed to see that milky drops of coffee marred the glossy rosewood surface in front of her. Just to make her entrance perfect, the mug's lid had come loose, letting hot liquid dribble out. Trying to look as if she were merely getting settled into her seat, Claire rubbed her arm over the table, blotting up the spill with her sleeve. Thank goodness she'd worn a dark jacket.

Tess, standing at the head of the table, made a show of frowning as she looked at her watch. She was attired in a stylish pink suit, but her bearing suggested she envisioned herself wearing a military uniform.

"So what's your excuse?" said the youngest woman, a sleek blonde whose silky hair cascaded to her cleavage. "Alarm didn't go off? Car wouldn't start?"

The man sitting next to Claire gave her a sympathetic look. A good-looking guy, with warm brown eyes and thick black hair. Probably close to her own age, thirty-five. He offered her an out, saying, "I heard a car wreck had traffic dead-stopped on the freeway."

"I'm sorry," Claire repeated. "It won't happen again."

No way was she going to tell them about waking up hot and sweating in the middle of the night, images from the nightmare still tumbling through her mind. Or about lying awake for hours, staring into the darkness, afraid to close her eyes. Or about finally falling into a leaden slumber, so heavy and deep that when the alarm went off, she was hardly aware of reaching out and turning it off before the void of sleep reclaimed her.

The other man chuckled. "Bet you blew us off for something more fun, right, sweetheart?" He was heavyset and balding, and he gave Claire a wink. "A little M.Q.? Got a hot boyfriend?"

"M.Q.?" Claire said. Was this some real estate term she'd failed to learn?

The black-haired guy whispered an explanation: "Morning quickie. Ignore him."

Claire returned the lout's wink with the glare he deserved. Frankly, she would have much preferred to be tardy because of a sexual romp than another nightmare. But there was no boyfriend. Only Zach, and that was over. Any day now she would receive the papers that made their divorce final.

"Behave yourself, George," Tess snapped, and Claire was pleased to see the balding man slump down like a cowed puppy. "That's no way to greet our newest associate. Everybody, meet Claire Scanlan. Claire, this is everybody."

Tess rattled off a string of names so quickly that Claire didn't catch them, although she knew who most of these people were. She'd seen their pictures on open-house flyers and read their profiles on the company Web site. They greeted her with cheerful hellos and small waves of their hands. All but the blonde smiled, though the balding man's smile came attached to a leer.

"Now back to business," Tess said. She was a tall, slender woman with champagne-colored highlights in her artfully tousled hair. Claire guessed her to be in her early fifties, but her hairstylist, shopping consultant, and personal trainer kept her buffed and polished enough to look at least a decade younger. "Claire, as you arrived I was saying that I had a call from a prospective seller this morning. When listings come in from someone who doesn't ask for a specific agent, I assign them in rotation, and it's your turn. Here's the information."

Tess handed a sheet of paper to the middle-aged redhead next to her, who passed it to the blonde. There it stopped.

"Wow. Ocean view, architect designed, hot tub, private screening room. I *so* should get this one. Since she wasn't here on time."

"Claire is here now," Tess said, "and it's her turn. You'll get the next listing, Avery."

"No fair. You said you were giving it to me." Avery arranged her face into a pretty pout. Claire could see the young woman's gaze shift from one member of her audience to the next as she assessed everyone's reaction.

Tess drew herself up even taller. "I'm always fair."

The man with black hair slid the paper out of Avery's grasp. He let out a low whistle as he read it. "Hey, Claire, you might be better off to let Avery keep this one. It's the LeGrande house."

That created a sensation. Everyone was suddenly on high alert. Several hands reached out to grab the paper, and there was a babble of voices:

"You mean Stefan LeGrande, the architect?"

"Talk about a place that's jinxed."

"No joke. Good luck selling that one."

"No way I'd touch that listing."

"Isn't that where a whole family got murdered?"

"Give it back," Avery demanded as she snatched the paper again.

Claire felt her breath catch. She had to force the air out of her lungs. "Did you say murdered?"

Tess tapped a pencil against the table, as if she were wielding a gavel. "Oh, quit acting like school kids, all of you. Avery, Claire, we'll talk about this listing when the meeting's over. Now, let's move on. We had four open houses yesterday, and I want to hear how they went. Who'd like to start?"

TESS McMILLAN'S OFFICE was designed to exude wealth, comfort and reassurance. Seeing her in this environment, sellers were eager to list their homes with Golden Gate, confident that Tess would get them top dollar. Buyers invested their dreams in her, believing that the homes they bought would let them prove, to themselves as well as to the rest of the world, they had achieved the pinnacle of success.

Claire understood the psychology behind the décor. The wealth part was obvious. Oriental rug, rosewood desk, works of art on walls and in niches—the room was full of beautiful objects and they all whispered *money*. The view of San Francisco Bay outside the window was perhaps the office's most expensive feature: a waterfront address in exclusive Marin County didn't come cheap.

It was the comfort part that was eluding Claire at the moment, as she and a scowling Avery Collier sat in twin leather chairs in front of the desk, facing their boss in her power seat on the other side.

"Claire was late," Avery pointed out to Tess for what must have been the twelfth time. "You already told me I could have this listing before she even got here."

The best tactic, Claire decided, was to be cooperative, keep the peace. Maybe that would make up for the faux pas of her late entrance. "Let Avery have it if she wants it. There will be other houses. I'm new, so maybe it's better if I wait and—"

"You're both new," Tess said. "You started last Tuesday, Avery the Tuesday before that."

"Oh," Claire said. "I didn't know that." She offered Avery a smile.

Avery swept her long blond hair behind her shoulders. "That still makes me senior to her."

"I lost two top agents a month ago. One moved back East and one had a baby." Tess pursed her rouged lips, expressing obvious distaste for both of those lifestyle options. "I figured I had two choices. One, I could replace them with experienced agents. Trouble is, experienced agents sometimes are tired and bored. They don't always have the kind of energy and enthusiasm we want here at Golden Gate Properties."

She glanced through the interior window that gave her a view of the large office "bullpen" where the agents had their desks. It occurred to Claire that Tess might be thinking of one person in particular. Maybe more than one.

"Two," Tess continued, "I could go with rookies. I decided there'd be an advantage to having novices who still find real estate fresh and exciting, who want a challenge, who are hungry and eager to make their mark. Your job is to prove me right."

"No problem," Avery said. "That's exactly what I intend to do."

Claire nodded. "Me too." She felt like she was losing ground here, although she wasn't sure what ground, or why.

"And I can do it with the LeGrande listing," Avery added.

"Frankly," Tess said to them, "I have serious doubts about accepting the listing at all."

"You can't turn it down. The place has to be worth three or four million." Avery didn't bother to filter the avarice out of her voice. "Think what the commission will be."

Tess tapped her perfect oval nails on her desktop. "It's a problem property. People may enjoy the thrills and chills of murder in books or on TV. But ask them to spend a few million bucks to make their home in a notorious crime scene, and watch how fast they back off."

"What happened there?" Claire asked. "Who was murdered?"

"You've never heard of the LeGrande case?" Avery looked shocked and delighted at Claire's ignorance. "A wacko drugged-out kid shot his family to death and then took his own life. About a year and a half ago. All the TV news shows covered it."

Tess nodded. "That's right. It got national coverage because the father was a famous architect."

Claire fingered the amethyst beads of her necklace. "I was living back East then. If the story made the news there, I missed it." Not that she'd been paying much attention to current events at the time. Zach's midlife crisis had led him to enroll in law school in Boston, and she'd been working long hours as a legal secretary to put him through. What she didn't discover until his graduation party was that her husband's quest to reinvent himself had also led him to a classmate's bed.

Well, Little Ms. Lawyer was welcome to the bastard. With luck, he'd make her life as miserable as he'd made Claire's.

Still, there were moments she missed him. A lot. Until law school turned him into a stranger, she had thought they were perfect together. Their interests had matched, and so had their dreams. He'd been kind, funny, supportive—her best friend. And never, until Zach, had she experienced such rapturous, delicious sex. She couldn't imagine having such intense pleasure with a man ever again.

Tears stung her eyes and she blinked hard to keep any from sliding down her cheeks. She didn't dare let Tess or, worse, Avery, think she might be crying.

She forced herself to tune back into what Tess was saying:

"Another drawback—the property is stale. It's been on the market for six months. Landry and Associates had the house on a three-month exclusive, and when it didn't sell, the listing went to Whitecap Realty. They couldn't move it either. I don't relish getting my distinguished rivals' leftovers."

"Why not?" Claire sat up straighter. "Let's grab the opportunity to show them how much better we are than either one of them."

Tess looked surprised. Then she smiled. "That's the right attitude."

"We could talk to the seller at least," Claire said. "And look at the house ourselves before we decide."

"We?" said Avery, blinking artfully shadowed eyelids.

"Excellent idea," Tess said. She scribbled something on a notepad, tore off the sheet and scribbled again on the one underneath. "It will be good experience for both of you. I was going to suggest tossing a coin for the listing. But having you both take a look is a better idea. The client can choose which of you he'd prefer to work with. Here's the address."

She handed one slip of paper to Claire and one to Avery. Like we're kids, Claire thought, so we won't squabble over who gets to hold the precious information.

"The seller's name is Ben Grant," Tess said. "His message said he'd be at the house until noon. I'll call his cell phone and tell him you two are on your way."

CHAPTER 3

The wind tugged stray tendrils of hair from Avery's hastily tied braid as she aimed her brother Kurt's Porsche 911 convertible around a switchback on Highway One. Thank God she had insisted that they take the Porsche to the LeGrande house. A sunny June day, vistas of green-and-gold hills with occasional glimpses of ocean, air scented with wild fennel and eucalyptus—the trip definitely called for a car like this. Sleek, black, and sporty. Totally awesome.

Claire had offered to drive, but when she led the way to a lime green lump of a Volkswagen in the parking lot, Avery balked. How could a top real estate agent impress clients in a car so uncool? As soon as she raked in a few fat commissions, Avery intended to buy a Porsche like Kurt's for her own.

The car whipped around the next curve.

"Whoa, slow down," Claire warned.

Avery risked taking her eyes from the twisting road long enough to glance at the woman in the passenger seat. Wisps of short dark hair flew around Claire's face. She looked concerned but not scared. Avery did her new colleague a favor and eased back on the gas pedal.

"Better?" she asked.

Claire smiled. "Much."

Avery figured Claire to be in her mid-thirties—perhaps not a full decade older than Avery's own twenty-seven years, but close. She was wearing midnight blue slacks with a matching jacket, and a strand of amethyst crystals that was to die for. Much too chic to be a Volkswagen person. What had Avery heard the old-style VWs called? Pregnant roller skates, that was it. The new ones like Claire's were slightly bigger, more like pregnant skateboards. No class at all. Nothing like the Porsche.

Avery was lucky, she knew, to have such a generous older brother. A few months ago, when she told Kurt she was sick of wasting her life in Texas, he totally understood. He'd fled from home himself. He encouraged her to come to California, fronted the tuition for her real estate classes, and was letting her stay in his apartment while she saved up to move into a place of her own. And she could borrow his car—well, he didn't know she was using it, but he wouldn't mind. The venture capital firm he worked for had sent him to Europe for several weeks, so it wasn't like he needed the Porsche himself. She was doing him a favor by giving it exercise.

The car cut the next turn too wide and veered over the center line.

"Watch out!" Claire yelped.

Avery jerked the wheel hard and swerved back into her own lane, just missing an oncoming pickup. The truck blared its horn as it blew past.

She glanced at her passenger again. Claire's hand was braced flat against the dash. Her foot was probably pressing an imaginary brake pedal right into the floorboards.

"Sorry," Avery said.

They swept down a long slope, angling toward the ocean. Sunlight glinted on the surface of the water. At the bottom of the hill they cruised by the turnoff to a village called Mariners Beach.

"Our road is coming up soon," Claire said as they started to climb again. "There, on the left. Highview Lane."

Avery made the turn. A narrow road twisted up, then leveled off along the ridgetop. They passed half a dozen houses. Widely spaced for privacy. Big decks and huge windows to take advantage of the view. Their price tags no doubt were huge, too. This was about as far from a sagging bungalow in a dusty prairie town as anyone could get.

"It must be that one at the end," Claire said, pointing. Avery couldn't see a house, just a driveway that began where the road stopped. They curled up a short hill and around some protruding rocks, and then . . .

"Oh my God," Avery murmured as the house came into sight.

It was all redwood and glass, twice the size of its neighbors, perched on the edge of a rocky cliff. Two wings with soaring rooflines made the house look like a bird in flight.

"This place is fabulous," she said to Claire. "How could it not sell? There must be plenty of people with money who'd love a house like this."

"A family was murdered here," Claire reminded her. "That scares people off."

"Trust me, if you avoid everyplace where bad things have happened, there'll be nowhere left to live." The ramshackle cottage she'd grown up in was a case in point. As far back as Avery could remember, nothing good had happened there.

To one side of the house, a garage with three doors faced a parking court. A silver Lexus was parked in front of the middle door. Avery pulled Kurt's car in beside it. It looked right at home. Driving the Porsche had definitely been the correct choice.

As she and Claire got out of the car, a man rounded the corner of the house from the rear, walking along a path of redwood decking.

"Hi there," he called. "I heard your car. You must be the agents from Golden Gate Properties. I'm Ben Grant."

"Oh my God," Avery whispered again as he drew nearer. This guy was gorgeous. Lean and tall—a couple of inches over six feet was her guess. Thick brown hair with just the tiniest touch of gray at the temples. Square jaw and chiseled features, all in perfect proportion. He was awesome compared to other men, just like the house was awesome compared to other houses. What did he do for living? This was the wrong part of California for movie stars.

She pulled off the rubber band and shook her golden hair loose from the braid, hoping the movement would make it gleam in the sun. Thank God she'd done up the braid. Otherwise, with the top down the wind would have knotted her hair into one big hopeless snarl. Claire's hair had gotten tangled but apparently she didn't care. She didn't even try to comb out the snarls with her fingers.

Avery extended her hand and a smile to Ben Grant.

Claire, though, got her hand out half a beat quicker. "Glad to meet you," she said as Ben grasped it. "I'm Claire Scanlan, and this is my associate—"

"Avery Collier." She increased the wattage on the smile. "What a beautiful house."

Her turn for a handshake. Ben's grip was warm, solid, strong. Qualities she liked in a man, whether you were talking about his character or important aspects of his anatomy. She nodded her approval.

"Yes, it's beautiful, no question about it." Ben looked toward the house and his face clouded. "Let's go around to the deck. With the previous real estate people, I tried to softpedal what happened here. But that turned out to be the wrong approach. So before we go inside, I want to tell you the whole story. That way you'll know what you're getting into."

Avery had to resist the urge to take his arm as she said, "Lead the way."

CLAIRE FOLLOWED Ben and Avery along the redwood path that skirted the house. She felt uneasy, though she couldn't explain why. The property was even more impressive than she had expected, and to be honest, so was its owner. Yet the moment she and Avery had pulled into the driveway, she'd been hit with an odd sensation that she couldn't shake. The day had darkened slightly, as if the sun had dimmed just the tiniest bit.

Residue from her horrid dream, she decided—the stain of last night's darkness seeping into the beautiful day.

As she reached the back of the house, she gasped in amazement. The deck extended the full length of the house. It was shaped like a big triangle, with a point at the center that jutted out from the cliff like the prow of a ship. There was nothing beyond it but sky and sea. Claire stepped to the railing. Looking straight down, she watched as the ocean waves slammed against the rocks and exploded into white foam.

Lifting her eyes, she noticed a bank of fog, the infamous Pacific marine layer, looming at the horizon. If the weather followed its typical summer pattern, the fog would move inland late this afternoon, obscuring the coastal hills in a swirling mist.

Right now, though, the air was clear and the sky overhead was a cloudless vault of blue.

Yet not quite as bright as it had been before they drove onto the LeGrande property.

"Come on, ladies, have a seat," Ben invited.

Claire turned and saw he had set up three folding lawn chairs in the shade of the overhanging roof. A thermos and three mugs sat on a molded plastic table.

"I brought coffee," Ben said.

He settled onto the center chair and began pouring. Avery sat to his left, hitching her chair closer to his. Claire shook her head at the younger woman's brazenness. Avery's hair was too long, her skirt too short, and her heels too high. Ben Grant seemed like a reasonable man—you'd think he would recognize the predatory look in Avery's eyes for what it was. But men were blind to that sort thing. Certainly her about-to-be ex had been blind to everything about Little Ms. Law-shark except her boobs and her ass and her long blond hair—which was just like Avery's, now that Claire thought about it.

"Claire? Coffee?" Ben's rich baritone broke into her bitter thoughts.

She sat in the remaining chair. "Thanks. This is very thoughtful of you."

His fingertips grazed hers as she took the mug he offered her. Claire was surprised to feel the pleasurable shock of electricity that zinged along her nerves.

Ben sipped from his own mug and gazed into the distance. "It helps if I have something to fortify me when I talk about what happened."

Avery leaned in closer to him. "You mean . . . the tragedy."

"Yes. My brother and his family—"

"Your brother?" Claire said. "Oh! I'm so sorry . . . I mean, for your loss." God, could she sound any more awkward? Why wasn't she one of those people who could express condolences with grace and ease?

"Thanks." Ben sighed. "This house was my brother's masterpiece. Stefan LeGrande, you may have heard of him. He would have hoped so—being famous was one of his foremost goals in life."

"I recognized his name," Avery said with a knowing nod.

Right, Claire thought. But you don't know him because of his architecture. To you he's a high-profile murder victim.

She bit her tongue though. Bad form to put down a colleague in front of a client. Instead she said, "He must have been truly gifted, to design a place like this."

"Yes, gifted," Ben agreed. "He built this house for his family, but he also intended it to be his showcase—a place where he could bring clients and put stars in their eyes about the home he could build for them. They lived here for only a couple of years before . . . well, before disaster struck."

Claire took a drink of the coffee. Rich and robust with a faint hazelnut flavor. She wished Ben had thought to bring cream.

She said, "By *they*, you mean Stefan and his wife and children?"

"That's right. This place was a dream come true for Jacqueline. She was Stefan's second wife. The love of his life—well, if you don't count himself." Ben gave a wry smile.

"What do you mean?" Avery cradled her mug in both hands.

"My esteemed brother was not only a world-class architect, he was a world-class egoist."

Ben paused, looking out beyond the deck. Claire saw a string of brown pelicans skimming through the air, following the line of the cliffs.

"Jacqueline was one of the most beautiful women I've ever met," Ben said. "It wasn't hard for men to fall in love with her. Unfortunately, one of those men was my nephew, Trevor."

"Her own son?" Claire was reminded of her lit class in college, reading *Oedipus Rex*.

"Stefan's son. His mother was Stefan's first wife, Rona. She walked out when the kids were small. Trevor was nine, I think. Melissa was about five. They were all pretty broken up about it."

"She just walked out?" Claire said.

"I don't know all the details. I lived on the east coast then, and my brother was always tightlipped about it. I think she got involved with another man."

"How could a woman do that, just leave her children behind?"

"Oh, that's not hard to imagine," Avery said softly, almost to herself. She was looking down, her face hidden behind a veil of blond hair, so Claire couldn't see her expression. But something about her tone made Claire wonder if Avery was speaking from experience. If so, had she done the leaving, or was she the one who'd been left?

Ben continued his story. "When the divorce came through, Stefan was granted custody. A few years later he met and married Jacqueline, and she brought her little daughter, Eden, into the family. Stefan designed and built this house, and everything seemed set for them to live happily ever after."

"So what went wrong?" Avery asked. She had set down her mug and was twisting a strand of her hair.

"I wish I knew. Trevor was a happy child, but that changed when his parents split. He turned angry and rebellious, started getting in trouble at school."

She released her hair. "Was his sister a problem child too?"

"No. Melissa was always the sweet and level-headed one. Took responsibility, had top grades, looked out for her new little sister. Eden idolized her." Ben shook his head. "Such a loss."

Claire felt her own pang of sadness for this girl, this family, whom she had never met.

"Things got better when Stefan married Jacqueline. Stefan was hopeful that Trevor had turned a corner. But then he hooked up with a druggie crowd. He was dealing and stealing, in trouble all the time. I attempted to reach out to him, but it's hard to be a good uncle from three thousand miles away. Trevor always brushed me off."

Claire nodded. "That must have been really difficult for you."

Ben sighed. "I keep thinking I should have tried harder. Maybe I could have done something to prevent what happened."

He poured himself more coffee and sipped it slowly. All three of them, even Avery, were silent until Ben was ready to go on.

"Stefan sent Trevor away to boarding school. At first we thought the school had worked a miracle, straightening him out. He graduated with honors, moved back home and enrolled at College of Marin."

"I guess the miracle didn't last," Claire said.

"Sadly, no. Trevor dropped out of his classes and fell back into old patterns. Stefan insisted he get a job, but

Trevor never could hold one for long. To make things worse, he developed an infatuation for Jacqueline. More than just a crush; he seemed obsessed with her. Being in the same house with him made her really uncomfortable. So Stefan booted him out. He gave Trevor two weeks to find a new place to live."

Ben picked up his mug and carried it to the prow of the deck. He turned and stared past them to the house. The look on his face made Claire's heart break.

He said, "Just a few days after that ultimatum, Trevor went on his rampage."

"What happened that night?" Avery asked.

"No one's sure. But here's how the police reconstructed the scenario. Melissa had a part in the school play—she loved the theater; she had tremendous talent. There was a rehearsal that night, and Stefan went to pick her up when it was over. That left Trevor home alone with Jacqueline. He tried to force himself on her and she fought him off. The rejection humiliated and infuriated him. So he grabbed the gun that Stefan kept in the house for protection and then—" Ben's voice broke.

Avery finished the sentence for him. "And then he shot her."

"Stefan and Melissa must have arrived home a few minutes later. They walked in to find Jacqueline dead and Trevor raging around with the gun in his hand. He shot the two of them in a panic. Then, in a fit of remorse, he killed himself."

"I'm so sorry," Claire whispered.

"What about Eden?" Avery asked. "She didn't die, did she? I heard it was four people. Did she witness the whole thing?"

"Thank God, Eden wasn't home. She was next door, sleeping over with a friend." Ben sighed. "She lives with me now. I'm the executor of Stefan's will, which left the house to her. We agreed that I should sell it for her. Neither of us could bear ever to live in it."

Claire said, "I understand completely."

"What a shame. It's such an amazing house," was Avery's comment. "I'd live here in a heartbeat."

"So I'm selling it. That is, I'm trying to. Two real estate firms have let me down. I'm hoping Golden Gate Properties will do better."

"You can count on us." Avery raised her mug as if offering a toast.

"I gave the first firm a ninety-day listing," Ben said. "I offered to renew it when it expired, but they refused to keep trying. They had lots of gawkers who wanted the thrill of peeping at a crime scene, but serious buyers ran away when they learned people were murdered here. So I went with a different company. Same thing."

"Too bad we have to tell people," Avery said. "I mean, look at this place. You can't tell anything awful happened here."

"We have to disclose it, though," Claire reminded her. "It's a legal requirement."

Avery dismissed the notion with a flick of her slender fingers. "That law is for real defects, like when the plumbing leaks or the extra bathroom isn't up to code."

Claire did her best not to sound exasperated. "The law covers anything negative that someone should know in order to make a sound and informed decision about purchasing a property."

Ben nodded. "Lots of people would consider this house to be bad luck. Whoever buys it could sue me and your company if they find out too late that it has such a bloody history."

"I know that," Avery said in a supercilious tone. "But it's silly to be superstitious about stuff like that."

"The whole house has been cleaned and re-painted," Ben said. "But whenever I'm here, I see them in my mind. Stefan, Jacqueline, Melissa, Trevor. I see what they were like when they were alive, and I see their bodies lying on the floor, the way they looked in the police photos. That's why I could never live here."

Claire closed her eyes. For just a second she could see the bodies too.

Ben set his mug on the plastic table. "I'm telling you all this up front so you'll know what you're getting into. Well, do you want to back out, or are you ready to go inside?"

"Inside, absolutely," Avery said.

"Right," Claire agreed. "We're going to do everything in our power to sell this place for you."

"Okay then. Come on." Ben moved toward the French doors that led inside from the center of deck.

"Wait," Claire said. "Let's go in the front door. I want my first impression to be the same as the buyers' will be when I bring them here."

Ben nodded. "Good thinking. This way."

Again Avery sidled up next to Ben for the stroll around the house. She might as well just go ahead and hold his hand, Claire thought. She was surprised to feel a pang of jealousy.

ARRIVING AGAIN at the front of the house, Avery noticed a man walking up the pebbled surface of the driveway. As he neared them he lifted his hand in a wave.

Ben waved back, calling, "Hey, Martin."

"Hi, Ben. Didn't realize you were here. Saw a couple of strange cars and thought I'd better check things out."

"I just picked up the Silver Bullet last week," Ben said. "Nice, don't you think? The Porsche belongs to these two—well, one of them, anyway."

Avery jumped in, eager to claim credit. "It's mine."

Ben introduced them. "Avery Collier and Claire Scanlan, meet Martin Roncallo. He lives next door, right over there."

Avery looked where Ben was pointing. All she could see was a gray slate roof peeking above a ledge of rocks. She turned to Roncallo and offered him her hand to shake, pleased that this time she'd beaten Claire to it. "A pleasure."

"Me too," Claire said in turn.

"Likewise." Roncallo's gaze lingered on Avery. She tossed a look of triumph in Claire's direction. This man wasn't so totally handsome as Ben—who was?—but a brushy black mustache and the gas-flame blue eyes under his wiry brows gave him his own brand of rakish charm. He reminded Avery of a pirate; all he needed was an eyepatch or a skull-and-crossbones flag. No wedding ring, she noticed. She'd been pleased to see that Ben wasn't wearing one either. Bare fingers didn't mean a man wasn't married, but a ring was usually intended to convey a message: *don't touch*.

"Avery and Claire are from Golden Gate Properties," Ben explained to his neighbor. "They're going to get this place sold for me."

Roncallo regarded them with sympathy. "Good luck. You two have your job cut out for you, considering the cloud hanging over this place." To Ben he said, "I don't suppose Eden is with you?"

Ben's grin was rueful. "You know the answer to that."

"Yeah, I know she refuses to come up here, but Lily keeps hoping. She misses having Eden right next door. We ought to get them together. It's been awhile."

"Eden would like that. Lily can come to our place. I'll call you soon to set something up."

"Good. Well, now that I've made sure you all aren't vandals—or, even worse, reporters—I'd better get back to work."

Avery couldn't contain her curiosity. "You work at home? What do you do?"

"I design computer games." Roncallo smiled at her, showing white, even teeth beneath his black mustache. Both the smile and the profession were promising. She'd read somewhere that game designers made big bucks.

"Lily—is that your daughter?" she asked.

"That's right. Ten going on twenty-two, all sass and mischief." He chuckled, a sound filled with affection.

Suddenly the pieces fell into place. "The sleepover was at your house, wasn't it? Eden was with Lily that night her family was killed."

A dark expression took over Roncallo's face, confirming her deduction. "Can't blame Eden for not wanting to come back to the old neighborhood, can you? Ben, I'll expect that call so we can find a way to get the girls together. Avery, Claire, good to meet you. I hope you get a smooth, speedy sale."

Avery watched as Martin Roncallo walked back down the driveway. Two intriguing men in the space of half an hour. Highview Lane was proving to be an interesting neighborhood. Ben Grant was more attractive than Martin Roncallo, but it was always good to have a backup plan.

Or a backup man.

That bit of wordplay made Avery giggle.

———————

THE FRONT DOOR was an oversized slab of solid dark wood. Carved into the panel was the large figure of a soaring seagull. Claire watched nervously as Ben set the key in the lock. He twisted the key and the door swung open.

She jumped back, reeling from the sudden stench of blood—hot, bitter, coppery.

Then the smell was gone. Had she imagined it?

Ben stood aside to let Avery cross the threshold. Neither of them seemed to have noticed the sharp if fleeting odor.

"Claire? Are you coming?" Ben asked.

"Of course." She flashed him a smile and stepped inside, forcing herself to take a deep breath. She smelled stale air and dust, the fusty quality you'd expect of any house that had been shut up for too long.

"Welcome to Stefan LeGrande's masterpiece," Ben said.

"Wow!" Avery said. "Look at this place."

They were standing in a marble-floored entryway. A skylight filled the space with soft, warm light.

Coming in farther, Claire saw that the entryway branched off to either side, forming a long gallery that linked the home's two wings. Straight in front of her, a step down from the gallery and separated from it by a polished wooden railing, was a vast living room.

Zach, Claire knew, would compare the room's size to a football field. Her best friend Lindsay would estimate how many times the little apartment that the two of them shared would fit inside the space. Claire had brought a metal tape measure in her purse. Before they left the house, she and Avery would get the exact measurements.

She ran her hand along the wooden railing. Smooth as satin. Stefan LeGrande had clearly understood the power of small yet sumptuous details. The high, vaulted ceiling, the gleaming hardwood floor, the stone fireplace—all these would be strong selling points.

The most appealing feature was the far wall. It was entirely glass, with French doors in the center that led to the deck. The room seemed to expand outward, becoming a part of the sky and the sea and the fog.

Something else Stefan LeGrande had known—how best to take advantage of a building's natural setting.

Ben joined Claire at the railing, as Avery pressed in on the other side of him.

"My brother had theories about how families live in public and private spaces. This wing," Ben said, pointing to the right, "contains private spaces: bedrooms, family bathrooms, the master suite. In the other wing you'll find public spaces: kitchen, dining room, the media lounge."

"What's this space here?" Avery swept her arm to indicate the huge room in front of them.

"Stefan called it the grand salon. It was a central gathering place, the pivot point around which the family's life revolved."

"And the media lounge? What's that?" Avery asked.

"A home theater," Ben replied. "I'll show you. Let's start the tour there."

"Go ahead. I'll catch up," Claire said. She stepped down into the grand salon and headed toward the glass wall, drawn by the view.

Instantly the air felt colder.

"Where did the murders happen?" Avery was asking as she and Ben walked together along the gallery.

The two of them disappeared through a doorway, so Claire didn't hear Ben's reply. But the chill in the air had told her—the victims had died right here. In this room, four lives had come to a sudden, brutal end in a tumult of rage and blood.

She could see no signs of the violence—too many months had passed, too much effort had been made to cleanse the house of the horror that had happened. All the place needed was an airing-out, a new family's energy and laughter.

Then her eyes closed and Claire saw them, as clearly as if they were still there. Four crumpled bodies, two by the fireplace, one by the glass wall, one in the center of the room.

Quickly she opened her eyes again, shook her head to scatter the images away from her mind.

The cold intensified, covering her arms with gooseflesh and turning her breath to an icy mist.

She tried to retreat to the gallery, but an unseen force blocked her way.

She'd run for the glass wall then. Open the door and flee onto the deck.

As Claire scurried across the room, something yanked on her shoulder. She tried to pull away. The painful grip tightened, binding her in place.

"Let me go!" She twisted her body, tried to lift her legs, tried to wrench herself free.

She couldn't move.

The room turned red. Again Claire smelled blood. Its metallic odor was stronger and sharper than before.

A voice hovered next to her ear, faint, a soft breath, barely a whisper: "Help me."

She wasn't sure she heard it at all.

Then, once more: "Help me!"

The whisper was nearly drowned out by a piercing shriek.

CHAPTER 4

"Claire! Are you all right? What happened?"
Ben's voice. Claire felt gentle hands on her arms, steadying her. A very different kind of touch from the cold wintry grasp that had clutched her a moment ago.

"We were in the kitchen and we heard you scream," Avery said as Ben, apparently satisfied that Claire would not collapse, released her.

"That was m-me?" Claire's voice was shaking. "I heard it too . . . but I didn't realize . . . you're sure it was me?"

She tried to laugh. Best to make light of the bizarre experience. Clearly neither Ben nor Avery had perceived anything out of the ordinary, except the shriek.

Okay, so maybe that was her own silly screeching. But then who had whispered words into her ear? Who had seized her shoulder? If Ben and Avery were off in another room . . .

"What was wrong?" Ben asked. "What made you yell like that?"

"N-nothing. I'm fine." Claire rubbed her arms. Her shoulder tingled where the unseen force had grabbed her. But the goosebumps were gone. The temperature of the room had returned to normal. Her heart, which had been banging against her ribs, was starting to calm.

Avery parked her fists on her slim hips. "A person doesn't scream over nothing."

Claire shook her head. "I–I had a bad dream last night . . . and now, all this talk about bloodshed . . . I guess my imagination ran away with me. I'm sorry if I scared you."

The word *sorry* echoed in Claire's brain. The refrain of the tune she'd sung earlier this morning when she arrived late for the Monday Meeting: *Sorry . . . sorry . . . sorry.* She was not getting off to a good start. She hoped she wasn't going to spend her entire real estate career making apologies. If so, that career would be brief.

But she wanted it to last for a good long time. She wanted . . . needed . . . to succeed at this. She offered a smile to Avery, her colleague, and a bigger one to Ben Grant, her potential client. "I hope I haven't given you a bad impression of Golden Gate Properties."

To her relief, Ben laughed. "A bad impression? Not at all. At least you're prepared now for some of the strange reactions you'll get from buyers."

"Let's get on with the tour then." Claire took out the little notebook she had in her purse.

The three of them spent the next hour going through the house. Avery cooed admiringly as Ben pointed out this special feature and that luxurious detail. Claire made careful notes about the top-of-the-line appliances, the sound system that piped music into every room, the climate-controlled wine locker. She ran her fingers over smooth granite countertops and satiny wood finishes. She jotted down the words Ben said about all the fine points of texture and color and angles and curves that were the signatures of a Stefan LeGrande design.

No more voices. No ice-cold air. No invisible hand clamping her shoulder.

The architect had built his family a truly exquisite home. You'd think such a house would have thrown a magic shield around the family, a protective barrier against the kinds of problems that beset people who lived in more ordinary circumstances. Clearly not, Claire thought.

In fact, maybe the house had made things worse. Except for its builder, the supremely talented Stefan, who could hope to live up to the standards implied by such perfection? Perhaps knowing he couldn't help but fall short was what had derailed young Trevor and set him on a course of destruction.

Martin Roncallo had mentioned a cloud over the house. Claire wondered if he had been using a figure of speech, meaning that the house had been made less attractive by the awareness that violence had occurred there.

Or did he, like Claire, experience that odd dimming of daylight when he stepped onto the property? Would Martin have heard the whispers if he had been with her in the grand salon?

By now they were back in the entrance gallery. As Ben opened the door so they could leave, he said, "I suppose we should talk about the price and a schedule for open houses and things like that."

Avery smoothed her hand over her long blond hair. "Have you thought about who you want to be your listing agent?"

Ben looked surprised. "What do you mean? I've already decided to give the listing to Golden Gate Properties."

Avery tilted her head coquettishly. "Well, sure, but Tess McMillan said you should choose one of us. Claire or me, I mean. Of course the whole firm will work hard for you. But it's customary to have one particular agent in charge of your listing."

"I don't see how I could go wrong with either one of you," Ben said—rather gallantly, Claire thought. "But if I have to choose . . . hmm, maybe I should spend some one-on-one time with each of you first."

"You mean, alone with you?" the blonde said. "What a good idea."

"Here's a plan. Claire, why don't you join me for lunch? Avery can drive her car back to the office, and I'll deliver you there later this afternoon. Avery, you and I can get together when I drop Claire off."

Avery frowned. "Well, I don't—"

Claire jumped in before she could finish. "That sounds great. Thank you."

Avery changed tactics. She erased her frown and beamed a big smile at Claire. "Tell you what, Claire. If you want, I'll let you take the Porsche back. It's a really fun car to drive."

Claire matched Avery's smile with one of her own. "That is such a generous offer. Thank you. But I don't dare take you up on it. I wouldn't trust myself with a car that's so exquisite." Or so expensive. The way the day was going, it'd be just her luck to get into an accident. No doubt the Porsche was insured, but insurance would pay only for the damage to the car, not for the wreckage of her career. It wasn't worth the risk.

Besides, time alone with Ben Grant was a highly appealing idea. And going first, getting to know this handsome man before Avery could get her mitts on him—the heavens were offering her an opportunity here. She did not intend to blow it.

DAMN! AVERY SLAMMED HER FIST against the steering wheel as the Porsche neared the stop sign at the end of Highview Lane. Without quite stopping, she pulled out onto the coastal highway.

So unfair. How could Ben Grant choose to meet with Claire first? He'd as good as handed her the listing right then and there. Sure, he said he'd get together with Avery before making up his mind. Big deal. Claire would get a chance to charm him over a relaxed lunch, and what would Avery get? Fifteen minutes and a cup of stale coffee in the conference room. The person who went first always had the advantage.

She zipped around a curve. The Porsche veered to the shoulder and the tires sent gravel flying. Avery jerked the car back into the lane.

She was so sick of coming in second. All her life she'd had to settle for runner-up, behind whatever someone else considered more important. Mama and her boyfriends. Daddy and his booze. Her brother Kurt and his ambition.

On her eighteenth birthday Avery had married Joey Burnside and they rode his Harley to Houston, fleeing the shithole town they'd grown up in. She was madly in love with Joey. Finally she'd found someone who thought she belonged in the winner's circle. But it wasn't long before she and the baby in her belly fell to second, third, fourth place behind Joey's chopper and his meth and his new buddies in leathers and chains. Her baby was only twenty-four hours old when Avery signed her over to the lawyer who promised he'd found the ideal adoptive family.

By the time she was nineteen, Avery was single again, living once more in her daddy's house and waiting tables at the Wagon Wheel Café. Only now she had to fight Daddy off. He had never messed with her when she was a kid, but now that she was divorced and clearly no longer a virgin, he decided the rules had changed. Late one drunken night he barged into her bedroom. She shuddered every time she remembered the heavy weight of his body falling on top of her, the rank smell of beer and sweat, the feel of her fingers sinking into his flabby flesh as she pushed him away. He had been too drunk to do anything, thank God, but she knew she couldn't live in his house any longer.

Avery slipped out of the house and walked around town aimlessly for the rest of the night. As soon as daylight came, she went to see her best friend Kaylee and begged for help. Kaylee and her new husband let her sleep in their spare bedroom. But six weeks later Kaylee's own baby was born and it wasn't a spare bedroom any more. Avery was ready to move out anyway. The idea of being in a house with a baby in it, someone else's baby, made her sadder than anything.

Well, all that was behind her now. She was on her way to the life she had dreamed about, the life she deserved.

If Ben Grant wanted to make a contest out of the listing for his house—well, fine. Avery intended to be the winner.

This time she was coming in first. And that stupid Claire was not going to stop her.

"Excellent," Ben said. He took a sip from the stemmed glass then set it down and nodded to the waiter, a skinny middle-aged man with a mustache so thin it looked as if it had drawn with a pencil. The waiter made fussy little movements as he poured wine into Claire's glass, filled

Ben's the rest of the way and set the bottle precisely in the center of the table.

Claire took a sip as she gazed at the sailboats bobbing in the marina. Excellent indeed—the sauvignon blanc was crisp and fruity and delicious, perfect for a sunny June afternoon. She probably shouldn't be drinking wine at lunch on a workday, but when Ben ordered the bottle she decided to let herself indulge in the interest of good client relations.

They were sitting under a wide umbrella on the second-floor deck at the Windward Restaurant, overlooking the ferry dock in Tiburon. A soft summer breeze caressed her cheek, and she imagined what it would be like to have Ben caress it too.

Stop thinking like that, Claire, she instructed herself. Remember, he's a client.

"Ready to order?" the waiter asked, pad and pencil poised.

"I'll have the Caesar salad," Claire said.

Ben ordered a sirloin steak, medium rare. The waiter painstakingly wrote it all down, then trotted away.

Ben lifted his glass. "To a successful sale."

"I'll drink to that," Claire said, clinking her glass against his. "A quick sale, no complications, and well over the asking price."

"I hope you're feeling better now?" Ben lifted his voice and his eyebrows, making it a question.

Claire nodded. "I'm sorry for acting so . . . so oddly back there."

On the drive from the LeGrande house to the restaurant, Ben hadn't brought up her strange behavior, for which Claire had been grateful. They had chatted about trivial, impersonal things—the weather, the scenery, a movie they'd both recently seen. The farther away they got from the house with its shadows and whispers, the more unreal the whole experience seemed.

"Maybe not so odd," Ben said. "Something about Stefan's house spooks people. At least you'll be able to empathize if a client comes to look at the place and runs out screaming."

Claire chuckled. "That will be an advantage, no doubt about it."

Ben leaned forward. "What happened, exactly? What did you experience?"

"I heard . . . I felt . . . well, it's hard to describe."

Did she dare tell him? The house was his responsibility. If strange phenomena were occurring there, he ought to know.

She glanced away, looking at the sailboats, the sunlight glinting on the water, the red geraniums in pots around the edge of the dining deck.

How could she convey what she'd experienced. She imagined the words tumbling out in a rush: *I felt the house go icy cold and saw the sunlight dim. I smelled blood and then I didn't. I saw bodies on the floor and then they disappeared. I heard someone whisper, asking for help, and then something grabbed me . . . and I . . . and I . . .*

The memory made her tremble, and she gripped the edge of the table, needing something solid and real to hang onto. She closed her eyes but the images kept crowding in, so she opened them again. Ben was looking at her, concern evident in his warm hazel eyes.

"What's going on?" he asked. "Are you okay?"

Claire made herself smile. What could she say that wouldn't turn his expression into skepticism or mockery? The last thing she wanted was for him to think she was some kind of nutcase.

"To tell the truth, Ben, I don't really know why I reacted like that at the house. I caught sight of something out of the corner of my eye and it startled me, that's all."

Ben grinned. "Not some sort of ghost or spirit, I hope."

"Of course not. Probably just a flock of birds flying past that plate-glass wall. My mind grabbed hold of whatever it was and ran with it. I've often been accused of having an overactive imagination."

"Accused? Harsh word. As if someone thought you'd committed a crime."

Picking up her glass, Claire stared at the view, which spanned Angel Island and the Golden Gate Bridge. In the distance she could see the towers of San Francisco.

As if she'd committed a crime. That was exactly how it felt at times. Grandmother Scanlan, who had raised Claire and her older sister, used to punish Claire for lying whenever she reported seeing or feeling something that Gram didn't believe. Zach's attitude had almost been worse. He would dismiss what Claire said, pronouncing it ridiculous or idiotic, or calling her a drama queen. Eventually she learned to keep her mouth shut. Nowadays, when strange things happened to her, she didn't really believe in them herself.

But she had no intention of telling any of that to Ben. Instead she said, "Your brother must have had a wonderful imagination. It shows in his house."

"Creativity was encouraged in our family. Even as a kid Stefan was our star. Our parents indulged him because his talent was so obvious. Though I have to say Dad didn't like it much when Stefan got creative with his name."

"What do you mean?"

"When we were growing up my brother was plain old Steve Grant. Just like I'm plain old Ben Grant."

"There's nothing plain about you." The words just flew out, much to Claire's astonishment. She felt herself turn beet red.

"You're too kind," Ben said. "But you have to admit the name is pretty ordinary. When brother Steve was at Cornell studying architecture he decided to tweak his name to make it sound more exotic and memorable. Steve morphed into Stefan. Grant was glamorized into LeGrande."

Claire laughed. "Apparently it worked. He became world famous."

"When I was a kid my big brother was my hero. There seemed to be no end to what he could accomplish. He opened his own firm straight out of grad school. Not many fledgling architects can do that and succeed."

"He went solo for his whole career?"

Ben scowled. "Well, he had a partner for the first few years, one of his classmates. But the guy didn't have Stefan's vision or skill. In fact, Stefan called him a no-talent bum. Finally he booted him out of the firm. Once he got rid of that liability, his career soared. As I recall, the man met some sort of tragic end soon afterward. A car accident, or something like that."

"While your brother became the famous Stefan LeGrande. Did you ever think about following suit? With your name, that is."

"You mean turn myself into Benjamin LeGrande?"

"You'd want a more unusual name than Benjamin, I think, to go with the grand LeGrande. Benedict, perhaps? Or how about Beniamino, like the sculptor Beniamino Bufano. That would give your name a nice artistic association."

"If Stefan wanted an artistic name, he deserved one. But I can't call myself an artist. Stefan was lucky—he found a way to express his creative vision and make money at the same time. I've had to settle for being a Sunday painter."

"You paint?"

"A little. I have more enthusiasm than talent."

"What else do you do?"

"For a living, you mean?"

Claire nodded, wondering if she was being too forward.

"I used to be a partner in a venture capital firm. I was in Boston, Cambridge actually, and when I joined the firm I had just earned a shiny, brand new Harvard MBA."

"Cambridge? What a coincidence. I lived there until just a few months ago."

"Really? It's a great city, isn't it. And most people would say I had a great job. I loved it at first, but the last few years were soul-numbing. When Stefan and his family died, I quit and came to California. I knew being executor of his estate would turn into a full-time job for a while. More important, I wanted to be here for Eden."

"Stefan's daughter. Your niece. The one who survived."

"His stepdaughter, actually, though he loved her like his own child." Ben pulled out a slim leather wallet. "I do too. She's a wonderful kid."

He slid a photo from the wallet and passed it to Claire. A posed school portrait, showing a girl of about ten. Pale blue eyes, blond hair that tumbled over her shoulders. She was gazing directly at the camera, offering the photographer a shy, sweet smile.

"She's very pretty," Claire said as she handed the photo back.

Ben nodded as he returned the picture to his wallet. "Smart as a whip, too. I'll have my hands full when she gets older."

"She's staying with you?"

"That's right."

"What about her father?" Instantly she regretted the prying question. None of your business, Claire.

But Ben didn't seem to mind. "For all practical purposes, she doesn't have one. Jacqueline's relationship with the guy ended right after their daughter was born. He used to visit Eden when she was little, and he claims he wants her to live with him when he gets out, but—"

"Gets out?"

"Of prison." Ben's expression turned dark. "Leo Hollister is a drug dealer, and a volatile, hot-tempered man. He's serving a sentence for assaulting one of his customers. No way is he ever getting custody of Eden. She and I are a family now and that's the way it's going to stay."

Claire shivered. The mention of Leo Hollister's name sent a chill through her, even though she had never heard of the man. How sad, how terrifying it would be to have a father in prison. And then to have your life wrenched apart by the kind of tragedy Eden had suffered—that was more than even Claire's overactive imagination could comprehend.

She was relieved to see the waiter with the penciled-on mustache returning to deliver their lunch.

She murmured a thank you as he set her salad into place in front of her. He then centered a platter with a steak and French fries squarely between Ben's knife and fork.

"Anything else I can bring you?" the waiter asked.

"Thanks. We're all set," Ben said.

"This looks delicious." Claire speared a segment of romaine and lifted it to her mouth. The lettuce was crunchy and cool, the dressing tangy with Parmesan and—uh-oh, garlic. It tasted wonderful, but she should have remembered that garlic was a key ingredient in a Caesar salad dressing. Garlic breath probably was not on the list of recommended tools for establishing a positive agent-client relationship.

Which reminded her—she was here with Ben on business.

"Would you like to talk about selling the house?" she asked. "Actually I'm surprised you're selling it. I mean, I definitely understand why you and Eden wouldn't want to live there. But if it was your brother's showplace, his masterpiece . . ."

Ben sliced into his steak, revealing the pink inside.

"I thought about turning it into a museum, but I figured it would just attract ghouls and voyeurs, people more interested in my brother's death than his architectural legacy. Another idea was to set up a foundation in his name and use the house as headquarters. I may do that, but I'll locate the office somewhere else."

"Keeping the house would probably be a financial burden," Claire said. "It must have been hugely expensive to build."

"It was, but Stefan had it completely paid for. There's no mortgage. The taxes and maintenance costs are high, but the estate is able to pay them. I want to get rid of the house for Eden's sake. She's terrified of the place. Refuses to go near it."

"Who can blame her?"

"A couple of times I took her to visit Lily Roncallo, who's her best friend. Eden started to cry as soon as we turned into Highview Lane. So now whenever the girls get together, Lily comes to our place."

Claire nodded. "I guess selling the house will be a good thing for her. Help her to heal from the tragedy."

"Exactly."

"Have you thought about the asking price? We might have to set it lower than you'd expect since it's been sitting on the market so long." She sighed. "Murder wasn't one of the market factors they taught us about in real estate school."

Ben poured more sauvignon blanc into her glass and then refilled his own. "We can wait until we get back to your office before we talk business. This is a get-acquainted session. We have a good meal and a good wine—and I, for one, am in charming company. Let's get to know each other better and enjoy a little of this beautiful afternoon."

"Yes, let's," Claire agreed. She was in no rush to get back to Golden Gate Properties and deliver Ben into Avery's clutches.

CHAPTER 5

To Claire's astonishment, the entire staff of Golden Gate Properties was in the office when she and Ben arrived. She would have expected them to be out with clients, or touring houses—anything besides turning to stare at her and her companion as they stepped off the elevator.

Avery marched toward them from the open bullpen where the agents had their desks. Her voice couldn't have been more honeyed as she greeted them.

"So glad you two could make it back. Where have you been all this time?"

Honey laced with battery acid, Claire thought.

"Sorry," Claire said before she could stop herself. She wished she'd bitten her tongue instead. She was definitely going to have to erase that word from her vocabulary. Why was she apologizing to Avery, of all people? Okay, it had been a long lunch, but she and Ben had never said what time they would return.

Glancing at the audience, Ben made a slight bow. "Claire, it's been a pleasure. Avery, if you'd care to join me, there's a place down the street that has a charming cocktail lounge."

"Sounds good. I'm ready." Avery was already carrying her purse. She hitched the strap higher on her shoulder and strutted to the elevator, tossing a smirk at Claire as she pushed the call button.

Claire smiled back. Avery probably thought she'd charm Ben into taking her out for an evening on the town. Or, more likely, a night on the mattress. And maybe she would succeed. Claire's mood, light until that moment, darkened at the thought of Ben and Avery in bed together.

The elevator door slid shut, and the two of them disappeared.

Claire sighed. As Ben drove her to her office, she'd tried to gauge which of them he was leaning toward, her or Avery, but he'd successfully avoided given her a clue.

Look confident, she told herself. She gave everyone a little wave as she walked back toward her desk. She lifted her hand extra high to greet Tess McMillan, the boss, who was in her office watching through the glass pane that looked out on the rest of Golden Gate's space.

George, the balding, heavyset guy who had been so annoying that morning, winked at her as she passed him. She ignored him but felt her teeth clench.

The agents' desks were arranged in two rows of three. As the newcomer, Claire had been assigned one of the pair at the rear of the bullpen. Avery had managed to score the desk in front of her, in the middle of things. The one next to Claire's was empty, its dark wood surface bare, ready to accommodate another new hire if Golden Gate decided to expand its staff. Five agents, six desks. She was in her own little Siberia back here.

She sat down and put her head in her hands. The way it was buzzing suggested that the sauvignon blanc, delicious as it was, might have been a mistake.

"So, Claire, how'd it go?"

She looked up. Perched on the empty desk was the black-haired agent who had been friendly this morning at the Monday Meeting.

"Oh, everything went fine. Sor—I mean, forgive me, I'm blanking on your name." Was *forgive me* an improvement over *sorry*? Probably not, Claire decided.

"Jeff Ortega." He put out his hand and she shook it; his grasp was firm and warm. "I probably should warn you—"

"About what?"

George pushed his corpulent self in between them. "Hey, sweetheart, you're gonna win, right? I got twenty bucks riding on you."

"About that," Jeff said.

"Win?" Claire said as that *uh-oh* feeling settled into her stomach. "Is there some sort of contest?"

"More like an office pool," George explained. "Me and the girls." He swept his hand back to indicate the two women hovering nearby.

"Just a little wager," said one of them. Short spiky red hair, probably in her mid forties. Office manager and receptionist, if Claire recalled right. Claire fished in her memory for the name: Marie, or Maureen . . . something with an M.

"I put my money on you. Actually, we all did," the other woman assured her, sweeping her hand to indicate the assembled agents. She was a slender Asian woman, maybe a couple of years older than Claire. Sleek dark hair hung to her shoulders. Claire remembered her name: Delia Chan.

"All except Jeff here." George thumped his colleague on the shoulder. "He's too chicken to place a friendly bet."

"What exactly are you betting on?" Claire demanded. "What am I supposed to win?"

"The listing for the LeGrande house," Jeff explained. "Tess told us how she sent you two out to the place so the client could decide between you. When Avery came back by herself, and said you'd gone out to lunch with the client, we all figured he'd made his choice."

Delia took up the story. "But Avery said no way. Not after you freaked out like you did."

"Freaked out? She said that? I never—"

"Don't worry, hon." The redhead with the M name patted Claire's hand. "Who doesn't get a little spooked on occasion?"

"What exactly did Avery say?"

Delia fingered a strand of her dark hair. "None of us really believed her. Well, I didn't anyway."

The redhead said, "She said she'd be going out with the client this afternoon, and she bet each of us twenty dollars that when she gets back, she'll have the listing. If she succeeds, we pay her. If the client picks you, she pays us."

"Each of us except Jeff," George pointed out again.

"Hey, it's not like I bet against you, Claire," Jeff protested. "I'm just not a gambling man."

"That's okay," Claire said. "I wouldn't take that bet either." And she fervently wished no one else had. It would hardly help her standing in the firm if people lost money, even twenty bucks, because of her. "But I appreciate the vote of confidence."

Tess came up behind the assembled agents. Her pink suit and champagne hair looked as fresh and unwrinkled as they had this morning. "Who's betting on what?"

"Oh, nothing," Delia said. She and the others melted away from Claire's desk.

Tess leaned against the empty desktop that Jeff had just vacated. "So how did it go?" she asked.

"Fine, just fine." The buzzing in Claire's head intensified as she remembered the whispering voice: *Help me*. "It's a wonderful house . . . if you don't consider the awful thing that happened to the family that lived there."

"So Mr. Grant has decided to go with Golden Gate?" Tess lifted a perfectly arched eyebrow, turning her words into a question.

"Yes, of course. I'm sure he has."

"And which of my talented and charming new agents has he decided to use?"

"Me. I hope. Unless he picks Avery."

"I see. Well, why don't you get started looking at recent sales of comparable houses, so we can begin thinking about how to price it."

Tess glided off, and Claire turned to her computer. Comparable houses, she thought as she pulled up the local real estate database. That's easy—I'll just look up every home sold in Marin County the last six months that has six bedrooms, boasts an ocean view, and was the site of a quadruple homicide.

AVERY KNEW she was in trouble when Ben Grant ordered a Diet Coke.

She had started out with high hopes. The Paradise Lounge was as romantic a place as she could have wished for. Deep red walls, soft music playing. Candles flickering in glass globes on low marble-topped tables. Thickly cushioned chairs on casters so people could pull up closer to the tables, or each other. At four in the afternoon, she and Ben were the only customers, which added to the atmosphere of intimacy.

They settled into a place in the corner, and Ben picked up the long printed list of wines the Paradise sold by the glass. He described the various vintages with knowledge and appreciation.

A short-skirted cocktail waitress appeared beside the table. Probably a college student, Avery decided, working part time. With her long blond hair, the young woman reminded Avery of herself a few years ago, though she'd never gone to college and none of the bars she'd worked in were anywhere near this classy. For once she was the one who got to be the customer in the company of the handsome man. How cool was that?

"Ready to order?" the waitress asked.

"Try this one, the Silver Creek cabernet." Ben was pointing, Avery noted with approval, to the most expensive wine on the list. He went on to praise its subtle tastes of vanilla, strawberry and, of all things, tobacco.

So she took his advice, expecting him request the same thing.

And then he went and asked for a Diet Coke. She felt like she'd been slapped in the face.

Not that she minded people who didn't drink. Goodness knows her whole family would have been better off if her daddy had quit guzzling all that beer.

But Ben didn't seem like a problem drinker, or a teetotaler, or an A.A. type. Ordering a soda signaled that he intended this to be strictly a business meeting, while she had in mind mixing business with pleasure. Her plan was to get him to relax and enjoy her company, so that he would invite her to join him first for dinner and then for the rest of the evening and then—she wasn't sure what would come next, but she was open to all sorts of possibilities.

Well, no reason the plan couldn't still work. She didn't need to get a man drunk to captivate him.

She leaned forward a bit to show off her cleavage, tilted her head and offered Ben her sweetest smile. "You're not going to have a glass of wine along with me?"

"Ordinarily I would, but as it happens, I had my quota for today at lunchtime."

At lunchtime. He meant with Claire. Damn it, he and Claire had enjoyed a glass of wine together, maybe two or three glasses. They had probably drunk toasts to the success Claire would have in selling the house. No wonder their lunch had lasted so damn long.

Avery crossed her legs, hitching up the hem of her skirt so Ben could notice and admire them. She had nice legs; men had been telling her that since she was thirteen.

He leaned back in his chair. Silence stretched between them like a taut rubber band ready to snap. Finally Avery broke it, saying, "So tell me . . . " But she couldn't think of a good way to finish the sentence.

Ben rescued her. "So tell *me*," he said, "what you think of my brother's house."

"It's totally awesome." She sat up straighter and gestured with both hands to show her excitement. "I bet I can sell it quickly. I don't know why those other agencies couldn't find someone to buy a great house like that."

He looked thoughtful. "Did you notice anything . . . out of the ordinary about it?"

"Are you kidding? The whole place is out of the ordinary. That's why it's so fabulous."

The waitress came back, placed paper coasters on the tabletop, and set down their drinks. Avery picked up her cabernet and sipped. She didn't know much about wine, really, but this one tasted lovely.

Ben ignored the Diet Coke. "True, but that's not what I meant. Claire seemed to perceive something . . . strange."

"Yeah. Wasn't that weird, the way she freaked out?"

"You weren't aware of anything that might make her scream?"

Avery shook her head vigorously, setting wisps of her hair flying. "Not me. Claire said herself it was her imagination running away." She extended her glass toward Ben. "Cheers. Here's to our partnership in selling that super house."

Ben still didn't lift his glass. "Avery, I've been thinking . . ."

Avery tensed. His tone and his body posture warned that she wasn't going to like what he'd been thinking about.

"You know, Ben"—she leaned toward him, spoke in a low conspiratorial tone, even though no one but Ben was around to hear her—"Claire seems to be, well, what my mama called high-strung. Kind of unstable."

"High-strung," Ben repeated. He smiled slightly. Reflected light from the candle on the table flickered in his eyes. Avery felt her heart jump. God, he was good-looking.

"You need someone level-headed like me, not some scaredy-cat. Someone who's enthusiastic too. Claire doesn't really like the house, it makes her uncomfortable, I can tell. But I love the place." She put a hand on his arm. "I'd do a great job for you, Ben."

"I don't doubt your enthusiasm for a minute. And that's a wonderful attribute, Avery. But Claire's reaction—it's as if she senses something about the house that you and I don't."

"What, like she really saw a ghost? You can't believe that. She's either a fake or a flake, take your pick."

"I think she has a vivid imagination, like you said. But buyers have imaginations too. Maybe hers will help her relate to their reactions to the house."

"Are you saying I can't relate to buyers?"

"Not at all. I expressed myself badly. Look, if I give the listing to Claire, you'll still make half the commission if a client of yours buys the house, right?"

"Yeah, but the listing agent gets half no matter who sells it, and the whole thing if she sells it herself. Please, Ben, I'll work really hard. I've already got a client who I know will be interested—" Okay, that last part was a fib. But surely the circumstances justified a little white lie.

"Excellent. Bring him around. Or her." Ben finally took a sip of his soft drink, then set down the glass again. "I wish there was a way to give the listing to both of you, Avery. But it seems that I'm required to choose between two excellent possibilities. For any other house, I'm sure I'd pick you. But for this one, my instinct tells me to go with Claire."

Avery felt the hot burn of tears and blinked hard to keep them from escaping her eyes. She was going to have to shell out sixty bucks to the people at Golden Gate, but losing that bet was the least of her disappointments.

"We'll still be working together," Ben said. "I'm looking forward to working closely with everyone at Golden Gate."

Avery nodded. She didn't trust herself to speak. She'd either sound angry or pathetic and needy, and neither of those attitudes would do her much good with Ben.

"So let's be friends," he said. "Enjoy the rest of your wine. Then we'll go back to your office and I'll take care of the paperwork."

"It's good wine," she said. Her hand was trembling as she reached for the stem of her glass. She downed the rest of the contents in one long swallow.

Damn it, this game wasn't over. She was going to sell that house, earn half the commission. She'd show Claire, she'd show Ben, she'd show them all. This time Avery Collier was going to win.

"The Champagne Express," Lindsay Berenger called out to Claire. "Now arriving on Track One. Toot, toot!" She emerged from their apartment kitchen, swinging a heavy bottle by its foil-wrapped neck. In the other hand she held two flute-shaped crystal glasses.

Claire laughed. "Don't carry it like that. It will spray all over the place when it's opened."

"No, it won't. I have a special touch with champagne bottles." Her roommate set the glasses on the coffee table and plopped onto the overstuffed armchair across from the sofa where Claire sat. Balancing the bottle on her knees, Lindsay stripped off the foil and removed the wire cage. "The secret is to hold the cork and twist the bottle, not the other way around."

"What are we celebrating?" Claire asked. She'd been working on the newspaper crossword puzzle but now she set it aside.

"How can you even ask? We're celebrating your successes, of course."

"My successes?"

"It's a red-letter day for you. You've listed your first house as a real estate agent, you've charmed a handsome and interesting man—"

"Charmed is overstating it."

"Not at all. He treated you to a lovely lunch, and he signed up to be your client despite having the office sexpot compete for his business. Certainly that qualifies as charmed. Whoops, watch out!"

The cork made a satisfying pop and flew across the room. White foam erupted out of the bottle.

"Warned you," Claire said.

"It's only a dribble." Lindsay grabbed a glass to catch the overflow. She filled both flutes and handed one to Claire. "Here's to a big fat commission and an even bigger romance."

They clinked glasses and Claire took a sip. The bubbles danced a pleasant little samba on her tongue.

"But don't let either one get too big," Lindsay added. "You can't move out for a long time. I need your help paying the rent." She settled back in the cushions and tucked her legs up under her. Claire always marveled at the positions her roommate could twist herself into and seemingly remain comfortable.

"I think you're stuck with me for awhile," Claire assured her. She was pleased to be living in Lindsay's apartment. Hers and Lindsay's—her mind still hadn't made the adjustment to thinking of this as home, not just someplace where she was staying on an extended visit.

She and Lindsay had been fast friends since their days at San Francisco State. They'd met as starry-eyed freshmen in the theater department, before their families persuaded them to switch to more practical majors than drama. In many ways their lives seemed to be in synch. Their birthdays were only two days apart, and though Lindsay's hair was redder than Claire's dark brown, they looked enough alike that people often mistook them for sisters. They'd stayed in close touch when Claire moved to Boston with Zach.

As it happened, she discovered Zach in bed with Little Ms. Legal-Beagle during the same chaotic week that Lindsay's live-in boyfriend announced he was taking a new job in Hawaii and leaving everything in their apartment behind, including Lindsay. For a long time afterward, their daily phone calls were all that kept either one sane. When Claire decided that her best course was to come home to the Bay Area, Lindsay had plenty of reasons, personal and financial, to take her in.

Claire ran a finger around the delicate rim of the champagne flute. "I hoped we were celebrating good news for you—like maybe you got promoted to be head of your department, or that hot stockbroker you've been eyeing has finally asked you out."

Lindsay laughed. "Don't I wish. That's why I always keep a bottle of champagne in the fridge—so I'll be prepared when something good like that happens. But this bottle was in danger of becoming a permanent fixture. I had to pry it loose from the clutches of the jelly spills and the containers of moldering leftovers."

"I didn't even know it was there," Claire confessed.

"Way in the back of the bottom shelf. You had to be on your hands and knees to see it. I put it there when I was expecting Michael to propose. I'm glad you've given us an excuse to open it up." Lindsay shifted in the chair, flinging her legs over one of the padded arms. "Okay, time to tell me all about Mr. Marvelous and the Magnificent Mysterious Mansion. All I've heard is the rough outline."

A sudden chill made Claire shiver. She felt a rustle of air near her ear, like someone's soft breath, and thought of the voice that had whispered to her.

"Mysterious is a good word for it, all right. Or mystifying—maybe that's better. I know you like to be precise about language." She paused, drank a little more champagne.

How much should she tell Lindsay? They kept few secrets from each other. But as much as they had in common, there was one key way they differed. Lindsay had a good imagination, but she kept hers firmly within bounds, applying it to the sets she designed for a community theater group and the publications she produced in her day job as a technical editor. She was level-headed and practical. If she could not take something in with her own eyes or ears or sense of logic, then it wasn't real.

Claire made up her mind. "You know, Linz, when I was at the house I had this really odd experience."

"Odd how?"

Claire fortified herself with another big gulp of champagne. Doing her best to keep her voice calm and her words matter-of-fact, she described the cold she had felt, the vision of bodies on the floor, the iron grip on the shoulder, the whispered words: *Help me.* Lindsay listened attentively, twirling a lock of russet hair and sipping from her glass.

"I know it sounds weird," Claire concluded. "I mean, none of that could really happen, right? But I don't know how to explain it, other than maybe I flipped out."

By now, both glasses were empty. Lindsay got up and refilled them.

"Okay, I take it back," she said. "This Ben guy? Maybe he's not Mr. Marvelous."

"What do you mean? Why not?"

"Well, it seems like he's into playing tricks at other people's expense." She returned to her chair and sat in it cross-legged.

"What trick?"

"He gets you inside the house. You feel strange sensations. You hear strange voices. What do you think is happening?"

Claire lifted her glass to her face and let the bubbles tickle her nose. "I wish I knew . . ."

"He didn't experience any of that, did he?"

"No, but—"

"So, maybe he faked it all to get a reaction out of you."

"Faked it? No way. How would you fake things like that?"

"Hidden speakers for the whispers. Fans and ice for the cold. I don't know how he managed to create that sensation of a hand clamping down on your shoulder, but I'm sure there's some sort of technology he could have used. There's technology for everything these days."

"Ah, but if it was faked, why didn't Avery notice anything happening?"

"The bimbo? From what you told me, she wasn't going to notice anything that wasn't a wallet or that other thing men keep in their pants. Besides, wasn't she with Ben in another room?"

"Why would Ben do something like that?" Claire protested. "What would he hope to accomplish? He's trying to sell the house, not scare people away from it."

Lindsay shrugged. "Who knows why men do anything?"

"Good point." Claire slumped back against the sofa cushions. She ought to feel relieved that Lindsay was offering a rational explanation. But she didn't want to believe that Ben was capable of that kind of deception. Nor did she want to think she could so easily be duped by such a hoax.

"Okay, here's one possible scenario," Lindsay said. "Ben doesn't really want to sell the place. You said it's not his, it belongs to his step-niece. As her guardian and the executor of his brother's will, it's his job to sell it on her behalf. He wants the house for himself, only it's way too expensive for him. But if it goes unsold long enough, the price will sink. Eventually Ben picks up the house at a bargain rate, and—"

"No way. He told me neither he nor Eden would ever want to live there."

"So he says. But how do you know he means it? Men lie all the time to get what they want."

"Zach did, that's for sure. But Ben—he's different, Linz, he seems . . . genuine, that's the word."

"Okay, he doesn't intend to move in. Maybe his plan is to buy it cheap and resell it for a huge profit. So he booby-traps the place, and triggers the devices just often enough to discourage anyone who might get seriously interested in buying it before he can drive the price low enough. Meanwhile he's making it look like he's fulfilling his responsibility to the step-niece by trying to get it sold."

Claire's head was buzzing. "I guess you could be right, Linz," she said glumly. "I don't know what think."

Linz jumped up to hug her. "Oh, hon, here we're supposed to be celebrating and I've gone and rained all over your parade. I'm sorry if I—"

She was interrupted by the trilling of Claire's cell phone. Claire got up to retrieve it from her purse, which she had dropped on the other end of the sofa when she got home. "Hello?"

"Claire, it's Ben Grant."

Speak of the devil. She pictured the energy waves from her conversation with Lindsay scooting through the air, reaching Ben, wherever he was, and giving him the impulse to pick up his phone.

"Ben! Funny, I was just thinking about you. Thank you again for giving me the chance to sell your house."

Phone to her ear, she wandered down the hall to her bedroom, out of Lindsay's earshot. Maybe she should ask Ben outright: Have you rigged up your brother's home to behave like a Halloween haunted house?

His voice was warm and rich. "I know you're going to do an excellent job, Claire. We'll make a great team, working together."

She felt herself flush with pleasure at the compliment. "Yes, I'm sure we will."

"Right now, though, I'm calling for social reasons, not business. I wondered if you'd like to have dinner with me tomorrow."

Her heart skipped a beat. "Dinner? God, I'd love to, but . . . well, you're a client. It's not really a good idea to mix business and pleasure."

"Don't worry, I'm not asking you for a date. Rather, it's a date, but it's going to be a threesome."

Uh-oh. Maybe Ben was up to tricks, after all, but a different kind than Lindsay suspected. "Um, Ben, look, I don't . . . I mean, somehow you got the wrong impression. Because I'm not . . . "

Ben laughed. "I don't mean that kind of threesome. My niece will be with us. I promised to fix her favorite lasagna for dinner. The recipe makes a huge amount, so I started thinking about who besides Eden I'd like to share the meal with. And the list started and ended with your name."

"Hmm, I do love lasagna."

"Think of it as a business dinner. Eden's your real client since officially she owns the house. This will give you two a chance to meet."

Claire's turn to laugh. "Since you put it that way . . ."

"We're on, then. How about six o'clock." He gave her his address. "I'd pick you up, but I'll be in the middle of massive preparations."

"That's fine. It's more businesslike if I drive myself. I'll be there at six."

A shiver of excitement rushed through her as she snapped the phone shut. Then she realized she'd let all thoughts of Ben's possible practical jokes slip out of her mind. She'd ask him tomorrow night for sure. Meanwhile, when she went to the LeGrande house in the morning to set up a lockbox, she would make a point of looking around for hidden gizmos.

When she returned to the living room, Lindsay was still sprawled in the chair, reading the sports section as she polished off her champagne. She gave Claire a questioning look but said nothing. One way they stayed such close friends was by adhering to an unspoken rule of not prying about potentially private matters.

But Claire knew Lindsay was curious. She said, "That was Ben. He invited me to dinner."

"Good. That will give you a chance to find out what's really going on. Just be cautious, okay? After all, you've been through, I don't want you getting hurt."

"I'll be careful, don't worry."

Lindsay set her newspaper and glass on the teak table beside her chair. "Speaking of dinner, who's up for takeout Chinese?"

CHAPTER 7

Claire was afraid to go to sleep.

She and Lindsay had talked all through a meal of mu shu pork and kung pao chicken and on into the night. When Lindsay wandered off to bed, Claire retreated to her own room, the smaller of the apartment's two bedrooms, and flopped down on top of the quilt.

When she'd moved in with Lindsay six months ago, Claire had painted the room a sunny yellow and set it up with the few possessions she'd brought cross country with her. The blue-and-gold quilt with its wedding ring pattern was one of her treasures. Gram had made it and given it to her for her eighteenth birthday. "For your hope chest," Gram said, as if young women still followed such an old-fashioned custom.

Most of the stuff in the rambling flat she'd shared with Zach had been tainted by his betrayal, so she'd been glad to leave it behind. It was mostly secondhand junk anyway. When Zach discovered belatedly, at age thirty-five, that his life's calling was to become a lawyer, he and Claire had sold almost everything they owned to finance his overpriced Harvard Law School education. His father and grandfather had been Harvard grads, so when Zach was admitted he insisted on carrying on the family tradition; a California school wouldn't do. So they moved from Berkeley to Cambridge and started fresh.

At first it was fun, scrounging for finds in flea markets and dusty secondhand shops. But the thrill quickly wore off. Their apartment was cold and drafty, and furniture that seemed charming on the seller's premises looked cheap and shabby once they got it home. Sanding, varnishing, and reupholstering might have helped, but who had time to do any of that? Claire was too busy grinding away at her mind-numbing secretarial job in order to support them, and Zach was buried in his books. Or so she had thought.

Now she was back in the Bay Area, starting over with a bed and bureau on loan from Lindsay's parents and a little walnut desk she'd discovered in an antiques store. And Gram's quilt.

Lying on top of it, Claire stared at the thin crack in the ceiling that reminded her of a snake. She should follow Lindsay's good example—brush her teeth, put on the old T-shirt she used as pajamas, try to sleep. It had been a long day following a restless night, and she wanted to feel fresh and upbeat in the morning—and even more so in the evening for her dinner with Ben. But though she was exhausted, her muscles felt tense and her nerves zinged with energy, a state Zach called "tired but wired."

And if she closed her eyes she might invite another nightmare.

She opened the book she'd started last night, a novel by one of her favorite authors. After flipping over several pages she realized that not one word had registered. She got up and paced, but the small space was too confining. So she tiptoed into the darkened living room, keeping quiet so she wouldn't wake Lindsay. She could make out the shape of the champagne bottle still standing on the coffee table.

Claire opened the sliding glass door to the balcony and stepped out. Cool, damp air cut through her grogginess. The apartments across the courtyard were dark. She leaned against the railing and watched the fog move in to shroud the hilltops above the roof of the neighboring building.

Nightmares. As a small child she'd been tormented by them. Too many nights, she woke up screaming. Gram would run into the bedroom to hold her close, rocking her and singing until Claire settled into peaceful sleep. In the morning, the pouches below Gram's eyes would show shadows the color of bruises, the effect of her disrupted night. Claire's big sister Cassandra, who shared the bedroom and whom she adored, would refuse to speak to Claire at breakfast or walk with her to school, punishment for making Cassandra lose sleep. By afternoon, though, they'd be on speaking terms again. "What was your scream-dream about last night?" Cassandra sometimes asked. Claire's reply was always the same: "I don't know."

As Claire got older, the nightmares haunted her less and less often. When her life was going well, she rarely had any at all. The whole time she was married to Zach, she had maybe half a dozen. Until the night of a law school graduation party held at the home of his litigation professor. Her boss made her work late that evening, so she told Zach she'd meet him there. By the time she arrived, the big Victorian house was crowded and noisy with drunken celebration. She couldn't find Zach anywhere. Finally, in search of a bathroom, she opened a door on the second floor. It turned out to be a bedroom, and one of the naked drunken celebrants on the bed was Zach. The other was Little Ms. Shyster.

That night she had her worst nightmare in years. Every two or three weeks since then, she'd suffered through another scream-dream.

Judging from the way she'd been thrown off stride all day, last night's must have been a doozy. Problem was, if anyone were to ask her what the nightmare was about, she'd have to give the same answer she gave Cassandra: "I don't know." She never remembered the content, just the terror of being chased by shadowy figures through swirling darkness, or dragged into a raging inferno, or smothered, or engulfed in a tide in which she would surely drown.

A brisk wind stirred, making Claire shiver. Time to go in. To go to bed. They were just dreams. Really, what was there to be afraid of?

Back in her bedroom, she noticed her amethyst beads lying on the bureau. She'd left them out when she changed out of her impress-the-new-colleagues outfit and put on jeans. She tucked the necklace carefully in its velvet case and put it in the bureau drawer.

She yawned. The bed with its rumpled quilt was tempting, but idea of waking up screaming was not. The clock on the nightstand showed 1:04. Not all *that* late. Why rush to sleep? Claire sat down at the antique desk and fired up her laptop so she could admire the Web page of the LeGrande house.

Earlier in the evening Ben had returned to the office—unaccompanied by Avery, as everyone noticed instantly. George, who just happened to have posted himself at the window facing the parking lot, reported that Avery got out of Ben's Lexus, slammed the door, and ran straight to her Porsche. She sped out of the lot, tires squealing, and nearly cut off an SUV, its driver leaning on the horn as she raced away. "Looks like she lost the bet," George announced. "Some of us are going to be twenty dollars richer."

Tess had whisked Ben and Claire into her office without saying a word about Avery. By the time Ben left, he had signed a contract, agreed on a multimillion-dollar asking price, and downloaded photos of the house from his flash drive. Claire and the spiky-haired redhead with the M name stayed into the evening to give the house its own page on the Golden Gate Properties Web site. The name, Claire learned, was Marlene, and its bearer turned out to be not only the receptionist and office manager, but also company's technology wizard.

Looking at the Web page now, Claire felt she felt proud and just a little smug at seeing the name CLAIRE SCANLAN shown as the agent to contact. So much nicer than seeing AVERY COLLIER. She imagined Avery looking the same page and feeling the twisted knife of jealousy. A mean thought, but Claire couldn't resist smiling.

A tap at the door. "Claire, you okay?" Lindsay asked.

So much for not waking her roommate. "Sure. Come on in."

Lindsay did, wrapping her terrycloth robe around her. "I heard noises on the balcony. I was afraid it was a burglar, but when I peeked out, no one was there."

"That was me. I'm sorry I woke you up."

"Glad I didn't call nine-one-one. I wouldn't have bothered you, but I saw the light under your door."

"Look at this." Claire pointed to her name on the computer screen. "I'm famous."

Lindsay stepped toward the desk. "Is that the house? How cool."

"There's a whole gallery of pictures here." Claire clicked through the photo tour—the redwood-and-glass exterior, the deck with its prow like a ship, the expansive view of ocean and sky. Then interior shots. How bare the rooms looked. She'd have to talk to Tess and Ben about staging the house by bringing in some furnishings, artwork, and green plants. If they could create a feel of warmth and luxury, that would heighten the appeal.

Although Lindsay, oohing and aahing, seemed to like it just fine as it was.

"Sold," she said. "How soon can I move in?"

"Might be a bit beyond your budget," Claire pointed out.

"I'll find a way. It's my dream house. Hey, it's anybody's dream house."

"Not for the family that lived there."

"Yeah, what an awful thing that was." Lindsay sat on the bed, and Claire saw her shudder. "So sad, what happened to them. I remember when it was all over the news. Hmm, maybe I don't want the house after all."

"I'm afraid that's how everyone will think." Claire stared at the picture on the screen, an exterior shot taken on a bright spring day. Clouds like cotton puffs hung in the sky and purple lupine bloomed along the ridge. "Who wants to buy a haunted house?"

"You say that like people expect ghosts."

"You think they don't?"

"Most people know better. The problem you're facing is that with all media coverage, people feel like they knew the family. Every time they think of the house, they think of that tragedy. It's hard for them to imagine turning it into a happy home for themselves. Your best bet will be someone who's never heard of the LeGrandes."

Claire hesitated, trying to frame her next words carefully. She could almost hear the mockery she'd get if she said them to Cassandra and Zach, and she didn't want to risk a similar reaction from Lindsay. "Suppose the house truly is haunted. What then?"

Lindsay smiled, apparently trying to lighten the mood. "In that case, why sell it? Keep it and charge admission—lots more profit to be gained that way. Wait—are you suggesting that the weird things you told me about were real? That you encountered ghosts or something?"

Claire sighed. "Of course not. It's just . . . well, they *seemed* real. And since I can't explain them . . . "

"Sure you can. Stress, excitement, lack of sleep. Though I still bet Mr. Marvelous has rigged up some sort of practical joke."

"Maybe so," Claire agreed, because it was the easiest answer. And possibly the correct one. There in the grand salon, the experience had seemed so true, so vivid. But now, hours later, its reality was beginning to crack and fade.

She brought up Google and typed in *Stefan LeGrande*. "I really should find out more about family and the killings. Buyers are going to ask lots of questions. I'd better be prepared with some answers."

"At least you can tell them it wasn't some lunatic who broke in randomly and killed everybody. The son did it and he's dead too. So the new owners don't have to worry about being in danger."

"Good thing," Claire said. This morning—had she been in danger? The whispered words, the icy grip on her shoulder—what would have happened if Ben and Avery hadn't come running?

Nothing, that's what. Everyone was right. She'd been spooked by her own imagination. A remnant of last night's nightmare, pushed to the surface by tales of murder. She tried to recall if that had ever happened before, a nightmare intruding like that into her waking hours, but she came up blank.

Lindsay stretched and yawned and pushed herself up from the bed. "I'll leave you to your research. Get some sleep tonight, okay?"

UNTIL AVERY SAW the LeGrande house, her brother Kurt's place had been just about the coolest place she could imagine. He had the penthouse suite of a hillside building in Sausalito. The whole front wall was glass, leading to a terrace that overlooked the marina, Angel Island and the Bay Bridge. The white-walled living dining space was larger than their daddy's entire house in Texas. Kurt had filled it with leather sofas, chrome-and-glass tables and lots of fancy toys, like a surround-sound music system and a plasma TV. When Avery moved in six months ago, she thought she'd died and gone to heaven.

Tonight, though, the apartment—in fact, the whole world—felt like hell.

She'd spent the evening downing the better part of a bottle of merlot she'd unearthed from Kurt's wine cellar—a hall closet really, but specially outfitted and temperature controlled—and watching old romance movies. But the films just made her sad. All she could think about was the sting of Ben Grant's rejection.

Then she made the mistake of looking at the Golden Gate Web site on Kurt's computer. Sure enough, there was the house, the name CLAIRE SCANLAN on prominent display. She sniffed back a sob. It should have said AVERY COLLIER. She was going to have to endure the humiliation of shelling out sixty bucks to the coworkers who'd taken her stupid bet. Claire was probably looking at her computer at this very minute, gloating.

Avery shut down the computer and climbed into Kurt's king-sized bed, sprawling in the tangle of satin sheets. He was in Europe, so he wouldn't care, and his was so much nicer than the single bed in the guest room she was using. But though she felt tired, and yes, admit it, a little soused, her eyes refused to close. Now, at one in the morning, she was moving about restlessly, footsteps swishing along the bare hardwood floor. The place was so damn empty! Much more space than could be filled by one person alone. She longed for someone to talk to, share her frustration with, someone who would take her side. But who? Kurt was due home soon—a few days, a week maybe, she wasn't sure when, exactly—but he wasn't here now, when a brotherly shoulder to cry on might do her some good. And it was way too late to call her friend Kaylee, probably two or three A.M. in Texas—Avery could never keep the time difference straight.

She found the merlot bottle and splashed the last of the wine into the glass she'd left with the rest of the dirty dishes piled up in the kitchen sink. Sipping as she went, she carried the glass out onto the deck. A thick, damp presence filled the air, making her shiver; it was beginning to obscure the lights across the bay. The Pacific fog bank moving in, she knew that. But it made her think of ghosts, which in turn reminded her of that idiot Claire causing a ruckus over nothing at the LeGrande house, as if she'd actually seen a ghost when everyone knew ghosts were nothing but a Halloween superstition.

So unfair. Today, for once, she had been the calm, level-headed one, but instead of being rewarded, she'd been shot down by a hysterical ninny. Today she had met not one but two of the best-looking men she'd encountered in a long time, and yet she was rattling around Kurt's apartment alone.

Either of the men would do, but Ben was the prize to go for. He was way better-looking, not that she couldn't have easily enjoyed Martin Roncallo's pirate-like allure. More important, Ben had sold her short.

Well, she'd show him. Show him and Claire and everybody at Golden Gate Properties. So what if he didn't choose her as his listing agent. She'd find a buyer anyway, sell the house, impress the hell out of everyone, ride into the sunset with Ben in his Lexus, leave stupid Claire in the dust.

GOOGLE CAME UP with an impressive 617,438 hits on Stefan LeGrande. Clicking through the first two or three pages of links, Claire found glowing descriptions and admiring reviews of buildings the architect had designed. Mansions for movie stars and ultra-rich CEOs, glamorous restaurants and resort hotels, the new De Crescenzi Arts Center in the Napa Valley. She'd fallen in love with that building when she and Lindsay attended a concert there; she'd had no idea it was a LeGrande design, but now she could see the characteristic touches. Every building pictured had some feature—the slope of a roof, the mix of glass and wood in a wall, the way light glanced off a marble surface—that reminded her of the house on Highview Lane.

Comments made about the man, rather than his work, were far less complimentary. Apparently Stefan LeGrande had been arrogant and narcissistic—a difficult person for clients and contractors to deal with.

Claire found references to several lawsuits for runaway costs, construction delays, and broken contracts. One plaintiff blamed LeGrande when a design flaw in his custom-designed house resulted in a fire that killed the man's family. Employees sued for discrimination and wrongful termination.

A tattletale blog called Archi-Talk dished a little gossip about the partnership breakup Ben had mentioned. Ben had told Claire that his brother dumped the partner because he was incompetent. Archi-Talk had a different explanation, claiming Stefan LeGrande's swollen ego didn't allow him to share top billing with someone equally talented. After booting his partner from the firm, Stefan trumped up complaints that forced the poor man out of the architectural profession. Bateman & LeGrande Associates became Stefan LeGrande Architecture.

Claire hoped an overblown ego wasn't a trait Ben shared with his brother. Ben didn't have that kind of I-am-wonderful aura about him, but some men—Zach, for instance—were good at using charm to mask their self-absorption. Ben's charm quotient was off the charts, which made her uneasy almost as much as it excited her. What did she really know about him after just a single day?

Finally she moved on stories about the LeGrande family's tragedy. She'd put them off until last, fascinated yet repelled by the promised glimpse into darkness.

Gruesome details in the written accounts confirmed what Ben had told her. What wrenched Claire's heart were the photographs—smiling portraits of Stefan and his wife and children, candid shots that revealed how they lived their lives. Suddenly they were real people, not just names in the history of the house she wanted to sell. Though she'd never met them, she felt an acute sense of loss.

This is how Ben feels, she thought. And his niece Eden. Only their loss is so much deeper, so much more profound.

Stefan's photos showed the fraternal resemblance to Ben. Stefan's hair showed more silver, but she could see it had once been the same dark brown. Both men had square jaws and chiseled features, though on Stefan's face the angles were sharper, the hazel eyes narrower and more penetrating. In one portrait, the eyes stared at the viewer in a way that made Claire squirm.

Ben, she decided, was much handsomer than his brother.

Jacqueline, Stefan's wife, was a stunning brunette, every bit the beauty Ben claimed she was. Even in still photos, she looked lively and animated. She flirted with the camera and whoever might view the pictures. With the tilt of her head and the light in her eyes, she enticed the observer to join her at whatever she was doing—riding a jet-black horse at the surf's edge, wielding a shovel at the ground-breaking ceremony for the arts center, dancing at a fundraising ball for the San Francisco Symphony. Claire could easily see how a teenage boy, even her own stepson, might succumb to Jacqueline's allure.

She found few pictures of Trevor. A tall, skinny kid with unruly hair and a blank expression, he retreated into the background of every shot he was in, looking away from the camera, standing so he was partially blocked by someone else's head. He looks so ordinary, Claire thought. Despite all their wealth and privilege and fancy houses, it must have been hard to be a child in that family, struggling to emerge from the deep shadows cast by Stefan's brilliance and Jacqueline's beauty. Only one photo gave her a good look at Trevor's eyes, and she kept gazing at them, trying to discern some hint of the lust or fear or rage or drug-addled paranoia that would drive him to grab a gun and kill himself and his family.

One shot, slightly blurry, showed a youthful couple with four-year-old Trevor and his infant sister. The caption revealed them to be Stefan and his first wife, Rona. Like Jacqueline, she had dark hair, but Rona, while pretty, lacked her successor's exotic appeal. She had one arm around her son and cradled baby Melissa in the other, gestures of love toward the children she would soon abandon.

Melissa's pictures disturbed Claire the most. A school portrait showed a fifteen-year-old on the verge of becoming pretty. The girl looked somehow familiar. Claire peered more closely at the screen. When might she have seen Melissa before? By the time she moved back from Cambridge, Melissa had died. And when Claire headed east, Melissa was only a fifth grader; she would have looked much different.

Then it hit her. Melissa's photo looked like her own sophomore-year portrait. Claire had detested that picture, but Gram loved it. Despite Claire's protests she kept a framed copy on top of the TV for years, until one day Claire managed to accidentally knock it over and break the glass.

Claire shivered. This was eerie, like peering backward through time and having the girl she'd been twenty years ago gaze back at her. Teenage Claire and Melissa both had long brown hair that hung past their shoulders, full lips and wideset brown eyes. Freckles, too—she wondered if Melissa had hated them as much as she did.

A string of links led Claire to a MySpace site maintained by a kid who'd been in Melissa's high school drama club. She'd been killed arriving home from a dress rehearsal, and the kid had posted photos he'd taken that night. The play was Thornton Wilder's *Our Town*. Melissa was playing the female lead, Emily Gibbs.

Claire couldn't believe it. She'd played Emily too. Nothing strange in that coincidence, she told herself. *Our Town* was classic drama club fare. Just about every good high school actress played Emily by the time she graduated.

One of the photos showed a scene from the third act, in which the newly deceased Emily sits in a chair that represents her grave. She and other departed residents are observing Grover's Corners from their vantage point in the town cemetery. Melissa sat stiffly in a calico dress, staring straight ahead, her face somber. She was taking her character's death seriously. Just a couple of hours later she would experience her own.

Claire shivered again. The bedroom had grown chilly. The fog had turned the summer night cold. Time to snuggle in under her quilt. Way past time really. With luck, she'd fall into a sleep so deep, no nightmare could reach her.

She started to shut off the computer, then had an idea she couldn't resist. Another Google search. She typed in *Ben Grant* and instantly got a tally: 21,300,000 results. None of the ones near the top of the list referred to the Ben Grant she had in mind.

Of course it was hardly an unusual name. Much more common than Stefan LeGrande. If she wanted to learn more about Ben, she'd have wait until tomorrow night.

RED, COLOR OF BLOOD, color of anger, color of fire. Out of the flames emerges a shimmering house of glass. Gingerbread turrets grow out of its corner; at the entrance hangs a mountain cabin's sagging wood-plank door. The angles of the roof lift like huge feathered wings. Their flapping and beating creates an icy gale, and as she watches the house rises up. She scrabbles to find something firm to hang onto, but the wind is too strong. It sucks her inside, where they, whoever they may be, are waiting.

Black, color of night, color of grief. She can see nothing in the overwhelming darkness. But she can hear noises—singing, sobbing, shrieking, sharp commanding voices that slice like razor wire. Then comes thunder, the roar of ocean pummeling land. A towering wave smashes down, shattering everything.

Claire woke up screaming.

CHAPTER 8

*S*he heard me!

I'm so excited. For the first time someone has heard me. I feel like jumping for joy, turning cartwheels, spinning in circles of delight. Except I can no longer move like that.

Three people came today—the lonely man who sometimes visits and two women, both of them strangers. And one of the women heard me.

I wish I could remember the name of the lonely man, but names were one of the first things to slip away. What remains with us are the emotions. If we knew someone in the time Before, the feelings we had for them are still with us, bright and clear. When the lonely man comes, I feel warmth, I hear laughter, just as I always did when he was around. For him, though, the warmth and laughter have vanished. All he has left is loneliness.

When I was alive, a friend told me about something called an aura. She said an aura is a field of energy that emanates from the physical body and surrounds it like a hooded cloak. I didn't understand auras then, but now I can see them. Everyone who comes to the house has one. It reveals the emotions that are strongest in a person's heart.

That's how I can tell the man is lonely. I'd like him to know that I still love him. But he believes that all of us are gone. When he comes here he's never aware of me, although today when I tried to speak to him I got close enough to taste the tears on his cheek.

I had no hope of reaching out to the pale woman with gold hair. She was aware only of herself. To her, everything is a mirror and she can't see past the shiny glass. Her aura shows layers of feelings—ambition, avarice, anger, and hidden underneath them all, the vulnerability of a frightened child.

The other woman is the one who heard me. She's different from the other one. It's like she's the mirror and the person who's being reflected is—me. Her hair is the color of chocolate, the same as mine used to be, and her face has a similar shape to the one I had, and she has freckles, only on her they look pretty. If I had been allowed to grow up, I bet I would have looked like her.

What I see in her aura is longing, though what she longs for I don't know. But it's another thing we have in common, because I'm longing too. I long for everything to be the way was Before. If that can't happen, I long to finish my task here so I leave this house and move on to the place called Forever.

I'm sure the chocolate-haired woman can help me. She heard me—now if only I can make her understand.

If only I hadn't scared her away.

I didn't mean to frighten her. My whispers were soft. My touch on her shoulder was gentle. I was just trying to get her attention.

That's something else I long for—to make a connection with someone. Ever since that fiery night— it seems so long ago—the one who's trapped here with me has been huddling in the far corner, blind and

*mute. He's a dense, dark presence not unlike the black
holes in the universe that I learned about in a science
class in the days Before.*

*Yet ever since the three people went away, something
strange has been happening. At first it puzzled me, and
then I realized that he's weeping. No tears, of course—
one of my greatest regrets about being trapped here
without physical bodies is this: we've lost the ability to
form tears to soak up our sadness and carry it out of
us. He's weeping even so. I've been trying to comfort
him, but without arms to put around him, I don't know
how. He doesn't seem to notice me at all.*

*But—weeping. I'm not certain if this is a good sign
or a bad one. Yet, for the first, time has stirred; the
energy in this house has shifted just the tiniest bit. And
it's because the woman with chocolate hair heard me.*

I hope she comes again.

She's our only hope.

"**G**ood morning, everyone!" Claire called cheerily as she entered the office, though cheery wasn't really how she felt. She had a headache, leftover from her latest nightmare. She'd delayed going to bed, and after her screams had brought Lindsay running to her room, she had been too keyed up to go back to sleep. So she had to get through today on maybe three hours of sleep.

The hell of it was, she had almost no recollection of what the dream had been about, just a hazy impression of a red reflection in a shiny glass window. Why should that be frightening? If her subconscious mind was going to torture her this way, it ought to at least grant her clear memories of the nightmares, to give her clues that let her exorcise the demons, whoever or whatever they were.

This morning the "everyone" she had greeted turned out to be Tess, George and Marlene. George sidled over as she set her purse on her desk in Siberia and took the last swig of blessed caffeine from her travel mug.

"Right on time this morning, I see," George said, running a pudgy hand over his balding scalp.

"You keep track of everyone's punctuality? There's no such thing as 'on time' around here except for the Monday Meeting."

"Just an observation." He waggled his brushy eyebrows, a bad imitation of Groucho Marx. "So no M.Q. today, huh?"

She remembered the acronym—morning quickie.

"George, you are disgusting." The words slipped out before she could bite them back. So much for her intention to forge friendly relations with all of her coworkers. She glanced around to see who had heard. Tess had gone into her office. Marlene, at the receptionist's desk, winked at her and applauded.

George seemed oblivious. "You know, you never have to lack in the M.Q. department. You can always give me a call." He patted Claire's shoulder, then strolled away, grabbing a scuffed leather briefcase from his chair as he headed toward the elevator. "Ta-ta, ladies. I'm off to see a client."

Marlene snorted. "Client, hell," she said as the elevator door slid shut. "His client's name is Jack Daniels. Want half my cheese Danish? I'm cutting calories." She took a pastry from a white paper bag and sliced it with a plastic knife.

"That guy is a harassment lawsuit on the hoof," Claire fumed as she went up to Marlene's desk. She brushed at her shoulder to dislodge any trace of his touch. "Why does Tess put up with him? His sales numbers must be off the chart, that's the only possible explanation."

"They are off the chart, all right—the bottom of the chart." Marlene swooped her hand down in a diving motion.

"Then why?" Claire repeated. Nodding her thanks, she accepted the chunk of Danish. Caffeine hadn't done much for her headache; maybe sugar would help.

"Brother-in-law," Marlene whispered conspiratorially. "Charity case. Tess hired him to keep peace in the family."

"Hmph. Some peace."

"It's some family. But don't worry. Tess is a great boss. You'll love it here. Just ignore George. Everybody will expect you to."

"Even George?"

"Especially George."

"Speaking of everybody, where are they this morning?"

"It's Tuesday, open house day. Didn't anyone tell you?"

"Oh, of course. It slipped my mind since I wasn't planning to go. Too many other things on today's to-do list."

Once a week, real estate companies in Marin opened their newly listed properties so that all the agents could preview them, but this morning she had a higher priority—another visit to the LeGrande house.

"Too bad it was too late to include that house of yours on the tour," Marlene said.

"We'll do next week for sure."

As Claire spoke, the elevator opened. Avery emerged, rubbing her eyes and wobbling on the high heels of her backless sandals.

"Well, good morning, sunshine," Marlene said. "Did you bring me my twenty bucks?"

Avery waved a greeting with her middle finger extended.

Tess picked that moment to come out of her office. "Avery, are you all right?"

Avery sank down onto her desk chair and pulled her long blond hair over her bloodshot eyes. "Fine. I overslept, is all." She lowered her head into her hands.

Overslept and overdrank, Claire thought. I know a hangover when I see one.

———·———

WHAT A DIFFERENCE a day makes, Claire thought as she drove past the Mariners Beach turnoff. Yesterday was sparkling and sunny. Today the fog bank refused to retreat and the sky was low and leaden. The distant vistas had disappeared, the world had closed in, what had been blue or green and gold was all shades of gray.

As she drove up the ridge and swung the Volkswagen into Highview Lane, the fog thickened into mist on the windshield and she had to turn on the wipers. It was as if she had driven right up into a cloud. She wondered how many days of summer sunshine the residents of Highview Lane were able to enjoy. Yesterday had probably been a rarity. She'd have to do a little research and find out; it was the kind of question buyers were likely to ask.

Claire knew fog. She had grown up in the fog zone—the outer Richmond, a district of middle class homes near the ocean in San Francisco, where some summers the sun was invisible for two entire months. She'd lived there while she attended San Francisco State, just a couple of miles south of Gram's house and plenty foggy itself. One of Zach's selling points for going east to law school was that she'd have the opportunity to experience what he, an East Coast native, called authentic seasons—winters with snow, autumns with glorious foliage, summers where a person could lie on the beach and swim in the ocean without freezing to death.

At the entrance to the LeGrande driveway she slowed to a halt. Maybe it hadn't been such a good idea to come to the house alone. What if she'd been by herself yesterday, what if Ben and Avery hadn't been there to free her from—

From what? A fantasized whisper? A sudden chill? A foolish fantasy about a hand on her shoulder? Get real, Claire. She shrugged her shoulders as if that would shake off any silliness. Yesterday her imagination had caught by surprise. Today she was prepared.

She pulled into the parking court. Getting out of the Volkswagen, she locked the door, then wondered why. Force of habit from living all her life in a city. There was no one here to break into it. She patted the car on the hood as she stepped away. She could almost hear Avery's sneering tone. "You want us to go in that? *That's* your car?" Avery had said yesterday when Claire offered to drive. "Let's take my car. More fun to ride with the top down."

To be honest, it had been fun, and she knew Avery was right about the VW. Successful real estate agents picked their wheels for their client-impressing potential. The Porsche was closer to the mark, although as a two-seater it wasn't really a practical choice for driving clients around since clients tend to be come in pairs, or even entire families. One of the items on Claire's long list of things to buy with her first commission check was a car that would help her project the right professional image. But she'd do it with regret. She loved her Volkswagen. She had bought it on impulse last fall when she decided to drive cross-country to California. The bright green color and jellybean shape made her laugh, and she'd been in need of laughs back then.

She approached the house, gripping her purse strap to hold it on her shoulder. Today the purse held a mini-toolkit, which made it heavier than usual.

The uplifted wings of the roof didn't appear to soar the way they had the day before; instead they seemed to be trying to hold up the thick gray sky and looked ready to buckle under the weight. Back off, Claire warned her imagination. I have work to do.

First task—set up the lockbox. She and Tess had agreed that posting a for-sale sign didn't make sense. The property was too expensive and too remote; a sign wouldn't draw serious buyers, just lookie-loos and vandals. The lockbox, though, was essential. The little metal container would hold the key to the house so agents could get inside and show the place to their clients. It didn't create much security risk since only agents could open the lockbox, using their own coded electronic keys. Each time someone opened the box a microprocessor inside would register the date, the time, and the agent's code number.

Claire hung the box by the brass light fixture next to the door. Instead of putting the key inside, she unlocked the big wooden door with the seagull carving and slid the key into her pocket. Taking a deep breath for courage, she counted—one, two, three.

Her hand gripped the knob but refused to open the door.

God, she could be such a wimp sometimes. The house was empty. What was there to be afraid of? Nothing except figments of her own silly imagination. It wasn't as though her nightmares could jump out of her mind and come to life in the house.

Bracing herself, she turned the knob. The door glided open. She flinched, half-expecting to be hit, like yesterday, with the acrid stench of blood—except the smell didn't come. Instead she caught a faint whiff of perfume, something floral. Gardenia maybe? Yes, that was it.

As she stepped inside the scent intensified and then was gone. Claire wondered if she had smelled anything at all.

She crossed the marble floor of the entry gallery and grasped the polished wooden railing that ran along the step-down edge of the grand salon.

"Okay, house, do your stuff. Bring it on."

Nothing happened.

She sighed with relief.

The house seemed smaller today, probably because the windows were curtained outside by fog rather than letting in light and expansive views. It was cold inside—even though she was wearing a turtleneck and a blazer, Claire had to rub her arms to keep from shivering. But it was chilly outside too. The house was no colder, really, than she would expect of any empty, unheated house in such weather.

Time to start the search. If Lindsay was right about Ben rigging the house somehow to play tricks and create illusions, then Claire was going to find it out.

She began with the grand salon, where yesterday's madness had occurred. It was the most likely place to uncover anything suspicious. At first she felt anxious, but she began to relax as she moved around the room and encountered nothing strange. No voices. No icy wind. No unseen forces grabbing at her. No visions of blood-soaked corpses.

And no technological gizmos.

Room by room she went through the entire place, looking for wires, speakers, projectors, fans, blowers— any kind of gadgetry that could be used to create bizarre special effects. She ran her fingers along the edges of floors and around the frames of windows and doors. Using the screwdriver from her toolkit, she unscrewed the plates covering electric outlets, light switches, intercom units, hookup points for the central vacuum system and the cable TV. Lindsay had told her what sorts of things she should look for.

She found nothing.

Claire had mixed feelings as she rose from the floor of the final closet and dusted her hands on the seat of her slacks. The good part was, no one had planted any devices to make mischief with. Despite Lindsay's suspicions, Ben was absolved.

Unless, of course, the devices were very well hidden.

The bad part was, this left her with no explanation for what she'd experienced yesterday except that maybe she was going a little crazy.

As SHE RETURNED to the entrance gallery, ready to leave, Claire caught a flash of movement in the corner of her eye.

She turned and gazed out across the grand salon. Nothing there.

Of course nothing was there. She'd searched the room thoroughly just half an hour before.

Then a face appeared, floating in the far corner of the room, right where the interior wall abutted the long expanse of glass.

Claire caught her breath.

No, wait, the face was outside, looking in. As she watched, a girl moved into view and pushed her face to the glass, hands cupped around her eyes to block the daylight as she tried to peer inside.

Who was this?

Had this kid, or someone, been outside yesterday? A prankster who'd figured out a clever way to scare people by transmitting a whispery voice into the house and making them think it was haunted?

Better see what was going on. Claire stepped down from the marble floor to the hardwood and strode toward the French doors centered in the glass wall.

Halfway across the space, she tripped over something and went sprawling. She landed facedown in the middle of the floor.

For a few seconds she lay there, stunned. Then— *bam, bam . . . bam, bam*—she heard two quick explosions, then two more. Gunshots? But they weren't loud enough to be inside the house, or even close by. Maybe it was a neighbor's car backfiring. Maybe she hadn't heard anything at all.

She gasped to regain her breath, which had been knocked completely out of her. The air she took in tasted like smoke.

Slowly she pushed herself up to a sitting position. The room spun, then settled back into its normal position.

What had happened? It felt as though she had bumped into something and tripped, yet nothing was there. She ran her hands across the floor, feeling for cracks or gaps in the floorboards that might have caught her toe. The surface was polished and smooth. Suddenly it turned cold under her touch, as if she were touching the frozen surface of a skating pond.

No, just part of it was icy, a patch of floor about two feet square, though the shape was irregular. She traced the edges with her fingers. The air right above it was cold too, up to about the height of her knees.

She had stumbled on a chunk of invisible, nonsolid ice.

The air by her fingers fluttered as if someone wanted to take her hand and help her up.

"I can do it myself, thank you," she announced. Not that she believed anyone was listening, but it was reassuring to hear the sound of her own voice, even if it quavered slightly.

Her left ankle twinged as she stood; she must have twisted it when she fell. But it seemed to bear her weight with no problem. A flutter of air brushed a stray lock of hair out of her eyes, and another tugged at the hem of her jacket to straighten it. The smoky smell had vanished, and the scent of gardenias drifted past her nose.

Claire swatted at the flutters as if they were mosquitoes. "Let go. Leave me alone."

The entire room was cold now, and the air had taken on a reddish tinge. She headed toward the French doors, her ankle protesting every step.

Ben had mentioned yesterday that the house key operated all the locks, including the deadbolt on the French doors. As Claire slid the key into its slot, she felt the merest puff of breath against her ear.

"He didn't do it," whispered the voice.

Claire fled through the doors. Never had she felt so grateful to be outside in the wind and fog.

"WHO ARE YOU?"

The voice came from behind her as she shut the French doors. Claire spun around to see a girl, maybe ten years old, standing out at the prow of deck, embraced by the railings as they came together in a V. Her long black hair was twisted into a single braid that fell across her shoulder. She had fair skin, bright blue eyes, cheeks made rosy by the stiff wind.

The face that had been peering in the window.

"I might ask you the same thing," Claire replied, stepping toward her.

"You first." The girl crossed her arms in front of her chest. She was wearing a purple fleece jacket.

"My name is Claire." She could hear the crashing of waves on rocks. Beyond the deck, sea and sky merged into a grayness that showed no line to mark the horizon.

"I'm Lily," the girl said. "Are you buying this house?"

"Actually, I'm selling it."

"Oh. Are you a real estate person?"

"That's right."

"I wish someone would buy it. It's a sad house with everyone gone."

"Are you the Lily who lives next door?"

"How did you know?"

"I met your father yesterday. He was talking about you."

Lily twisted her mouth. "I hope he said good stuff."

"He said you miss your friend Eden."

"Yeah, I guess so." The girl scuffed a sneaker along the decking. "It was nicer when she lived here. We could see each other every day. Now I hardly ever get to see her. And there's no other kids who live around here."

"So what brings you over to this sad house today?" Claire asked. It was too much to hope that Lily would respond with something like *I've been setting up tricks to scare people and I wanted to see if they worked on you*.

"Oh, nothing," Lily answered. "I like Eden's deck. You can get closer to the ocean here than you can at my house. Did you hurt yourself?"

"What?"

"When you fell in there." She gestured toward the French doors. "And then you were limping."

Claire glanced back at the house. Dark as the day was, it was still too bright to let her look into the interior. All she could see was the deck dimly reflected in the glass wall. The ghostly figures visible there were Lily and herself.

But a few minutes ago Lily had been up close, face pressed against the glass.

"Did you happen to notice what it was I stumbled over?" Claire asked. She recalled what the whispering voice had said: *He didn't do it*. Good to know, but who the hell was *he?*

Lily's shoulders shrugged inside the fleece jacket. "There wasn't anything. You just fell."

"What about a noise? Did you hear something go *bam-bam*?"

She shook her head. "No. It's been quiet out here."

Claire heard a faint voice calling: "Lily!" The girl didn't pay attention; perhaps she didn't notice it.

"When you come here to hang out on the deck," Claire said, "have you ever experienced anything . . . kind of strange?"

"What do you mean?"

"I don't know exactly. Heard a voice maybe. Felt a tap on your shoulder. Seen anything and then wondered if it was really there."

"You mean, like haunted house stuff?"

"I wouldn't say haunted. Just odd things happening."

The girl shook her head. "That's crazy."

"Lily!" the voice yelled, stronger this time but Claire still couldn't tell if it was a man or a woman. "Where are you?"

"Over here!" Lily yelled back. "I'm coming!"

"Is that your mother?" Claire asked.

"My dad. My mom lives in L.A. I gotta go now."

Lily took off running. Claire limped after her as she scurried around the end of the house. The wind was less fierce in the front, where the structure itself afforded some protection.

Martin Roncallo was in the parking court, standing next to her Volkswagen.

"Let me guess," she said with a smile. "You saw the strange car and came over to check out who's here."

Roncallo's responding grin showed beneath his heavy black mustache. "This time I was looking for my daughter. But I like the car. Shows you have an independent spirit and a sense of fun. You're one of the real estate ladies—Avery, is that right?"

Lily rolled her eyes. "Da-ad. Her name is Claire."

"Claire Scanlan. Avery is the colleague who was with me yesterday."

"Of course. The blonde with the Porsche. Can't believe I got you two mixed up." He put a hand on his daughter's shoulder. "Lily, you need to tell me when you're going somewhere."

"I didn't go anywhere. Just over here to Eden's house."

"This is somewhere. And it's probably somewhere you shouldn't hang as much as you do. Especially now that it's back on the market. You don't want to get in the lady's way."

"Oh, I'm sure she won't—" Claire began.

"You come over here all the time," Lily said, pouting.

"You do?" Claire said. Probably best not to ask him about his observations of peculiar phenomena. If his daughter thought the notion was crazy, it was unlikely he'd be more sympathetic.

"'All the time' is an exaggeration, wouldn't you say, Lily? But, yeah, I try to watch over the place for Ben.

And I do some yardwork and maintenance now and then, keep up the house for the sake of the neighborhood. My little way of honoring the LeGrande family's memory." He placed a hand on his daughter's shoulder. "Let's go, sweetheart, I can't be late for my client meeting."

She backed away. "I hate client meetings."

"I know, but Mrs. Applegate isn't available to stay with you, and I wasn't able to set you up a play date. Bring your book—you can read it in the reception area while I meet with my client. Afterward we'll get hamburgers, how's that?"

"Pizza."

"Okay, pizza then."

"And ice cream."

"My daughter, the international treaty negotiator," Roncallo said with a chuckle. "Just watch, Claire, she's destined for a diplomatic career."

Father and daughter strolled down the pebbled driveway, heading home.

I might as well leave too, Claire decided. The pain in her ankle settled into a dull ache as she circled the house, making sure it was locked and secure. She placed the key in the lockbox and drove away.

As soon as she passed Mariners Beach and turned inland, the fog abruptly disappeared. It was as if the Volkswagen had popped through a curtain into brilliant sunshine.

He didn't do it. Claire kept hearing the words, though this time she was certain it was her memory speaking, not the whispery voice.

Who was *he?* Claire wondered. And what was *it?* And why did the damn voice have to choose her to talk to?

Avery gulped another two aspirins and washed them down with strong French roast. One thing about working at Golden Gate Properties —the employee lounge had decent coffee. She got up from her desk to go refill her mug.

The office was empty except for Marlene at the reception desk and Tess, who was working on who-knew-what back in her inner sanctum. Avery had meant to go with Jeff and Delia on the rounds of agents' open houses, but by the time she arrived this morning they had already left. She'd never worked at a place where everybody was so damn punctual.

As she passed the reception desk, Marlene was talking on the phone and running fingers through her jaggedy red hair. "The listing agent can give you all that information," she was saying. "Her name is Claire Scanlan. She'll be delighted to hear that you're interested in the house. But she's not in the office right now. Let me give you her voicemail."

Avery didn't break stride. Marlene had to be talking about the LeGrande house. The one Avery should have been the listing agent for, not that silly Claire. Sounded like there was already an interested buyer on the hook. Probably someone who had called Ben Grant's previous realtor and been told that Golden Gate was now handling the property.

In the kitchen, out of Marlene's sight, she couldn't resist a triumphant pump of her fist. *Yes!* Opportunity was knocking.

She filled her mug with coffee, leaving half an inch in the bottom of the carafe so it wouldn't count as empty. That way she wasn't responsible for making a fresh pot.

Back at her desk she bided her time, drinking coffee and doodling on a notepad to look busy. As soon as Marlene went off on a restroom break, Avery checked the little list hidden at the back of her desk drawer. She'd made a point during her first two weeks at Golden Gate of sleuthing out everyone's voicemail retrieval code and other tidbits of potentially handy information. She punched in Claire's code and listened to the message, copying down the name and number that the caller had left. Then she hit the DELETE button.

She grabbed her purse and headed toward the elevator, waving her fingers at the receptionist, who was returning to her post.

"See you later, Marlene. I'm going to go catch up with the open house tour."

Avery left the building and crossed the sunny parking lot to the Porsche, where she could use her cell phone to make the call in private. Relaxing into the luxury of the black leather seat, she punched in the number.

"Mr. Burdick? I'm Avery Collier from Golden Gate Properties. I understand you're interested in the house on Highview Lane . . . Yes, that's right, she is the listing agent, but she isn't available. So I'd be happy to show you the house or do what I can to help you."

———•———

THERE WAS A SIMPLE EXPLANATION for the tumble she'd taken, Claire decided as she drove up the street approaching the Golden Gate Properties building. She'd simply been clumsy. She was suffering from a lack of sleep, and she'd been focusing on the girl's face at the corner of the big window, hurrying across the room to find out who the intruder was, and in her rush she'd tripped over her own feet. It could have happened to anyone.

And the *bam-bam* noise, the fluttering fingers of air, the whispered *he didn't do it?* She'd been rattled by the fall, that's all. After a tumble like that, naturally it would take her a minute or two to settle back into her senses. She'd half expected something weird to happen while she was in the house, and in her moment of disorientation, her imagination had obliged her.

As she turned into the parking lot, a black convertible sports car nearly cut her off in its haste to pull out onto the street. She caught of a flash of the driver's long golden hair.

Avery. Being rude and oblivious, as usual. Claire frowned.

But when she got out of the Volkswagen, the midday sun melted away her irritation. She lingered by the car, lifting her face to let the warmth touch her. Up on Highview Lane, she'd nearly frozen. That road was misnamed; on a day like this, Fogview Lane was more like it. And there were lots of days like this out there at the edge of the ocean. After several years of East Coast summers, she had almost forgotten how variable the Bay Area's weather could be, with all its little microclimates that meant any neighborhood could be hotter or colder or wetter or dryer than one just a few miles away.

Finally she made herself go inside, hobbling just a little. Her sore ankle was almost better. When she got off the elevator, there was no one in the office but Marlene. Hardly surprising—real estate agents didn't make money by sitting in the office. Right now everyone was touring open houses or taking a lunch break.

Yesterday at this hour she'd been at the umbrella table on the deck of the Windward, enjoying a good meal and fine wine with Ben Grant. The memory dampened her enthusiasm for the contents of the pale green paper bag that she'd picked up at Spuntino's deli on her way here. Spuntino's was always full of tempting delights, but she'd settled for a container of raspberry yogurt. Best to go light for lunch today, to save her appetite for the evening. Tonight she'd be with Ben again, savoring his homemade lasagna, which no doubt would be delicious, and his company, more delicious still.

Marlene was working on something at her computer. When she saw Claire she minimized the document she'd had up on her screen, leaving only the GGP logo screensaver visible.

"Hey, Claire, guess what," she said. "There might be a prospect for the LeGrande house."

"Already? Wow, that's great. Who is it?"

"I don't know. Some guy phoned this morning and said he's interested. I gave him your voicemail."

"Thanks. I'll call him back in a minute."

Claire dumped her purse and the paper bag on her desk and carried her mug into the kitchen. There she was greeted by the stench of something charred. Damn it, some idiot had left the coffee maker with the burner on and only a puddle of coffee at the bottom of the pot. The little bit of liquid had turned to scorched sludge.

The culprit was probably George, she decided. He was just the sort of inconsiderate jerk who would think making coffee was a woman's job, even though the office policy was clear: whoever drains the pot starts a new one.

Claire scoured out the carafe, scooped fresh-ground beans into the filter and poured water into the coffee maker. Her good deed for the day, she thought as the water began to drip through. The aroma of coffee filled the room but her desire for it had been killed. She poured herself a glass of water and returned to her desk.

The light on her phone that signaled waiting messages wasn't glowing. She picked up the receiver anyway and punched in her code. The little robot who lived inside the phone intoned in its flat mechanical voice: "No. New. Messages."

"Hey, Marlene," she said, "did the caller give a name?"

Marlene looked up from whatever she was doing at her computer. "The LeGrande house guy? Not to me."

"Damn. I wish he'd left a message."

"He didn't?" Marlene's forehead scrunched in puzzlement. "I'm surprised. He sounded so eager to talk to someone about that house."

Claire entered the code again, just to make sure. Same result. She sighed to release her disappointment. "No message."

Marlene shrugged. "I guess some people just hate voicemail."

"Well, if he's excited enough, he'll call back," Claire said. She popped the lid off the cup of yogurt.

While she ate, she began sketching out ideas for a flyer describing the house. She'd need flyers next

Tuesday for the brokers tour. Probably every agent in Marin County had been through the house at least once, so she'd have to think of some gimmick to make it seem fresh and appealing instead of stale.

Putting up the Web page had been easy because Marlene had done all the work. Designing the flyer turned out to be a challenge. Golden Gate had templates she could use but none of them seemed to fit this property. On the Web page they'd used lots of pictures to tell the story, but the flyer had room for only one or two. How would she capture the home's special qualities? The flyer needed a sales paragraph that would make the house sound sexy. Claire scribbled a first draft:

Picture yourself living in a contemporary mansion designed by an internationally renowned architect who has anticipated your every desire and provided for your every comfort. Enjoy the sunset as you entertain on your large redwood deck perched right at the edge of ocean. Unless, of course, the fog comes in and freezes your buns off, not to mention those of your guests. In that case, bring the people into the grand salon to relax by the warmth of the fieldstone fireplace, and hope nothing strange happens to creep them out.

Claire wadded the paper into a ball and tossed it into the trashcan.

The chime rang, signaling the arrival of the elevator, and Avery flounced into the office. "Hello, hello, hello," she sang out as she reached her desk, directly in front of Claire's. She plopped down a pale green deli bag of her own and, as Claire watched enviously, she arrayed its contents on the desktop—a fat roast beef sandwich, a bag of tortilla chips, a large container filled with a garlicky-smelling pasta-and-pesto salad, and three, count them, three chocolate chip cookies. Then she grabbed her mug and went into the kitchen.

Claire's mouth watered. She loved Spuntino's pasta salad.

Avery came back carrying the mug. "Thank God, someone made fresh coffee."

Claire glared at her and ate another spoonful of yogurt.

"Yogurt?" Avery said brightly. "Poor you. I can't stand that stuff."

"This raspberry flavor's not bad," Claire said.

Avery ripped open the bag of chips and held it out. "Want some?"

Yes, Claire thought. "No, thank you," she said.

"Are you dieting or something? You don't look that fat."

"Thanks, I think."

"I'm lucky, I've got this very active metabolism. It runs in my daddy's side of the family. Probably the only good thing he ever gave me."

Claire wasn't sure how to respond to that. "Enjoy your lunch," she said.

Avery sat down to her feast and Claire turned her attention back to her flyer, trying to ignore the munching sounds and mouth-watering aromas emanating from just three feet away. Finally she couldn't stand it any longer. "Avery? If the chip offer is still open, I'll take a couple."

Avery turned around and handed her the bag, still half full. "Sure. Help yourself. Take them all. I've got an extra cookie, too, if you're still hungry."

Claire helped herself to a handful of chips. "Don't tempt me too much. I need to save my appetite for dinner."

"Is it something special? Are you going out?"

"Well, actually, I'm having dinner with Ben Grant."

Avery looked stunned. "What! You have a date with him?"

"No, no. Of course not. Ben's a client. His niece Eden will be there. We're just going to get acquainted, that's all. The better you know your clients, the better you can help them."

"Jeez, I can't believe it." Avery snatched back the chip bag.

The phone rang on the receptionist's desk. As Marlene spoke to the caller she caught Claire's eye and pointed a forefinger in her direction, indicating that the call was for her. A moment later Claire's extension trilled.

"Hello. This is Claire Scanlan. How may I—"

A torrent of words poured into her ear. *"Hey great that's swell possible selling a grandmother house—"*

"Whoa!" Claire said. "Slower please. You said something about selling your grandmother's house?"

It was a masculine voice, and it didn't slow down much. "No, no, not my grandmother. The LeGrande murder house, the one near Mariners Beach where the famous architect's family was killed. You and your firm are selling it, is that right?"

Ah, this must be the man who called earlier and didn't leave a message. "Yes, indeed. Are you interested? I'll be happy to show it to you. It's quite a wonderful house despite its, um, gruesome history."

"Super. I can meet you there this afternoon. What time?"

Claire glanced at her watch. Almost three. Where had the afternoon gone? Did she have time to drive all the way back over to the coast, show the house, and return in time to get ready for her evening with Ben? Of course, it wasn't officially a date, so what did it matter if she didn't have on just the right clothes, or if her hair wasn't perfect?

"I thin it would work much better for my schedule if we could do it tomorrow morning."

"Doable for me. See you at nine? Nine-thirty?"

"How about nine-thirty. And what was your name again?"

"Griff Maxwell."

Claire laughed before she could stop herself.

"What's funny?" the caller asked.

"I heard your name as *Great, that's swell.*"

He obliged her with a chuckle. "People always tell me I talk too damn fast."

People were right, from what Claire could tell. "The real problem," she said, "is that I hear too slowly. How did you learn about the house so fast, Mr. Maxwell? Golden Gate just got the listing yesterday."

"Google Alert. I set them up for Stefan LeGrande and Highview Lane. I got an email this morning with a link to your Web page for the house."

"So you've had your eye on the house for awhile?"

"Sure have."

"Excuse me if I'm prying, but if you're that interested, then why haven't you already bought it? It's a new listing for us, but it's been on the market for months."

"What? Oh, I don't want to buy it. I want to write about it. Guess you missed that part too. I'm a reporter, *Marin Post-Ledger.*"

Post-Ledger. The words her brain had garbled into *possible.* The *Post Ledger* was the daily paper that covered the towns north of San Francisco. Tess subscribed to it for the office, though Claire rarely looked at anything except the real estate ads.

She felt a flicker of trepidation. "Write what about it?"

"I covered the killings back when they happened. Huge story around here, probably you remember. It was big nationally too. My articles got picked up all over the country. I thought it was time for a follow-up."

"Based on what? There's no news angle. Once you've made a quick mention of Golden Gate Properties, what else is there to say?"

"Plenty. I'll interview you, talk with some of the people who show up at your open houses. Here's a hook—you've got a house that's a double-edged sword. On the one hand it's an architectural masterpiece, right? But on the other hand, scene of a spectacular crime. So what are the challenges of selling a house like that? What are the attractions of buying it?"

"Thanks, Mr. Maxwell, but I think I'll pass."

"Hey, I'm giving you a super opportunity here. You can't buy publicity like this."

"It's . . . well, ghoulish. Our best marketing strategy is to downplay the tragedy."

"Look, when we meet in the morning I'll—"

"That's really not a good idea. I'm afraid I can't help you, Mr. Maxwell. An article like you're describing will just scare people off."

As Claire hung up, Avery swiveled around in her chair to face her. "Was that a reporter?"

"Yeah."

"And you blew him off?"

"Yeah, again."

"But why? You'd get your name in your paper."

"I can't see that some sensationalistic article is going to help us sell the house."

"Maybe, maybe not. People will still see your name, and they'll call you about other houses. Tess is always talking about how important it is to network."

"Networking happens when you actually meet people."

"It's more like having people find out who you are. What counts is that they know your name."

"Well, this isn't the best way to accomplish that. If this guy writes the article, it will pull all the weirdos and voyeurs in Marin County out from under their rocks, wanting to go see the place. And it will scare off all the serious buyers."

Avery shrugged. "I'd totally let him interview me. If you're so worried, maybe you shouldn't be the listing agent."

"And what, turn it over to you?"

Avery smiled. "Sure, why not?"

"Thanks, but I'll keep it."

"Okay. Doesn't matter. Things are going to work out for me anyway."

Avery's smile widened, giving her a cat-that-swallowed-the-canary look. Claire could almost see the feathers caught in her teeth. What was the blond bubblehead up to now?

Chapter 11

Claire double-checked the house number posted on the gate. Yes, this was the right place. Satisfied, she parked her Volkswagen at the edge of the road and took a good look at Ben Grant's home.

It couldn't have been more different from his brother's. Tucked into a woodsy corner of the town of Mill Valley, the gray woodframe bungalow nestled among trees and ferns and laurel bushes. Here and there, beds of impatiens punctuated the lush greenness with bright spots of red and pink. The yard was even bounded by a picket fence.

Desirable neighborhood, top school district, plenty of curb appeal—Claire realized she was calculating its market value in her head. A hazard of her new occupation. But she was here to have dinner with a client, so it made sense to be in her professional mode.

She twisted the rearview mirror down so she could see herself. Touched up her lipstick, adjusted the collar of her silk blouse and arranged the amethyst necklace so it fell just right. She was startled to realize she felt nervous about seeing Ben on his home turf. Okay, about seeing him again at all. Maybe she should admit it—her interest in him wasn't totally professional after all.

Her hair was in one of its rebellious moods, and she tried to comb the stray tendrils into place. For years, she'd worn it long and straight—a darker version of Avery's look, now that she thought about it. Zach had adored her hair that way, called it sexy. But when she made the decision to leave the son of a bitch and come back to California, she'd whacked her tresses short, a symbol of her new life, her new independence. The new style revealed waves and curls she'd never suspected, and her hair developed a mind of its own.

As she got out of the Volkswagen and started up the flagstone walk, Claire saw a flicker of motion behind a bay window. Before she could reach the front door, it popped open and a girl of about ten with a yellow ponytail stepped out onto the wide front porch.

"Hi, there," Claire said.

"Hi, are you Claire?"

"That's right. You must be Eden."

"Yep, that's me. Eden Hollister. We've been waiting for you. Come in." The girl beckoned Claire inside.

The door opened directly into a living room filled with old-fashioned furnishings—a camelback sofa with plush blue cushions, a pair of wingback chairs, glossy maple tables. Not exactly the contemporary look she would have expected of a brother of Stefan LeGrande, but cozy and homelike. An archway led to a small hall and from there, Claire guessed, to the bedrooms. Through a wider arch she saw a dining table set with three places and, beyond that, the door to the kitchen. Smells of onion and spices tickled Claire's nose.

"She's here, Ben!" Eden called, bouncing on her toes in their tennis shoes. Then to Claire, "I'll take your stuff." She gathered Claire's purse and the sweater she'd brought in case it got chilly later and disappeared with them through the bedroom arch. Claire hung onto the bottle of wine she'd brought.

Ben appeared at the kitchen door, wearing an apron of all things. His forehead glistened from the heat of cooking. He looked wonderful.

"Claire! So glad you're here." He quickly stepped forward, saying her name with such enthusiasm she half expected him to sweep her into his arms. He stopped short a few feet away, and she was surprised to feel disappointed.

"Glad to be here. You have a nice place."

"Thanks. I can't really claim credit, though. I rented the house furnished when I moved out here to deal with Stefan's estate."

Her eye was caught by a canvas above the blue sofa, a view of the coastal ridge near Mariners Beach, with the ocean beyond. At first glance the paint seemed to have been daubed on almost randomly. Yet the dots and dashes of color came together to create a lively picture. It was far from photographically perfect in its detail, yet it completely captured the spirit of the place. Stepping forward to admire the intricate brushwork, Claire noticed the signature in the corner: *B. Grant.*

"You painted this? It's beautiful."

"I told you I dabbled."

"That's so much better than mere dabbling."

He dipped his head modestly. "Thank you."

She held out the wine bottle. "I hope this is good. The manager at my favorite wine store recommended it for Italian food. You said you were fixing lasagna."

"Clos de Vignes zinfandel. Perfect. Come on back and we'll open this while I put the finishing touches on dinner."

Claire followed him into the kitchen. The appliances had to be two decades old at least, and the rest of the room probably hadn't been updated in fifty years. She immediately knocked forty thousand dollars off her mental price.

"Have a seat," Ben invited. Taking out a corkscrew, he used it to point to a pair of wooden stools pulled up to a butcher-block table. When the bottle was uncorked, he took three wineglasses from a cabinet, poured the zinfandel into two of them, and handed one to Claire. "Skoal," he said, lifting his glass.

"Cheers," she offered in return, and took a sip.

The wine was a deep rich red in both color and taste. Claire was no expert on the subtleties of flavors in wine, but she thought she detected a hint of raspberry.

Eden came into the kitchen, and Ben gave her the empty glass. "Hey," she said, "how come mine doesn't have any wine in it?"

Ben chuckled. "Fill it with whatever you like from the fridge. There's orange juice, water, milk, salad dressing—"

Eden made a face at Claire, to let her know Ben was teasing. "Can I have some Coke?"

"Mmm, I don't know . . ."

"Please!"

"Glad you remembered to add that word. What do you think, Claire? Is this enough of a special occasion for us to indulge her wishes?"

"Well, it's pretty special to me."

"Me too." He smiled at her. "Here's to sharing many special occasions."

The words made her heart flip-flop.

"Hey, wait, I want to toast too." Eden took a liter bottle of Coke from the refrigerator and sloshed some into her glass. "To a special occasion."

The bowls of their wineglasses touched, and the kitchen resounded with their musical ring.

"THAT WAS DELICIOUS." Claire sighed with satisfaction as she set her fork on her empty plate.

"Would you like some more?" Ben asked. "There's plenty left."

"Of course there is," she said. "You made enough to feed all of Mill Valley. No more for me, thanks. I've already indulged in twice as much as I should."

"It's health food, you know. All the basic food groups. Protein, vegetables, dairy, grain . . . "

Claire laughed. "Health food! Tell that to my waistline. You know, you're a great cook."

"Lasagna's not hard," Ben said dismissively, though he looked pleased.

"Maybe for you it's not. You've had lots of practice."

Eden blotted away her tomato-sauce mustache with her big cloth napkin. "Ben's says he's the chief cook and bottle washer at our house," she said. "And I'm the pastry chef."

"Pastry chef? Very impressive," Claire said.

"Is it time for dessert yet?"

"I think so," Ben replied. "Carry these plates into the kitchen and then you can serve it."

"I made my specialty," Eden said as she stacked the dinner plates. "You're going to love it."

"I can't wait," Claire said. "What is it?"

"A surprise. Just wait." Eden carried the plates into the kitchen. A moment later Claire heard them clatter into the sink.

Ben picked up the zinfandel bottle. It was empty. "Shall I find another bottle to open?" he asked. "Or are you ready for a cappuccino? I have a new espresso machine I want to play with."

"Cappuccino sounds heaven—"

"O-oh, no-o!" The wail came from the kitchen.

Ben jumped up. "Eden? Honey, what's wrong?"

"They didn't cook! They're all goopy!"

Claire followed him as far as the kitchen door. The oven door was hanging open. Sitting on the rack was a pan of what looked like underdone brownies. The lovely fragrance of chocolate filled the air.

Eden wiped at her eyes with a fat oven mitt. "I don't know what happened. I did it just like the directions said."

Ben was fiddling with the controls on the stove. "Did you turn off the oven just now?"

Eden shook her head, ponytail bouncing. "No. And it's on the right temperature too. I checked."

"Well, the oven is definitely off."

Uh-oh. Claire took a step back. Could strange powers be at work in this house too? Or maybe it wasn't the houses but Grant/LeGrande family that was haunted.

Ben said, "My fault, princess. I was supposed to leave it on when I took out the lasagna, wasn't I? So the brownies would bake while we ate. But I must have turned it off automatically, without thinking."

Eden sniffed. "You're always telling me, think first, then act."

"And now you see why. When you act without thinking you can screw things up, like I just did. We'll start them baking now. They'll be done in what, half an hour?"

The girl's shoulders sagged. "The oven has to heat up first. It will take forever."

Claire moved farther into the room. "What's that wonderful smell? Chocolate?"

"It got all ruined," Eden said apologetically.

"Really?" Claire made a show of inspecting the pan. She found a pair of potholders and lifted the brownies from the oven rack to the stovetop. "It looks perfect to me. My favorite dessert—how did you know? *Chocolat à la cuillère.*"

"No, it's not. It's—chocolate what?"

"*Chocolat à la cuillère*. Or in English, chocolate *á la* spoon."

Eden giggled.

"You've never tasted anything so delicious," Claire said. "All we need is spoons and bowls—"

"There's ice cream to go on top," Eden offered.

"Even better," Claire enthused.

As Ben stepped past her to his espresso machine on the opposite counter, he squeezed her shoulder and bent to whisper, "Thanks." His touch and his breath on her cheek made her dizzy.

When dessert had been portioned out into bowls and cappuccino poured into china cups, the three of them returned to the table. Claire tasted her brownie, which felt soft, warm and sensual in her mouth.

She washed down the morsel with a sip of cappuccino and then said, "You know, Eden, I met a friend of yours today."

Eden had to swallow a bite before she could say, "Who?"

"Lily Roncallo. I was up at your old house and she came over to say hello."

"You went back to the house?" Ben said, a spoonful of brownie and ice cream suspended halfway to his mouth. "Was everything all right? Did you . . . that is, did anything happen while you there?"

For a moment Claire's ankle throbbed as it had when she tripped over the invisible block of ice. The pleasant flavors of chocolate and coffee dissolved into the remembered taste of acrid smoke.

"No, nothing," she told him. "I was just there to set up the lockbox."

"Lily!" Eden looked wistful. "I miss her."

Ben said, "I saw her father yesterday, honey. Martin and I are going to make plans for you two girls to get together."

"I'm not going to her house. I'm not going to Highview Lane ever again."

"We'll arrange for Lily to come here," Ben assured her. "Or maybe we can meet her at the beach or a park for a picnic. Would you like that?"

"Just me and Lily. He can't come."

"Who can't?"

"Lily's dad. I don't like him."

"You don't?" Ben's surprise showed in his tone. "You've never mentioned that. Why not?"

"Because he teased me."

"About what?" Ben looked alarmed.

Eden shot a glance at Claire, then looked down at her plate. "Nothing. Just stuff."

Of course, thought Claire. The girl wouldn't want to talk about whatever it was in front of a stranger. Maybe she should excuse herself, ask to use the powder room.

But Ben seemed to have forgotten for the moment that Claire was there. He jumped in before she could say anything. "What kind of teasing?" he said sharply. "Did he hurt you?"

Eden fingered her long blond hair. "Not like you mean. He was making fun of my father."

"Stefan?"

"Lily's dad said I was the daughter of a jailbird. He made me so mad. That stupid Leo isn't my real father, Stefan was. What counts is who raises you, who's there for you. That's what my mom always said. So my real father was Stefan LeGrande, not some awful creep in jail. I'm never going to go live with him."

"Of course you're not, princess," Ben assured her. "You're staying with me, no matter what. You know we're a team now. We're family. When did this teasing happen?"

"A bunch of times. He did it on the night when . . . on the night . . ."

Suddenly Eden's fists were pressed tight against her eyes as she tried to choke back a sob.

Ben eased the girl out of her chair and into an embrace. After a moment her tears subsided. With quivering lips, Eden said, "I didn't mean to cry. It's just . . . I miss them. I miss my mother."

Ben hugged her tighter.

Claire said, "It's okay to miss them. Never let anyone tell you it's wrong to feel what you feel. I miss my mother, too, and I can't even remember her."

This piqued Eden's interest. "Why not? What happened to her?"

"She died in a car crash when I was a baby. My father too. My grandmother raised my older sister and me. The three of us made a new family."

"You mean like Ben and me."

"Exactly."

Eden slid back into her chair and spooned up a mouthful of the soft chocolate dough and ice cream. She seemed to be thinking things over.

Claire took a bite of her own dessert. "This is really very good, you know."

Eden smiled. "Yes, it is, isn't it? I'm going to make them half-baked all the time now."

"Does that make you a half-baked baker?" Ben asked.

They all laughed, even Eden, which led to more bad jokes and further mirth. The dark moment dissolved, and Claire began to feel more lighthearted than she had in a long time.

"EDEN'S A LOVELY GIRL," Claire said to Ben as she settled onto the blue cushions of the sofa in the living room. He took a seat in one of the wingback chairs and flicked on the porcelain lamp on the table beside it. Eden had been excused to watch a favorite TV program before going to bed.

"Isn't she," Ben agreed. "Lord knows I wish the circumstances had been different. But if we had to be dealt such difficult cards, at least Eden and I got lucky enough to play out the hand together."

"What is her father like, the one who distresses her so much?" Claire ventured to ask. "Does she look like him? Eden is beautiful, like her mother, but in the pictures I found on the Internet, Jacqueline's a brunette, dark and exotic-looking, while Eden's so fair."

"Leo Hollister. I've met him only a couple of times. He has blond hair, gray eyes. Eden takes after him. But just physically, I hope, not psychologically."

"She called him a jailbird. And you said he's been in prison. What's his story? If you don't mind telling it, that is."

"Oh, there's no secret there. Leo and Jacqueline knew each other growing up in Oakland. They had an off-and-on relationship—pretty volatile, from what I gather. In one of the *on* phases Jacqueline became pregnant. So they got married. Leo was obsessed with her—well, lots of men were, truth be told, she was an easy woman to fall in love with." His gaze shifted from Claire and he fell silent, as if his mind had drifted far away.

"And then came the *off* phase," she prompted.

His attention came back to her. "Off for good, as it turned out. Leo didn't much like the bonds and responsibilities that went along with marriage and fatherhood. One day he walked out on his wife and his baby daughter without a word. Then he got busted dealing drugs and phoned Jacqueline demanding she come down to the jail and bail him out. First time she'd heard from him in six months. Smart lady, she refused."

"You say lots of men fell for her. Was one of them you?" Claire was astounded to hear the question pop from her mouth.

Ben laughed. "Yes, for a time, I sure was. I was in San Francisco visiting Stefan and his kids, and I went into a bookstore to pick up something to read on my flight home. Jacqueline was working there. She had a smile that lit up the whole place. I still remember the perfume she wore. It smelled like gardenias. The store had a coffee bar and on impulse I asked her to let me buy her a cup when she had her break. Next thing I knew I had cancelled my return ticket. We went out every night for the next week. I thought I'd found heaven."

Claire knew the prick of jealousy she felt was totally unjustified. "But she was married to your brother."

"Not then, she wasn't. But Stefan had recently been divorced. Like an idiot, I proposed that he and his girlfriend of the moment double date with Jacqueline and me. The minute the two of them laid eyes on each other, something clicked. They went home together, leaving me behind with Stefan's very angry date. Jacqueline never looked back. Not at me anyway. The next day I bought a new plane ticket and flew back to Boston."

"How old was Eden then?"

"About three. Just barely big enough to be the flower girl at Jacqueline and Stefan's wedding. She carried gardenias, of course."

"So Eden has never really known her biological father?"

"Oh, she knows him, all right," Ben said. "Unfortunately Leo keeps popping back into the picture. When his ex married a famous architect he smelled money. He started coming around pretending an interest in Eden, demanding visits from his precious daughter. He threatened to fight Jacqueline for custody if she didn't pay him off."

"That's crazy. There's no way a court would favor him over her."

"No, but he managed to created a lot of hassle. He didn't really want Eden. What he wanted was an easy source of income."

"Extortion, in other words."

"Exactly. Eventually he was sent back to prison again on a parole violation. He sends letters to Eden constantly saying how much he loves her and begging her to visit him."

"Has she done that?" Claire asked.

"Only once. It upset her so much that now she wants nothing to do with him. He scares her. When he gets out, I'll look into getting a restraining order. She has no need for Leo. She had a good father in Stefan and now she has me."

"She uses Leo's name. She introduced herself as Eden Hollister."

"Stefan wanted to adopt her and make her a LeGrande, but Leo refused. Now I'm trying to do the same. Leo's determined to maintain his hold, though, especially now that he thinks his daughter is a wealthy heiress."

"And is she?"

"Actually, yes. But everything is in trusts. Her expenses are taken care of for now, but she won't get the bulk of the money until she's twenty-five. Leo has no hope of getting a dime."

Ben had been leaning forward as he spoke. Now he sat back. Claire thought he was gazing the painting above her head, his own rendering of land and sea. But it was hard to tell; in the dim light of the room, his eyes were shadowed.

What should she say next? Maybe now was the opportunity she had been waiting for, a chance to talk about the house. She could mention Lindsay's silly notion that Ben, or someone, had rigged up some sort of gadgetry to frighten off her and any buyer, and laugh it off together. She could confess that despite her earlier denial, strange things had happened to her today up on Highview Lane.

No. She wouldn't risk that.

"Ben," she said, not sure what words would follow.

"You look really nice tonight, Claire," he said.

She hadn't expected that, and for some reason it flustered her. "Oh! Thank you."

"I like that necklace. You were wearing it yesterday too."

Her fingers flew to the strand of amethyst crystals. "It was my mother's. I wear it sometimes for good luck."

"An heirloom then. It has a sweet, old-fashioned charm." Ben stood up. "I'm ready for another cappuccino, this one with a little brandy in it. How about you?"

Claire glanced at her watch. She'd been aware that the last glow of the midsummer dusk had disappeared from the sky outside the bay window, but she was surprised to see that it was nearly ten o'clock. The sensible thing would be to leave now and head for home. "I'd love another. No brandy though, please. I have to drive."

As he went into the kitchen she remained where she was, listening contentedly to the buzz of the grinder and whoosh of the espresso machine. When Ben returned he set the two cups on the coffee table, saying, "I'm going to check on Eden." He disappeared under the small arch that led to the bedrooms. A minute later he was back. "She's already asleep."

This time he sat on the sofa beside her, close enough that even though they weren't touching, the warmth of him prickled her skin. As Claire picked up her cup and saucer, her hand trembled, making them rattle.

"So good," she whispered when she'd taken a sip.

"Yes, very good." Ben took the cup and saucer from her and replaced them on the table. He slid his arms around her and pulled her closer.

"Claire . . ." he murmured, pulling her head to his shoulder and stroking her hair.

She inhaled deeply, taking in his spicy male scent. She didn't trust herself to speak.

His lips touched hers. She realized she had been anticipating this kiss, longing for it, since the moment she saw him in front of the house on Highview Lane. It was the fulfillment of a dream, a dare, a desire, and she wished it would never end.

Time spun and stopped. She didn't know how many minutes or hours went by, but eventually he murmured, "Sweet Claire, you could stay. But with Eden here . . ."

"I understand," she said, although all she really understood at the moment was the strength in his arms and the heat in her body.

His finger to her chin, Ben lifted her face and they kissed again, a kiss that promised pleasure to come.

She was skimming above the ground as she left his house. Arriving in her apartment building's parking lot, she wasn't sure how she'd gotten there. She'd seen nothing all the way except Ben's eyes, Ben's lips, Ben's beautiful face.

The apartment was silent and dark except for a single lamp that Lindsay had left burning for her. Claire drifted to sleep in her own bed, pretending it was Ben's.

PURPLE, COLOR OF BRUISES, color of jewels. A hand she cannot see is stringing gemstone beads onto a cord braided from strands of memory, dream, and desire. The last two beads on the string are eyes, and in their corners are tears of blood. Suddenly the cord breaks and the beads scatter. As she watches a young girl tries to gather them up, but the eyes roll beyond the girl's reach. Then a dark curtain woven of midnight drops on top of her, separating her from the girl and the gems. The cloth cloaks her head and smothers her face. She fights to pull it away, to escape the clinging folds, but it grips her until she can no longer breathe.

Gray, color of fog, color of regrets. Mist swirls about her ankles as she walks along a stone-strewn path along a ridgetop as sharp as the edge of a knife's blade. At the bottom of the steep slope to her left, ocean waves foam and ferment as they strike rocks made of heartbreak. Down the slope to her right is a valley filled with clouds. The girl waits at the far end, beckons her forward. She takes a step forward and her foot slips. She is falling, falling, falling . . .

Claire woke up screaming.

Chapter 12

I'm so frustrated. No matter how hard I try, I can't get the energy under control.

I know from a science class I took Before that people in the physical world have five senses. That's how they take in information, learn things, define what's real. Real to them, anyway.

So if I want to connect with them I have to give them something to see, hear, touch, taste, smell. Doing that is the way I can communicate with them.

The place where I now exist, caught between Before and the place called Forever, is full of energy, which can be whittled and molded and shoved around. It can be used it to make things that will hook into a person's senses in the physical world. And I try and try, but all my attempts are so clumsy. I work hard to make sights and sounds and fragrances—anything that will tell the people who come to this house that we're here and we need their help. But I don't yet have the knowledge or skill. What I manage to create is too puny for anyone to perceive, or it dissipates so fast they don't have time to notice it. Or else the power overwhelms them. They feel anguished or afraid without knowing why, and they run away.

When the woman with chocolate hair came back, I was really glad to see her. So far she's the only one who's been able to hear my voice or feel my touch, *even though she doesn't know it's me. I keep hoping I'll get my message through but all I've accomplished so far is to terrify her.*

The one who is trapped here with me is worse than no help. This time when the woman came, he was crouched in the middle of the room, right at the spot where he fell that fiery night. He had turned himself into a block of ice, solid and hard yet at the same time as insubstantial as air. The woman tripped over him and fell flat. When she got up she was limping, and I could tell she was in pain. A moment later she was gone.

If he's driven her away I'll never forgive him. We may never have another chance to make the truth known and prevent another tragedy. I told him so, but he didn't respond at all. He never does, which is why I'm so lonely.

Still, he has moved to the middle of the room. This is the first time he's crept away from the far corner.

What will he do if the woman comes again?

What will I do if she doesn't?

Chapter 13

"Morning, Linz," Claire said as she came into the narrow apartment kitchen.

Lindsay, dressed in an oversized San Francisco Giants T-shirt, was reaching into the refrigerator. Her dark auburn hair was still tousled from sleep. Emerging with a carton of orange juice, she returned Claire's greeting with a smile. "Well, hey, roomie, you're alive."

"Of course. Why wouldn't I be?" Claire opened a cabinet and took down two glasses, setting them on the tiled counter.

Lindsay kicked the fridge door shut with a bare foot. "The way you were yelling last night, I thought the bogeyman had crept out from under the bed and had you in his clutches."

"Oh, that."

"Third night in a row." Lindsay lifted an eyebrow in inquiry. "Is everything okay, Claire?"

"Sure." Taking the carton from her roommate, Claire poured juice into the two glasses. "Here you go."

Lindsay accepted her glass with a nod of thanks. "It's just that your nightmares seem like they're getting more frequent. More intense too, maybe. What was last night's about?"

"The usual, I assume, whatever that is. You know I can never remember my dreams, whether they're good ones or bad ones. It's so frustrating."

"All the changes you've been through in the last year, it's no wonder if things are getting stirred up in your psyche. A cross-country move, real estate school, a new job, the end of your marriage. Aren't your final divorce papers due to show up soon?"

Claire nodded. "Any day now." She hoped Lindsay didn't notice the shiver that the words *final divorce papers* had sent through her. Yes, it had been her own decision to leave Zach. Yes, she knew it was time to move on. But she had invested so many hopes and dreams in her marriage. She wasn't eager to receive the written proof that they all had failed.

"Well then, there you have it." Lindsay placed a sympathetic hand on Claire's shoulder. "Nightmare fodder for sure."

Claire looked at her juice, ready to lift it her lips. For just a second, an image floated on the orange surface. Then it vanished. "There was a girl . . ."

"A girl," Lindsay prompted. "In your dream last night?"

Claire stared into the glass, willing the picture to reappear, but the juice refused to cooperate. "I think so."

"Who is she?"

"No idea." The hell with it. She drank down the juice. That would teach it not to mess with her mind.

"Your inner child perhaps," Lindsay said lightly.

"Maybe . . . no, it's probably what this dream book I read once called 'day remnants'. I met two girls yesterday, ten-year-olds. Ben's niece and her friend who lives next door to the LeGrande house. I don't see kids that age very often, so it wouldn't surprise me if one or both of them made enough of an impression to sneak into my dreams."

"Makes sense to me. Speaking of Ben, how did last night go?"

Claire licked her lips, trying to recapture the luscious flavor and feel of Ben's kiss. All she could taste was orange juice.

Lindsay gave her a wicked grin. "That good, huh?"

"What do you mean?"

"You just made a little pleasure-moan."

"I did not!"

"Did too. So are you going to see him again?"

"Yes, I am, smartie. Tonight. And I intend to have a wonderful time."

"Another threesome? Is he cooking again?"

"No, a girl in Eden's summer arts-and-crafts class invited the whole group to a birthday sleepover, so Ben and I are going out to dinner. At the Petite Marmite, I'll have you know."

Lindsay whistled. "Fanciest place in Marin. So you're now officially dating your client."

"It's not a date," Claire protested, though she knew Lindsay was right. What's more, she no longer cared about the professional propriety of it; the notion of dating Ben delighted her. "It's more like a business meeting—Ben and I are getting to know each other so we can work better together."

"Right," Lindsay said. "And you're going to wear a gray flannel suit instead of that sexy black dress you bought."

"Black is businesslike." Claire had splurged on the dress on impulse with no clue when she'd get to wear it. It was almost as if she knew she would soon have the perfect opportunity.

"Sure it is. Well, have fun. Dine on something extravagant and expensive for me." Lindsay gulped the last of her juice. "Time to get businesslike myself and head off to the salt mines." As she sauntered out of the kitchen, she gave Claire a quick hug.

To CLAIRE'S DISMAY, George Pugh was hovering near the elevator when she arrived at Golden Gate. Shooting him a smile intended to be polite—they had to work together, after all—but not encouraging, she stepped briskly past him and headed for her desk.

Evidently he mistook her intent. He followed her to the back of the bullpen and parked his ample butt on the empty desk next to hers.

"Glad you could make it on time," he said as he loosened the knot of his necktie. The tie had a stain on it, Claire noticed, and his wrinkled white shirt was at least one size too small. "That's two days now. Out of three."

"I try to be punctual," she replied, keeping her tone crisp and professional. He was going to give her grief about her awkwardly tardy entrance to the Monday Meeting two days ago. Couldn't everyone just let it go?

But all George said was, "That's a good business practice."

"Yes, it is." She sat down, turned on her computer, picked up some papers, checked her empty voicemail— all signals, she hoped, that she was busy and he should go away.

He leaned forward, bracing his elbows on his knees. "I know lots of good business practices. The real estate business, especially. And I always like to help newcomers to the field succeed." He winked at her.

"That's nice." She made a show of bringing up the Multiple Listing Service on her computer and staring at the screen. *Go away now, George. Go away.*

"If you like, I could show some tricks." When she didn't respond, he added, "Professional tricks, I mean. Say, over dinner tonight?"

She couldn't believe it—was this jerk actually asking her out?

"Kind of you to offer. But I have an appointment tonight."

"Tomorrow then."

Whoops, she had been too polite. "Can't. I have an appointment then too." With her TV, but no need to tell him that. "And the night after that." And every night until the end of time.

"Next week then. I'll check my schedule." He slid off the desk, his feet in tasseled loafers landing with a thud. "By the way, I hope you're not in some kind of trouble."

Claire snapped her head around to face him. "Trouble?"

"Madame Boss said she wants to see you the minute you got in." Dusting his pudgy hands together, George ambled back down the aisle between the rows of desks.

"What!" Claire yelped at his retreating back. "Why didn't you tell me?"

Oh God, what now? Some kind of trouble. Claire tried to think of what she might have done wrong. She pulled a comb out of her top desk drawer and ran it through her hair. Gram had taught her a system for calming nervousness: take ten deep, slow breaths and think of something soothing. Claire was on breath number eight before a soothing thought came to mind: Ben.

Her heart was still pounding a moment later as she stood in Tess McMillan's open doorway. The owner and broker of Golden Gate Properties was seated at her vast rosewood desk, flipping through a sheaf of papers and jotting notes on a legal pad. She was dressed in another of her designer suits, its ivory color the perfect backdrop for her imposing gold jewelry and champagne-colored hair. Claire had thought the brand-new cream-colored blazer she'd put on this morning would be perfect attire for this job, but she could see that she might have to raise her wardrobe standards.

"Tess?" The name came out in a hoarse whisper. Claire cleared her throat and tried again. "Excuse me, Tess? George said you wanted to see me."

Tess beckoned her in. "Yes indeed, Claire. Come on in. Sit down."

Morning light filled the office. Outside the wide window, sunlight sparkled on the breeze-stirred waves and the white sails of the small boats that were riding them.

Claire edged onto the leather cushion of one of the visitor's chairs. "May I ask, uh, what this is about?"

Tess set down her pen. "I have good news for you, Claire. A possible buyer for that problematic LeGrande place."

Claire felt relief flood through her. "That's all? I mean, that's great. Who is it?"

"A couple I met last night at a dinner for one of my charitable groups. Paul and Nadine Johansen. They just moved here from Chicago; she's the new CEO of Marin Savings and Trust, and he's some sort of high-tech genius. They're renting right now, but they hate the place so they're primed to jump into a house of their own. I told them about your listing, and they think it sounds perfect. Nadine loves the idea of living in a LeGrande design."

"Wonderful!" Then Claire had a thought. "If she's familiar with Stefan LeGrande, she must know he was murdered there. Doesn't that bother her?"

"That didn't come up. They'll have to be informed of that detail, of course. But since they're new to the Bay Area, it may not resonate with them as strongly as it would with someone local. I doubt the story was as huge in Chicago as it was here."

"Makes sense. How do I get in touch with them?"

Tess handed Claire a business card. "She said she could make time in her schedule today. Go for it."

"Thank you, Tess!" Flashing her boss a grin, Claire stood up to leave.

She was halfway to the door when Tess said, "Oh, by the way. That green Volkswagen in the parking lot—it's yours, isn't it."

Claire stopped and turned. "Um, yes, that's right . . ."

Tess pursed her lips. "I was afraid of that." She started to say more, but Claire jumped in.

"Don't worry, I'm planning to get a new one as soon I can."

"Good. But you'd better take my car when you see the Johansens. Here." Tess tossed her a set of keys. Claire caught them on the fly.

Her mood soared so high that her feet barely touched the plush carpet as she went to her desk to make the call. It was going to work. She had found her calling. After giving up her early dream of a theater career, stumbling through a series of dull low-level marketing positions, chafing at the chains of her mind-deadening secretarial job in Cambridge, this was the perfect solution. It offered everything her previous jobs had lacked—independence, variety, rewards limited only by her own efforts and capabilities. Never mind Gram's doubts, Cassandra's smug superiority, Zach's sneers and putdowns and betrayals. She was going to succeed.

Five minutes later she had the appointment set up. She would meet the couple up on Highview Lane at two o'clock this afternoon. She headed to the lounge to get coffee, doing a victory dance as she went down the aisle.

Chapter 14

"People died in the house, right?" said the man in the passenger seat of Avery's Porsche. "It was a murder scene."

"Don't worry, Mr. Burdick." Avery laughed as she gunned the convertible around a sharp curve on Highway One. This car was the coolest ever. "All the blood and stuff like that was cleaned up. The whole place has been painted and refurbished. It's immaculate. Move-in condition."

"Good. Given the astronomical asking price, I don't want to have to invest more money right away into fixing it up."

Off to her left she could see the ocean glisten. The sun was shining for now, but wisps of fog were beginning to blow inland.

"It's true the house has an unhappy history. But what counts is the future." This had always been Avery's philosophy. If she had focused on the past, or even on the present, instead of what was to come, she never would have survived.

"Has it been ghost-busted?" Wayne Burdick asked.

Was he serious? Avery glanced at the client she'd stolen from Claire and was relieved to see he was smiling. A joke then.

She smiled back, a high-wattage beam intended to dazzle him. Strictly business, of course. An inducement to help persuade him to buy the house. She didn't plan to offer herself as a purchase bonus, but it wouldn't hurt to arouse his fantasies about how she might thank him for his signature on the sales contract.

Then again, maybe casting her lot with this guy wouldn't be such a bad idea. He was tall, fit and quite pleasant looking, even if his brown hair was thinning on top. His eyes, also brown, burned with a hot intensity that might be interesting to explore. The card he'd given her said he was a business consultant. Avery wasn't totally sure what meant, but he must be making plenty of money if he was thinking about buying a multimillion-dollar property.

But he wasn't Ben Grant—Ben, who on first sight had totally knocked her out of her boots. For the past two days he had been pushing his way into her mind until she could hardly think about anything else. Yet it was stupid Claire who got to go out with him last night.

One more time that life had been unfair.

So what if Ben and Claire spent an evening together. That didn't mean she'd snared him. Ben was one prize Avery intended to win.

Burdick repeated his question: "Has the house been ghost-busted?"

God, could he be serious after all? The last thing she needed was to have her client turn out to be a flake.

"Well, I haven't seen an actual certificate." She thought of Claire, the way she'd screamed over nothing. "But I can guarantee you, Wayne, there weren't any ghosts when I was there Monday afternoon."

"Damn. I was prepared to pay extra for a few ghosts. I was hoping to make the place a tourist attraction, charge admission. Come see the Highview Manor,

Marin's exclusive haunted house." He laughed, a nice laugh, and Avery, glad he was kidding, chuckled with him.

The Porsche swooped past the Mariners Beach turnoff and started to climb the ridge.

"Almost there," Avery said.

DRIVING TO HIGHVIEW LANE, Claire had to concede that Tess's midnight blue Lincoln Town Car was a more sophisticated automobile than her own lime-green jellybean. The handling was smoother, the leather seats were cushier, and the sound system far superior. But to be honest, she preferred the VW for its ability to make her laugh.

Besides, what if something happened to the Lincoln? State highway or not, the coastal road was treacherous—hilly, twisting, two narrow lanes carrying more traffic than they were built for. What if she lost control? What if an oncoming car cut a curve too wide and invaded her lane?

Her heart was pounding by the time she pulled into the parking court of the LeGrande house. The car's clock said ten to two. Good—she'd hoped to arrive early so she'd have a few minutes to check the house for—well, she wasn't sure for what, exactly, but she wanted to be prepared for anything strange.

As she closed the car door, she realized she wouldn't have that chance. Another car was pulling into the driveway, a dark green Jaguar. She waited where she was to greet the Johansens.

The pair that emerged from the car couldn't have been more unlike. The husband was large, blond, and Nordic-looking with warm blue eyes and a bushy reddish beard. He wore jeans, an untucked plaid flannel shirt and lumberjack boots whose laces were coming untied. His wife was a petite brunette in severely tailored gray pinstripes and high-heeled pumps.

"I'm Nadine Johansen," the woman said briskly. "This is Paul." Paul stuck out his big paw for Claire to shake.

"Pleasure to meet you. I'm Claire Scanlan. Thank you for coming. As I'm sure you can see, this is a truly spectacular house."

"I like it already," Nadine said. "We have friends who live in a Stefan LeGrande home in Los Angeles, one of his early commissions. You can see how his artistry grew between then and the time this house was built."

"Can't beat the setting," said Paul, who was gazing toward the ocean.

"Let's go inside," Claire said.

As she guided them toward the house, she was startled by another car that came zooming up the driveway. Paul and Nadine jumped out of the way. The car slammed to a stop a couple of feet from Claire.

Porsche convertible. Avery at the wheel, a stranger in the passenger seat. Damn.

"Whoo, that road is fun," Avery said as she got out of the car. Her cheeks glowed red from the wind, and her hair was plaited into the long braid she wore when she drove to keep it from tangling.

Her companion stood staring at the house. About Ben's height, but far less handsome. The Gingerbread Man, Claire instantly dubbed him in her mind. Everything about him was brown. Hair, eyes, dark chocolate polo shirt, caramel-colored slacks. Even his shoes were brown.

"So this is the haunted house," he said.

Uh-oh, what kind of ideas had Avery been planting in this guy's mind?

Claire pulled her aside. "What are you doing here?"

"Same as you. Showing the house to a buyer." Avery turned to her client. "Wayne Burdick, this is Claire Scanlan, one of my esteemed colleagues at Golden Gate Properties."

Claire had never before heard the word *esteemed* imbued with such venom. Thank goodness none of the clients seemed to have picked up on Avery's spiteful tone. They were too busy covertly looking each other over, assessing whether they were about to become rivals.

"Haunted house?" Nadine said, eyeing Burdick.

"Little joke," he said, meeting her gaze.

Nadine nodded. "It's Stefan LeGrande's own home, you know. The man was a genius."

"Everyone says so," Burdick agreed in a cool tone. "It'll be a real privilege to own the place."

"Shall we take a look inside?" Claire asked brightly before an argument could develop. She led the group to the front entrance and retrieved the key from the lockbox by the brass lamp.

"Look, Paul, a seagull." Nadine ran her fingers along the door panel, tracing a carved wooden wing. "Such craftsmanship."

Claire's breath caught and her muscles tightened as she fit the key into the lock. A moment's hesitation, then she threw open the big door.

Nothing inside stirred. No odor assailed her nostrils. The air in the house was a normal temperature.

She felt weak for a second as the tension rushed out her body. Then she stepped inside and held the door, inviting the others to join her.

"Welcome," she said, "to Stefan LeGrande's masterpiece."

"FABULOUS PLACE," Paul Johansen said to Claire for the tenth time. Standing at the point at the point of the prow-shaped deck, he planted his big hands on the railing and leaned out. "Look at that surf. Breathe that salt breeze. Imagine coming home to a view like this every night."

"It's yours for the asking," she told him. Right now that view was almost solid gray. The ocean was dark and a thick bank of fog was pushing toward the shore. Yet when she looked in the opposite direction, the sky to the east was still a bright blue.

Nadine stepped out through the French doors leading from the grand salon. The pinstriped woman was smiling. Good. That meant that the strange energetic force that operated in the house was continuing to behave itself.

In fact, Claire had just about concluded that her bizarre experiences had occurred solely in her imagination. Five people had just spent an entire hour poking through every nook and cranny, and nothing unexpected had happened.

She'd let Paul and Nadine wander through the house alone, nervous that they'd encounter something strange but knowing better than to hover at their elbows. It was hard for people to picture themselves living in a home with a real estate agent hovering at their elbows. The best tactic was to give clients free rein and let them form their own impressions. Avery, Claire noticed, had stayed right on her prospect's heels, chattering at him the entire time. If she were Wayne Burdick, she'd have been seriously annoyed. Fortunately the two of them had not stayed long—after a cursory tour, they'd dashed off, leaving the place to Claire and her clients for their leisurely inspection.

"So what do you think?" Claire asked as Nadine joined her and Paul at the deck rail.

"Marvelous place. It goes to the top of our 'consider seriously' list, don't you think, Paul?"

"Absolutely." Paul nodded his shaggy head.

"Right now, though," Nadine said, "I have to get to that shareholders' meeting. Ready, dear?"

Claire walked them to their Jaguar and gave them her card. "Any time you have questions, or when you want to see the house again, give me a call."

"Don't worry," Paul said. "We'll be in touch for sure."

Claire hugged herself with pleasure as she watched them drive away. They were seriously interested; she could sense it in the tone of their voices, their body language. What a coup that would be, to sell the house to the first people she showed it to. A place that had languished on the market for months, that everyone saw as a problem property, until she came along. Claire Scanlan, real estate miracle worker.

She tossed her purse onto the seat of Tess's car, preparing to leave, when she remembered the French doors. They hadn't been locked after Nadine came out onto the deck, and they needed to be bolted from the inside. Retrieving the key from the lockbox, she let herself in the front entrance.

The heavy door slammed shut behind her and the house plunged into darkness. It was as if she had suddenly gone blind.

Claire caught her breath, trying to calm her panic. She fumbled to open the door, but it wouldn't budge.

Where was the lightswitch panel? Next to the door somewhere. She ran her hands along the wall until she found, and pushed all the controls. Nothing.

Even with the fog coming in, the wall of windows should be letting in plenty of light. How could everything go black?

From the grand salon she heard someone moan. Another voice answered with a high-pitched wail.

Oh God. Heart hammering, she twisted the doorknob. It spun in her hand.

"Let me out!"

Have to get out of here, have to find light. Can't call for help, cell phone's in my purse on the seat of the car. What can I do?

She banged on the door, grabbed the knob, yanked with every ounce of her strength. The door popped open and she fled outside into the wonderful daylight.

Claire slammed the door shut and leaned against the carved seagull, gulping the cool, salt-tinged air. Her heart was still racing. Her whole body trembled.

What the hell was going on? Light couldn't just vanish.

And where had the voices come from? The wind had kicked up, rippling the lavender bushes and coarse sea grasses in front of the house, tossing the branches of the pine trees that stood farther along the ridge. But the noises she'd heard weren't the wind's rustling. They sounded human.

She had just spent an hour going through the entire house with four other people present, and nothing strange had happened. The minute she was alone, the place went wacko.

It was almost as if the house had chosen her to be its victim. But why? What made her so special in its eyes?

Now her addled brain was giving the house eyes.

Maybe she should give up, admit she wasn't the right person to sell the place after all. Tonight she could tell Ben that she was bowing out as his listing agent. Golden Gate could handle the sale, but someone else would have to head the team. She didn't need the aggravation.

Meanwhile, she still had to bolt the French doors.

She found a fat rock to prop the front door open, just in case, and went back inside. The light didn't dim; nothing appeared amiss. But as she stepped down into the grand salon, she could feel the energy in the room go haywire. Invisible lightning bolts were zapping around the room and ping-ponging off the walls.

This was too much.

Claire widened her stance and planted her hands on her hips, hoping to fake an appearance of strength and resolve. "Okay, whatever you are, I've had enough. Stop it right now."

Instantly the energy calmed.

Oh, my God, it worked. It took her a moment to get over the shock of success. She jogged across the big room to the French doors and secured the bolt. Now to get out of here.

Halfway back to the front doors and freedom, she felt the room turn to ice. The air shimmered and reddened until it seemed filled with a mist of blood. Its sharp odor stung her nostrils.

She started to run faster, but something, some force field, loomed in front of her, blocking her way. She dodged left, then right, trying to get around it, but it stayed with her like a guard on an opposing basketball team, obstructing her every move.

Trapped. She sank to the floor and pulled herself into a ball for self-protection.

Something touched her shoulder. She heard a faint whisper: "Stand up."

Slowly Claire uncurled herself and looked around. The room was empty. The red mist had dissipated, but her cream-colored blazer was stained all over with pinprick dots of spattered blood.

As she pulled herself to her feet, she felt a flutter of air brushing her hands and a soft breath tickling her cheek.

"Please listen," said the whisperer. Its voice was slightly stronger now. "Please help."

"Who are you?" Claire asked. "Wh-what's your name?" She couldn't keep her own voice from cracking.

"Please look. You can see what really happened."

Claire shook her head. "I can't see anything."

Then she did, the same quick flash she'd had on her first visit—four crumpled bodies scattered around the room, two by the fireplace, one by the glass wall, and one in the center, right where yesterday she had tripped and fallen.

She shivered. "Are you one of them?" she asked the voice.

"Please help. You can see what really happened."

I'm going crazy, Claire thought. I'm having a conversation with something that can't possibly exist.

She hurried to the front door and removed the rock she'd used as doorstop. Nothing impeded her progress.

As she pulled the big doors closed, she heard the voice: "Don't leave!"

Claire glanced back into the house. Across the grand salon, she saw a girl's face against the glass wall. Not Lily this time. Someone older yet not grownup, a girl with long brown hair and wideset eyes. It was like looking at herself long ago in a poorly silvered mirror.

The face began to fade; the mouth became the deck railing, the cheeks turned into sky. Then it disappeared.

Chapter 15

Claire drove away as fast as she could, jerking to a halt at the stop sign at the end of Highview Lane. Instead of pulling into the traffic on Highway One, she sat there for several minutes. She felt lightheaded, too rattled to drive, especially an expensive car belonging to her boss.

There was a bottle of water in the cup holder, and she splashed some on her face. She combed her hair and applied fresh lipstick—easy, normal, everyday activities that might root her again in the real world. Inspecting her blazer, she was amazed to see the tiny dots of blood had disappeared.

If they had really been there at all.

The soft music on the radio should have helped, but it couldn't push the whispered voice out of her mind. She tuned to a news-and-talk station. An argument about foreign policy blunders or the flaws in the healthcare system would be a better distraction. The host's bombast and the mindless slogans spouted by the callers would drive her crazy, but at least it would be a different kind of crazy.

She had to talk to Tess. There was no choice. The disclosure law required sellers of a property to divulge all of its known defects. If people being killed there was a problem, then surely disembodied voices, visions of corpses and weird manifestations of energy had to count as major flaws.

She wished she could avoid the whole issue. What if she handed the listing to one of the other agents—not Avery or George certainly, but Jeff Ortega or Delia Chan could handle it, assuming one of them was willing to take it on. Since she was the only person who perceived the strange powers, that would end the situation. But she was basing that notion on a very small sample—Avery, Ben, the buyers at the house today. Could she really be certain no one else would be beleaguered by the spirits, or whatever they were? Selling the house without disclosing their presence would put Golden Gate at risk for substantial liabilities. Yet announcing that the house was haunted would make the firm a laughingstock.

How would she ever explain all this to Tess?

And tonight she'd have to tell Ben. Either he'd get angry, or he'd think she was out of her mind.

A break in the line of cars. With a sigh, Claire pulled the Lincoln onto the highway. Keeping it firmly at the speed limit, she guided it over coastal hills back to Sausalito. By the time she reached the office, she felt like herself again. Except for the nervous flutter in her stomach and the heaviness in her heart.

As CLAIRE CAME into the office building's redwood-lined lobby, the elevator door opened to reveal Avery's client, the Gingerbread Man. Claire struggled to come up with his real name. Wayne, that was it. Wayne Burdick.

"Claire!" he said with a smile. "Good to see you. Avery and I have just been conducting a little business."

She smiled back warily. "Oh? What sort of business?"

"I'll let her fill you in on the details. But I think you'll be pleased." Giving her a wave, he sauntered out the front door toward the parking lot.

Claire found Avery upstairs, seated at her desk in the middle row of the otherwise empty bullpen. She was whistling a happy tune as she stuffed some papers into a manila envelope.

"Avery, what's up? I just saw Wayne Burdick in the lobby—"

"Did he tell you?" Avery looked up at her, blue eyes glittering with excitement. "He bought the house!"

"What!"

"He fell in love with the place. Well, I mean, who wouldn't? And it turns out he's a Stefan LeGrande fan. So we came right back here and I wrote up his purchase offer." She held up the manila envelope. "I'm on my way to take it to Ben."

"Wait! You can't do that."

Avery studied Claire with a look of consternation. "Are you all right? You look weird."

Claire ran a hand over her face. She was probably still pale. Or flushed. Or green around the gills. "I'm fine. Avery, you did tell Burdick about the murders."

"Of course I did." She sounded annoyed. "I know the rules." She took a hairbrush out of her big red leather pocketbook and redid her long blond braid. "Besides, he already knew. It doesn't bother him at all. 'What's past is past,' he said."

"And did you tell him the house is haunted?"

Avery laughed. "Oh, yeah. I told him it's our special deal. Buy today and get free ghosts." Pursing her lips at the mirror of her compact, she touched up her lipstick.

"I'm serious, Avery."

"What, just because you let yourself get spooked in there the other day? Oh, wait—you did it again, didn't you? Some stupid seagull flew past that big glass window and cast a shadow and you went all woo-woo. Wait till I tell Ben."

"Don't you dare. I need to talk to Tess and Ben before you do anything." Claire reached for the envelope. "Let's see the purchase offer."

Avery snatched it back. "Oh, no, you don't." She stood up. "Out of my way, please."

"You can't go to Ben. I'm the listing agent. The protocol is that you give the offer to me, and I present it to the client."

Avery slid out into the aisle. "Don't worry, you can do all the official stuff. But I already told him about it. He said I could fax it, but I prefer the direct approach."

The elevator that Claire had just left was waiting. Avery hopped in and the doors closed, making her disappear. If only she'd vanish forever. Sighing in frustration, Claire walked to Tess's office. Better get the unpleasant talk over with. The room was empty.

At the reception desk, Marlene was typing away at her computer. When Claire approached, the fuchsia-tipped fingers stopped flying. Marlene quickly minimized her document so Claire couldn't see what she was working on. Something personal, probably, rather than Golden Gate business. As if I care, Claire thought.

"Marlene, where's Tess? Do you know when she'll be back?"

Marlene ran her fingers through her spiky locks; the fuchsia nails clashed with the red of her hair. "Gone for the day. She went to a meeting for one of her pet causes, I forget which one. Can I help you with something?" She glanced at her screen, obviously eager to get back to what she was doing.

"No, that's okay." Claire wasn't sure whether Tess's absence was good news or bad news. Maybe she was foolish to worry. Here in the office, where the energy was calm and everything looked ordinary, her concerns seemed far less urgent. Why tell buyers the LeGrande house was haunted? They would never believe it anyway; she scarcely believed it herself. Mentioning the murders was disclosure enough; if people weren't upset by that, a few stray spirits wouldn't unnerve them.

Back at her desk, she picked up her phone and punched in Mrs. Johansen's number. "Nadine? This is Claire Scanlan . . . Yes, it was a pleasure to meet you and Paul too . . . I agree, it's a magnificent house. Listen, if you want, you'll need to act quickly. We've received an offer . . . No, of course I can't tell you the specifics. But I'd be happy to present your bid also, so the seller can make the best choice."

Nadine sounded enthusiastic. "I'll talk it over with Paul. We'll get back to you tonight or tomorrow morning."

All right! Claire thought when she rang off. If the Johansens bought the place she'd receive the full commission, instead of splitting the take with Avery. Normally Claire considered herself a generous person, and she was a little dismayed by the sense of satisfaction she felt at the notion of cutting Avery out.

The phone on her desk rang and Claire grabbed the receiver. Nadine struck her as a woman who could make quick decisions. It was too soon, but just maybe . . .

"This is Claire Scanlan. How may I help you?"

A babble of syllables poured into her ear. *"Hey there thatch a Michael Nore rain and sunny—"*

Her bubble of hope burst. "Uh-oh, you're that reporter, aren't you? But Michael Nore—that wasn't your name."

"Michael who? No, Griff Maxwell." He slowed to a pace that probably seemed painfully slow to him, but to Claire's ear was normal. "Thought you might like to know we're running on Sunday with an article about the house where the LeGrandes died."

"You're what! But I asked you not to."

"Doesn't matter. Like it or not, it's a good story. Readers will be fascinated. And Sunday's open house day. The article will draw you lots of visitors. What time does your open house start?"

"It doesn't. I'm not holding one." A decision she made right that minute. "Open houses for the public don't sell high-end properties. And we don't want lots of gawkers tromping around."

"Okay, I won't frame the story that way. But talk to me, show me the place. The article gets printed anyway. You might as well get your perspective in."

"No, thanks, Mr. Maxwell—"

"Griff."

"No offense, Griff, but I really don't see how talking to you is going to help me find that house happy new owners." She cut off further protest by hanging up.

AVERY BRAKED the Porsche convertible and stared at Ben Grant's house. How disappointing. A plain gray bungalow suffocating under a bunch of oppressive trees. Hardly more than a cottage.

She had expected something much grander.

When she called Ben to announce the good news, she told him she'd bring him the purchase offer. She knew he worked at home full time, handling all of the complicated issues of his brother's estate. She'd pictured a house that was—well, certainly not mind-blowing like Stefan LeGrande's, but way more impressive than this. Stefan's neighbor, Martin Roncallo, worked at home too, and while his house didn't come close to rivaling Stefan's, at least he had an ocean view to inspire his videogames.

Well, as her daddy used to say, you can't judge the horse by the barn. When the estate was settled, Ben would probably come into money and move up to a more suitable place.

And wouldn't it be fabulous if she moved there with him?

She removed the rubber band from the wind-resistant braid and brushed her hair to hang long and silky over her shoulders. For good measure she undid the top couple of buttons on her blouse to create a deep V-neck—perfectly proper, yet just a bit provocative in that way she knew men liked. She got out of the car and reached back inside to grab the manila envelope.

In the shelter of the front porch, she punched the doorbell and heard its deep chime. When Ben opened the door, she caught her breath. Never mind the house—she'd happily live in a mud hut if she could share it with a man this gorgeous.

"Hi, Avery." He was dressed in jeans and a black T-shirt tight enough to show off broad shoulders and a well-muscled torso.

She tilted her head and smiled, letting her tongue lightly flick at her lips. "Hello, Ben."

He reached for the envelope. "This is the paperwork for Burdick's offer?"

"Aren't you going to invite me in?"

"What? Okay, sure." He stood aside and let her step inside. "We'll have to be quick though. I have to leave in a couple of minutes."

Avery looked around. The furnishings in the dreary little living room weren't cheap, but they weren't new either, and they totally lacked style. When the right time came, a shopping trip was definitely in order. The only thing worth keeping was the painting over the sofa. Hills and sea, very nicely done. She could almost smell the salt air.

"Have a seat." Ben sat in a wingback chair, but he didn't ease back. He looked ready to jump up any minute. "Tell me about this bid."

She wished he would offer her a drink, or at least a cup of coffee. Why did he have to have some damn appointment?

"It's a very solid contract. A tad under the asking price, but close enough." Burdick's bid low by several hundred thousand dollars, but no point in making a big deal over that. Ben could always make a counteroffer. "And no contingencies, that's a big plus."

"How much under?"

"It's all in here." She patted the manila envelope on the sofa. "Very solid," she repeated. "I think you'll be pleased."

"Who's the buyer?"

"A man named Wayne Burdick. He's a business consultant, something like that. He knows a little about architecture, though, and he says he's always loved your brother's work."

"What about his wife and kids—do they like the place? I'd love to see a family living happily there. That would be the best tribute to Stefan."

"He didn't mention a family. I think maybe he's single." Wayne hadn't worn a wedding ring, she'd noticed that much.

Ben frowned. "It's a huge place for one person. He's planning to live there, right? Or does he have some other use for the house in mind?"

Avery put on her most winsome smile, trying to erase Ben's scowl. "Who would want to buy it and not live there?"

Before she could say more, a voice called, "Ben! I'm ready."

A girl—around ten years old, Avery guessed—bounced through an archway and into the room. She was carrying a pink overnight bag and box gift-wrapped in flower-patterned paper and rosy ribbon. Seeing Avery, she stopped short. "Oh! I didn't know we had company."

"Hello," Avery said. The girl wore shorts and sandals and a cropped pink top. Pink must be her favorite color. Her hair, long and blond like Avery's own, was done up in a ponytail.

Ben stood, a signal for Avery to stand too. "Avery, meet my niece, Eden Hollister." To the girl he said, "This lady is Avery Collier, honey. She works at Golden Gate Properties."

"Hi, Eden." Avery reached out to offer a handshake, a friendly gesture intended to please the uncle more than the niece.

Eden dropped the overnight bag and pumped Avery's hand with enthusiasm. "I'm very pleased to meet you."

Avery smiled at her. "Likewise, I'm sure."

"Hey, if you work at the real estate place, I bet you know Claire."

"Oh, I know Claire all right." She tried to make her tone light. The point of this visit was to sidestep Claire, not to bring the other woman into Ben's mind. But sounding resentful or annoyed or belittling wouldn't help her cause.

"Claire's nice," Eden said. "Isn't she, Ben?"

"Yes, indeed," Ben answered. "Let's go, honey. You don't want to be late. Isabel's dad is barbecuing burgers tonight, right?"

"Yeah, let's go. Bye, Avery." Eden picked up her pink bag and scooted out the front door.

Ben ushered Avery onto the porch, shutting the door behind them. "I'll look over the papers, give you a call tomorrow. Thanks for bringing them." He crossed the lawn to the driveway, where his Lexus was waiting.

Damn, Avery thought as she retreated down the flagstone walk. This encounter had not proceeded according to her mental script.

Adding insult to injury, the wind had stirred while she was inside Ben's house. The leather seats of the Porsche were littered with pine needles and dry leaves.

Chapter 16

Claire hadn't felt so pampered and contented in a long time. The Petite Marmite was the kind of place where the waiter whisked a crisp white linen napkin into your lap as you took your seat and refilled your crystal water goblet practically every time you took a sip. Her roast duck breast with glacéed apricots had been perfectly prepared and very satisfying. The pianist in the corner was playing romantic tunes, and the glow of candlelight was reflected in her companion's warm hazel eyes.

"Mmm, delicious," Claire said, spooning up another taste of the dessert she and Ben were sharing.

"Told you so," he said, smiling.

"You did. And you were right." She had balked at the idea of indulging in a rich dessert, but Ben talked her into splitting a serving of the house specialty, an extravagant concoction fittingly called Chocolate Passion. "You must have prior experience with this delectable concoction."

"I order it every time I eat here."

"And do you come here often?"

"Not really. I save it for special occasions."

She laughed. "I'm flattered that eating with your real estate agent qualifies."

"Oh, definitely. Special-est occasion I've had in a long time."

Claire ducked her head, hoping Ben wouldn't notice her flush of pleasure. He was the perfect paradox. When she was in his presence, everything seemed intensified—colors were brighter, flavors sweeter or spicier, sounds more musical. The air between them crackled with energy, and her nerves longed for his touch. Yet at the same time she was completely at ease.

It felt so good to be relaxed and comfortable in a man's company. That skill didn't come easily to her, a condition she blamed on growing up in an all-female household. She'd been a shy, gawky kid; in her high school social life consisted of hanging out with kids from the drama club. In college a couple of guys had broken her heart, but most of her romances were casual ones, lasting a few weeks and then drifting away.

Then she met Zach, who always had a knack for making her feel off balance.

The first time she saw him, he was in gray herringbone and a navy tie, staring at her across the table in a corporate conference room. The ad agency Claire worked for was wooing Zach's firm as a client, and she and her boss were making the pitch. Through their whole presentation, Claire was conscious that the eyes of the youngest, best-looking man in the room were fixed on her, as if willing her to screw up. She delivered her lines poorly, made a mess of running the PowerPoint show, and called three people in the room by the wrong name. Her boss was so angry, he refused to speak to her for the rest of the day, and Claire retreated into her cubicle in humiliation. That afternoon, Zach called to ask her out.

Her agency lost the account, but she won Zach. Six months later they were married. Now, after ten years of

passion, frustration, joy, disappointment, and anger—
and yes, love—it was over. Any day now, she'd receive
the papers saying they were officially unmarried
again.

"Claire?" Ben's voice pushed into her thoughts. "Is
everything all right?"

She looked up at him and smiled. "Of course. Why
do you ask?"

"You looked sad for a moment. Wistful."

She reached across the table and put her hand on
his. "Not at all, Ben. Here with you, I'm fine."

"Thank you. What a wonderful evening," Claire
said as Ben pulled the Lexus into his driveway. Her
Volkswagen was waiting by the gate to the white picket
fence.

"Care to come in for a nightcap?" he invited. "Last
night you passed up some excellent brandy. I should
warn you, though—there's no chaperone tonight.
Eden's at a sleepover."

"Yes, I know." As if she could have forgotten.

He got out of the car. Claire opened her door to
do the same. He quickly came around to her side and
extended a hand to help her out.

She'd almost forgotten what it was like for a man to
display such good manners. Zach had quickly given up
showing her that kind of little courtesy.

Ben didn't release her hand. She was standing so
close to him, the two of them wrapped in the night's
soft darkness. The breeze stirred the trees, whispering
that the two of them were alone together in the world.
She felt the heat of his body meet the heat of her own.
Her heart raced as Ben bent his head and kissed her.

"How about that brandy?" he said, his voice low and husky.

"I love you." A sudden, startling thought that she released to float away on the breeze. She almost didn't hear herself speak the words.

"What did you say?" Their lips were still almost touching. Claire could hardly breathe.

"I'd love to. But I . . . I should skip the brandy. Since I'll be driving home."

"Not unless you really want to." His arm around her, Ben guided her up the flagstone walk.

"EXCELLENT IS RIGHT. I don't know when I've enjoyed brandy this much." Curled up beside Ben on the blue couch, Claire turned the snifter in her hand, watching the amber liquid swirl. She inhaled the rich aroma— smoky, oaky, full of fruit and spice. As she took another sip, a pleasurable warmth spread through her.

"I've never enjoyed it in better company." He tightened his arm around her, and she settled her head against his shoulder. The lamp in the corner was turned low. A trio of candles burned in candlesticks on the coffee table, and classical music played on the stereo— Chopin, Claire thought, though she wasn't sure.

"That's a good line. I'll pretend I believe you."

"It's the truth." His lips brushed her hair. "I won't say there haven't been other women in my life. I've got some exes in my background—an ex-wife, an ex-fiancee, both way in the past."

"And Jacqueline, or so you said the other day."

"The briefest of flings." Though he looked away from Claire as he said the words. "I had a serious relationship going a couple of years ago, until shortly before I moved out here. She definitely didn't appreciate the fine points of brandy."

"What happened to her?"

"She left me for a man who drank vodka."

"Really?" Claire ran a finger along the top of Ben's leg.

"That's what broke us up, but actually it was over before that. She didn't want to leave Boston, and she didn't relish a long-distance relationship, especially with a man who was dealing with multiple deaths in his family. It turned out that giving emotional support was not one of her better talents."

"I don't suppose she graduated last year from Harvard Law School?"

"No, she's a fashion editor. What made you think of law school?"

"My ex likes vodka. And he was probably hooking up with his little sweetie-pie right about that same time."

"I'm so glad that happened," Ben said as he took her glass from her and set it with his on the coffee table.

"Why?"

"Because it means you're here with me."

The brandy flavored his kiss. So sweet. So delicious.

The kiss was gentle at first, but it kindled a hunger within her, a fire that swept from her lips to her loins. Claire's body, of its own volition, pressed tight against his. She kissed him back, harder and harder still, until they broke apart, gasping.

She ran eager hands over his body, savoring his warmth, his strength. Ben's lips found the tender hollow at the base of her throat, then glided down to her breast.

"More," she murmured. "Give me more."

A few minutes later, they were lying naked together in the smooth, fresh sheets of his bed, and he gave her everything she wanted.

GOLD, THE COLOR OF WEALTH, the color of skin gleaming in firelight.

By the hearth, a raven-haired woman slips silken straps from her shoulders and beckons.

A young man, his body aflame with desire, steps toward her, crossing a magic carpet that floats two inches above the floor. Beneath his bare feet, its intricate pattern shifts and reforms until it becomes a map of all the world's possibilities.

The room is a cage made of windows. Ocean waves batter the glass.

In the corner someone moves—a shadow, silent and dark.

Bam! Bam!

The woman spreads her arms like angel's wings. A red corsage blooms on her breast, and she falls. A bolt of lightning spins the young man in a circle and drops him to the floor.

The shadow circles the room, once, twice, three times. Waiting. Outside a storm rages.

The gale blows down the door and a man appears, wearing a shirt woven from discarded blueprints. Screaming louder than the wind, he rushes to embrace the fallen angel.

Behind him comes a girl, her face hidden behind a velvet mask. She rips off her mask and flings it away as she runs toward the storm. She looks back over her shoulder. Her face is a mirror and her brown eyes are imprinted with words: *Help me!*

Bam! Bam!

The mask hits the floor, turning into a tombstone carved of ice. The ocean shatters the glass and the room is engulfed in a tide of blood.

The shadow smiles and vanishes.

"CLAIRE, CLAIRE!"

Someone was shaking her, pulling her close. Her own body felt rigid and tense. She jerked away from the confining grasp.

She was in a bed, she could tell that. Her fingers searched for the comforting seams and stitches of Gram's quilt. Instead she felt a blanket, soft and fleecy. When she opened her eyes the window was on the wrong side of the room, and it let in too much moonlight.

"Claire, it's okay. You had a bad dream. Don't be frightened." Someone caressed her cheek and she remembered where she was. In Ben's house, in his bed, in his embrace.

"B-ben." Her voice sounded shaky. "I'm sorry. Was I screaming?"

"Wailing like a banshee. But that's okay." He kissed her forehead, then her temple. "I like banshees."

"Good thing." Tension oozed out of her until she was limp.

"Especially when they're as beautiful as you." He pulled her head to his warm shoulder.

She appreciated his attempts to cheer her, but the dream had left her feeling cold and gray, like ashes after a fire. "I thought tonight would be different. After what we did together . . . how could something so wonderful lead to another nightmare?"

"Hush, my beautiful banshee. Everything's all right. We all have bad dreams once in a while." He eased her against him, spooning his long body around hers, tucking the covers around them both. "Come on, let's go back to sleep. Things will look brighter in the morning."

Despite his reassuring words, she was still uneasy. She lay there, eyes open. In the moonlight, everything in the room was edged with silver. Ben's hand was cupped around her breast. His breathing was smooth and even, but she sensed he was awake.

"Ben? When they were killed—your brother and his family—how many people were in the house?"

"What? The four of them."

"You're sure? You're convinced of what happened?"

"Sadly, there's no doubt. Poor Trevor went berserk. He shot Jacqueline, then Stefan and Melissa, then himself. You know all that."

"I saw them. But I saw someone else too."

"Saw them? You mean in your dream?"

"I never remember my nightmares. But this one—I still can see pieces of it, Ben. Images, impressions. It's the first time that's happened."

He tightened his arms around her. "That's a good thing, right? The first step in taming the monsters that lurk in our minds to recognize them for what they are."

Tears stung Claire's eyes. "It's like—I wasn't in the scene but I could see it. I heard gunshots. I saw blood. There were five people, and one walked away."

"Who was it?" Ben asked.

She shook her head, feeling her hair touch his face. "I couldn't see him clearly. He was shadowy, indistinct. Or maybe it was a woman. I just don't know."

"Dream-foolery. That's all it was."

"What are you talking about?"

"It's a term my father used when my brother or I got scared by a nightmare. It means all the crazy, unrelated nonsense that your brain mixes together and serves up to you in your dreams. You've been hearing more than your usual dose of talk about violence and death, and I'm sure Stefan's house made an impression on you. Those are powerful elements. It's not surprising they'd combine with other random things to produce some pretty disturbing images. But they don't mean anything. It's just dream-foolery."

"What about the fifth person?"

"That's what I'm saying, Claire. There was no fifth person. Your brain made it up."

"But I'm certain—"

"Go to sleep now." Ben's voice was soothing. "Whoever you saw, if he comes back I'll protect you."

Soon his breathing, slow and regular, told her he was asleep. Claire squeezed her eyes shut, but she stayed awake for a long, long time. She thought she didn't sleep at all. Yet when she opened her eyes again, the bedroom was flooded with sunlight and Ben was gone.

Chapter 17

I'm in such turmoil. I don't know whether to be angry or elated.

I was furious when the one who's trapped here with me made the house go black. The woman with chocolate hair was so terrified she ran away. What would we do if he scared her off forever?

He didn't mean to frighten her. He was upset—we both were—when too many people arrived all at once. Except for her, they weren't welcome. Their auras clashed, full of anger and negativity, reminding us of the fiery night. He and I kept very still until they went away, hoping they wouldn't notice us. We were so happy when they left.

I can't really blame him for what happened next. When the big door opened, he didn't know it was the woman with chocolate hair, all alone. He thought they were all coming back and he wanted to make them go away. But he has even less practice than I do at making the energy behave the way he wants it to. No wonder his effort went haywire. Mine always do, too. When the woman ran out and slammed the door, I fell into despair.

But then she came back—came back and yelled at us! She acknowledged for the first time that we're here. I'm so thrilled that we've begun to communicate. She perceives what we do and she hears my voice. When *we show her what happened on the fiery night and tell her about the trouble that is looming, she'll know what to do. I have to trust her. There's no other choice.*

So instead of being angry at the other one who's trapped here, I'm grateful. Because of him, we're one step closer to breaking through to her. When the woman left he retreated into his corner, but now he has drifted closer to me, joining me in what I'm doing now.

I'm looking at the memories that are imprinted on these walls. If I think about them hard enough, if I can bring them out into the center of the room and put them in sharp focus, maybe the woman can see them. Then she'll begin to understand.

In the days Before, five of us lived in the house. We ate and slept here, had quarrels and laughed at jokes. We played and worked and studied. The grownups made love. And we dreamed our dreams.

One of us dreamed of building houses like ours all over the world and being celebrated for it. One of us dreamed of making this house into a happy home for the five who lived in it and being loved for it.

I dreamed of becoming an actress, a career in the theater. I loved being in the productions at school because playing a role gave me a chance to try on different lives to see how they'd fit me. The irony is, I never really got a chance to try on my own life. All at once, long before I was ready, it was over.

He—the one with me now—kept his dreams hidden. He's never told me what they were, but they must have been very powerful because he never dared to confront them. He latched onto drugs and sex and rebellion, pretending they were his dreams, but I could tell they were only bad imitations.

Only one of us, the youngest, still has dreams. Only she remains alive in the physical world. I'm so thankful she wasn't here on the fiery night, but I miss her terribly. She's never returned to this house. I wish I could touch her cheek. I wish I could tell her that we all loved her, and still do.

I am no longer capable of having dreams, but I do have a hope and a task to accomplish. I hope to make her understand what really happened, and I need to stop it from happening again.

Chapter 18

As Claire fought her way home through the morning rush hour traffic, her mood ricocheted all over the place. One moment her spirit soared, lifted by the joy she'd felt in Ben's company and the ecstasy of their lovemaking. A moment later it plummeted as blood-soaked images from her latest nightmare roiled through her head.

Who was the shadow? Could there really have been a fifth person in the house that night?

Behind Claire's Volkswagen, an angry driver leaned on his horn. In front of her, a battered pickup spewed smoky exhaust. Even with her windows rolled up, it seeped into her car. The acrid odor overwhelmed the delicate scent of the red rose pinned to the shoulder of her dress. No doubt the smoke was why her eyes were tearing up.

Until she woke up screaming, last night had been perfect.

She hadn't been expecting to find such passion with Ben, or anyone. She'd been avoiding relationships with men and the inevitable complications. The disaster with Zach had torn her apart, scraped her raw. Ever since her marriage exploded, she'd kept her feelings locked up for their own protection. In fact, she was beginning to realize that she'd kept them under tight guard for a long time, maybe most of her life.

So she'd been stunned by the suddenness with which Ben overcame her carefully constructed defenses. Never had she responded so quickly to anyone; it was as if an irresistible magnetic force pulled her to his side. What she felt for Ben was not only an amazing physical attraction but also a rush of deep affection. For the first time in her life, and this included her decade with Zach, Claire knew she was falling in love.

Then came the nightmare, and the disappointment of Ben's response. *Dream-foolery.*

Probably he'd been trying to comfort and reassure her. But she felt dismissed and diminished. When she woke up this morning and found herself alone in his bed and abandoned in his house, she couldn't help it— she'd broken down and cried.

Crawling out of the bed, she discovered her clothes neatly folded on a chair in the corner of the bedroom. Ben's doing—last night, in the heat and urgency of their desire, they'd simply dropped their clothing in a mound on the floor. When she put on the sexy black dress, it hung in wrinkles, as if she'd slept in it.

Her purse was in the living room. She'd left it next to a wingback chair, and now it sat on the coffee table, sharing space with a note from Ben and a drinking glass containing the red rose. He must have clipped it from one of the bushes in the yard. In the note he paid her several lovely compliments. He invited her to go with him to wine-tasting party that evening and apologized for his disappearance; he had a breakfast meeting scheduled with an attorney to discuss something pertaining to Stefan's estate. She vaguely recalled his mentioning the appointment at dinner. The invitation and the flower brightened her mood.

And then the memory of the nightmare had come crashing in.

Always before, though she could never remember them clearly, she'd assumed her scream-dreams were all similar—scenarios in which she herself was threatened by some unseen, unknown force. She wasn't sure what triggered them, but whenever she tried to trace a pattern, she realized that they occurred when she felt particularly angry, or frightened, or vulnerable, or overwhelmed with stress.

But since Monday something had shifted, and it had to do with the LeGrande house. She had visited the house every day for the past three days. Each time her presence had made something inside the house go crazy, and each night she had another nightmare. These dreams were different; they weren't really about her. Last night she hadn't even been present in the scene. She watched what transpired, the same way she'd view a video.

Lying in Ben's bed, she had watched four people die.

She had witnessed the murders of Stefan LeGrande and his family.

Claire shivered and rubbed her goosebumped arms. Okay, the images had been distorted and exaggerated. What she'd seen was the rush of emotions as much as the specific details of where people stood or what they did. But she had seen something true about what happened that night in that house above the ocean.

Five people were in that room. Four of them were shot to death. The fifth pulled the trigger and walked away.

She was absolutely certain the dream told the truth. So why had Ben tried so hard to discourage her from believing it?

CROSSING THE LAWN toward her apartment building, Claire saw the front door open. Lindsay dashed out into the sunshine, dressed for work in a camelhair jacket. Her purse was slung from one shoulder and she was carrying her briefcase in the other hand. Seeing Claire, she managed an awkward wave and hurried toward her.

"So how did it go?" Lindsay asked, dropping the briefcase on the grass to greet Claire with a hug. "Did Mr. Marvelous live up to his name?"

Claire wasn't sure how she wanted to answer that. "Linz, you have to try the Petite Marmite. It's fabulous. They have a dessert there to die for, called Chocolate Passion."

"Ah, Chocolate Passion." Lindsay gave her a sly smile. "And how about the other kind? Shall I take the fact that you stayed out way past curfew as a good sign? Did that sexy black dress do its job?"

Claire ran her hands over her hips, trying to smooth out the wrinkles and creases. "You know I never kiss and tell."

Lindsay laughed. "The hell you don't. I still have the recording I made of the blow-by-blow description you gave me of the first time you had sex with Zach. And I do mean blow."

"No, you don't," Claire teased back. "I burned your entire audio archive in the kitchen sink before I went out last night."

"Okay, so I don't have it on tape. But I still remember it vividly. I hope last night was half as good?" Lindsay made it a question.

"It was—indescribable."

"Uh-oh, something's wrong. I can see it in your face. If he hurt you, I will personally kill him."

"I appreciate that. But no, Ben was fine. Mr. Marvelous doesn't begin to describe him. Lindsay, the truth is . . . I decided I'm in love."

"Come on, Claire, a person who means those words doesn't say them in such a flat tone."

"I do mean it," Claire insisted. "Or I did last night. But then things got botched up."

"Oh, no! How so?"

"First off, I had another nightmare."

"While you were with Ben? Oh, sweetie, what awful timing!"

"This dream was different—so real. It was the LeGrande house, the night of the murders. I saw the four people die. Everyone says the son did it, Trevor. He killed the others and then himself. But he didn't shoot anyone, someone else did. A fifth person was there. Lindsay, I'm afraid it might have been Ben."

Lindsay burst out with a laugh. "Of course it was. You were right there with Ben, he was on your mind— maybe even on your body. What would be more natural than for him to insert himself into your dream?"

"A dream about murder?"

"Why not? You've been thinking a lot about those murders lately because they happened in a house you're trying to sell. That's what dreams do, right? They reflect things happening in your life."

Claire shook her head. "Not this one."

Lindsay ignored her. "I'll tell you who the fifth person was. It wasn't Ben, it was you."

"Me!"

"I read an article once that said our dreams are always about ourselves. You've been tired lately, nervous about the new job, you've met Mr. Marvelous, you're still stressed about Zach and the divorce. Your mind took all those churned-up emotions and blended them into a dream. And at a most inconvenient time, I might add."

"Inconvenient is right."

"Don't take this wrong, Claire, but remember meeting my friend Sonia Hirsch? You might find it helpful to talk this over with her."

Claire felt her face get hot. "You mean the psychotherapist? Lindsay, I don't need a shrink."

Lindsay looked hurt. "Just a suggestion. I'm not making light of your dreams. I know how upsetting they are. It's just that—well, they're dreams, that's all. Dreams reveal the state of our psyche. We all express our fears and anxieties in different ways. I do it by biting my fingernails and saying stupid things, which is what you probably think I'm doing right now. You do it by having bad dreams, and sometimes you imagine that the stuff you dream about is spilling over into your life when you're awake."

"I'm not imagining this, Linz. It's not dream-foolery."

"Dream what?"

Claire sighed. "It's an expression Ben used. He didn't take me any more seriously than you're doing." Or Gram, or Cassandra, or Zach . . .

"I am taking you seriously. Claire, you're my best friend. You know how much I care about you. I'd just like you to find some peace, that's all. These nightmares have been an issue for you for a long time. I think Sonia could help."

"I appreciate your concern," Claire said sulkily.

Lindsay gave her another hug. "I'll call you with Sonia's number, okay?"

"Sure. Whatever you say."

She glanced at her watch. "Oh God, look at the time. Gotta run, I don't want to be late. Are you okay?"

Claire nodded. "Have a good day."

"You too." Grabbing her briefcase, Lindsay started to cross the lawn, then turned to call back, "Don't wait up for me. That hot stockbroker I've been telling you about? He finally asked me out. If I'm lucky, I won't get home until way past curfew myself."

CLAIRE DIDN'T WANT to be late either, but by the time she showered and dressed and battled the traffic to Golden Gate's building, more of the morning had gone by than she'd intended. But it was worth it. Now that she'd taken the time to pull herself together, she felt better—calm, controlled, sensible. How dare Lindsay imply she needed a therapist's help? She was fine. A little tired, but who wouldn't be after several nights of disrupted sleep. She'd seen a therapist a couple of times right before she left Cambridge and all she got was a lot of blather and jargon. Sonia Hirsch wouldn't accuse her of dream-foolery, but when she unraveled all the psych terminology, it would amount to the same thing.

She arrived to find the office in a flurry of activity. Naturally the first person to notice her was George, who came out the lounge with a coffee mug and a pair of doughnuts as she got off the elevator.

"Hey, there, Claire," he said. "A little tardy this morning, aren't we? That's two days out of four. Your on-time average is slipping a bit."

"This is a real estate office, George. We don't keep regular hours. What counts is productivity."

"I keep regular hours."

Marlene, looking amused as she watched from the reception desk, cut in to say, "That's because Tess keeps you on a short leash."

George followed Claire into the bullpen. Claire hoped he'd stop at his own desk. It was in the front row, closest to Tess's office door. Claire guessed their boss assigned that one to her obnoxious brother-in-law so she could keep a close eye on him. But of course he continued past Jeff and Delia at their desks, following Claire all the way back to Siberia. He set his mug and a honey-glazed doughnut on the empty desk beside hers.

"I know why you're late," he said. He took a big bite of the other doughnut, cinnamon-dusted, and stood there chewing, waiting for her reply. When she didn't oblige him with one, he continued, "Bet you indulged in an M.Q. this morning"

"A morning quickie? Not me." She stuck her purse in her desk drawer and typed her password into her computer.

"Yeah, you did. You can't fool me." Sugary crumbs littered his lapels. "You've got that M.Q. glow."

By now all the others were watching. Claire felt herself flush. He was wrong about the timing, but did last night's passions and pleasures really show in her face? "What makes you think it's any of your business?"

He hooted in triumph. "Hah! I'm right."

What a jerk. She wanted to slap him. "You're projecting, George. I bet you're the one who had the M.Q., only you had to do it all by yourself. Go indulge your fantasies elsewhere." She reached over and snatched the honey-glazed doughnut. "And thanks for breakfast."

Delia and Jeff burst into applause. Avery, coming up the aisle, burst into laughter. With a shrug of his plump shoulders, George retreated.

Avery dropped into her chair and swiveled it around to face Claire. "You want that?" She pointed at the doughnut, now on Claire's desk. "I mean, if you do, okay. But the honey ones are all gone and they're my favorite."

"Help yourself," Claire said, although the permission was unnecessary since Avery was already taking a bite. "What's with the doughnuts anyway?"

"Delia closed escrow on a house yesterday. Marlene says when you do that, you celebrate by bringing in doughnuts for everybody. It's some kind of office tradition." Avery licked honey glaze from her fingers.

Closing escrow meant all the papers were signed, the money had changed hands, and the sale was complete. Which in turn meant the commission was in the agent's pocket. Claire waved at Delia. "Hey, congratulations! That's great."

Delia grinned and lifted her arms in a gesture of triumph.

The phone on Claire's desk rang. When she answered it, she was rewarded with a different kind of honey—the sound of Ben's voice. "How are you, Claire? I'm sorry I had to run out on you so early this morning. I couldn't cancel the meeting; Stefan's lawyer is going out of town today and we had some matters to talk about that couldn't wait."

"That's okay," she said. Avery was facing forward again, but Claire could tell she was listening. She was as obvious as a cat with its ears cocked back.

"There are things I'd like to discuss with you too," Ben said. "Is this a good time to stop by the Golden Gate office?"

Claire stared at the back of Avery's head with its flow of silky blond hair. "Let's do it somewhere else. Meet me in fifteen minutes at Spuntino's Deli."

Chapter 19

Holding coffee in pale green paper cups, Claire and Ben strolled beside the busy Sausalito street called Bridgeway. On the opposite side, tourists prowled through pricey shops and elegant galleries, but this stretch of sidewalk was open to the bay. Sunlight glinted off the water. Sailboats rode the gentle waves, taking advantage of the pleasant weather. Enjoy it while you can, Claire thought. The forecast called for the fog to roll in by mid-afternoon. Most likely the ocean beaches and ridges were already enshrouded in a cold, gray mist.

When he greeted her in front of the deli, Ben's smile had melted her heart.

They reached a bench facing the water and sat, Ben stretching his long legs out in front of him. "It's pretty here," he said. He draped his arm along the top edge of the backrest.

"Very," she agreed. She settled in comfortably, her shoulders against his arm.

"I miss Boston though." He drank from his green cup.

"I don't. I was so glad to leave. It's a nice city, don't get me wrong. But I didn't pile up good memories there."

"My plan's always been to go back there once the estate is settled."

Claire felt herself grow tense. There was a message here, but what? Was Ben saying, *Are you willing to come to Boston with me?* Or *I'm leaving soon, so don't invest yourself too much in this relationship?*

"Why leave? Northern California is a great place to live."

"For lots of people, it is. But for me, this will always be the place where an unspeakable tragedy occurred. For Eden too. Moving back East will be good for her. A fresh start in a new place."

"So . . . when are you leaving?" She took a quick sip of coffee to cover up the catch in her voice.

"That depends in part on how soon the house sells. I finally had a chance this morning to take a look at the purchase offer that Avery brought me."

"What did it say? I still haven't seen it. Avery won't show it to me."

"Doesn't matter. I'm turning it down. The price is so low it's insulting."

"You're not even making a counteroffer?"

"No. If the fellow's starting off this low, he's not going to come up to something reasonable. It's my responsibility to Eden to get the best price I can."

Claire was torn. A quick sale for this problematic house would be a coup for her professionally, even if Avery had found the buyer. Once she had the commission in the bank, she could get a fancy car to impress clients, even look for a place of her own to live, without a roommate who suspected she had mental health issues that needed a therapist's help. On the other hand, she was in no rush for Ben to leave town.

"I have another prospect, a couple named Johansen. They seem really interested."

"Hey, great. See, there's no reason to settle for this guy Burdick's lowball offer."

She took another drink of her coffee. It was hard to get a satisfying swallow through the plastic cup lid. "Have you really thought this through, Ben? You've had the house on the market for a long time with no takers. Maybe the price is too high."

"It's less than what the two previous real estate companies put on it."

Claire sighed. "Yes, but . . . pricing is such an art. Even my boss, Tess McMillan, who knows everything about real estate, wasn't sure what to do about this house. Normally we set prices by looking at how much comparable homes have sold for, but this house has no comparables. It's larger than most homes on the coast, and it's a signature work by big-name architect. Those factors raise the price. But then we have to consider the negatives, which are huge. Four people died there, horrible violent deaths, and the energy there is so crazy—"

"What do you mean, the energy is crazy?"

"I – it's just . . . people get weird feelings in the house, Ben. They experience strange sensations. Especially in the grand salon, where the family died."

Ben shook his head. "All I've ever felt in there is sadness. Which is natural enough; the victims were my family."

"I don't mean moods. I'm talking about things that actually happen. Strange noises, weird smells, whispering voices."

"Are you saying the house is haunted?"

"Of course not, but . . . well, yes, I guess that's one way to put it."

"And you've seen ghosts there." Ben looked amused.

"I haven't exactly seen them. But I've heard things, and felt things—"

"Didn't you tell me at lunch the other day that you've been accused of having a vivid imagination?"

"What you neglected to tell me is that you're such a skeptic."

"I want to be open-minded, Claire. Especially since this is clearly bothering you. Tell me what you saw."

"I did tell you. Last night, or rather, early this morning. In my dream—"

"Claire, I know the nightmare frightened you, but it's just a stew of images and feelings that your mind cooked up for some reason. Dream-foolery, like I said. It's not the same at all as actually seeing a ghost in the house."

"The house and the dream are tied up together. It's like . . . someone's trying to ask me for something, or send me a message." Her memory stirred with a faint echo of the whispered words: *Help me*.

"And you think a ghost is doing that? Who is it? My brother?"

"I don't know. But who else—" An image from the nightmare flashed in her mind. The girl's brown eyes with those words imprinted on them: *Help me*. "Melissa. I think it's Melissa."

Ben didn't respond. Claire looked at him. He was staring out over the water, perhaps watching the Larkspur ferry as it glided past Alcatraz on its way to the city.

"Sweet Melissa," he said finally. "Ah, Claire, I miss them all so much." He sipped the last of his coffee and crumpled the cup. "What do you think she's trying to tell you?"

"She's asking for help. She wants to tell me about that night. The dream was so clear, Ben. I watched the murders, like on a film. There were five people.

Trevor didn't shoot the others. He was one of the first to die, along with Jacqueline. Then Stefan came in with Melissa and the fifth person shot them too."

Ben was shaking his head. "There's nothing I'd like more than to believe Trevor was innocent. But he did it, Claire. I've gone over all the evidence, all the forensics, with the sheriff's officers who did the investigation. Everything fits. There's never been any doubt."

"Indulge me a minute. Suppose there had been a fifth person. Who do you think it could have been?"

"No one," he said sharply. "It's useless speculation." Then his tone softened. "It was just a dream, Claire. I wish I'd been in it. I would have protected you from the horror."

"But you weren't." Or was he? Claire bit her lip and looked away. She could almost see the shadowed figure from the dream hovering above the water. The shadow with no identity. She wished she could shake the feeling that it might have been Ben.

Before she could say more, his cell phone rang. He pulled it from his pocket and flipped it open. "This is Ben Grant." Whatever the caller said made him frown. He got up and walked down the sidewalk, away from her, to have the conversation in private.

She gathered the coffee cups and deposited them in a nearby trash container, then waited by the bench, watching a couple of seagulls squabble at the edge of the water. When Ben returned, his face was dark with anger.

"Is everything okay?"

"That was someone from the prison board. Leo Hollister got out of prison yesterday. Apparently he qualified for some kind of early release program."

"Eden's father? Are you going to tell her?"

"What purpose would that serve? It would just upset her. But he damn well better not try to disrupt our lives."

Claire glanced around, half expecting to see a menacing figure emerge from the crowd of tourists and shoppers. "Do you think he'll do that?"

"He doesn't know where we live, thank God. The only address he has for us is a PO box, and our phone is unlisted." He managed to put on a smile. "I hate to run off, Claire, but I have to pick Eden up from the sleepover and take her to her arts-and-crafts class. But I'll see you tonight, right? Are we on for that wine-tasting party?"

"What about Eden?"

"I've already lined up her favorite babysitter. It'll be less upsetting for her if we don't change or plans and routines unnecessarily."

"In that case, I can't wait to taste some wine."

"Me either." Ben pulled her into a tight embrace. As their lips met she felt last night's fire rekindle. She was vaguely aware of passersby dodging around them, but she didn't care.

AVERY GRINNED at the mouthpiece of her office phone. It was a trick she'd learned while working in the telemarketing boiler room of some scam corporation back in Texas. The job had been crappy and she lasted only a week, but one lesson from the training session had stuck with her: *A smile on your face puts a smile in your voice.*

"Don't worry about a thing, Wayne. Of course the owner is going to accept your bid."

"You're certain?" Wayne Burdick sounded skeptical and at the same time a little desperate.

"Well, maybe not your exact terms. You're kind of under the asking price. Any chance you could go a little higher?" Yesterday she'd been unsuccessful in getting him to goose up his offer, but it never hurt to try again. A higher price would mean a higher commission.

"I think my offer is fair, Ms. Collier."

"I told you, call me Avery. I like that better." She tried batting her eyelashes in case the flirtatious flutter would travel through the phone lines like the smile. "I'll see that the owner makes a reasonable counteroffer if he doesn't take yours outright. You know how these things work, back and forth, a little bargaining. And if this house doesn't come through, I'm sure I can find you a good one in your price range."

Burdick said, "I have my heart set on this one. Stefan LeGrande's home. That means something, owning a place designed by a big name like that."

"It sure does." She started doodling on a notepad— little dollar signs with frills and curlicues. "Don't worry. I'll talk to the owner and make sure a deal happens. I can be very persuasive."

That made him laugh. "Ah yes, Avery, I'm sure you can."

WHO WAS THE FIFTH PERSON? The question tormented Claire as she drove down Bridgeway on her way back to Golden Gate Properties.

No way could the shadowed figure in her dream be Ben. Or could it? He'd been in Boston on the fateful night. The next day he caught a plane to California as soon as he received the terrible news. At least that was what she'd assumed from what he told her and the news accounts she'd read online. But how did anyone know that he hadn't in fact arrived a day or two earlier?

The bad thing was, she could think of plenty of motives.

Long-simmering jealousy of his brilliant brother— hadn't she detected an undercurrent of envy in the way Ben spoke about Stefan?

An obsession with his brother's wife. Ben had been involved with the tempestuous Jacqueline first. He tried to seem nonchalant about her dumping him for Stefan, but Claire saw heat in his eyes when Jacqueline's name was mentioned. What if he'd spent years harboring a secret anger against them both? Or suppose he went to the house to win her back? She spurned his advances, throwing him into a murderous rage. Then the others walked in at just the wrong moment.

Money. Ben now controlled Stefan's fortune. Eden was the heir and now owned the LeGrande assets, but Ben, as guardian, executor, and trustee, was in charge. He made the financial decisions. Could be he'd decided to siphon the money into his own pocket.

A camera-toting tourist couple stepped off the sidewalk in front of the VW and she stopped to let them cross.

No, not Ben. No way. He was kind, tender, and even-tempered in a way she had rarely encountered in a man. He showed genuine affection for his niece, which she clearly returned.

Then why did he insist on dismissing the notion of the fifth person? Why not consider the possibility that someone other than Trevor pulled the trigger? Especially since he claimed he wished Trevor were innocent. Surely it would help Ben, and Eden too, heal from the trauma if they knew the truth about what happened.

Unless the having the truth come out posed a threat.

Unless Ben was the fifth person.

Claire sighed. How well did she know him anyway? They'd been acquainted for all of three days. Seventy-two hours. She'd never believed in love at first sight, and it certainly wasn't like her to jump so quickly and eagerly into bed with a man she'd just met. When she was with him, the magnetic pull between them was so strong, so intense, that all doubts disappeared. Yet as soon as she was alone again, they flooded in.

She could almost hear Gram's voice offering a favorite bit of advice: *Don't judge by what shows on the surface, Claire. People are rarely what they seem.* Gram generally trotted out this sage counsel when Claire or Cassandra was being catty about a classmate. Claire always assumed she meant that a person who seemed unattractive or unpleasant still contained hidden gold. But the reverse was also true. A thin layer of gold might conceal deep flaws.

When she reached the office, she headed straight for the ladies' room. Her head was pounding, and she was afraid that if anyone spoke to her, she would burst into tears. She spent a few minutes splashing cool water on her face and combing and recombing her hair. When she looked in the mirror it seemed to darken, as if the shadow of the fifth person had spread across it.

At her desk, she picked up the phone and punched in four-one-one for Information. "Please give me the number for the *Marin Post-Ledger*."

When she reached the newspaper's main switchboard, she said, "I'd like to speak to one of your reporters. His name is Griffin Maxwell."

Chapter 20

"Why the sudden change of heart?" Griff Maxwell said instead of hello. He'd arrived within fifteen minutes of Claire's call, which meant he hadn't worried about the speed limit as he rushed to Sausalito from the newspaper's headquarters in San Rafael.

She whisked him into the conference room, away from everyone else's inquisitive ears. He pulled out a small notebook and pen from the pocket of his ancient tweed sports jacket and plunked them onto the table's gleaming rosewood surface.

"I thought maybe we could help each other," she said.

Intense green eyes appeared at her through wire-rimmed glasses. "How so?"

His rapid-fire speech on the phone had made Claire picture someone tense and wiry. But the eyes were the only thing about him to confirm her expectation. The reporter turned out to be a big, shaggy bear of a man. He looked a bit out of place in the polished-wood, soft carpet, elegant-artwork, dress-to-impress environment of Golden Gate Properties. Bushy brown hair overdue for a trim. Jeans and work boots beneath the old tweed jacket. Claire felt slightly jealous. Normally she liked putting a little extra effort into her appearance, but right now she felt headachy and exhausted. The idea of indulging in the comfort of old, soft jeans held great appeal.

Next to the pad he set a miniature tape recorder.

Claire waved a hand to protest. "Put that away. I'm not giving an interview. I called because I need information about the LeGrande case."

"Aha. My point exactly." His syllables burst out like machine-gun bullets. "Anyone thinking buying that house wants the kind of info I'm putting in the article."

"No article. Please. Not yet anyway." She pressed her hands to her temples, hoping to lessen the headache.

"Then what sort of deal are you offering?" He sounded exasperated.

How could she put it so he wouldn't think she was a total flake?

She sank into one of the leather chairs and gestured for Griff to do the same. "I've . . . let's say I've come across something interesting related to the case. A theory about what happened that night. But I really don't know very much about the family, or the circumstances of their deaths. And apparently you're the local expert."

"Got that right. I probably know even more than the sheriff's department. I mean, they've got all these little crumbs of evidence—fingerprints, shell casings, stuff like that—but they never bothered to put it all together. No need, since they knew the kid did it. Readers want things like that assembled into a story."

Claire nodded. "Exactly. I need you to tell me what that story is."

"And in exchange I get . . . ?"

"Maybe nothing. Maybe an even bigger story, if my theory can be proved. Right now it's pure speculation. Nothing may come of it. For you, it's a gamble."

"Okay, I'll bite. What's the big theory?"

"Answer a couple of questions for me first. For starters, why is everyone so certain that Trevor LeGrande was the shooter?"

"Because he was a messed-up kid. Not to speak ill of the dead. And the gun was right by his hand with his fingerprints all over it."

"But why would he do something so awful? Hadn't his family been trying to help him?"

"Well, maybe. What looks like help to one person doesn't always look that way to another. According to sources I interviewed, Stefan and Jacqueline were about to throw him out of the house. Maybe that was a trigger. Anyway, Trevor had been doing drugs. The autopsy showed he indulged not long before the shootings. So he probably was out of control. That night he was home alone with this woman he had a crush on. Most likely scenario is he tried to rape her, she fought him off, he got pissed and shot her. Then he shot his father and sister when they got home, maybe to cover up what he'd done to Jacqueline, maybe just out of drug-addled spite. And finally he shot himself."

"Is there any evidence that he actually assaulted Jacqueline?"

"Forensic evidence? No. Maybe they fought about something else. But he'd been making unwanted advances, that's a known fact. Jacqueline complained about it to lots of people."

Claire nodded. Griff's version was consistent with the story Ben had told her.

Griff said, "Of course, if Trevor had the hots for Jacqueline, he wasn't alone. From what I could see, every man Jacqueline met came onto her, or wanted to. God, what a gorgeous woman." Claire wondered if he knew he was licking his lips.

"You knew her?"

"We'd met. As a reporter I cover a lot of ground. Jacqueline was big on the local circuit. Arts groups, do-good organizations, that sort of thing. Did some acting, community theater stuff. She tried breaking into the movies at one time. Probably the girl, Melissa, got the acting bug from her. Poor kid gets home from a school play rehearsal and *pow!*" He cocked his finger like a gun and aimed it at Claire.

"Did Jacqueline ever take any of those men up on their offers?"

"Not me, if that's what you're thinking. Can't speak for others. Wouldn't surprise me though."

"Seems like she had a good life going with Stefan. Why put it at risk by having an affair?"

Griff shrugged, shoulders riding up in the tweed jacket. "Depends on what you call the good life. Stefan LeGrande was totally focused on himself and his status as the great architect. He probably could've walked in on Jacqueline doing the pizza delivery kid on the kitchen floor and not noticed. Still, Stefan was a much better deal than her ex."

"Her ex—you mean Leo Hollister. The jailbird."

He gave her a grin and a thumbs-up. "Lady's been doing her homework. Hollister's a loser, been bouncing in and out of jail most of his life. He deals drugs without being smart about it, and he has a bad habit of getting violent when he loses his temper. Rumor was, he was Trevor's main source. Hook your customers then keep 'em supplied. Steady business that way."

"Couldn't be him, though," Claire murmured to herself. "He was in jail when the family died."

Griff apparently heard her. "No, he wasn't. He was out on bail."

"Really?" Had Ben told her Leo was in jail then or had she assumed it? Her headache lightened. Here was another candidate for the fifth person.

"Yeah, he got arrested for doing something stupid, probably another fight with a drug dealer, and then got bailed out. I interviewed him a day or two after the killings. You know there was a little girl who survived—"

"Eden. She wasn't home that night."

He nodded. "She's Leo's daughter with Jacqueline, and he wanted custody. But within a couple of weeks he had his sentencing hearing and was back in the slammer."

"Sounds like it's where he belongs. Too bad he's out again."

Griff grabbed his pen and notebook. "Yeah? Tell me more."

"All I know is, Ben Grant got a call saying Leo was released yesterday. But if he wasn't in jail when the family died, isn't he a possible suspect?"

"What do you mean?"

"Tell me, Griff, did the sheriff ever look into the possibility that someone other than Trevor fired that gun? Maybe an intruder trying to rob the place. Or someone with a personal motive—Leo, or a lover that Jacqueline jilted, or maybe someone who thought Stefan cheated him in a business dealing."

"You mean a client who hired Stefan to design a house that would impress the neighbors and got mad when everyone said it was ugly."

"Something like that. Anyone who might have gone up to Highview Lane, killed those four people, and left again."

"So that's your big theory. Trevor's been falsely blamed and someone else killed them." Looking at her with disgust, Griff stuffed his gear into his pockets and stood up. "Thanks for wasting my time."

"Wait! Sit down. Isn't it possible?"

"Hmm, I dunno. Sure as hell looks like an inside job."

"Why? What's so convincing?"

He sat again. "The gun and the fingerprints, like I said. And there was no sign that the LeGrandes were expecting company, or that anyone broke in. Besides, the timing would be tight. A neighbor heard shots and phoned 911 right away. Not a lot of time for an intruder to get away."

"Way out there, it would take a while for responding officers to arrive," Claire pointed out.

"True. And the intruder, if there was one, lucked out on the weather. It would have been hard to spot someone who didn't want to be seen. God, what a miserable storm. Driving rain, high wind—a tree blew down on the coast highway. That held up the cops some."

Suddenly images from Claire's dream swirled in front of her. She closed her eyes. *Outside a storm rages. Ocean waves batter the glass.*

Griff went on, "I heard the call on the police radio. By the time I got out there it was midnight and Highview Lane was jammed with cars. I had to park all the way out by the highway. Nearly blew off the ridge walking to the house. Got soaked clear through. Hey, you okay?"

"What?" Claire opened her eyes. "Fine. Sorry—" That word again. She bit it back. "By the way, did you ever talk to Stefan LeGrande's brother? A man named Ben Grant." She tried to make the question sound offhand.

"Sure. Your client, right? The guy selling the house. Lives in Boston. I interviewed him a couple of times. Tried to contact him for this follow-up piece but the number he gave me doesn't work." Griff leaned forward, elbows on the table. "Bet you've got his contact info. How about sharing?"

Not on a bet, Claire thought. "What did you think of him?"

"Straightforward guy, probably good company when he's not hammered with grief. Wait, you're not thinking he's your intruder?"

"Is it possible?"

Griff got up and started pacing in front of the picture window, scratching his chin as he thought. Behind him, boats bobbed in the marina and wind surfers scooted along the waves. "Hell, yeah, anything's possible. Closest surviving relative. Question is, was he really home in Boston that night? Cops here would have asked cops there to notify him about the deaths, but maybe they didn't go to his house. If they called a cell phone, he could have been anywhere. I'll have to check that out."

"Hold on, I don't want to be accusing anyone—"

"I won't mention your name. But you know, you're right. Everyone jumped to conclusions. Reasonable conclusions, but still . . . "

"What happened when you went up there that night? I know they wouldn't let you into the actual crime scene—"

"Couldn't get inside, no. But I saw it all. The blood, the bodies. I snuck back around on the deck." Griff grinned with pride at this achievement. "They had a guard posted, but what with all the rain and confusion, it wasn't hard to slip past him. All that glass, and the lights on inside, it was like watching a movie."

Claire made up her mind. "Can you come out there with me? I'd like to look at the house through your eyes, the way you saw it that night."

He grinned. "Past two days, you've shot me down whenever I suggested that."

"This is today."

He looked at his watch. Claire chuckled to see Mickey Mouse on the big round watch face. "Got an appointment in a few minutes. How about I meet you there at two?"

She agreed and walked him out of the conference room—smack into Avery's path.

"Oh, there you are, Claire. I need to talk to you." Avery's attention wasn't on Claire, though. She was giving Griff a smile and an appraising look. "Well, hel-lo! I'm Avery."

Griff smiled back and put out a paw for her to shake. "Griff Maxwell, *Marin Post Ledger*."

"Really? Are you a reporter?" Avery brightened. "What brings you here?"

"We were just talking about a place your company has for sale. The Stefan LeGrande house."

Avery laughed. "Did she tell you she thinks it's haunted?"

Griff threw a speculative glance at Claire. "Not in so many words."

"I sold that house, you know." Avery tapped herself on the chest, letting her fingers linger near her bustline. "Avery Collier, that's A-V-E-R-Y. Here, I'll get you my card." She trotted off to her desk.

Claire eased Griff toward the elevator. "No need to wait. I know you're in a hurry to get someplace." She pushed the call button, but the door didn't open. The elevator must be down on the first floor.

Avery was back in a flash, saying, "Here you are. If you have any questions, just call me. We had that house on the market for only two days, you know. Pretty impressive, selling it that quickly."

Claire put a hand on Avery's shoulder to back her off. "Don't pay attention, Griff. I'm afraid the announcement's premature. There's an offer, yes, but it isn't going to be accepted."

"What!" Avery whirled away, then faced Claire, hands on hips and gray eyes snapping. "That's not your decision to make. It's Ben's."

"And he told me this morning that he's turning down your client's offer."

"He can't do that!"

The chime finally announced the elevator's arrival. The door slid open.

Claire said, "Thanks for coming, Griff. See you at two."

"Sure thing." The reporter slid Avery's card into a shirt pocket but made no move to leave.

"What about a counteroffer?" Avery demanded, flipping back her blond hair. The volume of voice kept rising.

"There won't be one."

Since Griff wouldn't leave, Claire tried to maneuver Avery toward the conference room, but the annoying blonde stood fast.

"Ben can't say no. I promised Wayne Burdick he'd get the house."

"You should know better to make promises you can't keep."

"You bitch! It's your fault. You talked Ben out of the offer because you're trying to keep him all for yourself."

Suddenly Tess was there, stepping between the two women. Fire blazed in her eyes. "What in the world do you two think you're doing?"

Aiming a grin at Claire, Griff Maxwell slipped into the elevator and disappeared.

Claire fervently wished she could do the same.

Avery grimaced at her image in the restroom mirror. Tears had left dark mascara streaks down her cheeks. How could Claire do such a thing to her—sabotage a perfectly good offer, and then get Avery in trouble when she objected. Totally unfair.

True, Tess had been angry with Claire too. They'd both had to spend half an hour in the boss's office listening to her read them the riot act about what she called their "failure to maintain professional standards." Well, what could be more professional than actually bringing in a viable purchase offer? It was a perfect contract. So maybe the bid was a tad low, but the buyer was paying cash and not asking for any contingencies. What more did they want?

She knew what Claire wanted—the whole commission to herself, plus the seller as a bonus; it was clear she was putting the moves on Ben Grant. Being a stupid, selfish bitch—now that was a real violation of professional standards.

And now Claire had landed them both on Tess's shit list. That's not what Tess called it, of course. She called it probation, as if she were being kind by not sending them to jail. Avery knew when she signed with Golden Gate Properties that the deal was to have a three-month trial period so she and the company could see if they were a good fit. Claire probably had the same arrangement. But there was no reason they both couldn't make it. Why was Claire trying so hard to ruin her chances?

Avery scrubbed her face with a paper towel and carefully reapplied her makeup. She'd better get back out there. If she hid in the ladies room for too much longer, everyone would think that she was upset, or that Claire had gotten the best of her.

She blinked her eyes at the mirror. Better. Still a little red, but no sign left of the tears. She got out her brush and with fierce, determined strokes, she yanked it through her long blonde hair.

No way was she going let Claire get away with any of it.

WHEN THE PHONE RANG Claire was slumped at her desk, smarting from Tess's displeasure.

"Hello, this is Claire Scanlan." She forced herself to make her voice bright. "Oh, Nadine, it's great to hear from you. Have you and Paul come to any decision about the Highview Lane house? . . . Yes, the seller would be very receptive to entertaining your offer . . . You're right, there was one, but it's no longer on the table . . . Excellent!" No need to fake the brightness any longer. "Yes, I'll be out for awhile but I'll be back here at the Golden Gate office in the late afternoon . . . Four-thirty is perfect. See you then."

All right! The Johansens were coming in this afternoon to write up a purchase order. Claire could barely restrain herself from dancing on her desk. But after sitting through Tess's lecture, she didn't dare do anything that might not perfectly fit the image of a Golden Gate Properties professional.

She felt bruised by the reprimand. She'd handled the unpleasant situation as best she could. Avery was the one who'd been doing all the screaming. Yet somehow she'd managed to make Tess think that Claire, too, deserved a black mark.

Hopefully she hadn't done herself any real damage in Tess's eyes, or anyone else's. But she'd better do everything impeccably for a few days, just in case. Let them all see that she was indeed a professional—serious, dedicated, on top of the game. This little incident would blow over, and she wanted to make sure she came through it with her job secure and her career unscathed.

Ben's signature on the Johansens' sales contract would help a lot.

With luck she could hand him their offer when he came to pick her up for the wine-tasting party. She closed her eyes, picturing it—she opens the door, documents in hand. He reaches for the papers —no, he reaches for her. She steps into his arms. His lips find hers; his hands caress her body with their velvet touch. They melt together in a passionate embrace . . .

Her body grew hot, and she quickly shook her head to clear the scene from her mind. The visualization had strayed far away from the direction she'd intended it to go. So much better than the images from her nightmares.

Time to leave so she could meet Griff Maxwell at the LeGrande house. If she could get clear on what happened there, maybe these latest nightmares would cease. She grabbed her purse and headed out.

Passing Tess's office, she saw her boss at her desk, champagne-blond head bent over some paperwork. For half a second she had an impulse to ask Tess if she could borrow the Lincoln. But Maxwell wasn't a client—she didn't need to impress him. And she didn't want to push her luck with Tess. Her little green jellybean would do just fine.

AVERY EMERGED from the restroom with her head held high. She'd repaired the damage to her appearance, and if there was any damage to her ego—well, no way in hell was she going to let anyone know.

As she headed toward her desk, she saw Claire waiting for the elevator. She squinted, pretending to shoot daggers at the other woman with her eyes.

Stupid bitch. She imagined the dagger finding its mark between Claire's shoulderblades, and a very satisfying trickle of red blood staining her pearl-gray jacket.

Then she sat down and picked up her phone. It was going be hard to keep a smile in her voice this time.

"Bad news," she said when she got Wayne Burdick on the line. "Ben Grant told Claire he's turning down your offer."

"What! He can't do that. It's all cash, no strings. Did he say why?"

"He probably wants a higher price. I told you, your offer is low."

"And I told you, I can't go higher. That's all the cash I can come up with."

"What about a mortgage?" If Wayne had a few million in cash lying around, banks would jump over each other to make him a loan.

"Too much hassle and paperwork. I don't want to fuss with monthly payments. Look, you promised you'd persuade him to accept it. I've been counting on you."

Avery sighed. It hadn't been a promise really, just a teensy bit of bragging. But now she felt stuck. Okay, a real pro would figure a way to make this thing work. Technically, Golden Gate Properties represented the seller, not the buyer. Her job was to look out for Ben's best interest, not Wayne's. But surely the firm would be doing Ben a disservice to let him throw away this opportunity. What were the chances that the mismatched couple Claire brought to the house yesterday would actually want to buy the place? They didn't even like the same kind of clothes; they'd never agree on something big, like a house. Especially this house. She could see them now, showing off their new home to their fancy guests: *"And this is the grand salon where all those people got slaughtered. Isn't it charming? Don't you just love the view?"*

"Avery? Are you still there?" Wayne's voice jolted her out her thoughts.

Okay, she was going to make lemonade out this. "Of course I'm here. I'll go talk to Ben myself. We'll work this out to everyone's advantage. Don't worry."

An excuse to see Ben—that was the positive thing in all this. The thought of it made her heart beat faster. She would go to his house, plead her case, point out all the benefits of the deal—including all the extra-special ways she was willing to show him her appreciation.

Wayne said, "I'll go with you."

"What? You mean, to see Ben? No, I don't think so. Not a good idea."

"Sure it is. I want to meet Stefan LeGrande's brother. I'll lay my cards on the table, he can lay down his. When I do business, I like to know the person I'm dealing with. Besides, I'd like another ride in that cute little ragtop of yours. Let's do it now. I'll meet you at your office in a few minutes."

WISPS OF FOG blowing in from the ocean played hide-and-seek with the sun. The wind rippled through the sea grasses and tossed the branches of the pine trees and cypresses.

Pulling into the LeGrande driveway, Claire saw Martin Roncallo, with his shaved head and thick mustache, walking toward her from the direction of the house. He carried a pair of sunglasses in his hand. She rolled down her window. Fresh air rushed in, carrying scents of salt and evergreens.

"Hey there, Martin," she called.

Roncallo bent down to look at her through the window. "Hello, Claire. I was just checking on things."

"Good. It's reassuring to know that the neighbors keep an eye on the place. How's Lily?"

"Sweet as pie. She's hard at work in there, designing her own computer game." He pointed with the sunglasses toward his own house and shook his head, but his expression revealed affection and pride. "She says her idea's better than any of the games I've come up with. She can't wait to try it out on Eden, as soon as Ben and I can get those two girls together."

"Tell her I said hello."

"I will." He glanced back toward the LeGrande house. "As you can see, your customers have already arrived."

"Customers?"

"There's a couple of fellows up there who say they're waiting for you."

"Two of them? I was just expecting one."

"Well, you got two." He frowned. "Maybe I should go back up there with you, in case it's not who you had in mind."

"No, that's okay. Thanks anyway." She drove on to see an SUV in the parking court and, yes, two men peering into the windows at the front of the house. They turned at the sound of her car. Griff Maxwell, in his fraying tweed jacket, lifted a big hand to wave at her. The other man, shorter and skinnier, had topped his jeans with a khaki jacket with pockets all over it. A blocky canvas case hung from his shoulder on a wide black strap.

"Yo, Claire!" Griff waved as she got out of the VW and came over to greet them. "This is Kevin Underwood. Colleague of mine at the *Post Ledger*."

"Good to meet you." Kevin shook Claire's hand. A camera dangled from a thinner strap around his neck, and she noticed a tripod leaning against the wall of the house.

"You're a photographer?" She turned to Griff. "I thought we agreed that there wouldn't be an article, at least for now."

The reporter was already heading to the front door. "Never hurts to update the file shots. Let's go in," he called over his shoulder. Kevin grabbed the tripod and followed.

Using the key from the lockbox, Claire opened the house. As the carved wooden door swung wide, she caught her breath. No smells assailed her, no sounds, no blast of icy cold. *Please, Melissa or whoever you are. Be good. Don't let anything strange happen.*

They stepped into the entrance gallery, the grand salon open before them. Beyond the glass wall, the sky was a shifting pattern of misty gray and sunny blue.

"Wait a sec," Kevin said. "Let me get the empty room." He spread the legs of the tripod, mounted his camera on top. Claire and Griff kept motionless while he clicked a few shots. The house remained quiet and still.

"That should do it," Kevin announced, grabbing the tripod and pulling its legs together.

Griff bounded down the step into the grand salon. "Sure looks different," he said. "Someone did a hell of a job getting the mess cleaned up. You'd never believe how horrible it looked in here."

Claire stayed where she was, her hands braced on the railing. She was reluctant to venture into the big room. "Describe it."

The reporter crossed to the fieldstone fireplace. "Two bodies here, in front of the hearth. The grownups, Stefan and Jacqueline." He moved to the glass wall and stopped at the French doors that led to the deck. "The girl was right about here. Melissa." Then he paced the hardwood floor into the middle of the room. "And Trevor was lying here, smack in the middle, with the gun by his hand."

Claire shuddered. Griff was standing at the exact place where, two days before, she'd tripped over an invisible obstacle and fallen.

Griff swept his arm. "And the whole damn room was covered with blood."

She sat on the step and covered her face with her hands. She'd been right. Her first time in the house, she'd seen them, just a quick flash, four people lying dead in the precise places that Griff had just indicated. She hadn't known then who was who. Last night's dream had not only confirmed that earlier vision but had shown her how they died.

Claire shuddered. She wished she had gotten it wrong. Then she could blame her imagination for what she saw, instead of having to think that Melissa was sending messages from some sort of afterlife.

"How do you think the whole thing transpired?" she asked. "You're a writer, Griff. Tell me the story. How did the bodies end up where they were?"

"Okay. The official version, with a few Griff Maxwell embellishments for dramatic effect."

He moved around the room, acting out his role as he spoke. "Picture this. A November night, dark and stormy, rain pelting the glass. A fire in the fireplace, trying to make this big space cozy. Across the room there's a leather sofa. When I looked in through the glass, the table in front of the sofa had a couple of wineglasses, a fashion magazine, a science fiction paperback splayed open."

Kevin said, "Too bad the furniture isn't still in place." He was moving through the gallery, snapping pictures of the empty room from slightly different angles.

"I can visualize it," Claire said.

Griff continued his story. "So Jacqueline and Trevor are sitting there reading. His dad has gone to pick up his sister from a play rehearsal at school. The school's all the way over in Mill Valley, so that's going to take awhile, especially in the storm. Trevor's all alone with the gorgeous babe he's got the hots for. Good time to put the moves on her."

He reached out to embrace the air, acting Trevor's part. Then he became Jacqueline, making a shoving motion.

"She pushes him away. Maybe she smacks him hard or belittles his manhood. Whatever she does, his ego is hurt, he gets angry, he did some drugs earlier that have combined with the wine to mess up his head. So he gets upset and leaves the room. Jacqueline relaxes, crisis over. She goes to add a log to the fire. But Trevor comes back, and he's got a gun. She's pleading with for life when, *pow!* He shoots her."

By the hearth, a raven-haired woman slips silken straps from her shoulders and beckons. A young man steps toward her, crossing a magic carpet. In the corner a shadow moves. Bam! Bam!

"Was there a floor covering in here, Griff? An Oriental carpet maybe, something with a detailed pattern?"

"Yeah, a huge red rug covered with flowers and birds and stuff. How'd you know?"

Claire shrugged. "Lucky guess. Go on."

"Trevor can't believe what he's done. He hides in his room. Finally Stefan and Melissa get home. They come in from the garage through here"—Griff pointed down the length of the gallery to a door at the far end—"and when they get to right about there, where Kevin's standing, they see Jacqueline. She's lying in front of the fireplace covered in blood. They scream, and Trevor, who's in shock and scared shitless, comes back out. He's behind them with the gun. Stefan runs to his wife and just as he reaches her, *pow!* Trevor shoots him in the back."

The man embraces the fallen angel.

Griff pretended to fire a gun at the fireplace. Kevin came over to take a picture of the spot.

"Melissa is terrified. She runs for the door to the deck. It's her only hope for escape because Trevor's in this corridor here blocking the front door and the other exits. He chases her, and she almost makes it to freedom, but the door is locked. Before she can get it open, he shoots her too. Then he turns the gun on himself, and the rampage is over."

The girl runs toward the storm. Her eyes are imprinted with words: Help me! Bam! Bam! The room is engulfed in a tide of blood.

Claire rubbed her eyes, erasing the sight. "And that's the official scenario?"

"In essence." Griff blew imaginary gunsmoke from his fingertip. "I added some ruffles and flourishes."

Claire shook her head. It didn't fit. She'd heard two gunshots, and then the lull, followed by another two. In Griff's story, there would have been one shot, then three. If he was right, why did the dream give her the two-pause-two sequence?

Because Trevor didn't die last. The fifth person shot two victims, then two more.

Griff seemed to pick up her thoughts. "If you want, Claire, I could make up a new version that fits your theory."

Kevin said, "You mean the notion that someone broke in and shot them all?" Clearly Griff had filled him in on the ride over.

"No need," Claire said. "You filled in a lot of blanks for me. Thanks for your excellent performance." She clapped her hands in appreciation.

Kevin joined the applause. "Bravo!"

Griff smiled and took a bow.

Pushing herself up from the step, she stood on the gallery's marble floor and leaned against the railing. "A neighbor called the police, right?"

"Yeah," Griff said. "The guy next door."

"Martin Roncallo?"

"That's the one."

"I wonder why he didn't call after the first shot that killed Jacqueline. If the cops had come then, they might have prevented the others from dying."

Kevin, now by the French doors, said, "There's a pretty good distance between these houses. The noise of the first shot probably blended in with the sound of the storm. It's lucky he heard anything at all." He snapped another photo. "Okay if I take a few in the rest of the house?"

Claire waved a hand in permission. "Help yourself. Griff, follow along if you like."

"Coming with us?" Griff asked.

"I'll be along in a minute. You go ahead."

Claire watched the two men disappear into the kitchen. Once she was sure they were out of sight, she took a deep breath and counted to ten. Clutching the railing, she stepped down carefully onto the hardwood floor of the grand salon and waited. Would the air turn to ice? Would the room go dark? Would she smell blood, or camellias?

Nothing happened.

Exhale, draw in another breath. She let go of the railing and crept into the big room. "Melissa? Or whoever you are? Are you there?"

Still nothing.

The light seemed to dim, but maybe that was just the fog, lower and thicker than it had been just minutes before. All the blue was gone from the sky beyond the glass wall.

She stopped at the spot where Trevor's body had fallen on that stormy November night, where she herself had stumbled the other day. Reaching out with her foot, she tested the floor and the air just above it to see if she could feel anything solid. There was nothing.

Claire glanced behind her to make sure Griff and Kevin hadn't reappeared. The murmur of their voices reached her from somewhere deep in what Stefan LeGrande had called the public wing. The media lounge probably.

"Melissa?" she whispered. "It's okay, they're not in the room." Twice when the strange manifestations occurred, the house was empty except for Claire. But the first time, Ben and Avery had been inside, off in one of the wings. What mattered, apparently, was that Claire be alone in the grand salon.

She went to the fireplace and knelt in front of the stone hearth. This was the place where Jacqueline and Stefan had perished. Now she could feel it—the air was growing colder. She caught a whiff of camellias. Jacqueline's favorite perfume.

The chill deepened and the room grew darker. Claire saw thick fog pouring in over the deck outside. Still on her knees, she watched as a wisp of grayness seeped between the panels of the French doors. Like a tiny tornado it twisted itself into a shape that hovered in front of the glass. For just an instant Claire could see someone the face and form of a girl, sitting on a tombstone and dressed in calico. Perhaps she was Melissa, the daughter, the budding actress, who had almost made it to the safety of the French doors when a bullet ripped through her. But she also seemed to be Claire herself, an earlier Claire, giving a level stare to the woman she had grown up to become.

The girl melted away, became mist again.

Claire shivered. "Melissa? Did you know I played that part too? Emily in *Our Town*."

A breath blew softly across her cheek. She thought she heard a word—"Yes!"—but couldn't be sure.

Claire nodded. "I had a dream about the night you died. I saw five people here, not four."

A whispered voice, the same one as before: "You can see what really happened."

"Trevor didn't shoot anyone. He was a victim too."

"He didn't do it," the whisperer agreed.

A presence moved in close, as if Melissa had sat down next to Claire on the floor. Outside a hole opened in the fog, and a shaft of sunlight brightened the room.

Claire was whispering too. "Then who did? Who was the fifth person?"

Footsteps sounded from the direction of the kitchen. Griff's voice called, "Claire? You still here?"

The presence beside Claire crackled, as if it had been struck by a jolt of electricity. It rose up and began to float away.

"Don't go yet!" She put out her hand, wishing for something tangible to grab so she could pull the presence back. "Tell me who it was."

"Help me." The whispered voice was farther away.

"I'll try, Melissa," Claire promised. "I'll do my best."

Griff and Kevin appeared in the gallery. "Hey, Claire," Griff said. "Who're you talking to?"

Claire stood up and brushed her hands together. "Myself. Just making some mental notes about the house."

"We gotta get back. Kev has a school group he's supposed to shoot. Thanks for letting us in. I'll call you to follow up."

"Yeah, thanks. I got some good shots." The photographer snapped a picture of Claire and packed his gear into its case.

"I'm leaving too," she said. "Go on out and I'll lock up."

The two men went out the front door. Claire was about to follow when she felt a clutch on her sleeve.

"Be careful," whispered Melissa's voice. "The trouble is not yet over. You and others face grave danger."

Chapter 22

The whole way to Ben Grant's house, Avery rehearsed her speech in her head, the words that would convince Ben to accept Wayne Burdick's purchase offer. Wayne, sitting in the passenger seat of the Porsche, kept up a running stream of talk. He was apparently trying to impress her with his knowledge of real estate and architecture, but Avery wasn't really paying attention. She tried to make encouraging noises, like "uh-huh" and "that's great" and "absolutely," and just hoped she was murmuring them at appropriate moments.

"This is it?" Wayne said when she stopped in front of Ben's bungalow. "It's so . . . well, ordinary."

Avery nodded. "I know. Imagine living here when you could be in a huge house right on the ocean." She pushed a button to raise the convertible top; the last time she was here, she'd left the car open and the wind filled it up with leaves and twigs. She wasn't going to make that mistake again.

Wayne winked at her. "Not everyone appreciates an architectural masterpiece the way you and I do."

She hoped she wasn't making an even bigger mistake by bringing Wayne here. In real estate school, the instructors had emphasized that it wasn't the best strategy to let buyer and seller meet face to face before the deal was done. If this visit to Ben backfired, Tess might get even angrier than she was already. On the other hand, think how impressed Tess would be if she quickly closed the sale. The rules couldn't really apply to a problem property that scared most buyers off. You had to take some risks in order to sell a place like that, and if Avery was good at anything, it was taking risks. That's why she was here right now instead of stuck in her dead-end life in Texas.

Wayne placed his hand at the small of her back to guide her through the gate and up the flagstone walk. A breeze stirred the leaves of the trees; sun shone through the branches and dappled the lawn. Summer was much nicer in Northern California than in Texas. There the heat sucked her dry and left her limp. Here the air on her skin felt soft and warm, like a lover's caress. Her heart was racing with excitement. She was going to make this work.

The instant Ben opened his front door, all of the phrases she'd carefully practiced flew right out of her head. God, the man was gorgeous. Just the sight of him struck her like a physical impact, knocking her body back a step or two. She struggled to catch her breath.

"Avery!" he said. "This is a surprise."

She giggled, and hated herself for doing it. "A good one, I hope." When he didn't pick up the cue, she held out her hand to indicate the man beside her. "I want you to meet Wayne Burdick. He's the one who wants to buy your house."

Ben gave them a fleeting frown as he stepped out onto the porch, pulling the door closed behind him. Not the response Avery had been hoping for.

Still, he shook her client's hand. She decided to take that as a positive sign.

"Sorry you were dragged here on a wild-goose chase, Mr. Burdick," Ben said. "I appreciate your interest in the house, and I gave your bid a lot of thought. But as I explained to the listing agent this morning, I've decided to turn it down." He glanced from Wayne to Avery as he said, "Didn't Claire tell you that?"

Avery let herself touch Ben's arm. "I thought maybe if we talked it over, we could come up with a deal that would make you both happy."

Wayne gave Ben a pleasant smile. "I've followed your brother's career closely, Mr. LeGrande—"

"My name is Grant. The same as my brother's was, growing up. LeGrande was the identity he adopted along the way."

"Yes, I'm aware of that," Wayne said. "A marketing tool, you might say. A way to brand himself and his work. I thought he might have persuaded his family to switch to the new name too."

"Just his wife and children. They went by LeGrande."

"Let me be straight with you, Mr. Grant. You can't imagine how much it would mean to me to live in a house Stefan LeGrande designed. Especially this one—his own house, the one he lived in with his wife and kids, the culmination of all his design ideas."

"I appreciate your interest, Mr. Burdick, but unless you're prepared to change your terms, my decision has to stand."

Mr. Grant . . . Mr. Burdick. They were being so polite that Avery wanted to scream. She saw that Wayne's hands were curled into fists, though they stayed down at his side. She almost wished that he and Ben would go ahead and fight. Over the house. Over her. One time two guys had brawled over her in a scuzzy Texas bar where she happened to be working. One of them ended up in the emergency room with a broken jaw, while the other spent the night in jail. Of course she hadn't wanted either of those assholes. A fight between Ben and Wayne, though, two men with good looks and money —that would be more interesting. For one thing they weren't drunk. And they were evenly matched in height and build, so it could be a real contest. Ben seemed to be more muscular, though, so he'd probably have the edge. Which was fine with her.

Wayne said, "Unfortunately, I'm not in a position to pay more. But surely it would mean something to you to put the house in the hands of someone who admires LeGrande's work as much as I do."

"Can't we go inside and talk, Ben? I'm sure you two can reach an agreement." To persuade him, Avery arranged her face into the expression her brother Kurt referred to as her pretty pout. When she used it on him, she almost always got her way. She aimed it now at Ben, hoping he would be just as susceptible.

"Claire's handling the property," he said. "I thought that was clear, Avery. I appreciate all your effort, but if there's any negotiating to be done, she'll handle it. Mr. Burdick, I'm sorry I can't be more encouraging."

Avery felt like she'd been slapped. A black hole had opened inside of her and she wanted to crawl into it and disappear. No way, though, did she intend to let either of these two, especially Ben, see her disappointment.

"Okay," she said, making herself sound cheerful, "I'll talk to Claire some more about it. Thank you for letting us impose on you, Ben." She initiated a handshake and clasped his hand tight in both of hers. "If you ever want to see me—about, you know, anything—just let me know."

"About anything, you say?" There, he couldn't resist smiling. That was more like the reaction she wanted.

Behind her, she heard a car pull up. Easing his hand from her grasp, Ben looked out toward the road. His smile broadened to a grin. Losing his attention made Avery slide deeper into the black hole. Turning, she saw that a station wagon had nosed in behind her Porsche. The ponytailed girl she'd met yesterday got out of the backseat and closed the door, then waved as the station wagon drove away. She was wearing jeans and a T-shirt, with a pink sweatshirt tied by its arms like a cape around her shoulders. She came skipping up the walkway but stopped in her tracks when she noticed the group of people on the porch.

"Hey there, princess," Ben called. "How was your arts-and-crafts class?"

"Okay." The girl's voice sounded flat, a total lack of enthusiasm, as far as Avery could tell. Ben must be making her go to the class so she'd be out his hair during the day now that school was out for the summer.

"Hi, Eden." She beamed a bright smile of her own toward the kid. Ben seemed fond of his niece, and if Eden liked her—well, that couldn't help but give Avery a nice boost in his esteem.

"Hi." The girl barely looked at her as she trudged up the steps to the front porch. She sidled up close to her uncle and he put his arm around her shoulders. Nested against him, she asked, "What's going on?"

"Avery and Mr. Burdick came to talk to me about buying your old house. They're just about to leave."

Eden gaped at Avery, gave Wayne a longer stare, then turned to Ben. "I don't feel good. I'm going inside," she told him, and slipped in through the front door.

Well, that was rude. Hands on her hips, Avery frowned at the door as it closed. Her daddy would have been smacked her good if she hadn't given a civil greeting when guests came calling. She could see that Wayne was scowling too; he must be feeling as insulted as she was.

Best thing to do was make light of the situation. "Don't worry, Ben, all kids forget their manners sometimes."

Ben ignored her. He put his hand on the doorknob, preparing to follow Eden inside. "I appreciate your interest in my brother and his work, Mr. Burdick—"

"Then why not—" Wayne began, but Ben kept on going.

"If you're as well informed about Stefan as you seem, then you know as well as I do that I'd be remiss in my responsibility as his executor to sell the house for the price you're offering. Now if you two will excuse me, I have things to attend to."

Avery jumped in, trying to salvage the situation. "Well, anyway, we appreciate your time. I'll talk to Claire like I said. Look, here's my card. It's got my cell phone number on it. Call me and we can talk about, well, whatever you like."

When he didn't take her business card right away, she slid it into his breast pocket. He felt strong and solid beneath her fingers. She fantasized for a moment about how intensely pleasurable it would be to press her entire body against his, to let herself be consumed by the full power of his masculinity.

Then she turned away from Ben and tossed a fake smile to her client. "Come on, Wayne. Let's go."

Ben had held her hand longer than absolutely necessary. She would cling to that hint of encouragement. If only Eden hadn't arrived just then.

Again Wayne placed his hand on her back as they retreated down the walk. A gentlemanly courtesy?

Or was he were hoping it would be the first step to something more?

But she didn't want more with Wayne. Not really. Not if she could find a way to have Ben.

CLAIRE LOOKED at her watch again. Four-twenty. She was at her desk, nursing a cup of coffee and flipping through a sheaf of flyers. While she waited for Paul and Nadine Johansen to arrive, she might as well occupy her time by making herself familiar with all of Golden Gate Properties' current listings. At least, that's what she hoped Tess would think she was doing.

Truth was, the flyers were a blur. Her mind kept jumping from the Johansens to Ben and the wine-tasting party, and most of all, to the LeGrande house.

Trevor, the troubled son, had not killed three members of his family, and he had not committed suicide out of remorse or fear. Someone else had murdered all four of them, and the killer was still at large, posing a threat to other people who were unaware of the peril.

And she, Claire, was the only living soul who knew this.

What she didn't know was the identity of the killer or the potential victims, except for herself.

You and others face grave danger.

She also didn't know what to do about it. Tell the police? They'd ask her where she got her information, and when she told them, they'd laugh her out of the station and put her name in their file of known crackpots. Tell Ben? As a member of the family, he was a likely target, and if he was in danger he needed to know. But he already thought she was a little crazy for taking her nightmares seriously. Surely he'd dismiss a warning from a ghost.

Worse, talking to him could increase the problem. Ben himself might be the killer.

She didn't really believe it; she tried not to let herself even think it. But the gruesome idea kept skulking at the back of her brain, like a mugger hiding in a shadowed alley, ready to ambush her the minute she dropped her guard.

Closing her eyes, she tried to recreate the bliss she'd felt as they'd made love in his bed—the hunger and urgency leading to the moment of almost unbearable ecstasy, and afterward the languorous delight of lying together in a mutual embrace. The memory soothed her uneasy mood.

She couldn't deny that while a tiny part of her was worried, a much bigger part was eager to see him again. Tonight they would enjoy the wine-tasting party, and they would celebrate the good news about the Johansens' offer. Then they'd have a frank talk. If everything went as she hoped and intended, he would allay her suspicions and fears, and the evening would end in the same lovely way that last night had—minus the nightmare that sabotaged everything.

The phone rang on the reception desk. Claire heard the murmurs of her co-workers, first as Marlene interrupted her busy typing to answer the phone and then as Delia picked up the transferred call. She glanced at her watch. Four-thirty-five. Paul and Nadine would be here any minute. In fact, they were a little late. She shuffled the flyers into a tidy pile, returned a couple of stray pens to a desk drawer, and brushed some imaginary crumbs off her desktop. Not that it mattered; she planned to take the Johansens into the more elegant setting of the conference room.

Her first buyers, her first purchase offer. She felt a nervous quiver in her stomach. Tess's fault for including her in that lecture about professional standards, which only Avery really deserved.

Four-forty. Would the Johansens want coffee? Claire jumped up to make sure there was a fresh pot.

"Wish me luck," she murmured to Delia, who was now off the phone. "Clients coming in to write up an offer." Delia grinned and gave her a thumbs-up.

As Claire passed the reception desk, Marlene clicked the minimize button, making the document on her computer screen disappear.

"What's that you're always working on, Marlene?"

The receptionist regarded her with an air of wide-eyed innocence. The GGP logo danced back and forth across her screen. "Nothing."

"Hah. It's probably your secret plan to take over the company."

Marlene put a magenta-polished fingertip to her lips. "Shh, don't tell Tess."

The elevator chimed, signaling an arrival. "Hey, my clients are here," Claire said. She turned to greet Paul and Nadine with a big smile.

But it wasn't the Johansens who got out of the elevator cab. It was Avery. She mumbled hello to Marlene, glared at Claire and headed for her desk.

Claire took a seat in one of the chairs in the reception area. Might as well wait where she was. Surely her clients would be arrive at any moment. She poked at the magazines fanned out on a small table but didn't pick one up. She was much too jumpy to read.

Ten to five. The phone rang again. Marlene answered it, then punched a button and pointed to the extension next to Claire. "For you. Might as well take it right there."

Claire picked up the receiver and greeted the caller.

"Claire, this is Nadine Johansen."

"Oh, Nadine, hello! Are you and Paul on your way?"

"No, in fact I'm calling to cancel our appointment. Paul and I had a long talk this afternoon and, well, we concluded the Highview Lane house isn't right for us."

"What? But this morning you were so certain that you wanted it. If you want to see it again before you decide—"

"No, that's really not necessary."

"I don't understand. What made you change your mind?"

"To tell you the truth, Paul was at a luncheon this afternoon and mentioned the house to some colleagues. They bent his ear with all kinds of gory stories about the murders that happened there. When he got back to work, he did some Internet research, and what he found . . . I know you mentioned in passing that people died in the house, but we had no idea how brutal and traumatic the situation was. It's a much bigger load of negativity than we want the house we live in to carry."

"I see." Claire felt sick. She'd done more than mention the deaths in passing; she had made a full disclosure of the tragedy, just as she was required to do. "I'm sorry you've decided against the house, but I do understand. Why don't we set up a time and I'll show you some properties that might suit you better."

"Any house where people weren't killed would suit us better."

"I can promise you won't run into that problem with any of our other listings."

"As it happens, our schedules are jam-packed. Why don't I phone you next week?"

In other words, don't call us, we'll call you. "Fine," Claire said glumly. "I'm here to help you whenever you'd like."

She hung up and trudged back into the bullpen to get her purse. Time to go home and get ready for the wine-tasting party—at least she'd have that to redeem this distressing day. She and Ben wouldn't be celebrating after all, but she intended to enjoy the evening anyway. As well as get answers to some questions.

As she passed Avery's desk, the blonde looked up. "What happened, Claire? You look like someone ran over your puppy."

"I don't have a puppy."

"It was that woman you had at the LeGrande house yesterday, wasn't it. She said they're not going to buy it. Too bad."

Claire felt heat rush into her face. "You were listening in!"

Avery shrugged. "I can't help it if your voice carries."

"Not this far it doesn't. You used your phone to eavesdrop. Look, the button you've got pushed down is the one for the extension in the visitors area."

"Hmm. I must have pushed it by mistake."

Claire grabbed her purse and marched toward the elevator.

Marlene's voice stopped her. "Wait, don't leave yet. Another call for you."

She pointed to the visitors extension. Claire picked it up. "Hello, this is Claire."

"Claire, it's Ben. I'm afraid I have to cancel for tonight."

She felt her heart plunge to her toes. "You what? But Ben . . . "

"All day I've been looking forward to seeing you. But something came up."

That was all the excuse he going to offer?

"I see." She made her voice cold to keep it from revealing the depth of her disappointment. "What came up—can you tell me?"

"It's Eden. She's feeling upset. I thought we'd put the worst of it behind us, but all the talk about selling the house has dredged up the horror and grief. I need to make her my priority this evening."

"Of course you should. Tell you what, why don't I come over and join you? I'll pick up a pizza and some funny movies. That will help Eden put the distress out of her mind."

"Nice of you to offer, but I don't think it's a good idea. We'll get together another time."

"When?" She hated the desperate whine she heard in her voice.

"Soon. I'll give you a call."

He said goodbye. Claire stood there stunned, then slowly sank onto the visitors' chair. She heard Marlene clucking sympathetically.

When she looked up, she was facing the bullpen. Delia was paying no attention, thank God. But Avery was hanging up her own phone and smirking.

Chapter 23

Walking into her empty apartment, Claire was bent low, hand pressed against her stomach. The phone calls, first Nadine's and then Ben's, had been like two quick, sharp jabs to her belly. She flopped onto the sofa and doubled over, squeezing her eyes tight in an unsuccessful effort to keep tears from leaking out.

What the hell. Why not cry? It wasn't as if anyone would know. She was all by herself. Lindsay was the one who got to go out on a hot date tonight, while Claire was left to sit here rejected and alone, a failure at love, at her new career, at everything.

She pressed her face against a quilted throw pillow and let herself sob.

After awhile she could have sworn she heard Gram's voice. *"Go ahead. Indulge yourself in misery. Scream and cry and wail. That always improves the situation. I'm setting the timer."* And Gram would twist the dial on the old-fashioned plastic timer to make the bell ding in ten or fifteen or twenty minutes, depending on the nature of the hurt or disappointment that was making one of her granddaughters suffer. The rule was that for that entire time, the afflicted child had to wallow in her misery, complete with tears and curses and the beating of fists on a pillow. As soon as the dinger sounded, she had to quit and smile again. When the timer was ticking for Claire, it was amazing how often she got the giggles well before she'd used up her allotment of despair.

If the technique worked then, it would work now. Claire uncurled herself from the sofa and went into the kitchen, heading for the stove with its built-in timer. Thirty minutes ought to be enough. She punched in the numbers, then canceled them and started over. Better make it forty-five.

Turning from the stove, she noticed that Lindsay had come home between her work and her date. The evidence was there on the counter—the day's mail, neatly stacked. On top was a scrap of paper with the name and phone number of Lindsay's psychotherapist friend. Claire flipped it into the trash. Next to the envelopes and catalogues, Lindsay had set an unopened bottle of zinfandel, a corkscrew and a single glass. Taped to the bottle was another note in Lindsay's precise printing: *For celebrating, or for drowning your sorrows, depending on how you feel when you see what arrived today.*

Uh-oh. She grabbed up the stack of envelopes. It was easy to spot the one in question. Stiff and official-looking, it bore an imprinted return address: Middlesex County Probate and Family Court.

Her divorce decree.

Claire ripped it open. Given its cost and its significance, the document inside should have been embossed on heavy parchment and signed in gold or blood, maybe both. But it was a simple piece of paper stating that as far as the State of Massachusetts was concerned, Zachary Thomas Reynolds and Claire Elisabeth Scanlan Reynolds no longer were husband and wife.

She carried it to the sofa and stared at it for a long time. Then she leaned her head against the cushion and gazed at the blank white ceiling.

It was over. Done. After more than a decade of love and hurt and anger, of dreams formed and dreams destroyed, Zach was out of her life. She was free.

Her new life was truly beginning.

Why did she feel so cold and empty?

She didn't move until she was jolted by the timer's loud, insistent buzz.

AVERY WAS SITTING on the terrace of her brother's penthouse, well into her second glass of wine. She was thumbing through a fashion magazine, looking up from time to time to gaze at the amazing view. Sunset had tinted the landscape. Sailboats crossed gold and bronze waves as they headed back to their marinas; the hills across the water had taken on a purple hue. What a great setting for two people in a romantic mood. Too bad she was here all alone.

Heaving a sigh, she downed the rest of the wine, then frowned at the empty glass. She should have brought the bottle out here with her. Oh well. Probably time to go inside anyway. It was getting too dark to see the pictures in her magazine, and the breeze had turned cold. A thick plume of fog was moving across the bay from the Golden Gate. In an hour or two the whole area would be socked in.

The evening stillness was broken by the first few notes of Shania Twain's song "I Won't Leave You Lonely"—her cell phone's ringtone. She fumbled the phone out of her pocket and said hello.

"Howdy, sis."

"Kurt!" So good to hear the deep rumble of her brother's familiar, comforting voice.

"Everything going okay back there? How's the new real estate gig?"

"Fine. Just fine." No point in going into details about her spurned purchase offer or Tess's unjustified anger. "Are you liking Europe? Where are you? Still in Paris? Or is it Rome by now?"

"Actually I'm in New York. We wrapped up the European project early. I'm hopping a plane tomorrow at the crack of dawn, which means I'll be home by lunchtime. Just wanted to let you know."

"Omigod! Tomorrow? That's . . . that's super, Kurt. I can't wait to see you."

She rang off and panicked as she gathered up phone, wineglass, bottle and magazine and hustled them all inside. God, tomorrow. It would take her a week to get the place cleaned up. In the time she'd been living alone, she'd been—well, not sloppy, exactly, but housekeeping hadn't been on the top of her priority list. She'd been really busy after all, what with finishing up her real estate classes and hunting for job and getting acclimated at Golden Gate Properties. And a girl needed to go shopping sometimes, and have the occasional date, not that any of those had worked out lately. Besides, a little clutter never bothered her.

First thing to do was put fresh sheets on her bed. Probably best not to mention that she'd been using his bedroom instead of the guestroom he'd turned over to her. And she'd better move the cosmetics that were scattered all over his bathroom. And clean up the kitchen. And vacuum. Where was the vacuum cleaner? Kurt must own a vacuum cleaner.

Once again the cell phone warbled its country tune. She dumped the other items she was carrying on the kitchen counter. Just as she hit the talk button, the wineglass, which had landed on its side, wobbled onto the floor and shattered.

"Damn!" she said. "I mean, hello."

The caller chuckled.

"Kurt? Is that you again?"

"This is Ben Grant, Avery."

"Ben! For real? I'm mean, it's great to hear from you." She put her hand over her heart to calm the sudden pounding of her heart. Her shoe crunched on broken glass as walked with phone to the living room. "To what do I owe this honor?"

Passing a gilt-framed mirror, she paused to smooth her hair and pinch some color into her cheeks. Sure, Ben couldn't see her, but it probably worked on the same principle as *A smile on your face puts a smile in your voice*. If she looked sexy and beautiful, she would sound that way too.

He was making his voice low and sexy. "I have a little proposal for you, Avery. To make up for turning down Wayne Burdick's offer. I was impressed today when you brought him see me. That shows courage and enterprise."

"What, are you changing your mind?"

"About the offer? Probably not. But about other things . . . I'm willing to reconsider. To let you persuade me."

"Other things . . . you mean Claire? You might drop her and make me the listing agent?" She wondered what had gone sour between Ben and Claire. Clearly something had turned him off where she was concerned. Their phone call late this afternoon, when Avery had just happened to be listening in, proved that. Ben had canceled their date on such a flimsy excuse.

Well, the reason didn't matter. What counted was that Claire's problem was turning into Avery's opportunity.

"That's one possibility. Could I see you tonight, Avery? We can talk about it. And I have a surprise for you." His voice was a lion's purr. Her fingers found the hot, magic place between her legs.

"Ooh, I like surprises. Shall I come to your house?"

"Actually, I'd like to meet you at Stefan's house. The surprise is waiting there. Say, in half an hour. I think we could have a very good time."

"Oh, yes, Ben," she breathed. "I'm sure we can. I'll be there, ready for . . . well, anything."

The instant the call finished she ran to the shower in Kurt's bathroom. Cleaning up for her brother would have to wait. To get to Highview Lane in half an hour, she needed to leave right away. That meant she had to set the world record for speed primping if she was going to make herself look irresistible.

WHEN AVERY cut her headlights, the entire world went black.

She got out of the Porsche and stood there for a moment in the whipping wind, her hand on the door so she would stay tethered to something solid. There were no streetlights up here on Highview Lane, and the LeGrande house, just a few yards away, was totally dark. She thought there would be a security light, but the bulb must have burned out. Driving in from the coast road, she had noticed a lighted window at the Roncallo house, but from here she couldn't see it. She looked up toward the sky. No stars, no moon; they had been obliterated by the thick blanket of fog.

Unable to see, she realized that her other senses were paying sharp attention. She could hear the *shussh-*

shussh of the surf below the ridge and the rush of the wind as it shook the invisible plants and trees. The mist turned into an icy drizzle that pricked her face like tiny needles and left her skin damp. She shivered. She should have worn a jacket over her thin lacy top and the narrow band of cotton that was her skirt.

Ben wasn't here yet; the Porsche was the only vehicle in the parking court. Maybe it would be better to wait for him inside the house; with luck it be warmer. Avery recalled that Kurt kept a flashlight in the trunk. She felt her way around to the back of the car and dug it out. The beam was weak but better than nothing. At least it showed her where to put her feet. She stepped cautiously in her spike-heeled sandals, reassured by the crunch of pebbles under her toes and the solid feel of the earth. Taking the key from the lockbox, she opened the door.

"Okay, ghost, here I am," she announced. Not that she believed in any such thing. But submerged in darkness, the house took on a spooky quality it didn't have in daylight.

The air inside seemed to ripple, as if her words had dropped like a stone into a still pool of water and set in motion a series of tiny waves.

Catching her breath, she stepped into the entrance gallery, leaving the door open just in case. Her heels clicked on the marble floor; there was no other sound. She pointed the flashlight in front of her. The meager beam didn't penetrate the black void that was the grand salon. The house was cool inside, but at least she was out of the wind.

All at once she was aware of a presence behind her—the faint heat and the slight gravitational pull of another body. Before she could react, a veil fell over her eyes. She screamed. The flashlight clattered to the floor and its beam went dark.

Unseen hands tightened the blindfold with a tug, then caressed her shoulders. Strong arms enfolded her in a tight embrace. "Hello, Avery."

"Ben!" She went limp with relief. "You frightened me."

"I didn't mean to. Tonight, my sweet, is about excitement and love, not fear."

He kissed her neck, making her tremble. His hands glided down her sides to her hips and up again until they were squeezing her breasts. She sighed and leaned into him. He released her, and she felt bereft.

Then he lifted her, his arms supporting her knees and her back, like a man about to carry his bride across the threshold of their new home. "Come with me. I have everything all set."

Secure in his grip, Avery felt him step down. They must be going into the grand salon.

"Why the mask?" she asked. "It's totally dark in here anyway."

"It heightens the pleasure, don't you think, my sweet? When you can't see, other sensations are intensified. There's no such thing as total darkness, you know; even in here, we'd get used to the low light and begin to see things. This way, we won't have that distraction."

"Are you wearing one too?"

"Of course. It's shoved above my eyes right now. But as soon as we're settled I'll put it in place."

He carried her to what she guessed was the middle of the room and gently set her down. To her surprise, she was lying not on the bare hardwood floor but something soft and cushiony.

"I made us a bed, Avery. I hope it will be comfortable enough." He lowered himself beside her and gathered her into his arms. His mouth on hers tasted of mint, spice, heaven itself.

He undid her buttons and her lacy top fell away. His eager lips discovered her throat, her shoulder, the soft mound of her breast, the hard nubbin of flesh at its tip.

"Oh, Ben," she moaned. His name became part of the air she was breathing. She pulled him closer, lifted her breast to his tongue like a sacred offering. Running her fingers across his eyes, she discovered the smooth, satiny surface of his mask.

"I told you, my sweet, I don't need to see you to appreciate how beautiful you are."

She opened his shirt, exulting in the muscular firmness of his chest. She unzipped his jeans and shuddered with pleasure as she touched the hard treasure within. In an instant they were naked, their bodies entwined. He was right, she realized. She didn't need eyes. Her hands, her mouth, her body told her everything she needed to know.

"Ben!"

Everywhere he touched her a fire ignited, until her whole being blazed with heat. When she felt him above her, poised and ready, she pulled him deep into her innermost part and let the flames consume her.

"Oh Ben oh Ben oh Ben oh oh *oh!*"

"Beautiful Avery. I love you."

After that they both lay still for a long time, arms around each other, her head pillowed on his chest. She couldn't remember the last time she had felt so happy.

He brushed a strand of hair away from her ear, and as he did the air nearby fluttered. She thought she heard something, the barest hint of a whisper.

"Don't believe him."

But the warning was so quiet it didn't sound like a voice at all, just an echo of fear from her own foolish, distrustful heart. Her last doubt vanished as he held her closer and began to kiss her and thrill her all over again.

CLAIRE WAS CURLED UP in the overstuffed easy chair, wrapped in Gram's blue-and-gold quilt, when she was roused by the ringing of her cell phone. On the TV, a baseball outfielder bobbled a catch as the scores of the evening games crawled across the bottom of the screen. God, they were on sports already? She must have dozed through the entire eleven o'clock news.

She had spent the evening sitting in a deep funk in front of the TV. When the timer sounded, signaling the official end of her pity party, she tried to talk herself into an upbeat mood, but it hadn't worked. She hadn't even opened the wine Lindsay had left. It would have been too tempting to gulp down the whole bottle.

The phone rang again. Who would call so late? She hoped Lindsay hadn't run into trouble on her hot date. Rubbing her eyes, Claire untangled herself from the chair. Where was the damn phone anyway? The third ring pinpointed its location as her purse, still on the sofa where she'd flung it when she came in. She fished it out and said hello.

"Claire!" said the caller in an impossibly cheerful voice. "You'll never believe what I just did!"

Not Lindsay. The voice was familiar but Claire couldn't place it. "Who is this?"

"Three guesses."

She felt a headache begin. "I'm not in the mood for games. Tell me who you are or I'm hanging up."

"Wait, Claire, don't. I'll give you a hint. What if I tell you the LeGrande house is haunted after all. In fact, it has the most charming and sexiest ghost you can imagine."

"Oh God, this is Avery, isn't it?" Claire pressed her fingers against her throbbing temples.

"Congratulations, you're a winner. But that's the only prize you get. I win everything else."

"What are you talking about, Avery? It's late, I was asleep, just get to the point."

"I just wanted to tell you I spent a totally amazing evening with a totally hot guy named Ben Grant. And I do mean hot. He's going to reconsider the Burdick offer, and he's making me the listing agent, too."

Claire sank down onto the sofa, shoving aside the envelope she'd restuffed with her divorce decree. "Ben's not doing any of that. No way."

"Oh yes, he is. You might say we sealed the deal tonight." Avery giggled.

"You're high on something, aren't you?"

"You bet. You'd be high too if you'd had an experience as incredible as the one I just had. But it's never going to happen to you, Claire. Not with Ben. Goodnight now. Sleep tight."

The line went dead. Claire threw the phone across the room.

AVERY FLIPPED HER CELL PHONE SHUT and turned onto the coast highway. She wished she could have seen Claire's face. Maybe it had been a little bit mean to make the call, but she couldn't resist sharing the joy she was feeling. In a way she was doing Claire a favor, giving her a heads-up that she was losing out on the listing and on Ben, too. She wouldn't be hit with the shock tomorrow in front of everybody.

Mist swirled in front of her headlights as she negotiated the hilly curves. Even away from the ocean's edge, the fog was heavy. As she swept past the Mariners Beach turnoff she had to turn on her windshield wipers so she could see where she was going. Good thing the convertible top was up or she'd get soaked. At least there was no traffic to contend with. She was alone in the black of the night, the only car on the road.

Well, not quite alone. It almost seemed as if Ben was riding with her. Her skin still tingled as if his body were touching hers. His words of love filled her mind. Claire might not believe her, but everything she'd said was true. Ben had promised to make her his listing agent and let her present Wayne with a counteroffer. She would have no trouble negotiating a deal that Ben would accept. Especially now that he'd shown her some exquisitely pleasurable ways to persuade him.

She'd been disappointed that they couldn't spend the entire night together, but she tried to act understanding when he explained that Eden, at ten, was too young to stay by herself past midnight. Of course Avery had been left alone plenty of nights when she was that age, even younger, and she'd fared all right. But the fact that Ben was concerned for his niece was probably a good sign. And they had a whole future of nights to spend together.

Faith Hill's song "Love Will Always Win" was playing on the CD and Avery sang along as she drove. From Mariners Beach the road turned inland, climbing over the coast range in a series of tight switchbacks. Drizzle was making the pavement slick, and she fishtailed around a tight turn. Better slow down and concentrate. When she yanked on the wheel to skid around the next turn, the car shuddered. It wasn't responding the way she was used to. Nothing better be wrong; Kurt would have her hide if he got home tomorrow and his precious Porsche wasn't in perfect shape.

The darkness shifted; light from somewhere was entering the car. A glance at the rearview mirror showed a pair of white headlights behind her, growing larger and larger as the vehicle approached. Jesus, what an idiot, that guy was coming way too fast. And no place on this stupid road to pull over and let him pass.

The driver's horn blared. Avery floored the gas pedal, trying to get the Porsche out of his way. The road coiled around to the left, but the Porsche went straight, flying into the air. She saw it strike a tree, felt it crash-land and somersault down a rocky slope. As it came to rest she heard first the sound of her own screaming, and then the rattle of the wind in the eucalyptus leaves, and then nothing at all.

PLUCKING HER PHONE off the carpet, Claire took a deep breath and scrolled through the phone's address book until she reached Ben's number. Did she dare call him? It was late; she should wait and deal with it in the morning. Anyway, she didn't believe a word Avery said.

But . . . why would Avery make up a story that could so easily be proven wrong? And Ben *had* broken their date. What if he'd dumped her so he could take Avery out instead? How could he even think of doing that after the love they'd shared, the beautiful intimacy? Had that been just a fling for him, a one-night stand? Last night she'd felt so close to him. Today she had learned, over and over, that she didn't know him at all.

Avery, in her gloating, had insinuated that something sexual happened between her and Ben. What had she promised him, and what had he promised her in return?

Claire punched in the call. Ben's phone rang and rang, until finally his voicemail kicked in. She disconnected without leaving a message and went into the kitchen to set the timer. Thirty minutes, that's what she'd allow herself. By then she should be weary of weeping and drained of tears.

YELLOW, THE COLOR OF WARNING, the color of a blond woman's hair. The woman picks up a brush whose bristles are made of treachery and smooths flaxen locks over bare breasts. Suddenly someone she cannot see seizes the hair. Invisible hands braid it into a thick rope and loop it into a noose around her neck. A bird, huge and dark, grabs the noose by its knot and the woman screams. Its stout wings are tipped with fire as it lifts her up and flies away with her.

The owner of the hands is as translucent as a shadow. It turns to the people waiting in line. A child, another child, a man, a woman. The shadow kneels by the first child and looks into her eyes. The eyes are two windows. One sees the past, the other sees the future. Both eyes are filled with blood. The shadow locks its unseeable hands on the child's shoulders. "Come with me," it croons. Its tongue, forked like a snake's, flicks over dry lips as it bends to bestow a kiss. "I love you."

Claire woke up screaming.

Chapter 24

Melissa!
    What a beautiful word, like music.

The woman with chocolate hair sang those syllables; she was addressing them to me.

Melissa! The sound was familiar, comforting. I wonder if that was my name?

The word echoes off the glass and hums in the corners. Melissa! Her saying it gave me hope, and listening to it encourages me.

Without it I would be feeling bleak and afraid.

The house has gone dark. The energy in here has turned hot, and it's slinking around the edges of the room. None of that is our doing, the two of us who are trapped here. Two people were here, and they're the ones who roiled the air. The pale woman with gold hair was addled with hope and desire. The man lying with her was also lying to her. I tried to warn her, but the only words she ever hears are the ones she wants to believe.

The other one who is trapped here has moved closer to me. I've been trying to sneak into his corner, but he's pushing me forward. Everything that's happened since chocolate-haired woman first arrived has changed him. Now I can feel him expand and grow stronger, and I'm so glad. I'm going to need his help very soon. I can't do this alone.

The energy is drawing back, gathering force, like the ocean forming a monstrous wave that will crash down and destroy everything in its path.

Not even on that night was I so frightened.

Chapter 25

"Where would I find books on dreams?" Claire asked the sales clerk, a woman in her fifties who had glasses perched on her nose and gray hair that was cropped short like a boy's.

"You mean advice how to live your dreams? Try self-help, it's behind the business section."

"No, I'm interested in interpreting dreams, the kind you have at night while you sleep."

"Oh, in that case you want the psychology section. Over there." She pointed to a section of blond wooden shelves near the racks of magazines and the little café.

Claire said her thanks and meandered through the store on a circular route, inhaling the fresh paper-and-ink smell, pausing to flip open a book when an alluring cover beckoned from a display tables. She'd awakened this morning feeling exhausted and out of sorts, as if the heat of her anger toward Avery and Ben had left her with a fever, and for her, bookstores were always soothing. On her way to work, she'd impulsively detoured to the Marin Book Emporium in search of solace and, she hoped, a few answers.

For the past five nights, she'd been wrenched out of sleep by a nightmare. All her life she'd experienced scream-dreams, but this was the first time she'd had so many in a row. Each night they'd become more vivid and disturbing, and now, for the first time, she was remembering more than bits and pieces when she awoke.

Last night and the night before, she'd felt as if she were witnessing actual events. She'd watched as the members of the LeGrande family were murdered. She wasn't quite sure exactly what this latest nightmare wanted to show her, with its snakes and dark birds and nooses, but it had left her with the same conviction that what she'd seen was real, not merely a construct of her imagination. Real and yet not real—more like watching a fantasy movie than a documentary film. She had been peering through lenses of symbol and metaphor, seeing the truth of the events, not the facts.

Arriving in the psychology section, she began to scan the shelves. Perhaps some of the volumes on these shelves would help her make sense of it all.

IT WAS LATE MORNING by the time she arrived at Golden Gate carrying the white plastic bag that held her new books. As she came off the elevator she took a wary look around for George but didn't see him. Thank God for that—she was in no mood for him to give her grief about tardiness or make sly digs about her sex life.

Avery wasn't there either, the little coward. Of course she didn't dare show up and face Claire.

But everyone else was present. She waved to Tess in her office and exchanged greetings with Marlene Murphy at the reception desk and Jeff Ortega, who was just coming out of the lounge with a mug of coffee and something wrapped in a napkin.

"Doughnut Day again," Jeff informed her, holding up the napkin to reveal chocolate sprinkles. "There's a few left if you want one."

"Wow, Golden Gate's on a roll. Escrow closings two days in a row. Congratulations, Jeff."

"Unfortunately, the congrats aren't mine. Delia won a double-header this week. She's the doughnut queen, just like yesterday." Jeff pointed with his doughnut to Delia Chan's desk. Delia peeked around a bouquet of roses and grinned. The flowers were probably a thank-you from her client.

Claire smiled back. The corners of her mouth fought against turning upward, and she hoped Delia couldn't tell. Her glum mood wasn't her colleague's fault. "Then my congratulations and admiration and envy all go to you."

Delia hooked her silky black hair behind her ears. "Be prepared when you close your own sale—nothing feels like the first time."

"How are things going with the LeGrande house?" Jeff asked. "Have any buyers seen a ghost yet?"

"Not that they've reported to me." A perfectly accurate answer. Jeff hadn't asked about her own experiences.

"Don't worry, someone will," Delia said. "Any house that has a history like that, people expect it to be haunted. If it's not, they're disappointed. This listing I had once—an old lady had died there. So many people asked if her spirit was hanging around that I was tempted to rig up a white sheet to come flying out a closet."

Claire nodded. "At the Monday Meeting, everybody warned me that buyers shy away from properties that are connected to a death."

Delia laughed. "Oh, I'm not talking about buyers. These were people out for a thrill. Just wait, you'll see."

Claire dropped the bookstore bag and her purse on her desk, checked her voicemail and went to fetch a doughnut. Only two were left, coconut and maple glaze. All at once, the act of choosing seemed overwhelming. She took them both and carried them into the privacy of the conference room.

All morning she'd put off calling Ben, that betrayer, that user, that trifler with emotions. She was afraid of what he might say to her, and even more afraid of what she might say to him. She'd hoped he would call her first, and she'd worn a jacket with big pockets that would hold her cell phone and let her grab it quickly when it rang. Every moment it didn't ring added to her wretchedness. She couldn't move forward until she knew the truth behind Avery's phone call, and she needed to have that explanation come directly from Ben. Fingers trembling, she punched in his number.

No answer on his cell phone. None on his home phone either. She left the same message on both: "Ben, it's Claire. Call me the instant you get this. It's urgent."

She sat at the rosewood table with her head in her hands. Then she slowly worked her way through both doughnuts, alternating bites of one with bites of the other, making herself savor each and every sugary, fattening morsel.

It didn't help. When she finished licking her fingers, she didn't feel any better. In fact, she probably felt worse. She balled up her napkin and swiped away at the crumbs she'd dropped on the tabletop.

"Claire?" The voice made her jump. Marlene was leaning in through the doorway. "Call for you. Should I put it through to the phone in here?"

Finally! Thank God.

"Ben Grant?" Claire's voice squeaked when she said his name, and she hoped Marlene didn't notice. "I've been expecting to hear from him."

"Nope, it's Wayne Burdick. He wanted Avery, but when I said she's not here, he asked to speak to you."

Her mood had just been uplifted. Now it sank like a rock. "The Gingerbread Man."

"Who?"

"Never mind. I'll take the call here. Thanks."

When the extension rang, she picked up the receiver. "Mr. Burdick? This is Claire Scanlan."

"Claire, I'm trying to reach your colleague, Avery Collier. She was supposed to call me first thing this morning, but I haven't heard from her. Do you know where she is or how I can get in touch with her?"

"No, I don't. But I'm happy to help you if there's something I can do."

She heard Burdick sigh. "Just pass along the message, will you? Tell her I want to talk to her."

So Avery and Ben were both incommunicado. As Claire hung up, a picture floated unbidden into her mind—the bedroom where she and Ben had shared such incredible passion and pleasure. Only now the woman in the bed wasn't Claire. She was a lying, scheming, conniving, manipulative blond bubblehead.

As she went back to her desk, Claire felt tired and headachy. Feeling this way was getting to be a bad habit. Not to mention the fact that the damn doughnuts were fighting a war inside her stomach.

Passing Tess's office door, she peeked in. Her boss had pencil in hand, reviewing what looked like financial statements. Today's chic suit was navy blue and had epaulets at the shoulder, making Tess look like a military commander. Claire straightened her posture and quickened her pace, determined to appear professional and productive.

First order of business—find other houses to show the Johansens. A professional wouldn't let a pair of willing buyers slip through her fingers. So what if they didn't want the LeGrande house. That didn't mean they weren't eager to buy a home; all she had to do was find the right one and they'd come running back.

She jotted down everything she could recall that Paul or Nadine had said about the place—compliments, complaints, offhand comments—and constructed a list of the features they seemed to looking for. Logging onto the Multiple Listing Service, she scrolled through the properties for sale. Surely there was one that matched the Johansens' requirements.

She came upon a photo of a Mill Valley cottage similar to Ben's. The distressing image of Ben and Avery in bed together popped back into her head. Then the image flickered, then zoomed in on Avery's face and—what was that? A noose of blond hair wrapped around her neck.

Claire tumbled back inside her nightmare. She dodged the flaming wings of the dark bird, darted away from the fork-tongued shadow with unseeable hands, hovered over the line of people waiting for the shadow's kiss. Two children, a man, a woman.

Then she felt herself blink, and the spinning subsided. She was sitting at her desk again. Everything was normal and ordinary except that she was out of breath and her heart was racing.

The words Melissa had whispered to her yesterday echoed in her head: *Be careful. The trouble is not yet over. You and others face grave danger.*

"Hey, Claire, you okay?" It was Jeff, coming to his desk with another cup of coffee.

Claire looked up, pushing back a lock of hair that had fallen over her face. "Sure, fine. Why?"

"For a second there you looked a little like you might be getting sick."

She managed a smile. "A momentary twinge, that's all. Guess I overdid it with the doughnuts."

Reassured, he chuckled. "If Delia keeps up her pace, we're all going to be on permanent sugar highs."

As he settled in at his desk, Claire reached for the bookstore bag she'd stashed under her desk. If her nightmares were going to disrupt her days as well as her nights, she might as well read up on ways to decode their secret meaning.

She had just flipped open the cover of the first book when Marlene's voice rang out: "Hey, have any of you heard from Avery today?"

"Nope," Jeff said.

"Not me," Delia echoed.

A man was standing in front of the reception desk, drumming fingers on the polished wood. Fair-haired, slim, medium tall. Claire was sure she'd never met him, yet he seemed familiar.

She got up and approached him. He was casually dressed—jeans, western-style plaid shirt, black cowboy boots—but there was air of money about him. Claire was willing to bet that every item of clothing bore an expensive designer label.

"Hi, I'm Claire Scanlan. Are you here about the LeGrande property? I'm the listing agent, but I know Avery's been working on that one too."

The man shook her hand but didn't smile. His gray eyes showed worry. "I'm Kurt Collier, Avery's brother."

"Pleased to meet you." That's why he looked familiar. He reminded her of Avery. Now that she was looking for it, the family resemblance was obvious, though Kurt had a smoothness, an aura of class, that his sister lacked. Just being related to her was reason enough to look worried, in Claire's opinion.

"Do you know where she is?" Kurt asked. "I'm a little concerned about her."

It was two in the afternoon. Surely Avery and Ben were out of that damn bed by now.

"I'm afraid I don't," she said. "She didn't tell me her schedule for today." Claire thought of the noose of hair and shivered.

"Me either," Marlene said. "But as I'm sure you know, Kurt, in this business we don't keep track of each other's comings and goings."

"What's made you worried?" Claire asked.

Kurt shifted his weight from one booted foot to the other. "I've been letting Avery stay with me these last few months while she gets settled. I left in April for an extended business trip in Europe."

"Europe," Marlene said dreamily. "Must be nice."

Claire glanced at her, then noticed the document on the computer screen. It bore a title: *The Case of the Desirable Debutante: Chapter 12*. So that was it; Marlene was a closet novelist, writing on company time. What genre, Claire wondered—mystery, romance or porn?

"A successful trip," Kurt said, drawing back Claire's attention. "But when I got home a couple of hours ago—well, something's not right. My place is a wreck, broken glass on the floor and stuff tossed all over. And my car's missing. Before I call the cops, I want to talk to Avery to see if she knows what happened. I don't want to get her in trouble. But she's not answering her cell. It won't even give me her voicemail."

The elevator chimed and they all turned to see who was arriving. Kurt let out a disappointed sigh when the door opened to reveal, not Avery, but George. He sauntered out, chomping on a candy bar. To Claire's annoyance, he wandered over to join the threesome at the reception desk. No one greeted him.

"The car that's gone," Marlene put in. "Is it a Porsche convertible? Black with a tan leather interior."

"That's the one. How did you know? I'm going to be real upset if that baby's been stolen."

"Hey," George said as he wiped chocolate from his mouth with the back of his hand. "That's Avery's car. Something happen to it?"

Kurt frowned. "Avery's car!"

"Well, we thought so," Marlene said. "She's been driving it the whole time she's worked here. Don't worry. When you find Avery, you'll find the car."

"But she has her own car. A Toyota Corolla. I bought her a used one when she got here from Texas."

Marlene made a face. "Hmmph. If I had a choice, I'd pick your Porsche too. Avery probably took a client to see a property."

"I hope so," Kurt said, though he didn't look as though his mind had been set at rest. "It's just that, well, I probably shouldn't say this, but she gets herself into scrapes from time to time. That's what makes me apprehensive."

He looked around and Claire realized he was addressing the whole office. Jeff and Delia were avidly listening in, and Tess had come out of her office.

Claire said, "I don't know if this helps, but I spoke to her last night. She sounded, well, upbeat would be a good way to put it." There were more precise words she could use—gloating, triumphant, high as a kite—but she didn't want to invite questions about the purpose of Avery's call.

"So did I," Kurt said. "I phoned from New York and she sounded okay. What time did you talk to her?"

"I'm not sure . . . wait, I do know. The eleven o'clock news was just over."

"So if anything went wrong, it must have happened this morning." He shook his head. "I can't believe it. Ironic how that timing worked, isn't it. Everything goes okay the whole time I'm gone and then falls apart at the last second."

Tess stepped forward, taking charge. "Of course we're ready to help in any way we can, Mr. Collier. But I'm sure Avery's fine. There's no real reason to think there's a problem."

Kurt smiled bleakly. "Maybe you don't have a reason. But I know my sister."

And I had Avery show up in a scream-dream, Claire thought. A feeling of dread began to gnaw at the pit of her stomach.

"Excuse me, I'm going to go make a call," she said. "I know someone who might have seen Avery more recently than any of us."

She slipped into the conference room again and sank into a chair. Damn it, Ben, you better answer this time. As she took her phone out of her pocket, it rang in her hand, and she jumped. "Hello?"

"Claire," said the caller. "Can you get to Spuntino's Deli right away?"

"Ben? Is that you? I was just about to call you. Again," she added pointedly. "Is Avery with you? Her brother is here and—"

"Avery? No, I'm calling to talk about her. I need help, Claire. Can you take Eden for the night? I need a place to hide her."

The tension in Claire's gut tightened. "Hide her? From what?"

"Her father. Leo Hollister called this morning, threatening to take her away. Said he's coming to the house and won't leave without her. Thank God she was at her arts-and-crafts class, but I don't dare take her home. I've brought her to Spuntino's. So far she thinks we just came for a treat. I haven't told her about Leo. Before I do, I need to know she's got a safe place to stay. Somewhere he won't find her, with someone she likes and I can trust. It can't be one of her friends, they're too easy to track down."

"Oh, God. Of course I'll take her, Ben. Are you certain there's no way Hollister might think of me?"

"I can't see how, unless he was lurking outside the house Wednesday night when you were there. Did you see anything suspicious in the morning when you left?"

"No, nothing." Though she'd been in such a spin at the time that Hollister could have been standing by Ben's gate and she probably wouldn't have noticed.

"We made such an effort to keep him from finding out where we live. I can't believe he found us so quickly."

"Spuntino's, you say. I'm on my way."

She ran back to her desk, loaded the books into their bag, grabbed her purse. As she rushed past the group assembled at the reception desk, everyone pelted her with questions.

"Who did you call?"

"What did you find out?"

"Did you reach Avery?"

"Do you know where she is?"

"Where are you going?"

Claire punched the elevator button. "Sorry, it's an emergency. I'm sure Avery will turn up soon." She didn't add, like the proverbial bad penny.

The elevator doors opened and she jumped inside.

Chapter 26

Stepping through the door into Spuntino's, Claire was greeted by a feast for her nose—the pungent odor of garlic, sharp scents of cheeses, herbaceous smells of basil and olive oil, the yeasty aroma of fresh-baked bread. One side of a wide aisle was lined with glass cases filled with deli goodies and pastries. Shelves on the other side displayed jars and bottles and boxes of exotic and expensive gourmet treats. Yet none of it tempted her, even though she had eaten nothing so far today except for the two doughnuts. She had no appetite; anxiety was twisting her stomach into a knot.

At the rear of the store was a small seating area, a few tables inside and a few more in a tiny, fern-filled garden. Claire found Ben and Eden sitting outside at a round wrought-iron table, the only customers braving the gray, chilly weather. Ben had on a corduroy shirt to help block the cold. Eden's pink hoodie sweatshirt matched the puddle of melted gelato in the small metal bowl in front of her. She was aimlessly stirring the liquid with a spoon. By her place were some colored pencils and a drawing pad, the top sheet still blank.

Ben rose from his chair when he saw her. "Claire! Thanks for coming." He gave her a hug. She responded by standing there stiffly, and she turned her head when he tried to kiss her cheek. Her reaction seemed to bewilder him. "What's wrong?"

"We'll talk later," Claire told him, nodding toward his niece. She wasn't doing this favor for Ben. She was doing it for this girl who'd had so much sadness in her short life. "Hello, Eden."

Eden didn't look up. "Hi, Claire."

Ben gave her a long questioning look, then said, "I need some coffee. May I bring you some?"

"Please," Claire said. "Milk, no sugar."

"Would you like anything, princess?" he asked Eden. "More ice cream?"

"No, thanks." She set down the spoon and slouched in her seat, thrusting her hands deep into the hoodie's pockets.

"While we were waiting for you, I explained to Eden what's going on," Ben said.

"Good," Claire replied. "When you come back you can explain it to me."

He started to say something more, then shrugged and went into the shop.

There were only two chairs at their table. Claire found one at another table and dragged it across the mossy brick patio. When she sat down, the metal mesh seat sent a wave of cold through her summer-weight trousers.

"I hear I'm going to have an honored guest tonight," she said to Eden.

"Who's that?"

"You."

Eden looked up at her for the first time. "What do you mean, I'm an honored guest?"

"When Ben asked if you could stay with me tonight, I got really excited. I haven't had a sleepover in a long time." True, she'd spent the night with Ben, but that wasn't the kind of sleepover she meant. "I'm sorry about the circumstances, but I'm delighted that you and I will have a chance to spend some time together."

"Ben says Leo the Creep got out of jail. He wants to take me away with him. So I have to hide."

"That's probably a good idea for a day or two, until the situation can be worked out."

Eden tugged on a strand of hair that had worked loose from her ponytail. "I'm never going to live with Leo. Not ever."

"That's true," said Ben, who at that moment had come back into the garden. He was carrying a tray that bore three pale green paper cups. "Why should you go live with him when you and I have a good home together? Here, I know you said you didn't want anything but I brought you some hot chocolate."

"Thank you," Eden said, taking the cup he handed her.

Claire took hers too. The warmth in her hands felt good. "So what's the plan?"

Ben set his own cup on the table and sat down, putting the tray aside. "I'm not sure I've thought it through well enough for it to qualify as a plan. I can't take Eden home in case Leo's waiting there to cause trouble. Even in prison, he may have had ways to find out who her friends are, or mine, so I don't want risk having her stay with any of them. But you're new in our lives, Claire. There's no way he could know about you. You're the best solution."

"As I said on the phone, I'm happy to take her." At least Ben preferred her to Avery when it came to entrusting his niece with someone.

"We're both grateful," he said, and Eden nodded. "Do you mind taking her shopping? She'll need some things since we couldn't go home and pack a bag. A toothbrush, maybe a change of underwear." He pulled out his billfold and gave her a sheaf of twenties. "Here's. a hundred dollars. Keep track of what you spend and if it's more than that, I'll reimburse you."

Eden perked up just a little. She poked at a smudge on the front of her hoodie. "Can I get a new top? This one's got ice cream drips."

"Sure," Ben said. "Why not?"

"What will you be doing tonight? While I'm at Claire's."

"I'm going to go back to the house and wait to see what Leo does. If he shows up, I'll call the police. I've already talked to our lawyer about a restraining order to keep him away from you, but since the weekend's coming up, it may be take some time to get one issued."

"What about Avery?" Claire asked before she could stop herself.

"What about her?" Ben looked puzzled, as if Claire had changed the subject.

But she really hadn't. She was still talking about Ben's plans for the evening. Her real question was, will Avery keep you company as you wait for Leo? Spend the night with you, now that Eden won't be there to know? However, with Eden right there she certainly wasn't going to ask outright.

She took a long swallow of coffee before she said, "Avery phoned me last night and said . . . well, that you were going to take the listing for the house away from me and give it to her."

"That's ridiculous. Why would I do that?"

Because she slept with you and you wanted to return the favor in some way. How's that for a possible reason? Still, she tried to feel reassured by his response. "So it's not true?"

"Of course not. You've been doing an excellent job." He put his hand on Claire's.

"Thanks. But my point is, people have been looking for Avery today. No one knows where she is. Her brother showed up and he's worried. Since you were with her last night—"

"No, I wasn't," he said. She liked the words, but she didn't like the way he looked away from her when he said it.

Eden said, "Are you talking about the lady who came to the house yesterday? The one with long blond hair."

Ben nodded. "That's the one."

"She came over the day before too." Eden took another sip of her hot chocolate.

"I have no idea where she is today," Ben said. "She said nothing yesterday that would give me a clue. Why is everyone so concerned? She probably decided to go somewhere for a long weekend. If Monday rolls around and no one's heard from her, I could see it, but this is a matter of hours, not days."

"I don't know," Claire said. "I just have a bad feeling." *Because in my dream, that long hair Eden mentioned was wrapped like a noose around Avery's neck.*

Ben slid a small photo out of the pocket of his corduroy shirt and gave it to Claire. "Here, this is Leo Hollister. There's no reason to think you'll see him, but just in case, it would be a good idea to know what he looks like."

Claire studied the picture. Gray eyes stared back at her, cold as stones. The photo was a head shot, badly lit. The contrast was too sharp, throwing parts of the face into deep shadow. Hollister looked thin, almost gaunt. His hair, the color of dead grass, was in need of mowing. A couple of days' worth of whiskers showed on his cheeks and a meager mustache lined his upper lip.

"Don't tell me I look like him," Eden warned.

"You don't. You never could. Not on the worst day you'll ever have in your life." Putting the photo in her purse, Claire pushed back her chair and stood. "You ready to be my honored guest?"

Eden nodded. "Let's go."

Ben caught them both in an embrace. "My two favorite ladies. Have fun tonight, and take care." He gave them each a kiss, a light one for Eden on her forehead and a deeper, more lingering one on Claire's lips.

The kiss felt genuine, but Claire knew from experience how meaningless a kiss that seemed heartfelt could be. She had trusted Zach's kisses, his embraces, his passionate lovemaking right up until the moment she discovered he was treating Little Ms. Lawyer the very same way.

His two favorite ladies, Ben called them. At least when it came to Eden, she could believe he was telling the truth.

EDEN SLID another slice of pepperoni pizza from the box of Claire's coffee table and put it her paper plate.

"That was a super movie," she said as she settled back next to Claire on the sofa.

"I thought you might like it." Claire hit the button on the remote to eject the DVD. Pizza and movies was the best way she could think of to pass the evening with a ten-year-old girl she barely knew. *The Princess Diaries* had turned out to be a good choice. "Want to watch another one?"

"Maybe in a minute." Eden held the paper plate under her chin as she bit off the tip of the pizza wedge. She'd explained to Claire that she was eating that way to keep tomato sauce from splattering on her new sweater, which she had insisted on wearing home from the store. Claire had suggested using a paper napkin as a bib, but Eden had rolled her eyes at the total lameness of that idea.

The girl had perked up a bit during the shopping expedition. The two of them made a game of seeing how far they could stretch Ben's hundred dollars, buying a toothbrush, a hairbrush, scrunchies for her ponytail, panties and socks, a big T-shirt to sleep in, and two tops. That left just enough for pizza and a couple of DVD rentals. As they were leaving the mall, Eden spotted this sweater, lavender with pink stripes, and fell in love. Claire bought it for her as a gift.

They'd seen no sign of anyone resembling the photo of Leo Hollister, either at the mall or around Claire's apartment complex. As soon as they were inside, Claire locked the door behind them and went around to make sure all the windows were secured. Then she ordered the pizza, an extra large in case Lindsay would be joining them. While Eden got out paper plates and napkins, Claire poured Coke for her guest and opened a bottle of wine for Lindsay and herself. Just as the pizza arrived, Lindsay called with the news that the hot stockbroker had shown up at her office with flowers and an invitation to dinner. So Claire and Eden were spending the evening alone.

Now Eden looked thoughtful, her mouth chewing pizza while her eyes stared at something far away.

"Which movie would you like to see next?" Claire asked.

"I'm deciding." The girl turned to face her. "Did you ever want to be a princess? I think it would be cool."

"I've noticed that Ben calls you princess sometimes."

"Yeah, but that doesn't mean I'm a real princess."

"What would it take to make you a real princess?"

"Three things." She ticked them off on her fingers. "Your parents have to be a king and queen. You have to be beautiful. And you have to have jewels."

Claire laughed. "I don't think beauty is a requirement. And you don't become a princess just because you have jewels. It's probably the other way around—you get the jewels because you're a princess."

"You have good jewels for a princess."

"I do?"

"You know that purple necklace you had on when you came to our house for dinner? That's a good princess necklace."

Her amethyst crystal beads. "I guess you're right. I never thought of it that way."

Eden sat up straighter. "Can I see it?"

"Sure. I'll go get it." She went to the bedroom, took the velvet case out of her bureau, and brought it back. "Here you go."

Eden ran her fingers over the soft nap of the box and flipped up the hinged top. Only a single lamp was burning in the living room, but the amethysts caught enough light to sparkle. "Ooh, that's so pretty. Can I try it on?"

Claire lifted the necklace out of the box and fastened it around Eden's neck. "It's lovely. Here, come look at yourself."

Near the front door hung a mirror. She and Lindsay used it to make last-minute checks for uncombed hair or smeared lipstick before they left the apartment. She led Eden there.

"Wow," Eden said admiringly. "It goes perfect with my new sweater. Dark purple on light purple."

"Very nice." The colors did go well together, though the sweater was too casual a style for the necklace. Claire saw nothing to be gained by pointing that out.

"Where did you get it?" Eden asked as they went back to the sofa.

"It belonged to my mother. I wear it for good luck sometimes, because it makes me feel close to her."

"She died when you were little, didn't she? That's what you said the other night."

"That's right, she did."

"I have some of my mom's jewelry too. Ben's saving it for me, for when I get older."

"That's good. It's important to have things to remember her by."

Eden fingered the amethyst crystals. "Is it magic?"

"The necklace? Not that I'm aware of." In fact, the thought had never crossed Claire's mind.

"It looks like the kind of the necklace that would be magic. I bet you just have to know the right set of magic words."

"Maybe so. I don't know any magic words though."

"Me either. If I knew any, know what I'd do?"

"No idea. Tell me."

"I'd—I'd make my mom be alive again. I'd make all of them be alive, Mom and Stefan and Trevor and Melissa." Eden blinked, and Claire saw a tear slide down her cheek.

She put her arm around Eden's shoulder and drew her close. "Oh, sweetie, I wish there was some kind of magic that could do that."

"That girl in the movie, the one who finds out she's really a princess? She reminds me a lot of Melissa."

"Anne Hathaway, the actress? Melissa looked like her?" Claire hadn't noticed any such resemblance when she looked at Melissa's photos on the Internet. The person she thought Eden's stepsister looked like was Claire herself.

Eden nodded. "Melissa was really pretty like her, and she had that same kind of long dark hair. The princess's mouth is bigger though. She was going to be an actress too. Melissa, I mean."

"So was I, once upon a time," Claire told her. "That's something she and I had in common. I even started out in college as a theater major, before my grandmother persuaded me to study something more practical."

"She should have told you to follow your dreams," Eden said solemnly. "That's what my mother always told us."

"Good advice," Claire agreed.

"Melissa wanted to be an actress, and I'm going to be an artist, and Stefan was an architect. He used to say everyone in the family would have an A-list profession. Trevor didn't know what he wanted to be, so Stefan would make up jobs for him. He'd say Trevor could be an acrobat, or an astronaut, or an animal trainer, or an apricot picker, or an ambulance chaser, or an automatic pilot."

"An automatic pilot?" Claire repressed a smile.

"Yeah. I don't even know what that is. But Trevor liked the idea. I remember one time Stefan told him that's what he could be, and Trevor said, 'Yeah, I'm going stay an automatic pilot for the rest of my life.' " She bit her lip. "I bet he would have been a good one too."

"I'm sure he would have."

Eden found a napkin that been stuffed between two couch cushions and used it to dab her eyes, which had suddenly gone damp. "I don't know why everyone always says Trevor killed them."

That caught Claire by surprise. "You don't think he did?"

Eden clamped her eyes shut. She was trembling and Claire hugged her tighter.

"Eden? Are you okay, sweetie?"

Claire's cell phone rang. Her first thought was to ignore it. But what if it was Ben? If he couldn't reach her, he'd worry that something bad had happened, that Leo Hollister had caught up with her and Eden.

She gently withdrew her arms. "Let me get this, sweetie. I'll be right back."

The phone was on the kitchen counter. She thumbed the talk button and said hello.

"Claire Scanlan?" A male voice. Not Ben's. Could Hollister have tracked them down?

"Yes," she replied warily.

"This is Martin Roncallo, on Highview Lane. Listen, you better come up here right away. Something strange is going on at the vacant house."

Her grip tightened on the phone. "The LeGrande house? What you do you mean, strange?"

"Peculiar noises, weird lights—I can't tell what's happening." Roncallo's voice sounded rushed and nervous. "I went over and took a look, but I couldn't find any way to get in. No smashed windows or anything. If someone broke in, I don't know how they managed it."

"I appreciate the alert, Martin, but you need to call the sheriff's department, not me."

"I did that, but who knows when they'll get here? We're in the middle of nowhere. Everybody out here complains about how slow the emergency response times are. And a strange noise in an empty house isn't going to be at the top of their priority list. By the time the cops arrive, the house could be trashed, or burning down."

"What could I possibly do?"

"The house is your responsibility, isn't it? You're the one with access to the lockbox. You'll have me as back-up. Together, we can probably handle the situation until the cops arise. Scare off the trespassers or whatever."

"How about Ben Grant? Did you call him?"

"Tried to. Left a voicemail. Who knows when he'll get it. When I couldn't reach him, I figured I'd better call you."

Claire tried to think it through. She felt pulled to go up there. She'd been entrusted with an irreplaceable architectural treasure; what a tragedy if something happened to the house on her watch—especially if she ignored a request for help and chose instead to watch another DVD. Besides, despite what Martin said, the police probably would arrive by the time she could get there.

Martin's voice summoned her from her thoughts. "Claire?"

"Okay. I guess you're right. I'm on my way."

Claire rang off and quickly punched in Ben's number. A busy signal. She returned to the living room, where Eden regarded her with wide frightened eyes.

"What's going on?" Eden said. "Why do you need to call the police? Did something happen to Ben?"

"No, sweetie, I'm sure Ben's fine. But we need to go to your old house and check something out."

"No!" Eden pulled back into a corner of the sofa, drew in her knees, and lowered her head. She looked as if she were trying to protect herself from a beating. "I won't go."

"I know it's hard, Eden, but you have to come. I can't leave you here by yourself." Claire sat beside her and rubbed the girl's back, the only part of her that was exposed.

Eden's voice was muffled. "I'm never going to that house again."

"Tell you what, sweetie, we're stopping first at your friend Lily's house. That was her dad on the phone. You can stay there with her while he and I go make sure the other house is okay."

Claire heard soft sounds of crying.

"I wouldn't ask you do this if it wasn't an emergency. It will be a very brave thing for you to do. And I know Lily will be happy to see you."

Finally Eden sat up. She rubbed her face with the sleeves of her new sweater.

"I'll come with you," she said. "I don't want to, but I will."

"Thank you."

"But only to Lily's. I'm not going back to my old house." She ran her hand along the string of amethyst beads. "Can I wear the necklace? For good luck."

Claire started to protest. She could just see it getting broken or lost as the two girls played princess. She didn't dare take that risk. The necklace was much too precious to her.

But looking at the plea in Eden's eyes, she relented.

"Sure. For good luck. We'll put it away when we get back home. Come on, we need to leave now."

Claire held out her hand and smiled at Eden as she grabbed hold.

Chapter 27

All the daylight had bled from the sky by the time Claire turned the Volkswagen onto Highway One. She took a quick glance at Eden in the passenger seat. The girl was curled up, huddled against the door. Her eyes were closed, but Claire didn't think she was asleep. Too much tension in the way she was holding her body.

Twisting up the hill, they left the last of the houses behind and entered a thick grove of eucalyptus trees. Fog obscured the treetops and swirled out above the road. Claire shivered and turned up the heater. She should have worn something heavier than the cardigan she'd thrown on over her T-shirt and jeans.

They reached the crest and began the long descent toward the ocean, negotiating the series of sharp S-curves. Claire hugged the right-hand side of the road, the upslope side. To the left, the land dropped away into a deep valley.

Eden made a sound, something between a sigh and a whimper, but she didn't stir. Claire felt alone in the darkness, just the hum of the tires and the drone of the engine for company. They had encountered almost no other cars. A good thing. This road was treacherous enough with having to second-guess other drivers.

Swinging around a switchback, she saw a large tree looming straight in front of her. Its bark was torn, and broken branches hung at crooked angles, like arms about to reach out and grab her.

She jerked the wheel but it wouldn't turn. "Oh God! Eden, hang tight!"

The tree rushed closer. Claire braced herself against the impact. But at the instant she expected to crash, she found herself tangled in the branches, looking down as the car plummeted down the steep slope.

Only it wasn't her Volkswagen that she saw falling. It was a different car—a small, black convertible.

Before she could react, she dropped back into her own driver's seat. The road swung to the right and so did the Volkswagen, holding firmly in its lane.

In her rearview mirror she thought she saw a noose and its victim dangling from one of the branches. *Avery.*

She felt like she'd been punched in the gut. Her head began to spin and her stomach heaved. She was afraid she was about to be sick.

"Claire?" Eden sat bolt upright. "What happened? You yelled."

"Nothing happened, we're fine."

Eden coiled around in her seat to look out the rear window. "We almost hit that tree."

"No, we didn't. Don't worry, sweetie, everything's okay." A lie, but an excusable one, Claire thought. Truth was, she didn't feel anywhere close to fine. She felt queasy and dizzy and upset that there was no place to pull over and catch her breath.

The fog turned to drizzle. Claire flipped on her windshield wipers and was calmed a little by their *swish-swish* rhythm.

They were approaching the intersection with the road leading into Mariners Beach. A country store sat at the corner, the sole commercial enterprise in the village. The sign was dark, which meant the store was closed. A single street lamp illuminated the parking lot, its light haloed by mist.

Claire steered into the graveled lot and stopped as wooziness overtook her again. She rested her head on the steering wheel until she felt steadier.

She got out her cell phone.

"Who are you calling?" Eden asked nervously.

"The police," Claire told her. "I want to tell them I think a car went off the road back there where that tree was." She also wanted to make sure that officers were on their way to the LeGrande house. And she'd try again to call Ben.

Eden was clutching the amethysts around her neck. "Why do you think so?"

"Just a guess, sweetie. There were some broken branches, and—damn."

"What's wrong?"

Claire snapped her phone shut. "I can't get a signal."

"Was somebody in the car? Are they dead?"

Her mind flashed on the noose hanging from the tree. It marked Avery's grave, she was certain of it. She could almost see Avery's body lying broken in the tangled wreckage of her brother's car.

You and others face grave danger.

Was Avery one of the others? The way she drove, an accident would be no surprise. But what if someone had deliberately forced her off the road?

"I hope no one's dead, sweetie. I'll call from Lily's house, and the police will go find out what happened. If anything happened at all." She turned the key in the ignition. "Let's go."

Eden was bent over, arms wrapped tightly around herself. "Maybe we should turn around and go home."

Claire made herself sound calm. "We'll go home just as soon as the police make sure everything is okay at your old house.

"The same police?"

"Different officers, I'm sure. Checking the house won't take long. Of course by the time I'm done, you'll be having so much fun with Lily that you won't want to leave."

Eden sat up again. A smile flickered on her lips. "I'm glad I'll be seeing Lily."

"Me too." What really made Claire glad was that she had a safe place for Eden to stay while she was next door at the LeGrande house.

Back on the coastal road, they rode in silence as Claire replayed the last few days in her mind. In her phone call last night Avery had mentioned the LeGrande house, saying it was haunted after all. Had she gone up to the house? Maybe she'd placed the call from there. If so, it was possible that she'd had an accident on the way home, going off the road and plummeting down the steep hillside. But what evidence did Claire have? Nothing except the strange sick feeling that hit her when she saw that broken tree.

Besides, Avery claimed she'd just been with Ben. And Ben had been at his own house with Eden. Claire recalled how Ben had made sure Eden was asleep before enfolding Claire in his embrace on the living room sofa. Had he done the same with Avery, this time letting passion carry them to the ultimate fulfillment?

She was about to ask Eden what time she'd gone to sleep last night. Before she could, the girl broke the silence in the car.

"Do I have to be nice to Lily's dad?"

"It's generally a good strategy to be nice to people," Claire replied.

"Even if you don't like them?"

"Even then. That can make it harder though."

The couple of times Claire had met Martin Roncallo, he'd had struck her as pleasant enough. But she had revised that opinion down a few notches when Eden told her and Ben about the way Martin taunted her for having a jailbird father.

"Just remember," she added, "being nice doesn't mean you have to let people tease you or push you around. It's important to stand up for yourself."

No response but a deep sigh. Claire figured Eden must be girding herself for her first visit to Highview Lane since the night her family was killed. Perhaps now was not the best time to ask about last night.

Looking over, she thought she saw the glisten of tears on Eden's cheeks but there was so little light in the car that she couldn't be sure. She set a reassuring hand on the girl's knee. "It's a brave thing you're doing, Eden, coming with me to your old house."

Eden put her own hand on top of Claire's. "Can I tell you something?"

"Of course."

"I saw it."

"Saw what?"

"That night when they all got killed."

"What do you mean? Ben said you were at Lily's."

"I was. But then . . . I got mad at Lily's dad because he was saying mean things. So I said I was going to the bathroom. We were all watching a movie, like we did tonight, you and me. It was a really exciting movie so I didn't think they'd would notice if I was gone for a while."

"You're saying you went home?"

"I was going to get Stefan and make him come back and tell Lily's dad he had to be nice. It was raining and I got soaking wet. The front door was locked. I rang the bell but nobody came. So I went around the house to the deck. Sometimes my mom and Stefan forgot to lock the double doors there that go into the big room."

Her hand tightened on Claire's and she sniffled. "What happened then?" Claire asked, adding, "You don't have to tell me. Only if you want to."

Eden gulped and went on. "At night when you're on the deck you can see right into that room like it's a movie. But a person inside can't see out very well. The glass gets all full of reflections."

"Right. I know how that works."

"I ran straight for the doors so I could get out of the rain. But they were locked too. I was going to pound on the glass but first I looked in to see if anyone was in the room to let me in. There was a fire in the fireplace and it looked all cozy. And then . . . and then I saw my m-mom. She was lying in front of the fireplace. At first I thought she was just resting and getting warm. She liked to do that—like a cat, she said. But she was curled up funny and she had b-blood on her."

Her voice quavered. "Then I saw T-Trevor. He was on the carpet in the middle of the room. He was all bloody too."

"What about the others? Stefan and Melissa."

"They weren't there yet. But a man was sitting on the couch. He was holding a g-gun."

"What! A man—who?" The fifth person. The nightmare was right.

Eden shook her head. Her ponytail brushed Claire's hand. "I don't know. I never saw him before. He had a big brown beard."

Not Ben. Even though they hadn't met often, living a continent apart, surely Eden would have recognized her step-uncle. Claire was surprised by the intensity of her relief.

"The man was smiling," Eden said. "He had his arms stretched out on the back of the couch like he was all relaxed, and in one hand he had the gun. I was so scared. He looked right at the double doors and I was afraid he could see me after all."

"What did you do?"

"I couldn't move. I was too frightened. I stood there getting wetter and wetter. A couple of minutes later I heard a noise. I thought maybe it was the wind but the man heard it too. He got up and crouched down behind the arm of the couch, on the side close to me so no one could see him from the entrance gallery. That's when Stefan and Melissa came in from the garage, all happy and laughing."

Eden pulled her hand away from Claire's and covered her eyes. "They saw the others on the floor, and Stefan ran to my mom, and Melissa ran to Trevor. The man jumped out. He yelled something at Stefan and shot him dead."

"Oh, sweetie. I'm so sorry . . . "

"Melissa screamed. The man got between her and the front door, so she ran to the double doors where I was. She was about to open them and run out, but the man shot her. She—she crumpled up right at my feet, only the g-glass was between us."

They had reached Highview Lane. Claire turned off the highway into the narrow dead-end road.

"I was afraid the man would look at her and see me there. So I ran back to Lily's as quick as I could. Her dad had already called nine-one-one. The rain and wind were letting up so he heard the last two g-gunshots."

A dark-colored sedan was parked in front of the first house on the lane. Claire halted her car behind it, at the edge of the road. Cutting the engine, she pulled Eden toward her. The girl fell against her shoulder and dissolved into sobs.

The drizzle quickly coated the car windows with moisture, diminishing and distorting her ability to see outside. Claire and Eden were shut into their own tiny, isolated world. Claire did the best she could to comfort the girl, though she could feel tears welling up in her own eyes.

Her dream was confirmed again. Two shots, which killed Trevor and Jacqueline. Then an interval before two more shots took out Stefan and Melissa.

Finally Eden's weeping subsided. Claire reached to open the glove compartment, where she kept a packet of tissues. After a bit of fumbling she found it and offered it to her passenger.

"Thank you." Eden wiped her eyes and blew her nose.

"May I ask a question?" Claire asked. When Eden nodded she said, "Why didn't you tell anyone? All this time, people have been blaming poor Trevor."

"I was going to, but . . . well, I was scared. Lily's dad got all crazy because I was outside when he heard the gun go off. He didn't know I went back to my house. He thought I just went outside for a minute for, you know, some fresh air."

"Even though it was raining so hard?"

"I used to walk in the rain a lot. I thought it was fun. Only, ever since then I don't like it any more."

"That's understandable. I wouldn't like it either."

Claire felt the girl shiver. "Before I could explain, the police came. He made me and Lily wait in her room with the door locked, and he went with them to see what happened. By the time they got back, they had this whole story figured out about how Trevor killed everyone and then shot himself."

"Did the police ask you about what was going on in your family?"

"A little bit. But I didn't say very much and they stopped asking."

"Why not tell them?"

"What if the man wanted to kill me too? If I told about him, he might come find me."

"The police want to help keep you safe. But they can't do that if they don't know what really happened."

"It was too late. Everybody in the world knew it was Trevor." Eden was hanging on tight to the amethysts. "I wasn't sure any more if I saw the man kill them or if my mind made it up. Maybe I was too dramatized to remember it right. Maybe nobody would believe me."

"I think the word you want is traumatized," Claire said. "And I believe you."

She gave Eden a hug, and Eden hugged her back. Soon the girl stopped trembling.

"There's a water bottle in the cup holder," Claire told her. "Why don't you dampen a Kleenex and wipe your face? I'm going to try my phone again. The reception might be better up here on the ridge. Then we'll go on to Lily's. We're almost there."

While Eden followed her suggestion, Claire fiddled with the phone. Still no signal.

She started the car again and drove the short distance of Highview Lane. "Tell me something, Eden. What did the shooter look like? Do you remember?"

Eden hesitated before she replied. "He had a beard, like I said. I sort of forgot until yesterday."

"Ben said you got upset yesterday. Is that why, because something reminded you of the man?"

"I guess. I don't want to talk about it any more. There's Lily's driveway."

Claire made the turn and stopped in front of the Roncallos' garage door. No sign of any police vehicles. Maybe they had gone straight to the LeGrande house.

Martin and Lily's home was built of redwood, stone, and glass. It resembled its next-door neighbor, though it was considerably smaller and much less breathtaking, Lights at the front entrance were ablaze to welcome them.

They got out of the Volkswagen. Mist dampened Claire's face. The wind carried the smell of salt and seaweed, hinting at all the mysterious life that dwelled in the ocean.

Eden stood still for a moment, arms folded to protect her from the chill. She looked toward the house where she had lived, where her family had died. It was shrouded in darkness, and Claire figured that even in daylight the stand of pines and the configuration of the ridge would hide most of the house from view. But she was certain that Eden was seeing it with stark clarity.

She put an arm around the girl's shoulders. "Come on. Let's go see Lily."

The front door opened before they could ring the bell. Martin Roncallo stood there, hands extended in greeting. The grin beneath his thick mustache looked frozen in place, and his eyes refused to look at them. "Glad you're finally here. I've been worried, thought you'd never make it. Come in, come in." He swallowed hard, then grinned again.

Claire shivered. Something was wrong.

"Eden, don't go in there," she warned, just as Martin caught Eden in a hug. He made a quarter turn that carried her across the threshold.

Lily appeared in the foyer behind them. "Eden!" she squealed, and the two friends fell into each other's arms, blond and brunette heads pressing together.

As they pulled apart Lily looked up and caught Claire's eye. Her cheeks were blotchy and stained with tears.

"Eden!" Claire called. "Come with me."

A shadow stirred inside the house, and someone else came into view. When Eden saw the man, her face filled with terror. She ran back and threw herself against Claire.

Claire heard Lily shriek as the man grabbed her and placed the barrel of a gun against her ear.

"Eden's staying here, Claire," Wayne Burdick said. "And so are you. Or Lily dies."

Chapter 28

Claire's heart jumped as she pulled a trembling Eden close. The girl buried her face against Claire's shoulder.

Her nightmare flashed into her mind. This was what her latest scream-dream was trying to tell her. It was not just showing her Avery's death, but warning of other deaths to come, including her own.

Four people at the mercy of a shadowy figure. A child, a child, a man, a woman. Eden, Lily, Martin, and herself.

A warning, but no clue about how to prevent any of them from dying. What was she going to do?

"Get in here!" Burdick demanded.

Clutching Eden, Claire angled herself against the doorframe as she tried to catch her breath and think. If she could keep the door from closing and trapping them inside, they might have a better chance to escape. Though the odds seemed nearly insurmountable, so long as Burdick was holding the gun to Lily's head.

"Please, Claire," Martin begged. "You have to come in. He means it when he says he'll kill her."

Claire didn't move. She looked not at him but at Burdick. "Why? What is this all about?"

The overhead light in the foyer made the sweat glisten on Burdick's forehead. "It's a trade. Give me Eden and I'll let Lily go free."

Lily was crying again. "Daddy," she whimpered.

"Quiet, you," Burdick demanded, jabbing her head with the gun barrel.

Martin stood there looking helpless, clenching and unclenching his fists. "I'm sorry," he said to Claire. "When he showed up here and made me call you—well, you see why I had to do it."

"You're in real estate, Claire, you know how deals work," Burdick said. "Each side gives something and each side gets something in return."

Eden mumbled something into Claire's jacket. Claire couldn't make out the words. She bent her head closer to Eden's. "What, sweetie? Tell me again."

"It's him. The m-man who sh-shot everybody."

"Shut up!" Burdick yelled. "What is she saying?"

Claire's eyes scanned the foyer. Floor paved with terra-cotta tiles. A small table with a mirror above it. A pasty-looking Martin Roncallo slumped against the wall. She saw nothing she could use as a weapon.

"I don't understand," she said. "Just because Ben Grant won't sell you the house you want—"

"He damn well better if he wants Eden alive. That's the trade I'm offering. Lily for Eden. Eden for the house."

"But there are so many good houses, Wayne. What could possibly make this one so important?" She mentally inventoried what she had in her purse. Nothing heavy. Nothing sharper than a nail file or car keys.

"It's my house!" Burdick's face flushed. "Don't you get that? All those ideas that made him famous—they're mine. He stole them. He stole everything from me!"

Red, color of blood, color of anger, color of fire. Out of the flames emerges a shimmering house of glass . . .

The image burst into Claire's mind, strange yet somehow familiar. She squeezed her eyes shut, trying to see it more clearly. "He?—you mean Stefan LeGrande."

Burdick snorted with disgust. "The revered, celebrated asshole Stefan LeGrande."

Eden's head shot up, though she didn't move from Claire's side. "D-don't you call my father that!"

"What—revered, celebrated? Those are compliments, Eden."

"No, I mean asshole, you asshole!"

Burdick chuckled without mirth. "Oh, you're a feisty one. Just like your mother, Jacqueline, who I must say did not go to her death quietly. She was hospitable enough when I arrived, despite the fact we'd never met. She even gave me wine. But she struggled too hard when I wanted to make love to her after shooting that boy."

Martin's jaw dropped. "You killed her? I thought Trevor—"

"Stefan killed my family. We lived in a house, a prototype design. We had both of our names on it, but, sadly, it was all Stefan's work. It looked good, lots of glass and wood, and was built to code, but it turned out Stefan's design had fatal flaws. When the house caught fire, the flames spread much too quickly. He and I were at an architectural conference in Chicago, but my wife and daughter were home. They got trapped inside. You can't imagine how horribly they died."

Red, the color of fire . . . Claire broke into a sweat. She'd seen the house burn in one her nightmares. The image had been lost to her waking self until Burdick's story resurrected it.

"Olivia was only two, born the same year as Stefan's precious Melissa."

Melissa, Claire thought. The one who'd been reaching out to her, through her dreams, through the bizarre things that happened when Claire was in the LeGrande house. Melissa, help me. You asked for my help but I can't give it unless you help me first.

"I'm sorry for your loss," she said softly, as if sympathy was going to win him over, divert him from his dreadful plan. "You're the partner, aren't you? Roger Bateman."

"Can you believe Stefan had the nerve to blame *me* for the fire? He spread rumors and lies about me and kicked me out of the firm I'd built for him. Thanks to him, the Architects Board pulled my license. He destroyed my family and my livelihood."

"I heard you died. A car accident . . ."

"I staged it. Stefan had destroyed Roger Bateman. It served my purpose better to become someone new. As soon as that house over there is mine, I can set about to restore Roger Bateman's reputation. And Eden's going to make it mine."

Eden shot Claire a frightened glance. Twisting the amethyst necklace in her fingers, she said, "N-no, I'm not."

"Yes, you are. Come here, sweetheart." He held out his free hand, the one without the gun. "Don't worry, I'm not going to hurt you. I need you alive."

Eden took a tentative step forward. Claire gripped her shoulders to restrain her.

"What about Lily?" Eden said. "Will you let her go?"

Martin made a strangled sound.

"Of course I will, sweetheart. I said I would, didn't I?" Burdick's tongue flicked over his lips as he smiled, just like the forked snake's tongue from last night's dream.

Claire had no doubt that he intended to kill them all.

———•———

"EDEN!" Burdick's voice was sharper. "Quit stalling." He pushed the gun harder against Lily's head and Lily squealed.

Claire's cell phone rang. Without releasing Eden, she took it from her pocket and flipped it open.

"Don't answer that!" Burdick yelled.

"I have to. It's Ben. You don't want him to be worried." She pushed the talk button and spoke as rapidly as she could. "Ben! Have you been looking for us? I've brought Eden to Highview Lane to see Lily . . ."

They were all staring at her. Four pairs of eyes No, five, she realized with a start. The mirror on the wall held the image of a teenage girl with long brown hair.

She kept babbling into the phone. "You know how the girls have been wanting to get together. We got here at nine-eleven and we'll be going home soon if they ever get done playing cops and robbers—"

Burdick growled and lunged for the phone. He still held the gun but it was no longer pointing at Lily.

Claire heard a soft voice whisper: "Throw me the phone."

Glancing at the mirror, she saw Melissa's image nod. She heaved the phone as hard as she could, hitting the teenager's face. Martin jumped, and Burdick whipped the gun toward the sound of breaking glass.

"Run!" Claire yelled.

She grabbed Eden and pulled her out the door. A gunshot whizzed past them, splintering the Volkswagen's windshield.

Too risky to run for the car. "This way," Claire urged, tugging Eden around the side of the house, away from the lights in front. A cold wind was rushing off the ocean.

Eden stumbled along beside her. "Where are we going?"

"I don't know." Claire was shivering. "But we have to get away from here."

Another shot rang out.

Eden stopped and turned toward the sound. "Lily!"

Claire grabbed her arm. "Stay here, Eden! Push yourself flat against the wall."

"But Lily and her dad might be hurt!"

She pressed fingers against Eden's lips. "Keep your voice quiet. The best thing we can do for them is get away and get help. Hopefully Ben got my message and is sending the police."

"Your message?"

"I said *nine-eleven* and *cops and robbers*. It was all I could think of."

"That's good," Eden said. "He'll figure it out." But she sounded unsure.

"What you and I have do is to figure out a place to hide."

"I know—my old house."

Burdick's voice cut through the night. "Eden! Come back here. Claire!"

Claire shook her head. "We can't go down the driveway to the road. He'll see us." For the first time since leaving there, she wished she was in Massachusetts. Back east, oceanfront houses were linked with grassy lawns or sandy beaches, instead of being separated by steep hills and rocky terrain.

"There's a shortcut, a path along the cliff. This way, come on."

Eden took her hand and led her toward the ocean's roar. They kept close to the wall of the house, then the railing of the Roncallos' back deck. The fog made the darkness impenetrable. Claire wished for moonlight. Even a clear sky full of stars would have cast a helpful glow.

"Claire! Eden!"

Claire looked back. A silhouette that had to be Burdick appeared at the corner of the house in the spill of the driveway lights.

"He's coming!" she murmured.

"Follow me," Eden said, letting go of the deck rail. "I think the path starts here."

"Are you sure?" The ocean was crashing almost directly beneath them. A false step, and one of them, or both, would plunge to the wave-swept rocks.

"Sort of sure. It's been a long time. And I've never done it at night before."

"Better let me go first," Claire said. She crossed her purse strap over her body so the purse wouldn't swing. Feeling in front of her with her foot, she stepped when it found solid ground. The wind was stronger away from the house. Her hair whipped into her eyes.

Another gunshot sounded, and Eden cried out.

"Eden!" Claire asked in alarm. "Are you hit?"

"N-no." She made a sound like a sob. "I'm okay."

"Thank goodness. I know this is hard. Let's go. We have to stay quiet," Claire warned. "If we're loud he'll know where we are."

"He already knows. The b-bullet went right by me."

"Remember, he can't see us. He's shooting blind. We'll be all right if we keep moving."

Claire took two or three steps, then heard another cry and the sound of small rocks tumbling. "Eden!"

"I'm okay," she repeated. "My foot slipped a little."

"Get down on all fours. We'll be safer if we're low to the ground, from bullets and from falling too."

Claire helped Eden get to her knees, then lowered herself. Crawling made it easier to maintain her balance, though sharp rocks and thorny brush brought pain to her hands and knees. Progress was slow. Why did everyone on Highview Lane have to build their houses so distant from their neighbors?

At least they'd heard nothing more from Burdick—no shouts, no gunshots, no sounds of sliding stones or breaking branches that might suggest he was in pursuit.

The track grew narrower until it became a rough, sharp edge, both sides falling away steeply. It was hard to get her hands and knees to maintain a grip. Claire heard Eden whimper, as if she was softly crying.

"Eden? Are you all right?"

"I don't think we're on the path anymore, Claire. And my knee is bleeding."

"Hang in there. We've almost made it," Claire reassured her, though she had no idea if this was true. "Lean to the right if you can. On that side you won't go very far if you fall." It wouldn't help Eden to mention that falling to left would lead to a fatal plunge to the ocean.

"Let's stay here. It's so dark, we're hidden good enough."

"Too cold. We'll freeze." Too dangerous, we'll fall.

Claire inched forward. Hand, foot, hand, foot . . .

A yelp, and the sound of rocks tumbling.

"Eden!" Claire cried. She twisted around but could see nothing.

Rocks tore at her hands as she scrambled back to where the girl should be. Eden wasn't there. Her heart sank.

Oh God, please let her be all right.

"Eden!"

No answer but the ocean's roar.

She came upon a large gap in the skinny line of rocks, a place that had seemed solid enough when she traversed it a moment ago. Her weight must have begun to dislodge them, so that they crumbled when Eden reached them, carrying her away.

"Eden!"

This time, faintly: "Claire!"

To her astonishment, the voice came from the ocean side, yet not far below her. The roar of the surf was much farther below. Eden must have landed on something, but what? And how was Claire going to get her back up? Especially when she couldn't see.

Except she could see, just a little. A faint glow illuminated a spot on the face of the cliff.

She heard a whisper: "I want to help you."

"Melissa, is that you?" she whispered back.

The glow darted about like a flashlight beam, then fixed on a protruding ledge a few feet below. Eden was on her back, gasping as if the air had been knocked out of her. She looked startled when the light found her.

"Eden? Oh wow, I was afraid you were in the ocean. Are you hurt?"

"Can you see me, Claire?"

"A little bit."

Eden sat up, then stood gingerly and shook her arms and legs. She'd have bruises tomorrow for sure, but it looked to Claire as if nothing was broken. Yet. There was still the matter of Eden getting up to the top again.

"Stretch up your arms," Claire instructed. Eden did. The top of the cliff where Claire sat was about three feet above her extended fingers. She examined the cliff face, seeking out handholds and footholds so she could guide Eden up.

The beam of light skipped away, leaving Eden in the dark. "Don't go," Claire protested.

The light flashed past her face and then settled on a scraggly bush. Melissa's voice whispered, "Sweater."

What did that mean?

The light run up one of Claire's arms, down the other. "Sweater," the whisper repeated.

"I get it," Claire said.

She took off her cardigan and tied a sleeve to the bush. She pulled on the branches; they were skinny but strong, and the bush seemed solidly rooted.

The light darted back to shine on the girl on the protruding rock. Eden was pressing herself as tight as she could to the cliff face.

Claire tossed her sweater over the edge. "Eden, look up. Take hold of my sweater. You can use it like a rope to climb up with."

"I can't."

"Sure you can. It's tied to a bush, good and secure. As soon as you're high enough, I'll grab onto you."

Eden reached up with her right hand, tugged on the dangling sleeve. It didn't give.

"Come on," Claire urged. "You can do it. One hand at a time. Brace your feet against the cliff."

Biting her lip, Eden managed to grasp the sleeve with her left hand, placing it just above the right one. She found a foothold and boosted herself up.

"That's the way," Claire said. "Now the right hand above the left."

Inch by inch, Claire guided Eden up. Melissa's light followed her, letting them both see what they were doing. As soon as Eden was high enough, Claire gripped her under her shoulders and pulled her the rest of the way. When she was safely on top, she gathered her into a hug.

"Thank goodness," Claire said. "I'm so glad you're safe. I was scared when you fell like that."

"I was scared too," Eden said. "Wasn't it good I had your necklace on? It brought me luck."

"So it did. How do you feel? Is anything painful?"

Eden shook her head. "That was a good idea with the sweater."

Claire said, "I'm glad it worked." Thank you, Melissa, she added silently.

She untied the sleeve and put the cardigan back on. She'd been so focused on Eden that she'd forgotten the cold, but all of a sudden she was freezing.

"Where do you think that guy is?" Eden asked. "The man with the gun."

"I don't know. I hope he's given up on looking for us."

"What about Lily and her dad? Do you think he hurt them?"

"I hope not."

"Maybe we should go back and see."

"Not a good idea. Let's keep going. We have a better chance of being safe if we can make it to your old house." Claire glanced toward where she thought the house should be. To her surprise she could make out an edge of the soaring roof and the jutting prow of the back deck. "Look, Eden, we're really close."

Eden didn't speak for a moment, and Claire wondered what she was thinking of this first shadowy glimpse of the house she had avoided for so long. Finally the girl said, "Okay then. Let's go." She stood up and Claire could tell she was pointing. "This way—I see the path! It's right over there."

Sure enough, Claire could see it too, a track that ran parallel to the rocky ledge they had been traversing, just a few yards further back from the cliff. The soft beam of light preceded them as they scrambled down into a rocky trough and up again to the path.

"I didn't know you brought a flashlight, Claire. Why didn't you turn it on sooner?"

"I didn't bring one." How could she explain that Melissa was guiding them? "I guess our eyes are just getting used to the dark."

Eden didn't reply, so Claire couldn't tell whether or not she believed her. The light brightened the way until they were safe on the deck behind the LeGrande house.

"H-how are we g-going to get in?" Eden asked, her teeth chattering from cold, or from the adrenaline rush of her brush with death.

"I have the key to the lockbox," Claire said. "But I don't want to go around front in case Burdick is watching the house."

"What'll we d-do then?"

"Let's break the glass on the French doors. If we're lucky it'll trigger the alarm, and the alarm company will send the police. Hopefully Burdick won't hear the noise. Come on, help me find a rock."

They explored the first few feet of the walkway that led around the house from the deck. Claire spotted a good, round stone, a little bigger than her fist.

"Let me do it," Eden said. She wound up as if she were pitching a softball and heaved the rock through the glass. Claire felt through the hole for the latch to the deadbolt, then remembered a key was needed to unlock it even from the inside. So they kicked out more glass and crawled through the hole into the grand salon, where they stood up and dusted themselves off. The light followed them inside.

"Now what?" Eden asked.

They couldn't call for help because Claire no longer had her cell phone. But the alarm must have sounded, neighbors would have heard the gunshots, with luck Ben had decoded her message. Surely help was on the way.

"I think we just wait for the police," Claire told her. "Let's find a room where we can turn on some lights that Burdick won't see from out front."

"The media lounge," Eden said. "It doesn't have windows. This way."

She was halfway across the big room when a hand reached out of the gloom and grabbed her. Her shriek curdled Claire's blood.

"I knew where you'd go." Burdick's voice. "You're not the only ones who can get in by breaking a window."

"Claire! Help me!"

Not a ghostly whisper but Eden screaming.

In the minimal light Burdick looked like a dark shape buried in shadows. His arm was locked around Eden's neck. Claire saw a glint off the gun barrel and knew the weapon was aimed at her.

She felt weak-kneed and dizzy. Any moment he could pull the trigger and she would die.

But for Eden's sake she tried to make her voice strong. "Don't you dare shoot. Let Eden go."

A slight ripple in the darkness as Burdick shook his head. "No way. I need her."

Eden thrashed in his grip. "Lemme go! Lemme go!"

Burdick began backing toward the front door, dragging Eden with him, holding the gun steady. "Don't worry, girlie. I'm not going to hurt you. You own this house. I need you alive until we sign the sale papers."

"No!" Eden landed a kick on his shin. "Never!" Claire saw Burdick wince.

"Damn you, kid." He grabbed the girl's throat and began to shake her. Eden cried out.

Claire took a sharp breath. If Burdick was going to kill her, she might as well make her last act a heroic one. If she could knock him off balance, maybe he'd release his grip on Eden. She pulled down into a partial crouch and charged.

The gun fired and she felt the bullet whisk past her ear. Then her head connected with his solar plexus.

With a grunt Burdick fell, but he knocked her down with him, and they landed in a tangle. She heard the gun go off again.

Eden sank to her knees beside them.

Claire tried to untwist herself and get upright. The girl looked dazed but unhurt.

She yelled, "Go, Eden! Run!"

Eden scrambled to her feet, and Burdick reached out to seize her.

A snapping sound, then something rattled and clattered like hailstones beating the ground.

"Oh, no, Claire! He broke your necklace!"

As Burdick lunged again for the girl, an icy gale swirled through the room. Eden gasped as she suddenly flew up into the air, and Burdick howled in pain.

Claire was kneeling, feeling queasy, out of breath. She quickly examined herself. No blood that she could tell, no searing pain. The gunshot must have gone wild.

The light in the room gradually brightened.

She felt flutters of air by her hand. As she tried to shoo them away, they became solid, like fingers, a hand grasping hers to help her up.

Burdick howled again. He was bucking and writhing on the floor as someone—just the hazy outline of a young man—kicked him in the ribs and the groin.

Claire heard a whisper: "We're helping you."

"Thank you," she replied.

Eden was floating horizontally in the air, about four feet above her tormentor. It looked to Claire as if she were being carried in someone's arms, leaning against someone's strong chest. The same someone who was administering the kicks.

Burdick fell silent, except for an occasional moan. He curled up on the floor, his hands cupped over his private parts. He struggled to sit up, then flopped back with a *whoomph*.

Eden was lowered to the floor. She stared at Burdick, then at Claire, eyes wide with disbelief. Her arms hugged the hazy outline as if the young man were solid and real.

"Are we okay now?" she asked.

Claire looked down at Wayne Burdick. She had the impression that someone was sitting on his chest. As she watched, the vague image coalesced into a girl's translucent face, framed by long brown hair.

Melissa. She was smiling.

Claire smiled back. "I think we're fine."

Eden's voice got small. "I'm sorry about your necklace."

Her mother's necklace! Claire had forgotten. She looked around in dismay. The amethyst beads had scattered and rolled all over the room. Oh, God, she hoped she could find them all.

"Don't worry, Eden, it's just a necklace. Want to help me gather these up?"

They were down on the floor chasing beads when they heard a voice at the front door.

"Police! Open up!"

CLAIRE UNBOLTED THE DOOR and Eden pulled it wide. Two sheriff's deputies stepped inside, guns drawn. And behind them, approaching from the parking court, was—

"Ben!" They both yelled his name at once.

Ben ran toward them, scooped them into a three-way hug. "Thank God!"

"That's him," one of the deputies said, pointing into the grand salon. His partner found the control panel and all at once the room was flooded with light. Her face buried against Ben's shoulder, Claire heard the click of the deputies' shoes on the marble floor of the gallery and the softer tap as they crossed the hardwood surface to where Wayne Burdick lay groaning.

Eden was first to pull out of the embrace. As the officers rolled Burdick over and handcuffed him, she ran to tug on the sleeve of a uniform.

"You have to send somebody next door right away. My friend Lily . . ." Her lip trembled as her voice trailed off, as if saying what might have happened to Lily would make it real, make it too terrible to bear.

The officer, a short man with a reddish mustache, was gentle. Once Burdick was secured, he rose and set a hand on the girl's shoulder. "Your name is Eden, isn't it? It's already being done. Some of our buddies are next door and the ambulance is on the way."

"An ambulance? Is Lily hurt? And her dad? Will they be okay?"

"Wish I could tell you that. All I know is, they're in good hands." Stepping away from her, he sent an amethyst crystal skittering across the floor. "What's all this stuff?" He swept an arm to indicate the scattered beads.

"My necklace," Claire said. "It broke." Hand in her pocket, she clutched the three beads she'd managed to pick up before the police arrived. "Look, there's another call you need to make. I think a car went off the road—"

The officer was instantly alert. "Where?"

"On Highway One, a couple of miles east of Mariners Beach. You'll see a tree near the road with broken branches."

The officer went off to call in a report just as a couple of detectives arrived.

"We thought all hell had broken loose up here," said one of the new arrivals, a woman around Claire's age who introduced herself as Sylvie Cappolino. She raked a hand through her short black hair. "Three separate nine-one-one calls and an alert from an alarm company."

"One of the calls was from me," Ben said.

Eden clutched his hand. "You figured out Claire's message? That was smart of her, wasn't it?"

"Sure was." Ben slid his other hand around Claire's waist.

Cappolino added, "The others came from neighbors who heard the gunshots."

For the next hour, Claire sat with Ben and Eden on the step between the gallery and the grand salon, answering the detectives' questions. Despite all the hectic activity going on around them, the energy in the house felt calmer than it had since Claire first stepped inside five days ago.

An ambulance arrived and paramedics carted Burdick out on a gurney. Cappolino supervised the departure. When she came back, she said, "I don't know how you two managed to inflict such damage on that guy. Not that he doesn't deserve it, but the tech said with the injuries he's got, it's like somebody stomped him with steel-toed boots."

As Eden started to speak, Claire tousled her hair, a signal to keep quiet. "I guess it was adrenaline," Claire said. "You don't know what you're capable of until you have to protect the life of a special kid like this."

When Cappolino finally said they were free to go, Claire rose from the low perch feeling stiff and numb. Next time she had a listing for an empty house, the first thing she'd do would be to stage it by bringing in some furniture. Soft, cushy furniture, she'd insist on that.

"Come home with us?" Ben suggested, sliding his arm around her. "Of course, after a rough night like this, you might feel more comfortable sleeping at home in your own bed."

Eden seemed to miss the meaning Ben implied in the words sleeping and bed. "Yes, please come. You can stay in my room."

"Thank you," Claire said. "That's a kind invitation. I think I'll take you up on it." She wondered for a moment if she should find time later to discuss the phone call she'd gotten from Avery, but she dismissed the thought. Claire was now certain that Avery's assertions were lies. Ben's actions tonight told her she didn't have to worry about who held his affections.

As Ben was about to open the front door, Eden held back. "Wait, I want to thank the man who helped me. Where did he go?"

"What man?" Ben asked. "One of the police officers?"

"No, the man who picked me up when that bad guy tried to grab me."

Ben gave Claire a puzzled look. She shrugged and shook her head. Apparently Eden hadn't recognized Trevor. Just as well. This wasn't the time or place to go into complicated explanations. She wondered if she could ever explain to Ben what had happened. She was only beginning to believe it herself.

They started again to head outside. This time it was Claire who hesitated. Feeling fingers flutter against her shoulder, she paused to see who was trying to get her attention. Not Ben, not Eden, all the sheriff's officials were too far away.

"Look down," came the whisper, and she did.

Arranged on the floor at her feet was a sparkling circle of amethysts.

SUDDEN LIGHTS. Shouting voices.

Avery stirred. It was night again—black, cold, damp. Or had it been night all along? No, the last time she drifted toward wakefulness she'd seen sunlight. Or maybe that was a dream.

She tried to move, but couldn't. She was still trapped, twisted metal pinning her into place. Everything hurt. The cloud of pain settled over her again, and she sank back into the welcome darkness.

"Hey, here it is!"

"This way!"

"Damn shame, what a car!"

"Driver's inside. Poor woman."

Loud voices hammering on her head. Avery groaned.

"Hey, she's alive."

"Quick, let's get her out of here."

"Lady, can you hear me."

Warm hand touching her cheek. She moved her lips, tried to form words.

"What's that, lady? Say it again."

Head bending close. Breath smelling of spice.

"Take me home," Avery murmured. "Take me home."

Chapter 30

So happy. So proud . . .

Our task is done. People in the physical world know the truth. My brother and I are no longer trapped here. Our little sister is safe and she knows in her heart that we love her.

So does the lonely man. I was thrilled to see him sweep her into his arms, and the chocolate-haired woman, too. I can't call him the lonely man anymore. His aura has changed, announcing his happiness.

My brother—and what a joy it is to have that word reappear in my vocabulary—showed such courage. And I did my part as well as I could. It's the hardest role I've ever played, more demanding even than Emily in Our Town. *Only two people in the audience even know I was there on the stage, yet I can hear the bravos and the thunder of applause.*

I couldn't have done it without one of those people, the woman with chocolate hair. She heard me. She understood my words. She gave me back my name Melissa!—and made me confident of my own power. I wish I could thank her, but all I could think of to do was to collect and present her with the scattered purple stones.

The passage has opened and a shaft of pure light beckons us. The ones who went before, our parents, are waiting and we'll greet them with joy. I wonder if, from time to time, we'll be able to slip into the physical world just long enough to make sure that the people we care about there are all right, to tell them we love them, our voices the softest of whispers.

My brother and I are ready at last. Together we float into the place called Forever.

"Thanks for the interview, Claire." Griff Maxwell flipped his spiral notebook shut and pushed the stop button on his pocket tape recorder.

"You probably gave me more information than I gave you." Claire leaned back in Ben's desk chair. She and the reporter had retreated to his small study so they could talk quietly, away from the chatter of all the visitors in the living room—Lindsay and other friends, Ben's neighbors, Claire's Golden Gate Properties colleagues— all of them eager to express concern and hear the juicy details of last night's events. She swiveled the chair a little so she could gaze out the window at the satisfying sight of Eden and Lily at play the sun-dappled backyard. Lily would be staying with Ben and Eden for a few days until her father was released from the hospital.

Griff shrugged his big shoulders and reached for his glass of lemonade. Even with the window open, the room was warm. Fine with Claire; she'd had enough fog, wind, and cold to last a long while.

"I've been hanging out at the jail and the cop shop for a long time." The reporter zipped through the words as if he were playing them on fast-forward. "Wouldn't be good at my job if I hadn't figured out how to get people there to talk to me."

Some of what he'd learned from his sources, and told Claire, were things she already knew. But many details were new to her. For instance a can of gasoline had been found in the trunk of the car that Wayne Burdick had left parked at the mouth of Highview Lane. Apparently his plan had been to kidnap Eden and then kill Claire, Lily, and Martin, setting the Roncallo house on fire to make their deaths look accidental. When Claire and Eden bolted, Burdick shot quickly at the father and daughter, then chased the two escapees. But he was distracted and his aim was off. Martin had suffered a flesh wound in the leg; Lily, thank God, he'd missed entirely.

"I'm glad to know Leo Hollister is still in prison," Claire said.

"Yeah, he won't be up for parole for at least a year. It was Burdick made those calls to Ben pretending to be the prison official and Hollister. He seems to be good at faking voices. I think he was trying to stir things up. If he could get Ben and Eden to change their routines, he might be able to get at Eden more easily. He must've felt he struck gold when Eden went with you; he figured you'd be concerned about the house so he could lure you up there."

"He was right about that, sadly. I can't believe I didn't notice him following us from Spuntino's to the mall to my apartment."

"And he followed Ben when he picked Eden up at her class and brought her to the deli. But think about it. Brown hair, brown eyes, tall but not super tall. Average-looking guy, really. You wouldn't even notice him once he put you on the lookout for Hollister, who's big and blond and rough around the edges."

"He went to a lot of trouble figuring it all out."

"He's been obsessed getting revenge on Stefan LeGrande for years. He got a settlement for wrongful termination and breach of conflict when LeGrande forced him out their architectural firm—he had some money left from that, which is what he planned to use to buy the house."

"So that's why couldn't go higher on the price," Claire said. "It was all the cash he had, and he couldn't get a mortgage because he had no credit under his false name."

"He got a huge amount, several million, but it didn't make up for the loss of his family and his reputation. I've got a buddy who writes about architecture, and he thinks the truth is that it was Burdick's own design flaw that made the fatal fire so intense. But Burdick couldn't accept the truth; he wanted to make LeGrande pay. Burdick did a lot of research on the family so he could figure out how to make that happen. The ID Eden made convinced the cops that he killed the four of them up on Highview Lane. Trevor's exonerated, not that it does the kid any good."

"It means a lot to Ben and Eden." Claire looked across the study to the bookcase behind Griff. On an eye-level shelf was a photo—six people standing in the prow of the oceanfront deck, Stefan's family plus brother Ben, visiting just a couple of months before the murders.

"Sure, of course it would. Now the authorities are looking at Burdick for killing Rona."

"Stefan's first wife?"

"Yeah. Supposedly she left a note saying she was running away with another man and was never heard from again. She and Stefan were having a really rocky time so no one was surprised. Now the cops are guessing she was Burdick's first murder."

Claire shuddered. It was hard to imagine that anyone—even a mad man—could be so cold-blooded.

The small chair Griff was sitting on creaked as he stood up and relieved it of his weight. "Well, better get going. I'm glad Burdick didn't add four more victims to his tally last night."

"You think *you're* glad!" Claire was surprised that she could actually chuckle. She stood, too, and shook his hand. "All this certainly gives you plenty to write about."

He grinned. "Yeah, they'll have to give me a whole section of my own in the Sunday edition."

Lindsay poked her head through the doorway. "Ben's going to take the girls back to the hospital to see Lily's dad. He wants to know if you'd like to come."

"Sure. Griff's leaving anyway. Let's go."

THEY STOPPED to buy flowers on the way. Claire selected two bouquets. When they got to Marin General, Claire was gratified to see that Martin's color was good and his mood surprisingly jovial. While the girls entertained him, she left one bouquet behind and slipped away to look in on another patient.

In contrast to Lily's dad, Avery looked wan and fragile; she was hooked up to an amazing number of tubes and monitors. Claire thought she was asleep and started to tiptoe away, but her brother Kurt, sitting by the bed, beckoned her in.

"How is she?" Claire asked.

"The doctors say they're hopeful about her prognosis. Eventually she'll be as good as new." He squeezed Avery's hand and smiled at her with affection. "Hear that, sis?" Then he turned back to Claire. "I heard you're the one who told them where to find her."

Claire nodded.

"I want to thank you. They said that down in that ravine where she was, it could have been weeks before anyone found her. Your tip saved her life. We owe you a real debt of gratitude."

"I can't take credit. It was a lucky guess." Claire was startled to realize she knew that wasn't true. The strange things she saw, her bizarre experiences, the messages in her dreams—they weren't luck, they weren't her imagination. They were real, even if they were real to no one but herself.

She would have to start paying closer attention.

"I'm just glad my hunch turned out to be right," she told him.

Avery's eyelids flickered and opened. She turned her head toward the voices. "Claire."

"Hi Avery." She held up the vase of flowers. "I hope you like aspidistra."

"Pretty." Avery managed a half smile, which quickly faded. "Claire, it wasn't Ben, was it?"

"You mean, the man you made love to at the LeGrande house the other night? No, it was your client, Wayne Burdick." This was more information she'd gleaned from Cliff. "It turns out he's a really bad guy. He tampered with your car and then, just to make sure, he bumped you off the road."

"Why?" Avery's voice sounded hoarse.

"He wanted the LeGrande house badly. Apparently he was angry because he thought you screwed up his deal with Ben, so he decided to get revenge."

Claire pulled up another chair to the bedside and gave them a summary of what she'd learned about Wayne Burdick. Avery seemed to be dozing in and out, but Kurt listened attentively and Claire knew he'd pass the story along.

Before long she got up to leave, not wanting to overtire the patient. "See you tomorrow, Avery," she said softly.

"Just wait, Claire," Avery murmured. "If Burdick isn't buying that house, I'll find someone else who will."

Claire laughed. "That's the spirit. I can see you're going to be just fine."

WHEN THEY GOT BACK to Ben's, the visitors were gone, and they settled in for a quiet evening. While the girls watched TV in Eden's bedroom, Ben and Claire sprawled on the living room sofa, teasing each other with hints of pleasures to come.

"I'm sorry I can't ask you to stay the night," Ben said, then he dipped his head to give her another long delicious kiss. "But with two kids in the house . . ."

She laughed. "I understand. With Lily in Eden's extra bed, there's no room for me."

"Will you come over tomorrow?"

"Of course." How could she contain herself for that long? "Tell you what, I'll to treat them to a movie. A double feature, popcorn and all. That will give us a few hours all to ourselves."

"Deal," he said, kissing her again just as her cell phone rang.

She took it out onto the front porch to answer it, relishing the balminess of the summer air, the music being played by insects in the grass. "Hello?"

"Claire? This is Nadine Johansen. Paul and I have been talking and, well, we'd like to look at that house again. We just can't get it out of our minds. Any chance you could take us up there tomorrow?"

Yes! "Absolutely. I'd be delighted." They set a time early enough to allow her to be back for the movie matinee.

As she rang off, ready to hurry back to Ben, she realized that Eden had slipped out on the porch to join her. "Claire, can I ask you something?"

"Of course, sweetie, what is it?"

"That man last night . . . "

"You mean Wayne Burdick?" Claire frowned at the thought of him.

Eden shook her head. "No, the other one, the one who lifted me up. He reminded me of my brother Trevor."

All the admonitions Claire had heard for her entire life pushed into her mind, ready to spill out of her mouth. *Don't be silly, it was your imagination, you're making it up, it never happened.*

"Yes, sweetie. He reminded me of Trevor too."

"He was real, wasn't he." A statement, not a question

She pulled Eden into a hug. "Yes, he was. For now, though, let's make that a secret between us, you and me."